How it all began

In London, in the summer
in full swing, Mark Gunn and Sylvia Fordred, two young Private Investigators, who have set up in business together, are given an assignment which is very different from the usual fare of errant spouses and routine debt inquiries. It takes them across the Channel to France and on by boat to Naples and Haifa, and has them reaching into their past, separate and collective, to face an uncertain future.

About the authors

DA Kent is a pen name, a name chosen with reference to the county of Kent and the initials of two writers.

Both authors have drawn on their extensive travels and experience within the field of private investigation and probate research. They came together with a story to tell, and, using their skills and knowledge, have brought Dateline Haifa, the first of the Clements Chronicles, to life.

First published in Great Britain in 2019 by Wealden Strand Publishers @wealdenstrand

Paper Edition ISBN   978-1-9161801-1-6
eBook Edition IBAN 978-1-9161801-0-9

DA Kent

Dateline Haifa

WEALDEN STRAND

Dateline Haifa

Jonathan Jones had lived in Chartrettes, a little town caught on the curve of the Seine, as long as he had lived anywhere. He often told people that. He had made good friends there. Despite the Occupation, and the occasional little unpleasantness, he had no especial cause for concern when he wandered into town for his accustomed drink with Jean-Paul Bossis at the bar and tabac. With his newspaper under his arm, he kissed his wife, Louise, the love of his life, and set out in the sunshine. He never saw her again.

He knew something was amiss immediately he arrived home. The gates were wide open. He had closed them; they always did, nowadays. Her voice was stilled. Two cigarette butts were on her clean kitchen floor. A cup lay on its side, cradling the dregs of her coffee, on the counter. He knew instantly that she had been taken and that he was alone. In years to come, he would torture himself with thoughts as to whether, if he had been at home, they would have taken her. The truth was, the house had been watched carefully, their movements monitored. There was nothing either of them could have done.

Chapter 1

Sylvia Fordred fiddled in exasperation with the unwieldy lock at Number 3, Clements Court, and bounded up several flights of ill-lit, narrow stairs, cursing the treacherous holes in the matted carpet, summoned by the imperious clamour of the telephone, catching it just before the caller rang off, trying not to sound out of breath. London was impossible to get around at the moment, with the Olympics in full swing, surging, jolly crowds and searing heat. In this weather, it was a mercy that the 'bunker,' as the office was affectionately dubbed, never got any sunlight. It was perishing cold in the winter but that seemed some time away. 'Good morning, Clements Enquiry Agents, how may we help?' Sylvia fiddled with a pencil stub as she listened to Edward Cumberland, her attention gradually narrowing from the office surrounds to the sheet of paper and sketched notes she was making, bent over the desk. Periodically, she lifted a hank of tawny hair out of her line of sight, caught by the unusual element of excitement in Edward's normally measured and calm tones. 'Mr. Jones was booked to arrive on the Night Ferry at Dover two nights ago and he did not keep an appointment for dinner at Simpsons last night?'

'That's correct.' Edward's voice hinted at puzzlement. 'Utterly out of character for Mr. Jones. Cumberlands have handled his affairs for over forty years, even after he married and moved his farming business over to France. He has never missed an appointment. Absolutely punctilious. I have to say, we're worried.'

This sounded rather different from the usual fare of errant spouses and recalcitrant debtors, entertaining though that often was. Sensing the note of urgency, Sylvia suggested:

'We could come over this afternoon if that suits?'

Edward's relief was almost tangible. 'That would be marvellous. As soon as possible, really. I've got a completion to do now, just round the corner, then lunch with the old man. I'll rustle up Louis as well. Shall we say three o'clock?'

Sylvia held her hand over the receiver as a whirlwind burst through the door, weighed down by a heavy holdall and a camera. The inevitable string of curses rang out in the background as the door to what was known as the 'props cupboard' was wrenched open and kicked shut. It had seen better days, like the rest of the bunker; those hinges needed replacing. An afternoon in Edward's more civilised surroundings sounded tempting.

'Sorry about that. That was Gunn. Three o'clock is fine. We'll see you then.'

Replacing the receiver, she turned to face her colleague. She always liked hearing about his exploits. 'What a night,' he groaned. 'Met up with the old Free French crowd. Only meant to have a quick snifter. And before you ask, yes, I did get round to the Imperial this morning. Caught the lecherous old sod in the act. Got him bang to rights. Better get these developed this morning. Who was that just then?'

Mark Gunn and Sylvia had met some years

ago, sheltering from pounding rain in a bookshop on the Charing Cross Road. They had been friends ever since, although he drove her to distraction as regularly as the morning pips on the wireless, and 'partners in crime' at Clements, as they liked to tell people, for the past couple of years.

'Come on, let's have a cigarette and a coffee and I'll fill you in,' she smiled, liberating one of his cigarettes. Continental adventures had given both of them a taste for coffee and on his way from the Imperial, Gunn had picked up a pound of the precious stuff from a merchant in Old Compton Street. One of their first acquisitions for the bunker had been a decent coffee pot; a necessity rather than a treat, as they often worked late on cases.

'Right.' Sylvia sipped at her cup, savouring the taste. Despite his foibles, Gunn made an excellent coffee. 'In a nutshell, elderly gentleman, English, lived in France for thirty years or more as a farmer. Highly respectable. Managed to survive the war; should have been in London for an appointment at Cumberlands and then dinner with his bankers at Simpsons last night – a celebration for the opening ceremony apparently. He didn't show up for either. Not a sign, not a word.'

'Must have been something serious to duck out of dinner at Simpsons,' Gunn grinned. 'Assuming he even arrived in London of course.'

'And Edward sounded decidedly ruffled. Not like him at all. I'll give you a hand with your photos and the report and then we'll head over to see him and Louis.'

Sylvia noted Gunn's raised eyebrow; he had

9

picked up on Edward's departure from the norm too. Nothing usually perturbed that Battle of Britain flying ace. In the dark room, she cast an appraising, perfectionist eye over Gunn's handiwork. Their dark room was at the back of the office in an alcove to which Gunn had added some doors and panelling he had found on a bomb site in Whitechapel last year. There was barely room to swing a cat in there, but tolerance and experience of working in even more cramped and dangerous conditions allowed them to work together like gears meshing in a decent car. Gumshoes on a shoestring, they often quipped.

'I reckon Vera will be pleased with these,' she commented. 'And we could make a small fortune, flogging them to one of those shops in Berwick Street. Anyway, the sooner we get our report to her, the sooner we can put our bill in.'

Vera had turned up at the bunker one day, and instructed them directly. Usually, instructions on such delicate matters came through their growing network of solicitors, but Vera was quite a 'gal.' She came across initially as one of the most embittered, vindictive people they had ever met, with language that would have made a navvy blush but she turned out to have a twinkle in her eye when they sat her down in the most respectable chair they could find, plied her with coffee and cigarettes and coaxed the sorry saga out of her.'

Born into a family of wealthy publicans in the East End, she had married, far too young, a man who turned out to be a drunkard and a wastrel. Vera had left him one day with their little girls in tow; a brave move, as there was nowhere for her to go really, as her parents had retired to the country and died prematurely. She managed by a stroke of fortune to get herself a job as secretary to a Member of Parliament.

While working for him, she met Wilfred, a naval officer; some years her junior and devilishly handsome. They married when her divorce came through and settled by the coast. More children followed. Just as she thought they were safe, with the war finished, (the second they had lived through), and heading for the sunny uplands of retirement, she discovered Wilfred was having an affair with a 'flibberty-gibbet' by the name of Prudence. Nasty little piece; Vera had some pithy comments to make about her. The upshot was that Vera now wanted a divorce and to drag him through the mud.

Gunn had spent a few entertaining evenings following Wilfred from work at the Ministry of Defence to the front door of the Naval and Military Club and had, having bought the doorman a few drinks, discovered he was meeting Prudence at the Imperial Hotel in Bloomsbury. With a raging hangover, he had somehow got himself over there this morning, flirted with one of the chambermaids and got her to knock on the door of room 31, calling 'Room Service!' in dulcet tones. Wilfred had opened the door ready to give her a piece of his mind, as they hadn't ordered anything, with a scantily clad Prudence behind him, but Gunn was ready with his camera and had time to get some excellent shots before legging it down the corridor and squeezing into a service lift with the chamber maid, emerging into an alley which led him around the back of the British Museum. He was glad to see a few curators back at work; the building, always a favourite of his, had suffered some damage in the Blitz. A couple of them gave him a strange look as he dusted himself down carefully. That lift was not designed for two.

He made a mental note that he owed the chambermaid 10 shillings for her willing assistance. There was a network around town and it was always best to keep staff sweet. Word would spread if he didn't unbuckle the silver and equally it would spread if he did. It was a relief to have the pictures, he thought, as he typed up a letter on Clements paper to Vera, while Sylvia sorted the photos into order. Vera insisted on corresponding through a Post Office Box; she didn't want any of Wilfred's relatives nosing about and did not entirely trust her daughter not to tell him. Feisty old bird seemed to relish the cloak and dagger side of things. Perhaps she might make a good recruit.

They decided to treat themselves to lunch out at a Lyons Corner House, as a reward for their work on Wilfred and an early celebration of Edward's new assignment. Pushing aside the remains of his rather non-descript soup (water with a heavy-handed dose of pepper), Gunn looked across at Sylvia. They made a formidable duo, he thought. The son of a French woman and an Englishman, Gunn had grown up in France before being sent to England to school in the thirties. He had joined up in 1939 and served in North Africa and Syria, at one point fighting Vichy units near Damascus, which amused him once the bullets had stopped flying about. He had been co-opted into the SOE and jumped more than once, breaking an

12

ankle and a collar bone separately. He had been arrested twice and was among the prisoners who had escaped following the RAF raid on Amiens prison in February 1944. He had made his way back to England and went back over on 6th June in the gliders.

Gunn relished what his old headmaster would have called 'high jinks' and 'piracy.' Stunts like the raid on Wilfred and Prudence in Room 31 definitely fell into that category. It was true to say though that working with Sylvia had polished up his more cerebral side. She was rather a dark horse. When he first met her, she was doing some sort of secretarial work with the army; didn't let on much but nobody ever did. She had landed a job at the Nuremberg Trials and, when that came to an end, declared she never wanted to work for anyone else again. Women were being steered firmly back into the home now the war was over but Sylvia had no home to go to. So they had pooled resources, taken a lease on Clements' Inn with the last of Gunn's 'demob' money and a little bit she had put by, and started in business straightaway.

Edward was an old friend of Sylvia's family; Louis Wonzowicz, his partner, had served in the RAF with him. They had been among Clements's first clients. Who on earth was this Jones character, he and Sylvia mused, as their taxi purred towards Queen Anne's Gate (they had no desire to join the perspiring hordes on the underground.) Why had he got under Edward's skin?

Chapter 2

These questions were still taxing them as they arrived at Cumberlands' offices. The bells at Westminster Abbey were just striking three. Edward, most unusually, was in the foyer before Cathy, his well-spoken but slightly scatter-brained receptionist, and Joan, her quick-witted sidekick, could even offer them a cup of tea. Edward's father, senior partner in Cumberlands, disapproved of Joan and her huge bulk and broad Cockney accent and didn't want her anywhere near clients. He was hardly ever around nowadays to witness what went on, which was fortunate, as the clients loved her. She never forgot a face or what they took in their tea.

'Shall we go straight up to the meeting room?' suggested Edward. 'Louis will meet us up there.' He seemed on edge. Joan and Sylvia exchanged glances before he led the way upstairs.

The contrast between Edward and Louis always struck Sylvia, whenever she saw them together. Louis was slight, dark and excitable. Edward was blond, patrician and courteous. They could hear Louis loudly berating one of the girls from the bank on the telephone as they walked upstairs; they could never spell or pronounce his name properly, to which he took great and vociferous exception.

'We won't be needing tea or indeed anything at all for the next hour or so' Edward pre-empted Joan briskly. She nodded at his retreating back and shook her head. Gunn winked at her, rolled his eyes in sympathy and followed Edward and Sylvia, his hands

14

firmly in his pockets. Making one of his 'points,' as Sylvia had been heard to observe more than once. Having finished terrifying the hapless girl from the bank, Louis followed them down the corridor, which was lined from floor to ceiling with bound volumes of law reports, in date order. Sylvia wondered idly if anyone ever bothered to take one off the shelf; they looked in such pristine condition.

The meeting room was panelled and discreetly furnished. A pair of Stubbs flanked the fireplace and a decanter of brandy and a set of highly polished Napoleon brandy balloons sat on a felt marker on the long oak table, which gave off a slight hint of beeswax. Edward offered Sylvia and Gunn a seat either side of the table, motioning Louis to sit at the end, and poured a decent measure for each of them. He sat with his fingers steepled in thought for a while. Then, unusually for him, he opened proceedings with no preview or preamble.

'How confident would you two be about an enquiry in France? It's a highly sensitive matter, maybe a little dangerous. I'd hate to think of it being bungled in any way; the consequences could be dire.'

Gunn bridled a little at the inference that he and Sylvia could be involved in any 'bungling' whatsoever. Clements was a highly professional outfit, as Edward well knew. He was about to add that they would expect suitable remuneration and a decent operative budget, when Sylvia shot him one of her warning glances. He decided to sit back and listen. He was very good at that when he wanted to be; it unnerved people. Edward could do with a bit of unsettling sometimes.

'Without wanting to state the obvious,' began Sylvia, 'We can see you are very concerned about Mr Jones's welfare. Have you thought about ringing the local gendarmerie? Or even talking to the police here?'

Louis leant forward. 'Miss Fordred,' he stated emphatically, in clipped tones. 'I must tell you from the outset, we cannot involve the police in this matter, in any jurisdiction.'

Sylvia knew better than to ask why not. She was in no mood for one of Louis's tirades.

Edward raised a hand in a gesture of peace. 'Look, I am sure you would handle the matter in your usual exemplary fashion. It's just that we are committed to client confidentiality and we have no desire to involve country gendarmes, bringing their mud and gitanes into the equation.'

He paused, took another sip of brandy and then went on to explain that Jonathan Theophilus Weston Jones was born in the 1880s into a farming family of some note. He was sent away to school but, as he intimated on more than one occasion, he always preferred farming to any other career.

'Nothing out of the ordinary so far,' Sylvia observed. Edward nodded in agreement.

'Indeed. But then, his life changed. His father died in 1908 and Jonathan came into some money. That summer, he decided, on an impulse, to accompany some friends to see the last stages of the New York to Paris automobile race, just as it arrived in Paris. While he was there, he met the lady who was to become his wife, Louise Marie Vogel, from Austria originally. It was what the French call a coup de foudre.' Gunn tried not to wince at his accent.

Edward went on to explain that Louise and Jonathan were married the following year and decided to live in France, buying a small farm near Chartrettes, south of Paris. Jonathan had settled happily there with Louise, only returning to London once a year to keep his appointments with this office. Nothing changed in the routine until the recent war. Then, tragically, Louise was arrested and deported. Being married to an Englishman did not preclude her being on a train east in 1942.

'Unfortunate,' Gunn remarked dryly. 'Why on earth would a woman living on a farm be of interest?'

'She was Jewish, that sufficed,' Edward murmured, almost to himself. 'Still, one thing that remains with me is that Mr Jones told us that the SS arrested Mrs. Jones, not the local gendarmerie, as was the more usual method in France.'

'A little odd, but not necessarily significant.' Sylvia looked up from her notes.

'Agreed,' Louis put in. 'Miss Fordred, Mr Gunn, I will come straight to the point. This firm is – and has been for many years – on a generous retainer from the Jones family trust. Mr Jones was a broken man when we saw him here last summer. It would be most remiss of us not to take action.'

'Money no object then,' Gunn quipped.

'Sorry, couldn't resist that!' Giving him another warning look, Sylvia observed:

'So, in summary, you need us to find out whether he ever made it to London. And if he didn't, then we need to broaden our investigations into France.'

'Got it in one.'

Edward seemed to relax visibly. By the time Sylvia and Gunn left the office, bidding a quick farewell to Cathy and Joan, they had a long list of potential leads, including Mr. Jones's London Club, his favourite restaurants, the manager at Drummonds Bank and his stockbrokers. They affected a polite but studied nonchalance at the cheque Edward had written them, until they got round the corner.

'I almost feel like framing this and putting it on the wall at the bunker.' Gunn smoothed it at the edges and put it in his pocket. 'Better pay it in before the bank closes though. Then I'm off for another snifter and dinner with a certain chambermaid. Early start tomorrow – how about I get the first train to Dover, to see if our Mr Jones ever made it to back to Blighty?'

'I'll go round the hotels then; maybe start with the Club,' said Sylvia. 'I suppose he could have changed his plans; might not be such a creature of habit as Edward imagined. Wonder if there was any other family – cousins maybe? They didn't say. Rather cagey, weren't they?'

Turning at a sudden commotion behind them, they spotted Joan moving amazingly fast through a group of excited American athletes who were ready for a night on the town. Like Moses parting the Red Sea, Gunn thought, or a dose of salts.

'Here,' she panted. 'Got something for you.'

She produced a small rusty key; to a mortise lock, Gunn noted. 'Mr Jones gave this to me last year.

Told me to make sure to keep it very safe. Keep schtum, know what I mean?'

Before they could ask her what exactly she did mean, and why she hadn't handed the key straight to Edward or Louis, the crowds swallowed her up again. Shaking his head thoughtfully, Gunn pocketed the key.

Waving to him as he descended into the underground, Sylvia realised she was right by Somerset House, with an hour to spare before it closed for the evening. The sky was turning black and she hadn't brought an umbrella. She crossed the quad, noticing the great stones blackened by grime and repairs, but it remained a magical place as far as she was concerned. As the first gusts of rain came, she picked up her step and, handbag over her head, dashed to the entrance and bundled through the doors, just as the rain threw itself against Somerset House and London. Shaking her head free of the rain drops that sprinkled her hair, she made her way into the gentle hum of study. She didn't notice the louche individual slouching out through the foyer, noting her entry as he left, collar up and cigarette firmly tabbed to his lower lip.

The Search Room contained row upon row of volumes documenting births, marriages and deaths going back to 1837. Sylvia marched straight over to the 1880s section, notepad and pencil in hand. By the time the miserable old trout at the front desk had announced that the Search Room would close in fifteen minutes, she had the sketchy beginnings of a family tree. Why did he have to be called Jones, she sighed, as she queued up with her docket to order the certificates she needed.

Deciding that was quite enough for one day, she made her way to the bus stop through the rain and then home, which had been, for the past year, a room in a Georgian house in Tufnell Park, owned by two parsimonious doctors. The house was dark, so tall that it cast a gloomy shadow, even in the summer, over what passed for a garden. The other houses cast equally large shadows, making the road look forbidding, even on a sunny day. A doodlebug had scored a direct hit opposite, which let a little light in, but it was getting quite overgrown.

Basic hardly began to describe Sylvia's room. Last winter had been so cold that her window had frozen on the inside. The bunker almost seemed warm and palatial by comparison. There weren't even any curtains when she moved in. A supercilious young stockbroker had the other room downstairs. She knew he smuggled his girlfriend in for the odd overnight stay; rather a sourpuss. Apart from the odd terse run-in about the kitchen and bathroom (why did they think she would want to steal their milk and where else was one meant to dry one's nylons?), their paths scarcely crossed. She preferred it that way. It would do for now. It was a roof over her head. That mattered more than anything. A few more cases like Mr Jones, she thought, as she walked towards the house, smiling at the gaggle of children playing in the street and the ginger cat that always waited for her return.

A figure emerged from the shadows on the opposite side of the road and disappeared nimbly into the bombsite, releasing a strong scent of buddleia. He looked vaguely familiar, Sylvia thought, but you got all sorts of strange people wandering past nowadays. She let herself in through the door, its rather grand stained glass panels belying the Spartan interior.

Gunn, meanwhile, had had a snifter too many with the chambermaid, whose name, he had discovered, was Dolly, and was already late for dinner at an old friend's bistro on Greek Street. Still, he could count on Dimitri to work his charms on young Dolly. After the usual scolding and the flurries of self-deprecating apologies, dinner was good and the wine, for London, was drinkable. Then Gunn escorted a tipsy Dolly down to Piccadilly Circus, found her a cab, unbuckled the proverbial silver and sent her happily on her way.

Satie, one of his musical heroes, liked a stroll in the rain, or so Gunn had once read. He approved of that. Declining a cab, he decided to head for his digs in South Kensington on foot. A good stride away, but it would give him time to clear his head in time for the busy day ahead in Dover. He made his way back to his lodgings just as the pouring rain redoubled its efforts. This was getting personal now, as was the front door being locked and the lights out. Gunn sighed, and hoisted himself up via the porch and drain pipe to the first floor. He slipped his fingers in beneath his window and twisting his shoulders heaved the heavy sash open and rolled headfirst into his room, bumping up against the sagging wardrobe which contained his other suit.

So much did not stack up about Jones but he was in desperate need for some shuteye right now. Tired though he was, sleep did not come easily to Gunn. Thoughts of the war fluttered through his head, juxtaposed uneasily and bizarrely with lines of poetry he hadn't thought of since boyhood –something about a promise.

More than once, he retreated from his bed to his armchair for a cigarette and an abstract gaze into the night beyond his window. Giving up altogether on sleep at around 5 am, he washed, dressed and let himself out of his lodgings the same way he had come. He saw no need to disturb the slumbers of the rest of the house, which consisted of Mrs. O, a sharp-tongued landlady with arms like ham hocks (her stentorian and self-righteous snoring could have woken the dead, he thought irritably, during his vigil), a retired veteran of 14-18, a spinster who had lived in China in the thirties (some said she had been a missionary before succumbing to gin) and a cellist at the Royal College. Gunn had always been a man who enjoyed a mixed crowd. Some might say he took it a little too far sometimes. Hands in pockets, raincoat slung over his shoulder, he sauntered down the garden path, hopped over the gate and set a course for Victoria Station and Dover, the lock and key of the kingdom. He would see if he could penetrate it.

Chapter 3

By the time Gunn was making his way down to Dover docks, the white cliffs towering above him, seagulls busily flying to and fro with their harsh cries, Sylvia was enjoying a welcome cup of tea with Albert, concierge at Claridges. What he didn't know about his 'regulars,' as he liked to call them, was scarcely worth knowing, but Albert was the soul of discretion. He did have a soft spot for Sylvia though; dating back to her childhood days when she was taken there for tea as a 'special treat' by her aunt. A small child, even one on its best behaviour, had been an unusual sight in those magnificent surroundings. In any case, he had started work early; the place was heaving, and he welcomed the chance to take the weight off his feet.

Albert, Sylvia noted, was worried about Mr Jones and seemed genuinely relieved to pour out his concerns. Mr Jones's annual visit was a regular fixture in the calendar, throughout the twenties and thirties. Sometimes, Madame Louise would accompany him, and Albert would be charged with finding the best seats in the house at the theatre. This year, his favourite suite had been reserved, but he hadn't shown up. Albert was adamant about this – if he had decided to stay at his club instead, he would have let them know.

Her next stop, at Albert's suggestion, was Rules. Mr Jones had not been there this summer. Nor had there been any trace of him at his club. After a visit to the library to consult Debrett's, Sylvia wended her way absently back along the Strand towards

23

Clements Inn and the bunker. It was beginning to look as though Mr Jones had never made it over here. Unless Gunn found any clues at Dover, that trip to France was becoming a reality. France was a part of her life she had put in a distant compartment.

As Sylvia pushed open the door of the bunker, and picked up the post, which was stuck halfway through the letterbox, (not more bills, surely,) Gunn pushed open the door of the Hotel de Brussels in Beach Street. He settled himself in the snug, turning his card rail ticket over in his fingers while he waited for the early morning shift of customs men to trickle in, confident that a few pints would elicit some useful information.

A couple of hours and more than one dip in the expense account did indeed pay dividends. Gunn returned to Dover Priory station, purchased a morning edition of the Daily Sketch, and hopped back and forth, change jiggling in his pocket while he waited for a ruddy-faced charwoman to finish her conversation on the only functioning public telephone. Shaking his head at the animated discussion of Mrs Duckett's bunions, he smiled thanks as the charlady finally emerged, holding the door open for him. He put his money in the slot, almost bursting with impatience as the operator put the call through in languid tones. Someone was already queuing behind him but he saw no particular need for any discretion.

'Sylvia, listen, one of the Customs chaps remembers Jones well. Heath, his name is. Been here since the 20s. Decent cove, bit of a fossil though.

Anyway...' Gunn broke off, glaring at the pale, lugubrious man peering right in at him; his facial features scarcely discernible. He looked rather unwell but how incredibly rude. Suddenly, the old adages about 'walls having ears' and 'careless talk costing lives' flashed through his mind. Grubby telephone boxes probably had ears too. 'Look – Damn, here's the train. See you back at the bunker.'

Gunn dropped the receiver and ran to the train, reaching for a carriage door and swinging up and in without a second to spare, as the locomotive drew out of the station and started building up steam.

'Gunn, are you still there?' Sylvia had not registered the last comment about the train. 'I meant to say, could you call in at Simpsons on your way? See if Jones cancelled that meal? Gunn?'

There was some slightly wheezy breathing on the other end of the line and a discreet cough, before the receiver was replaced. Bemused, Sylvia continued working her way in her usual methodical fashion through the day's post. A receipt for a quarter's rent from their landlord (good thing he hadn't been upstairs lately and spotted Gunn's dark room, otherwise he might start charging them more.) A decent cheque from some solicitors in Wembley accompanied by a fulsome letter of thanks for their help in tracing a particularly slippery former client, and, even better, finding out that he had ample money to cover his debts. They would appreciate some assistance with a few more cases and suggested a meeting at their offices in September, after the holiday season. Vera would be paying them soon too for Gunn's jaunt to the Imperial Hotel.

Things were looking up. The summer was always a little quieter in their line of work, with the courts being shut in August and the holiday season generally. If they did end up having to go to France, this wouldn't be a bad time. She wouldn't let Gunn go alone; she trusted him, of course, but this was definitely a job for two. She would just have to try and brush aside the memories it would provoke, and the sadness she had kept locked firmly away for years, and keep her business brain engaged.

She pulled out the sketchy notes she had made at Somerset House on Jonathan Theophilus Weston Jones. Born in 1884 to Henry Theophilus Jones (that's where it came from) and Olivia Harriet Weston. An older brother, Clarence Walter Weston Jones, born in 1881. Killed at the Battle of Loos. A lieutenant in the King's Royal Rifle Corps and he hadn't married. Henry, their father, died in 1908, confirming what Edward had outlined, and Olivia in 1919. So that would have meant that Jonathan was the sole heir. Not much on the Joneses in Debretts, but a full entry on the Westons; probably where the money came from. Both parents were only children. Louisa Vogel was noted in Debretts as Jonathan's wife. Daughter of Samuel and Cecilia Vogel, of Vienna and, more recently, Paris. They hadn't yet updated the entry to record her death.

Gunn folded his paper. He could not concentrate and in any case was not overly concerned with the Olympics, which London had somehow been foisted with, despite the privations of what remained a wartime economy. That cove at Dover Priory had rattled him a little. Something definitely did not sit right. A cold hard dash of logic had it that there would be no reason for anyone to be keeping tabs on him or Sylvia. They were, after all, on a private commission, and the circle of knowledge was pretty tight from what he could tell.

All the same, he decided to wander the length of the train on a just in case basis, making his way along the corridor. As an American GI had observed to him in '44, 'no harm, no foul, bud.' As the train chugged along underneath the cliffs of England, normally a part of the journey he loved, Gunn suddenly came face to face with old 'Lilychops' from the telephone kiosk, sitting in an empty compartment. 'Blimey, he must have got a move on to catch the train,' thought Gunn. Lilychops seemed startled to be confronted directly and made to get up, but Gunn had him in a choke hold.

'What the hell do you think you are doing?' hissed Gunn.

Before Lilychops could respond, the ticket collector appeared at the end of the corridor. 'Tickets please, ladies and gents,' he called cheerfully. Lilychops took advantage of a momentary loosening of Gunn's grasp to duck under his arm and flee.

'Folkestone Central,' called the guard on the platform. Lilychops pushed the door open and got out. Gunn let slip a resounding 'Bugger!' as Lilychops tore down the ramp towards the exit, to the horror of the mother with three children in the next compartment. 'I do beg your pardon, madam,' he apologised. Realising he had become one of those people his own mother had always instructed him to

27

avoid, Gunn gave a rueful chuckle and tried to focus on his paper again. Old Lilychops would now have at least an hour to wait for the next London train and the tea at the little station cafe was, from what Gunn could recall from his schooldays, going backwards and forwards to Paris, pretty vile.

Well, that had shaken him off, but then there were bound to be more where he came from. He started to feel a little uneasy about Sylvia being alone in the office. If that ticket collector hadn't happened along just then, he might have got something out of him. They might have to talk to that shower at Cumberlands about a higher budget at this rate. It certainly seemed that Jones had not made it to England this year, and they were not the only people interested.

Gunn was first off the train when it pulled into Charing Cross, and sprinted up to Clements Inn, taking the steps several at a time. Sylvia was quietly writing up the accounts ledger. Over a much-needed coffee, Gunn recounted the day's happenings; the confirmation from Heath that Mr Jones came to England once, and very occasionally twice a year. It tended to be in the early summer and he had not been through this year. Sylvia told him about her findings at Somerset House and at the library, and at Claridges and Rules.

'Oh, did you manage to get to Simpson's? I wasn't sure if you heard me; line went a bit funny.'

Gunn told her about Lilychops outside the telephone box and on the train. Sylvia frowned. 'Funny, but I think someone was lurking outside my house last night; just caught a glimpse out of the corner of my eye.'

Locking the door to the bunker with more care than usual, observing their strict 'clear desk' policy, they went their separate ways – Gunn to check out Simpson's and Sylvia to meet Edward and Louis and suggest a retainer for this new phase of the investigation. Simpsons confirmed, after the usual to-ing and fro-ing and the passing of a ten shilling note in the passing handshake that Mr Jones had not arrived and indeed they had had no word from him 'whatsoever.' Gunn turned that over as he strolled back along the Strand towards Aldwych.

'Whatsoever.' That was pretty categorical for those stuffed shirts at Simpsons, beyond their usual facade of utter discretion. He turned on his heel and returned to the restaurant and, having unbuckled another note, came away with the impression that Simpsons were, for reasons they could not identify, very concerned about a valued customer. Gunn paused and cadged a light from a passing Marine. Something was amiss. He had the sense that a trip to France might be a necessity, not a luxury on Edward's tab. He hoped Sylvia would be able to work her magic on Cumberlands.

Fortified by one of Joan's special cups of tea, Sylvia was already ensconced in the meeting room at Cumberlands. Louis was in Court at an emergency hearing before one of the High Court Masters; an issue had arisen over the lease of one of his tailors in the Piccadilly Arcade that simply couldn't wait. It would be difficult to discern which of them would be more ill-tempered, Edward joked, as he took a seat opposite her. 'Oh, to be a fly on the wall!'

'Anyway.' He cast an appreciative and slightly wistful eye over Sylvia, thinking how much her green dress suited her colouring. 'How have you been getting on?'

Sylvia gave him a carefully adulterated version, which included the odd specimen who had flitted across the bombsite opposite her house and Lilychops, but not what Gunn had done to him. Edward had a peculiar fascination with the life of an enquiry agent, or at least his perception of it, but he could be terribly prissy at times, for somebody who had been in the air force. Sylvia loved to tease him, assuring him that it wasn't a dark art.

The upshot was, Mr. Jones had not made it to England. Many people seemed to be concerned about it. Some appeared less than savoury. If Cumberlands were adamant about not involving the police or consular officials in their inquiry, presumably they would now require Clements Investigations to take things further and would be prepared to come up with the 'necessary.' She outlined the preparations that would have to be made and the steps they would need to take in France, and took some more careful notes. Edward confirmed that Mr Jones had a very distant cousin on the Weston side in Dorset, several times removed and he had already been in touch. 'Sounded as if he was at death's door,' Edward commented. Anyway, he had heard nothing since before the war, although that was not unexpected; they were not that close.

'You drive a hard bargain, Miss Fordred.' Edward sighed as he took out his fountain pen and wrote out another, even larger cheque to cover up-front expenses. Sylvia eyed him thoughtfully. He usually had to get his father's authority before he so much as bought a box of matches. First yesterday's sizeable cheque, now this one; whatever were they getting themselves into?

'But seriously, please don't hesitate to ask if there is anything – anything at all that you need. Here's Quentin's card, by the way.' Edward had told Sylvia that Cumberlands' correspondents in Paris, Cabinet Meunier, would be at their disposition in case of emergencies. He had already briefed Maître Meunier by letter.

Edward frowned fleetingly, as if it were an afterthought.

'Seriously, though, Sylvia, I wouldn't like to think of you going over there on your own but ...this Gunn character....seems a bit rough around the edges, can't put my finger on it...I mean, would you trust him?'

'With my life' came the emphatic reply, as Sylvia took her leave.

Edward raised an eyebrow the merest fraction of an inch. Deep in thought, he made his way back up to his office, not stopping for his usual chat with Cathy and Joan. He did not know what to make of Gunn. He didn't like the cut of his jib. In his time in the RAF, Edward had fought alongside men from outside his social world. He valued them and held them in the highest esteem and would always stand a drink for them. But Gunn, well, he was a different kettle of fish. He disturbed Edward's carefully crafted world view and style. Gunn was neither an Englishman nor a Frenchman; at least being the latter could have excused him. He was between two worlds and thus worthy of suspicion. Even his war service had been irregular for the most part, serving with Stirling and then the SOE. Not quite the right team.

Anyway, if that clown let the slightest harm come to Sylvia, he would cheerfully throttle him with his bare hands. He and Sylvia went back a long way; their families had been friends, although this had come to an abrupt end. He never knew why, but he and Sylvia had continued to exchange letters when they were away at school. He had been off somewhere with the RAF when the news had come through about her father, but his parents had remained tight-lipped, still nursing some kind of grudge. Now they were steering him inexorably towards Caroline, the bovine daughter of friends from his parents at the tennis club.

Actually, he should have been setting up exchange of contracts right now, on a house in Hampstead belonging to yet another of his father's Cambridge contemporaries. It could bloody well wait. Scowling, Edward screwed up the piece of paper with the details on it and threw it against the wall. Ringing down to reception, and telling Cathy in no uncertain terms that he was not to be disturbed for at least an hour, irrespective of who it was, he unlocked the top drawer of a large cabinet belonging to his father. The secretaries had gone home early. Now was his chance. Fortified by a large slug of brandy from the meeting room, he took out a large file on Jones, marked 'Confidential.'

Back at the bunker, and in equal need of a drink, Sylvia poured a measure of whisky for herself and a more substantial one for Gunn. Grinning his thanks, he observed 'here's mud in your eye' and threw a good portion of the 'life giver' down his throat. He set his glass on the desk and watched as the tawny spirit settled down. He looked over at his colleague.

'Well, this is a rum do. Money thrown at us, everyone we meet as twitchy as hell, and we can hardly move without stumbling over some cove in the shadows like some character from some ghastly provincial two-hander at Retford Rep.'

'I can't understand it,' Sylvia agreed. 'The whole thing doesn't really ring true.'

'Not for a minute. I wonder if old Louis knows more than he lets on. He was pretty quiet the other day, apart from warning you off about the police. And I don't think you could put it all down to him being worn out after tearing that girl from the bank off a strip, either.'

'I think we had better put Chartrettes at the top of the agenda.' Sylvia reached for the battered school atlas from the shelf, and her father's copy of Baedeker. 'South of Paris, isn't it?'

'Indeed. Other side of the river from Fontainebleau.'

'So you know it?'

Gunn narrowed his eyes. 'Not really. My parents took me to some friends at the Chateau de

33

Sermaise when I was a boy. Beyond that, I have little memory of the area. Now Paris I do know.'

'I can imagine.' Sylvia pursed her lips in mock disapproval. 'Some stories to tell?'

'In the right company.'

Gunn closed the subject. 'Shall I get tickets for the boat train for the day after tomorrow? Should be fairly easy; every bugger is coming in rather than leaving.'

'Fine by me' said Sylvia. 'Now, about money and exchange controls...' She was about to tell him about Cabinet Meunier.

'Not a problem. We'll use the old Stavisky method. Just unbelt some money that a friend of mine in Hatton Garden can turn into gold. Works like a dream. Trust me. Voice of experience and all that.'

Privately, Sylvia felt rather relieved to have Cabinet Meunier's business card. She wasn't sure she liked the sound of this Stavisky method, even with the voice of experience in charge of it. Life with Gunn had always been entertaining. Now, she felt as if she were in a novel written by a madman, with no familiar landmarks.

Chapter 4

On the top deck of the SS Isle of Thanet, Sylvia and Gunn were enjoying some afternoon sunshine. It had been an incredible couple of days. Sylvia was not at all sorry to see the back of Tufnell Park for a while. One of the doctors had shot suspiciously into the hall as she set out, canvas holdall slung over her shoulder. Goodness knows what he thought she had in there. She had given him a cheerful wave in farewell.

Gunn had faced down another interrogation from Mrs. O, his landlady. She never missed a trick. Giving her a couple of months' rent had shut her up. Gloria, the old China hand, had given him an unladylike conspiratorial wink as she stirred some disgusting-looking porridge. 'The stories she could tell would fill a book,' Gunn thought, as he headed for the underground.

Idly watching a seagull trying to keep pace with the ferry, Sylvia chuckled as she recalled Gunn's face when he had appeared, tickets in hand, to discover Joan ensconced tightly behind a desk.

'Christ,' he had grumbled sotto voce. 'We'll need a bloody extension at this rate. How will she manage the stairs?'

'Well, a few more cases like this and we can take the whole building over' Sylvia replied, happily.

'Don't you worry, Mr Gunn' Joan had said, watching Gunn and Sylvia scurrying back and forth like a pair of ants, in and out of the props cupboard, carrying out final 'pre-op' checks (old habits died hard). She was amused to watch Gunn taking things out of the bags and Sylvia putting them back in. 'I'll look after the place for you. Keep it ticking over. Fancied a change from those stuck up gits at Cumberlands anyway and this is right on my bus route. You concentrate on finding Mr Jones. Real gent, that one.'

Both fell silent as the coast of France drew nearer, lost in thoughts and memories of their own. Each had a complex relationship with France, rooted both in childhood and in the fall of France in 1940. Sylvia's father had been a wine importer and her earliest and sunniest memories were of trips to Epernay and Bordeaux, in an overloaded Citroen supplied by her father's company. The last time she had seen her father was when he had put her on the train at the Gare du Nord for her journey back to boarding school in England. He had written regularly but then darkness had fallen; the end of her childhood. She often told herself, when she felt very alone, that this was an experience shared by many. It didn't make it easier.

Sylvia instantly knew she was 'home,' as she still thought of it, as they negotiated customs and immigration, by the evocative smell of gitanes. A hot, dusty ride to Amiens and finally they were on the Paris train. Gunn's mind was racing as the city he loved so much drew closer. As they chugged through the suburbs, he realised Sylvia had fallen asleep with her head on his shoulder. He was reluctant to move her, although his arm had gone to sleep. He stayed stock still, deep in thought, for the rest of the journey.

'Sylv' he said 'Wake up, sweetheart. We're here!'

Normally, he would have known better than to call her 'Sylv' or 'sweetheart.' However, Sylvia scarcely seemed to notice and to be almost in a world of her own as she stood on the platform and he passed the bags down to her, including far too much of the props cupboard. 'Thought we were meant to be travelling light, not going on a sodding Thomas Cook's tour,' he grumbled. Most of this would end up in the consigne, if he had his way. It struck him then how little he knew about Sylvia; she never mentioned her family. He only knew she had been married in 1943, and widowed almost immediately. She rarely let her guard slip. Watching her, lost in thought beside the train, he sensed the vulnerability under that prickly exterior.

'Gare de Lyon next,' said Gunn, as he joined her on the platform. 'There's a bus right outside. Then, I don't know about you, but I am going to need a large snifter.'

The familiar sight of the squat clock tower on the Boulevard Diderot caught Gunn's eye as the bus pulled in to the Gare de Lyon. He grinned at a memory or two, despite the press of cinq à sept humanity on the bus. Sylvia looked at him inquiringly. Gunn considered for a moment and then offered:

'Oh, I got stuck up behind the clock face in '43. Some damn fool op coming into Paris, got rumbled by the Germans and the French police. Had to stick a knife in my contact, who was working for the police. They chased me into the station and they

37

spent hours, combing every damn train in and out. Meanwhile, I found a door, prised it open and ended up observing their scuttlings from behind the hour hand. Most unedifying it was, too. Right, let's find our train.'

Sylvia never knew quite what to make of Gunn's stories. She followed him obediently off the bus and along to the huge ticket hall. It seemed unusually thronged with humanity, even allowing for rush hour. They soon established that there had been some flooding further south and there would be no more trains to Chartrettes, or indeed anywhere near it, that evening.

'Well, let's use some of Edward's money,' suggested Gunn. 'I know a little place in Le Marais.'

'Le Marais, isn't that the Jewish area?' Sylvia didn't know Paris terribly well; it had been a while since she last passed through. Right now, anywhere with a clean bed and somewhere she could have a wash and brush-up after that bus journey sounded good. Gunn always had a certain style and, despite the waves of exhaustion lapping over her, she was rather curious to see some of these old haunts and to see Paris through his eyes. That snifter sounded tempting, and she realised they had scarcely had a bite to eat all day.

'Yes, it is.' Gunn shouldered their bags and led Sylvia firmly out to the taxi rank. Poor girl was dead on her feet. 'No more buggering buses. Hate them. Rather take a cab.' The pair waited, content in the hum of noise about them and a cigarette each from the packet that Gunn had gleefully bought at the tabac at the station entrance.

A cab drew up and Gunn threw their bags into the boot, held the door open for Sylvia, and followed her in, folding his frame in after her. He leant over to the taxi driver. 'Hotel Le Vau. Rue du Plâtre.' He leant back and looked at Sylvia. 'Little place I found in 46. It will do. Now, hang on tight, taxi drivers around here are a little enthused at the best of times.'

He wasn't joking, thought Sylvia, feeling slightly dizzy as she followed Gunn into a tall building which had seen better days. She was only half-listening to him rattling on to Madame at the front desk, who had greeted him like an old friend, about the unprecedented shortage of hotel rooms, probably due to the problems on the trains. They followed Madame up the stairs, pressing the light switch at every stairwell, to a room at the top.

'Voilà, Monsieur et Madame Gunn' She rattled an impressive bunch of keys and opened the door with a magnificent flourish, as if ushering them into the best suite at the Ritz. 'Bienvenue à Paris!' Giving them a lascivious wink, she added 'Félicitations!' and commenced the steep descent back to her desk.

The view out of the window was stunning; the rest of the facilities not so impressive. The bed, which was huge and sagged in the middle, had an old red counterpane draped over it. It looked as if it dated back the Revolution. Clouds of dust billowed out if you so much as touched anything. The walls were a brown colour; that was probably all the nicotine over the years.

'That bed has seen some action.' quipped Gunn.

'I suppose you would know all about that!' retorted Sylvia.

A quick wash and brush up later, using the rather grubby facilities at the end of the corridor (Sylvia shuddered to think who else was using them; certainly someone with most unpleasant habits) they sallied forth into the street.

'So, a snifter and then dinner, Mrs Gunn?' came the suggestion. Sylvia could sense he was pleased to be back in Paris, possibly a little too pleased with himself, but she nodded in agreement. 'We could have a stroll and see what we come across.'

'Why not?' Sylvia was tired, but felt the need to stretch after having been cooped up for so long on the train. 'Any particular direction in mind?'

'Hmm, left on the Rue des Archives, coming up in a minute, then a right past the Theatre des Blancs Manteaux, then a right and a left down the Rue des Rosiers. Slap bang in the middle of the Jewish district. There's a damn decent restaurant down there.'

'He clearly knows his Paris,' thought Sylvia.

Another hundred yards and they were there; through the noisy Jewish deli and down the rough steps into the restaurant, spit and sawdust and Jewish food from back east. Gunn visibly relaxed as they followed the waitress down the steps into the bustle and hum and the music. The waitress, whose hair was cut straight across her cheek bone and as sleek as a crow's feather, insisted that a party at a long table squeeze up to make some room. Her tone brooked no resistance.

Gunn and Sylvia sat down and he ordered them vodka –Polish and ice cold, as a palate cleanser. He smiled at Sylvia, who was looking about her with some curiosity.

'First came here in 45, just after the Germans were cleared out.' Gunn pointed back to the stairs. 'The deli was a little empty, but they were getting back in the saddle. 'I had meatloaf and carp, not on the same plate mind, too much vodka and then fell out onto the street at around breakfast time, which led me to Les Halles, strong coffee, bread and apricot jam.'

'You'd better order.' Sylvia was dazed. 'It looks amazing. I wouldn't know where to start.'

Over dinner, and more vodka, they talked about Chartrettes. It was difficult to make many plans before they got to the house. Presumably Mr. Jones had neighbours. Maybe the local shop or auberge could shed some light.

'It's good to be in France again.' Sylvia sat back contentedly, letting the alcohol course through her veins. She told Gunn about her father, and how he had died in the summer of 1940, when France fell. Her mother had walked out on them many years previously. As a result, Sylvia had become the ward of her aunt Hortense although she was at boarding school in Folkestone. After her father's death, she became rebellious and disaffected, spending most of her time working out how to escape from school. The final incident had involved the local boys' school. She hastened to add that nothing untoward had gone on.

41

'That's where the resourcefulness comes from. I knew it. Good thing I wasn't in the vicinity,' commented Gunn.

Eventually, she was expelled. The headmistress told her never to darken the doors of the school again. Aunt Hortense died not long afterwards. The old bat's friends spitefully told her at the funeral that this was due to her disgraceful behaviour. The family doctor later assured her that this was unlikely to have been the case. Yet Aunt Hortense had changed her will and left her house and seven mangy cats to the local Cats' Home, with just a small allowance for Sylvia to eke out an existence in London. Her father's estate had been held in trust for her and she would come in to it in a few years.

She had enrolled on a secretarial course, and then worked for a law firm in the West End, dealing with high profile divorces. One evening, she had met Richard, a young Canadian officer, at a dance. They were married within six weeks, at the local Registry Office, with two strangers pulled in from off the street as witnesses. Their happiness was short-lived; Richard was killed in Italy. Sometimes, she wondered whether she had dreamed the whole thing. She had received a sweet letter from his parents in Manitoba, offering her a home with them, but after years of being under someone else's control, that was the last thing she wanted.

Sylvia rarely told people about her marriage. It had only lasted a few weeks and scarcely seemed real now. Sometimes it crossed her mind that it might have complicated things with the trust, which Edward's firm was managing.

'One up on young Master Cumberland,' Gunn remarked.

She had joined the army, before going over to work at the Nuremberg trials and the rest, as they say, was history. Fuelled by vodka, she leaned across the table.

'You've never told me about your family. I mean, was there ever a real Mrs. Gunn?'

The effect was astonishing, like shutters being pulled down on an Oxford Street shop window. Gunn parried the question, saying he was far more interested in hearing about her antics with the other little minxes in the dormitory. The conversation turned back to Clements and plans for the future. Much later, they staggered out of the restaurant, arm in arm.

In no time, they were back at Rue de Plâtre, just before Madame locked up for the night. They clattered up the stairs.

'I would carry you across the threshold, Mrs. G,' offered Gunn, 'But in my present condition I might drop you.'

He gallantly averted his gaze while Sylvia got ready for bed and then stretched himself out on the floor, on an old army groundsheet which Sylvia had stuffed into one of the bags, thinking it might come in useful.

After a while, he ventured: 'Sylv?' Then, after a pause. 'It's bloody uncomfortable down here.'

Back came the retort 'Don't even think about it!' A rock-hard bolster, and a huge cloud of dust, flew towards him. 'Anyway, this bed's shot to pieces. You're probably better off on the floor. Night.'

Gunn punched the bolster a few times, more in hope than in expectation, and then stretched out like a cat and flirted with sleep. For the most part, it eluded him, though he did dream for an hour or two and found himself again behind a clock face. He woke with a start. He needed a cigarette, but did not wish to disturb Sylvia, whose even breathing spoke of decent sleep.

He unfolded his clothes and drew them on, picked up his shoes and padded out into the dimly lit corridor and down the stairs. At the bottom, he sat and put his shoes on, and slipped past the snoozing night porter and out into the street. It was 5 am. He was beginning to make a habit of this, he thought.

Back in London, Edward had also had a patchy night's sleep, after a steaming row with his father. He did not like what was alluded to in the Jones Confidential file one bit. Much of it was in German; even the part that was in English made little sense. 'Assets of importance.' What the deuce was that supposed to mean? He had tracked Joan down at Clements, secretly rather admiring her gumption, although nobody could make a cup of tea quite like her, and established that Sylvia and Gunn had already left for France, were probably in Paris already and yes, she would contact him immediately if she heard from them.

He had placed an urgent call to Maître Meunier last night and instructed him that the pair were on no account to proceed any further without first speaking to him. He had a fleeting fancy to get on the next boat train and go to Paris himself. Then, he remembered the Tennis Club Dinner that night, with Caroline and her parents. There would be hell to pay if he didn't turn up. He paced up and down, watching the clock, willing it to get to a civilised hour in France.

Quentin Meunier finally took a call from Edward at around 11 am. He had been much too busy, and the curves on his new secretary far too interesting to make too much time for a former RAF pilot, a man that the aesthete in Meunier regarded with a certain amused contempt, his war having been spent in a villa in the hills outside Marseille. He had been a resistant of the last hour, just to make sure, and he glided through life like a cat on a smooth surface. He smiled, and allowed a sip of coffee to pass his lips before speaking to Edward and confirming that he had yet to receive any visit or call from Gunn or Sylvia.

Chapter 5

While Edward was digesting the less than reassuring news from Meunier, Sylvia and Gunn had made their way to the Gare de Lyon and found a direct train to Chartrettes, fortified by strong coffee and croissants. Sylvia had been less than appreciative about being hauled firmly out of bed by Gunn.

'God, my head,' she groaned. 'All your damn fault. Plying me with vodka.'

Some hours later, they alighted onto a deserted platform and made their way out into the dusty streets. A group of elderly men were playing pétanque. They looked up from their game to acknowledge them as they passed.

'The mayor will know there are foreigners in town in about five minutes' observed Gunn, somewhat moodily. 'Nothing we can do about that though. Might as well get a cab, if that's possible around here.'

He looked up and down the Rue Joffre in front of the station. There was one tired long-nosed Citroen Black. A taxi sign was bolted to its roof. Sylvia dug his ribs. 'Let's get that one; can't see any others.'

Gunn grunted a response, something Sylvia could not make out. She cleared her throat.

'What did you say?'

'Nothing.'

'Right, well, let's get this taxi. We haven't got all day. I'm not sure when the trains stop running back to Paris. Don't want to be stuck here all night.'

'All right' he said, absently.

46

Sometimes, Sylvia thought, Gunn's moods were very difficult to fathom. Coupled with those impenetrable silences, they could be really irritating. She much preferred him when he was teasing her and regaling her with his stories, incredible though they often seemed. Would she ever be permitted to get to know the real Gunn? What would that be like? Exasperated, she turned to him.

'Look, what is your problem with this car?'

'It's the make and colour of Citroen that the Gestapo used to use.'

'For goodness sake. Well, it will have to do,' she said, testily. She consulted her notebook. 'Edward said he had a smallholding out on the eastern edge of town, in the Bois de Saint Denis. An old hunting lodge.'

Gunn opened the door of the Citroen to allow Sylvia in, grumbling to himself before stepping in behind her. He was clearly going to be as much use as a lead parachute today, she thought crossly. Well, as usual in these situations, she would have to take control. She decided to ignore him.

Leaning forward, she instructed the driver:

'La ferme de Monsieur Jones, s'il vous plait. Au Bois de Saint Denis.'

Gunn noticed that the driver knew straight away where to go. No questions asked. Rather a taciturn sort. Presumably, though, Jones and his missus would have been accustomed to taking cabs from the station. Edward and Louis had mentioned that the couple often went to Paris in those carefree pre-war days. It wasn't exactly far.

Soon, the Citroen was speeding through the forest, following the line of the river. The River Seine, thought Sylvia. In her guidebook, she had read that they once produced grapes in the area but the vines had all succumbed to phylloxéra. She wondered what Mr. Jones had been cultivating. The Citroen came to a smooth stop outside the gates of an old house. It made her think of Le Grand Meaulnes. French had been one of the few lessons at school where she had paid attention. With its shutters firmly drawn, the house looked as if it had closed itself up against the world.

'Vous voulez que je vous attende, madame?' asked the taxi driver.

'Bien sur,' Sylvia smiled, folding a note of considerable size into the driver's calloused paw. He grinned and settled back in his seat, his cap pulled over his eyes. Sylvia shook her head and stepped out of the Citroen followed by Gunn.

The hunting lodge was probably 16th century, stone and wood with a low and tight stone porch, leading onto a stone path, slick with last winter's moss. They crunched through the gates and over the gravel towards it. A few weeds were peeping through.

'Doesn't seem to look after the outside much, does he?' Gunn commented. 'Poor old boy. Maybe he lost heart when his wife was killed. And he is getting on, I suppose.'

Sylvia went up to the door while Gunn peeled off and nosed about the side and back. There was no response to her knock but she had not expected one. She followed in Gunn's footsteps and found him at a small arched door at the foot of some steps below ground level. He looked up at her.

'Remember that key? Fifty francs says it opens this door.'

Gunn blew at the keyhole. There were fairly fresh scrap marks around the lock. Somebody had been here, not so long ago. Could have been Jones, of course. He turned. Sylvia was close, peering over his shoulder. Her scent was good. She reminded him of someone. Closing his eyes for a moment, he observed: 'Interesting how the taxi driver knew exactly where to go, without question. What does that suggest?'

Before Sylvia could answer, Gunn fished in his pocket for the key and looked about him. There were two stable blocks, a barn with a hayloft and beyond them a line of trees, hunting ground. He shook his head. 'The Gestapo had a listening station in Chartrettes.'

'Relevant?'

'Not a clue.'

Gunn shrugged and handed the key to Sylvia. 'Want to do the honours?'

Sylvia was becoming a little weary today of rhetorical questions and cryptic utterances. What was the matter with him? They had both supped deep of the horrors of war, for God's sake. Opening the door with some difficulty, she made her way inside.

Gunn continued his patrol of the outside, taking his camera with him. One thing he hadn't minded bringing from the props cupboard was decent photographic equipment. The house and grounds, as he had remarked earlier, looked slightly unkempt. Pieces of masonry were falling off. That roof needed attention. Whoever had been here recently hadn't come to help with maintenance; that was for sure. His reverie was broken by a scream which turned his blood to ice. What had he been thinking of, letting her go in on her own? 'Sylv?' He rushed round to the arched door and found her in a corridor.

'Flies. Swarms of them. And the smell. Oh God, I think I'm going to be sick.' She pushed past him, into the open air.

She was right. The smell transported him back to somewhere he had no wish to revisit. She had obviously opened another door somewhere and released these pestilential creatures.

'Hope they don't carry disease,' he thought, fastidiously. 'They probably do; typhus, bubonic plague, all sorts.'

He felt Sylvia's hand in his.

'Come on. We can do this.'

Gunn wrapped a handkerchief about his nose and mouth, and pushed at the wooden door with a scuffed shoe. The door swung lazily open, and he could see into some kind of dining room or salon, buzzing with angry flies. There was a brass door stop at his feet. He picked it up, feeling the weight in his hand. It would do. He threw it at the middle of three windows and the ancient glass crumbled rather than smashed, giving the flies a sudden exit route.

Jones was sitting foursquare on one of the dining chairs, his hair still thick but heavily grey, his nose sharp. His mouth was open and his throat cut and crusted black with blood. Gunn took a few shots of him. It seemed faintly disrespectful. There was no sign of a weapon.

'Let perpetual light shine upon him,' he heard Sylvia say softly.

'Sylv, we're going to have to involve the gendarmes' he said gently, after a moment.

'But Louis said…'

'Sod Louis. Those old boys by the station clocked us. The taxi driver knows we're here. Think about it. The last place we want to be is in some stinking French gaol. Trust me. I reckon we have about fifteen minutes, if we're lucky, before our driver finishes his kip and starts wondering where we have disappeared off to. Better have a look round, I suppose. Nothing we can do for the poor bugger now.'

The salon would have been a magnificent room once; gracefully proportioned though sparsely furnished. It looked as if someone had been emptying it. Perhaps, as Gunn suggested, the old man's heart had gone out of the place after his wife's shocking death. Sylvia's eye was caught by a beautiful walnut writing desk. The lid was down and the drawers pulled out, as though someone had been rummaging through. She gave one of the drawers a hard tug. Jammed tightly into the back was a large wallet stuffed with photographs. She put it into her handbag.

Gunn, meanwhile, had wandered outside again with his camera. He had noticed a few more outbuildings to the side of the house. Two of them had been used for animal feed, presumably before the war - no animals in evidence now. A third, larger building caught his eye. It was not locked.

A moment later, he exclaimed:

'Sylv, come and take a look at this.'

Sylvia followed the sound of Gunn's voice, with a final regretful glance at the dead man. She picked her way across the yard, the long grass brushing her ankles. He was waiting in the doorway of one of the outbuildings. His normal sangfroid had slipped a little; he seemed almost happy, inviting her in without due ceremony.

The barn was long and low, and had a couple of old fruit wagons in storage against the far walls, Gunn grabbed her by the elbow and pointed: 'Look.'

Sylvia was not sure what she should be looking at. She peered along the line he was indicating, noting a thick layer of dust on the floor, which had been undisturbed for some time, and the faint indentations of a trail of footprints in the soil. It might have been a long time since anyone had been there but it was clear they had been, nonetheless. She looked at Gunn and he grinned.

'I think we should, don't you?'

The trail came to a halt at the far wall, having skirted a stack of barrels, old brick and crumbling mortar. Gunn leaned in, placed his cheek to the wall and squinted along the eyeline. 'Got it.' He fished a clasp knife from his pocket and, releasing the blade, started to lever at one of the bricks which was slightly proud of the wall. It fell, with a soft crump. 'I reckon we'll find something in there.' Gunn stepped back so that Sylvia could inspect the opening.

She peered in to a small hollowed-out recess and, as she felt her way, her fingers came across the comforting solidity of an iron cash box. She eased it out. The key was still in it. She turned it, and drew out a pile of documents. One looked like a will. There was also a stack of letters and a photograph of a lady that she took to be Louise Vogel.

'I think we should go straight to the gendarmerie and report Jones's death,' said Gunn 'My instinct is to keep this lot with us and go through it later. Lock the box up and leave it here empty. Don't say anything in the car.'

Putting the documents into her handbag with the photographs from the writing desk, Sylvia followed Gunn back down the drive, where they found their driver just coming round from a deep sleep. Gunn opened the door for Sylvia and then leaned forward to speak to him:

'La gendarmerie, s'il vous plait. Aussi vite que possible.'

'Oui, monsieur' came the response.

Soon, the Citroen was dropping them off outside a low, modern building. The tricolore flew outside.

'Let me do the talking, Sylv.' Gunn turned to her. She nodded. A new assertive, decisive Gunn, with a dash of chivalry added to the mix, was emerging. The sulks and the morose silences annoyed her, but this other aspect was strangely attractive; back on familiar ground, no doubt. Reproving herself for thinking such things with that poor old man lying dead just up the road, she walked into the gendarmerie with Gunn. A young gendarme was manning the desk, reading a book. He sprang out of his chair as they approached, quickly putting his kepi on.

Gunn presented himself as a British officer, formerly of the SOE, who had come to visit an old friend, Mr. Jones and to introduce him to his fiancée, Miss Fordred. Nice touch, thought Sylvia, looking down at Richard's ring, which she had put back on for the trip, just in case. He had found Mr. Jones dead, with his throat cut. The gendarme made furious notes as Gunn spoke. Gunn noted that in his professional judgment, Jones had been dead a week or so. He asked when the last time was that anyone else might have paid Mr. Jones a visit.

The gendarme paused in his writing and shook his head. 'I have no idea, M'sieu. We used to drop in when passing but Mr. Jones is – was – a private gentleman, although always courteous and kind.'

After a few more formalities, the gendarme noted down Meunier's address; Gunn was deliberately vague about where they were staying, explaining their plans would have to change now. They were allowed to go on their way. He hoped that Monsieur Gunn and his fiancée would enjoy the rest of their stay. It was a short walk back to the railway station.

'Great cover story,' Sylvia began.

Gunn seemed not to hear her; he was deep in thought. She tried again:

'Look, there's the train, that's good timing.'

By four o'clock, they had found their way to the Tea Caddy, which stood opposite Notre Dame and

Saint Julien-le-Pauvre, the oldest church in Paris, Gunn told Sylvia. He had come out of his reverie, thank goodness. It was hard to reach him when he went into one of those. 'Thought after the day we've had, a decent cup of tea would be just the thing. None of that gnats' piss.'

His expressions amused Sylvia. They were starting to creep into her vocabulary too. She would have to be careful not to try them out in the wrong company. Gunn had acquired a taste for English tea over the years and the Tea Caddy had always been a favourite haunt of his.

'Came here with Dad' he remarked. 'Just before I came over to England for school.' He never talked about his family much, thought Sylvia, although she had spoken to his father a few times on the telephone. This turned out to be another of his non-sequiturs.

She changed the subject.

'I love the china. Aunt Hortense used to have Willow Pattern.'

After a light lunch, they ordered another pot of tea and began to sift through the photographs. There were the usual wedding pictures and ones of the couple as they got older at the house. Some of the photos were from an earlier date and of a more private nature; there were several of Louise at Deauville in a bathing costume and, similarly attired but in soft focus, by the lake at the demeure. Others showed her with someone who looked very like her, endorsed 'Louise and Marguerite at La Demeure' on the back.

'He must have really loved her,' said Sylvia.

'That definitely comes through in the photography' Gunn agreed. 'How awful.'

They sat in silence for a moment, drinking their tea.

'Shall we have a look at these papers then?' suggested Gunn. 'Quite a few of them, aren't there?'

He began leafing through some letters. They were in German, but he could make out a few familiar names.

'Sylv, you speak German. Take a look at all these while I pop out for a newspaper, then we'll have a look at the rest together. I need to get some fags too. There's a tabac just the other side of Shakespeare and Co. Shan't be a minute.'

Sylvia started to read the letters. A large batch were from Mr. Jones's sister-in-law, a personal assistant to a high ranking official in Berlin, who was protecting her Jewish roots in return for favours. That much was clear. What was also clear was that Marta Vogel (not the other girl in the photographs then, thought Sylvia) had been sending letters and documents which she had copied to her sister in the period up to around 1939. Sylvia guessed it was a kind of insurance, though not one that had done Louise much good. Maybe not Marta either.

Gunn returned, a copy of Le Figaro in his hand. He skimmed through the report on yesterday's athletic events at the Olympics, and an article on the Berlin blockade. His attention was drawn to a piece below on the acquittal of one Friedrich Otto Heinz Mueller in some 'épuration' proceedings in Berlin. He remembered that the French didn't refer to this process as 'denazification.' Mueller had been on the General Staff and had also spent time in France, near

56

Melun, before being recalled to Germany. It was a very short article, as they tended to be. Other priorities were taking over. The world was changing.

'Friedrich Otto Heinz Mueller,' he reflected aloud. 'One lucky bastard, by the sounds of it.'

Sylvia looked up sharply.

'What about him? Marta was working for him in Berlin before the war. Louise's sister. I reckon they were having an affair. Look at this.'

She showed Gunn a picture of a beautiful woman, immaculately dressed, with the address of a Berlin photographic studio stamped on the back, and the handwritten phrase; 'Mein Liebling.'

Gunn raised an eyebrow in enquiry as Sylvia carried on. 'Judging by these letters, and I've just had a quick scan so far, Mueller was setting frameworks in place to allow senior Germans to escape Europe and into the wide blue. I mean, I'd heard of this being done, but Mueller was clearly way ahead of his time.'

'Any other names in there?'

'Plenty. And I would wager a shilling or two that most of them have since been cleared by tribunals. Otto Neumann, now he was sentenced *in absentia*. I remember typing that up. He was in charge of one of the death camps. Said he would survey the camp and could see nothing but rotting flesh. That was how he perceived his prisoners. And Wilhelm Beck too, his henchman. From what I can remember, they were picked up, let go and then disappeared. God. This is amazing stuff.'

'Reckon people were after these letters?'

'Almost certainly.' Sylvia narrowed her gaze. 'Why else kill an old man? Gunn, what have we got ourselves into?'

They turned their attention to the will, their heads close together, totally absorbed. It was short, type-written and relatively simple, signed by two witnesses – French names, probably neighbours. It followed the format Sylvia recognised instantly from her days with the solicitors.

'I, Jonathan Theophilus Weston Jones, being of sound mind and testamentary capacity, hereby revoke all other wills, codicils and other testamentary dispositions.

Following the deportation in 1942 of my dear wife, Louise Vogel, I leave my estate in its entirety to my sister-in-law, Marguerite Cecilia Werner, formerly Vogel, now believed to be in Haifa.'

A 'care of' address was given for an Aaron Vogel in Haifa. The will went on to stipulate that all papers in his possession should be given to Mrs. Werner.

'Well, you could see from the photos that she was close to Marguerite,' said Sylvia. 'I only found the one picture of Marta. I don't understand this. Why didn't he leave his will for Cumberlands to sort out? Could he not have given it and the papers to them, instead of hiding them in a wall? Or do you think that was what he was planning to do?'

'Wait. What's this?'

Gunn drew out from the bundle a scrap of paper, on which, in a shaky hand, was written 'Mannfred Brand' and 'Lothar Kaltenbrunner,' next to it. In another column, the name 'George Cumberland' was underlined several times.

'George Cumberland' exclaimed Gunn. 'Isn't that Edward's father? Did you know he was German?'

'Oh, I always knew that. He's been in England for ages. I didn't know what his name was before though. Edward's mother is English. As a family, they were always more English than the English. I think he was educated over here and then went to Cambridge. I do remember something of a kerfuffle when he was picked up and taken to the Isle of Man; it took them a while to catch with him. Kicking and screaming, no doubt. That wasn't long after he...'
Sylvia stopped, and looked embarrassed. After a second, she added:

'They soon let him go. Probably couldn't abide him in the camp a moment longer.'

'Huh,' Gunn sipped at his cooling tea. It went down well. 'I would have left him on the Isle of Man or made him swim. Reckon he has such sympathies?'

'Quite possibly.' Sylvia turned the question over in her mind. 'After all, with a son as a Spitfire pilot, he would be hidden in plain sight.'

'Of course, and let's be clear. Edward, for all his skills as a pilot, isn't the sharpest tool in the box.' Gunn set his cup down. 'Not being too harsh, but I wonder whether he was given his current position.'

'He was.' Sylvia shuffled uncomfortably. She had a concern for Edward, nothing more. He was upright and basically decent. In some very dark hours at school, she had looked forward to his letters. 'So, let's accept George is a sympathiser and part of this

59

network or framework of Mueller's. What do we do? We can't give the papers to Edward now. His father would get them off him straightaway. I know what he's like.'

'I wonder if we've been set up? These papers are dynamite. Presumably, that's why we've had these goons following us.' Gunn paused, and looked at Sylvia. 'I think we should get down to Haifa pdq, find the family and hand them over.'

Sylvia thought for a moment.

'Won't we have to report in, though? It'll look funny if we don't. I mean presumably there is some sort of murder investigation going on in Chartrettes now. Whoever is on the trail will soon get wind of that. Should we go and see Meunier now and get some money from him, just to make an appearance?'

Gunn shook his head.

'Absolutely not, Sylv, they could be waiting for us at his office. We'd be walking straight into a trap. We need to get out of here. It could turn nasty. In fact, I'm not sure if you shouldn't go back to London, give Edward some cock and bull story to fend him off, keep him off our backs, and just carry on as usual. I'd rather you were safe. I mean, I've done this type of thing over here, and with the greatest respect…'

'I'm not leaving you,' she said firmly.

'I don't know, Sylv.' He sighed, and took her hand in his. 'All right, here's what we do. We'll get ourselves some wheels, drive down to Marseille, then get the boat to Haifa. That in itself could be tricky. You know what the situation is over there. Don't worry about money. I'll get us some. Before we go though, we'll telegraph Meunier, say we are going to Switzerland and will be in touch on our return. Then, if Cumberland does send any of his goons after us, they will be going in totally the wrong direction.'

Sylvia put the papers and photos carefully back into her handbag, and they settled up with la patronne, before heading to the PTT to send the telegraph. At the hotel, which they now affectionately called 'the fleapit,' they told Madame they were off to the country for a while and paid her to keep the room for them. Gunn told Sylvia in no uncertain terms to pack lightly. This was no sodding picnic. They would need to keep their wits about them. They would catch some sleep wherever they could, but they needed to leave Paris now and keep moving as fast as possible.

'You finish packing and I'll go and organise some money and a car,' Gunn spoke over his shoulder as he left. 'I have a few old friends who can help or will help. I will insist.'

Chapter 6

Gunn prowled through Paris as if it were his personal domain. In a way, it was. As a boy, his father had given him a Metro ticket every Saturday and told him to choose a different ligne and navigate his way back on foot. The city had put its memory into his bones that way. It had been useful in '43 and '44, and got him out of more scrapes than a ship in dry dock. He strode down the Rue du Roi de Sicile, ducked down a courtyard and crossed over a back gate into the Rue de Sevigne, took a right down the Rue de Jarente without a pause and then another right into the Rue Necker. He knocked on a large wooden door. A concierge let him in at the passing of a folded note and he headed across the courtyard and up a flight of old stone steps around a galleried landing to Apt 6. He rapped smartly three times in staggered cadence. The door opened and a familiar looking face opened the door halfway, puzzled. Gunn pushed his way in.

'Salut, mon vieux. Been a while.'

Alex Le Puce smiled. 'Four years?'

'Four years and I have some business for you.'

At the word business, Le Puce grinned and welcomed Gunn in. 'Some good business, I trust?'

'Really good.' Gunn was not in the mood to muck about. He fiddled with his jacket cuff and tugged at a thread while Le Puce poured them a cognac each. The seam split and Gunn allowed three slim gold plaques to slip out and into his hand. 'This kind of business.'

Alex grinned, and handed Gunn a glass. 'The kind of business I like. I think I can help.'

'Yes, you can.'

Gunn's gaze was steady as Le Puce screwed a jeweller's eye glass into his good right eye, his left being a rosette of puckered flesh from a beating too far at the boxing booths of Menilmontant in 1937. He had not been a bare knuckle fighter, but a bookie's runner. He had tried to rip the bookie off and taken a pounding for his presumption.

Le Puce inspected the gold plaques and let the eye glass drop into the palm of his right hand. He set it on the table and looked at Gunn.

'Good stuff,' he observed. 'The Stavisky method never gets old. For these three plaques I can offer you $250. Allows me a bit off the top.'

'A bit?' Gunn mused. He would argue for sake of form and appearance, but felt reasonably comfortable, with another five plaques sewn into his collar and waistcoat. 'Not good enough.'

'What can I say? It is the market.'

'Your innocence would win you a Cesar and a night with Arletty.'

'Ha, well, her cunt is international, or so she said, and I am a Pole.'

'No, you are not. Your mother was a Pole and your father was a poilu and you were born three streets back. And you can still do better.'

'Oh, you are not a reasonable man.'

Le Puce grimaced and poured them both another drink. Gunn raised his glass and they clinked rims. Gunn observed:

'No, and I never claimed to be.'

'Putain.'

'Of course.' Gunn's tone became brisk. 'So, you can do better, and by better I mean \$250 and that new Simca 8 of yours in the courtyard.'

He raised a hand to stifle a protest. 'No, that car is for hire and your friend and mine, Jacques Berger, can pick it up and bring it back. I will leave 100 francs under a condom in the petrol cap.'

'How will Jacques know where to pick it up?'

'Well, give me your telephone number and I will call you and tell you where I have left it and Jacques can pick it up.'

Gunn knew he had won.

'Deal?'

'Deal.' Le Puce stood up.

'When do you want the money and the car?'

'Now?' Le Puce shrugged. 'Impossible.'

'Quite possible.' Gunn stood up. 'I am lacking patience today.'

Le Puce knew better than to argue with Gunn when he adopted that tone. He remembered it of old. He sighed, went and got the money and then, rather reluctantly, handed over the keys to his pride and joy.

Twenty minutes later, Gunn drew up outside the hotel. Sylvia had just come downstairs with one large canvas holdall and another smaller one.

'That's my girl.' he said, getting out to open the door. 'On y va.'

It was getting quite dark now. As Gunn negotiated the narrow streets, heading south, he stole the odd glance at Sylvia, lost in thought beside him.

64

'It's been quite a day, hasn't it? Finding Jones like that. I mean, despite everything we went through for all those years, it came as a shock. Almost felt we knew him, too. You must be exhausted. I suggest we get out of Paris and as far south as possible tonight. Then we'll find somewhere for some shut-eye, off the beaten track; we'll camp out. Good thing it's quite warm.'

'Camping? Have you got a tent in the back?' Sylvia asked, absently.

'No buggering tent.' Gunn was amused. 'What do you think I am, a frigging Boy Scout? We need to keep mobile. I think there's a rug or something though.'

She was wearing a black cardigan with lots of little buttons of different colours; very demure. He realized they looked exactly like the cover story they had given to the gendarmes and which they were going to stick to now; a former British officer with his fiancée, touring round France.

At Queen Anne's Gate, George Cumberland slammed the telephone down on Meunier abruptly.

'Switzerland,' he snorted derisively. 'A likely story!'

He had called in at the office on his way to the club, to pick up some petty cash. He had been only too pleased to take the call which Cathy had put through to him. Cathy, with the attention span of a goldfish, had completely forgotten that calls from Meunier were meant for Young Mr Cumberland and him alone. Edward was out doing a completion in Fleet Street. That, George thought, would keep the stupid boy out of mischief for a while. Serve him bloody well right in this weather. Young whippersnapper was becoming quite defiant.

'No,' he shouted, as Cathy appeared with a weak cup of tea, just before she left for the evening. One thing Joan (that fat old mare) used to have in her favour was that she made a decent cup of tea. That was all. Cathy was useless. Not even attractive either.

'Take it away' he almost screamed. 'Get out.'

He noted what Meunier had said about Jones's death having been reported to the gendarmerie by an English officer and his fiancée. That would be all over the newspapers soon, in France as well as here. They needed tracking down soon. One thing was for sure, they wouldn't get very much further, even with all the money his idiot son had given them. That should make things simple. He wagered they would soon be back in London. Better make a call just in case, and get a watch put on the railway stations. It would be useful to know when to expect them. He could hear Louis in the conference room, down the corridor, working on some litigation. Closing the heavy door to his office as a precaution, he lifted the receiver and spoke in low tones:

'Hier ist Mannfred Brand am Apparat.'

Sylvia and Gunn had got out of Paris just in time. The Simca 8 had already cleared the banlieue and was on the Route Nationale. They stopped at the first petrol station they came to, for some food supplies, some water and a coffee each. They also picked up a Michelin Guide, as Sylvia had left the

Baedeker back at the fleapit. Gunn thought it was probably out of date anyway.

'It's getting quite late' he commented. 'I wouldn't mind getting past Troyes and then we'll stop for a kip. You forget how big the distances are here, don't you?'

As they drove through the darkness, they talked again about the papers they had found at Chartrettes. In the folder with the photographs, Sylvia had found another compartment containing love letters between Louise and Jonathan. The paper was thin and delicate, and the writing very close.

'It feels almost as if we are intruding, looking at these,' she commented, 'But we'll have to, won't we, to get the full picture. And then there's this German network. I guess the papers will explain old Cumberland's involvement. There's obviously something in it. I genuinely don't think Edward knows.'

'We'll go through it all properly on the boat. You can sift through all the German and talk me through it, and we'll put it all together in a report. And I might just see if I can get a message to this Aaron Vogel cove in Haifa. By the way, I never asked you. How did you learn that infernal, buggering language?'

Sylvia frowned.

'Don't call it that. It was the first language I spoke.'

'Sorry' said Gunn. 'Rude of me. How did that come about? Didn't you tell me once you had French grandparents?'

67

She explained that her mother was indeed half French, which was how her father had got into the wine importing business. They had lived between England and France; something of a peripatetic existence. She had an older sister, Madeleine. When she wasn't quite two years old, her mother had had an affair with one of their suppliers, who had a small cognac house in the Charente.

Gunn looked at her sharply. 'Whereabouts?' he asked.

'I'm not sure; near Cognac itself, I believe. Why do you ask?'

'Oh, I knew a girl called Madeleine from the Charente once, but I didn't think…' Gunn frowned. 'Anyway, go on.'

'My mother took Madeleine one day and just walked out. She would have taken me too, I suppose, but I had chickenpox. So I stayed with Daddy. He used to say I was the apple of his eye. I always thought it was a funny saying.'

'But you were just a little scrap. I don't understand how anyone could do that.'

Stories of abandonment always upset Gunn. His own childhood had been a happy one, with two parents who had loved him. Like Sylvia's, it had come to an abrupt end with the death of his mother and being sent to school in England.

'Well, I never saw either of them again,' continued Sylvia. 'I presume they stayed with this guy at his cognac house. Aunt Hortense never had anything to say about Mother; just a load of vitriol and venom. I don't think they made it, I never heard. But I was so small, I never knew them anyway.

Daddy had to keep running the business of course, and travelling, so he employed a German nanny, Jutta. She was the nearest thing I had to a mother, I suppose. That's why I speak the lingo.'

'What happened to Jutta?' asked Gunn.

'I've often wondered that. When Daddy decided to send me back to England to boarding school, she went back to Berlin. I think she married her childhood sweetheart. Goodness only knows what happened to them both. He probably had to go in the army and ended up on the eastern front. Jutta may have been killed in one of the raids. I think they lived quite centrally. We did write for a while, until the war started.'

They drove on, in companionable silence. Gunn pulled off the main road a few miles short of Troyes.

'I'm bushed,' he admitted. 'Let's get our heads down for a few hours. Nobody about.'

Gunn pulled the Simca in off the road, behind a screen of trees, just enough to make sure a casual glance would not pick them up and not far enough to get the car bogged down. He handed Sylvia the picnic rug from the boot, excused himself and went for a cigarette. The air was warm and heavy, so close he could almost wear it.

He drew heavily on his cigarette. He had picked up the habit as a boy when helping out at a racing stable, much to his mother's irritation, although he had never been quite sure whether her irritation had been due to the habit or his working at a racing stable. Not quite the thing. He smiled to himself and stretched his limbs. The Simca may have been new but it was somewhat lacking in the comfort department. Le Puce's weak spot was, and always had been, new cars although now it looked as though he had graduated from stealing them to buying them, more or less legally.

He made himself comfortable on the edge of the blanket and looked over at Sylvia, who was fast asleep. That one could kip for England, he thought. She looked incredibly peaceful. He tucked his jacket around her and eventually drifted off into an uneasy sleep of his own. His mind had centred on another hot summer's night in France when he had slept under the stars with another girl beside him. Only now she had Sylvia's face. Surely...

Gunn woke with a start. The birds were singing and it was getting light. He gently shook Sylvia awake.

'Rise and shine, sweetheart. Time to get back on the road and find somewhere for a coffee and a wash and brush up? I'm going to have to get some more fags, too.'

Sylvia commented, as they drove along, on how lovely the area was, with the half-timbered houses. Gunn told her they were probably 15th century. Soon, they were in open countryside, driving through an avenue of poplar trees. It made her think about trips around the country with her father.

'Of course, they were planted to allow Napoleon's army to march in the shade,' Gunn grinned. 'Or so the story goes. There was a crueller version told by a Marine I once knew. Hard bastard. Loathed the Germans but really hated the French.'

'That would have made things awkward' Sylvia observed.

'Well, not as far as he was concerned.' Gunn shook his head. 'He was itching for an excuse to kill a Frenchman. Finally did so in Syria. Several of them.'

'Several?'

'Well, they were only Vichy so I couldn't give a damn' remarked Gunn. 'Funnily enough, I met one when I was in France in 44. Used to work for Vichy, and yet somehow got himself in with the Allies and the FFI. Came from the Charente, funnily enough. Amoral bastard. Profile like a Sphinx after a decent meal. He was trouble.'

'Didn't anybody investigate him?'

'Oh, he investigated himself apparently.' Gunn shrugged. 'I love this country, but it drives me to drink sometimes.'

He paused and let the silence drift a moment before offering an observation.

'Talking about amoral bastards, I reckon Le Puce would sell us out. What say we dump this car, somewhere between Dijon and Macon, borrow another car and leave this in payment?'

Sylvia's mind was spinning. Her world of certainties was running away from her. Only a few days ago, she was in Tufnell Park, arguing with the stockbroker over use of the kitchen and bathroom, and flitting in and out of London's archives and libraries and meetings with clients. Now she was in France, a country she had left as a child, on a mission she had thought she understood and which she knew was always going to be difficult, but which now seemed dark and dangerous. And she was on the way to Haifa with Gunn. She had told Edward that she would trust him with her life. She had no choice now. He seemed to know what he was doing but…

'Want to take the wheel for a bit?' he asked.

He watched her for a while as she drove, and then dropped into a deep sleep. This time, it was Sylvia's turn to nudge him awake.

'We're in Dijon. And you were talking in your sleep.'

'I deny it all' Gunn rubbed his eyes and stretched his frame. 'Shall we find somewhere to get something to eat, and maybe switch cars on the edge of town?

They parked outside a two table sports bar at the back of the cathedral and stopped in for breakfast and a spruce up. Smearing apricot jam on her bread, Sylvia observed;

'We're making good time.'

'We are, but the car is beginning to get to me. Le Puce will sell us out, I'm sure. He has sharp ears. Word will filter through to him that we have something other people want.'

Chapter 7

Balancing uncomfortably over the hole in the ground in the WC at the back of the café, which was slippery and none too clean, Sylvia wondered how Gunn proposed to achieve the next stage of his plan. As if in answer, he appeared next to her with his razor as she brushed her teeth at the unisex sink and combed her hair. They shared a mirror.

'Feels ages since I last had a shave,' he commented. 'Ready for our next little adventure? Just do exactly as I say, sweetheart, don't worry. If we head out towards Longvic, that will get us on the right road.'

Gunn opened the driver's door for her.

'You can drive again for a while.'

Shutting the door on Sylvia, he looked up. The wind was shepherding some heavy clouds their way. It was going to be a hard rain falling. He flicked up the collar on his jacket out of instinct and got in the passenger seat.

'Let's go. And don't spare any horses. It is going to chuck it down.'

Sure enough, just a few miles short of Beaune, the rain began to spill. It was bouncing back up from the road, such was its velocity. Gunn peered through the windscreen, the valiant efforts of the windscreen wiper being in vain. 'Charming.'

'Should we stop or carry on?' Sylvia bit her lip. She did normally enjoy driving (she had learned in the army) but the gear box was heavy and the tyres slick with rain.

'Pull over here, on the left. I've just spotted a petrol stop. We can fill the spare jerry can up with petrol and wait for the weather gods to stop fooling with us.'

The petrol stop consisted of one pump and a tumble-down workshop leaning heavily in on a country cottage. 'Le patron' looked like Jean Gabin's older, more fatigued cousin several times removed and with the addition of a moustache that would have seen service with Napoleon's cavalry at Austerlitz. Gunn trotted over, shook the man by the hand and came back with something approaching a smile on his face and oil on his hand.

'He doesn't think it will last. He's got a Citroen under wraps at the back. He would be prepared to do a deal.'

'Worth a look?'

'I reckon so.' Gunn wiped his hand on the inside of his jacket pocket.

'He wins, we win. Let's give it a few minutes and then talk business.'

'While you do that, I'll go and ring Joan,' said Sylvia. 'I won't tell her where we are, of course. But we do need to know what's been going on in our absence.'

Sylvia shut herself into the telephone box and was soon through to one of the 'demoiselles' and then Joan. It was reassuring to hear Joan's voice though not what she had to say. Joan explained that she was receiving some mysterious calls, where the person just hung up. Old Mr Cumberland had been on the telephone four times, she said, demanding to know where they were. Young Mr Cumberland had turned up at Clements, leaving a message that they should ring him straightaway. Otherwise, things were ticking over nicely. The Wembley firm had confirmed the appointment with several new instructions for a few weeks' hence. A couple of other divorce cases had come in but they could wait until their return. Oh, and Cathy had left Cumberlands after the old man had been particularly ghastly once too often.

'Don't know how she stuck it out so long,' observed Joan. 'Listen, ducks, I know you can't say much. But be careful. That old git, Cumberland seems to have a bit of a bee in his bonnet. I know Mr Gunn will take care of you but I worry about you both.'

Thoughtfully, Sylvia walked back across the road towards Gunn. It felt as if something had walked over her grave. She told him about Edward's visit first.

'Nice of him to care,' commented Gunn.

'His father is onto us though,' she said. 'He's phoned the office four times.'

'Bound to happen, I suppose.' Gunn shrugged. 'But we do have a head start and we are a little bit smarter than that old square head. You didn't give Joan any inkling of our whereabouts?'

'No.' Sylvia shook her head. 'I just said something vague about Switzerland.'

'Good girl. Not a million miles from here, so quite plausible. And it ties in with the story we fed Meunier yesterday' He looked at her. 'You're shivering. Come in out of the rain. I've had a look under the oilskins at the car. It's a 1934 Citroen 7A. Front wheel drive, all steel body in great nick. Used

75

to belong to the old man's son but he was killed in 1943, trying to blow up the local telephone exchange. Not many klicks on the clock. I vote we turn the Simca over and get the Citroen plus a few francs and a tankful of gas.'

'Just make sure it starts first, and that he hasn't been keeping chickens in the back seat. And bring the rug and the Michelin guide.'

Gunn reappeared with the car a few minutes later.

'Hop in! Bloody sight more comfortable, this car.'

'You and your cars!' Sylvia smiled. 'Like being on a day out with Mr Toad.'

Having listened absently for a few minutes to a lecture on the virtues of the Citroen 7A, Sylvia began:

'Gunn, I've got a bad feeling about this. Old Cumberland is in this up to his neck. The thing is, he has friends in very high places in the establishment so even if we gave the papers in to the authorities, it wouldn't make the slightest difference. He'd wriggle out of it. And we would still be his targets because we know the truth. Probably just me, actually.'

'Why do you think I'm so keen to get us to Israel?' asked Gunn. 'Quite apart from getting the will to Marguerite of course? They'll know exactly what to do with the papers there, I can assure you. And why do you think he is just honing in on you? We haven't had an awful lot to do with the repulsive old sod, have we? It's mainly been Edward and Louis giving us our instructions on all the cases.'

Sylvia looked ashen.

'Sylv, come on, spill the beans,' he urged.

Sylvia explained that, when she was about sixteen and had lost her father, she and Aunt Hortense were summoned to a meeting at Queen Anne's gate, to discuss her father's will. Aunt Hortense had to go to the dentist urgently, so Sylvia ended up going to the appointment on her own. Cumberland had told her that her father's estate was all tied up in trust for her until she reached the age of twenty five. No provision had been made for her mother, who had married the man from the cognac house, or for Madeleine.

'Well, you know I was expelled from school at around that time. He started talking about that. He seemed outraged at me having gone off the rails. I'd always been scared of him. I'd seen the way he treated Edward.'

Gunn felt a momentary pang of sympathy for Edward, as he did for anyone who had an unhappy childhood. Overtaking a camionnette, he said gently:

'Go on.'

'He made a pass at me. You know, sexually. It was horrible. If Joan hadn't rescued me, I don't know what would have happened.'

It was Joan who had dried her tears and taken her round to Claridges, to wait with Alfred for Aunt Hortense.

'And nothing did happen?'

'No, but I was so terrified. I've never...you know, mentioned this to anyone. He would only have twisted it round so it looked as if it was my fault.'

'Well, I'm not letting you out of my sight now. Thank God Joan came waddling to the rescue.

If, once we are back in London, I find he hasn't already been taken out, I will wring his frigging neck. Right. Let's get on that boat as soon as we can. I think there might be a sailing later tomorrow which we could make. It's going to be packed to the gunwales but let's see if the Stavisky method can work its magic.'

They drove hard, stopping only for a coffee break or two and the occasional 'pit stop.' They ate sandwiches at the wheel. As they hit the road, south of Lyon, with Gunn grumbling under his breath about missing a meal there, the weather finally began to clear. They were on a decent stretch of road and the Citroen followed through on wheels. It had the instincts of a cat but more of a forgiving nature. Gunn was becoming rather fond of it.

'Gunn,' Sylvia suggested. 'Why don't I do a pretext call to George and see if I can put him right off the scent?'

'Too risky,' commented Gunn straightaway. 'Words like 'head' and lion's mouth' spring to mind.'

'Not if I do it in German. It's just that today is his day for going to the office, taking out all the petty cash and then getting blotto at the Club. Anyway, they'll have a new receptionist, and she won't recognise my voice.'

'Want to go through your cover with me? And your alter ego?'

They did this all the time back in London, joking about their alter egos, saying that the bunker was getting far too crowded and deciding which one would have to be killed off next. They would run through their pretexts together, suggesting small adjustments here and there. That was how they got their results. Gunn pulled up at the next telephone box. There was nobody about. Often, as in England, there were queues outside telephones.

'Right, make yourself scarce, Gunn. You know I don't like anyone listening when I am doing this.' She added: 'Unless you want a slap.'

'I'll look forward to that.' Gunn smiled, as he sat down outside for a stretch. Sylvia really was good at this, he thought; cool and unflustered. He liked watching her at work, although he wouldn't want to get on the wrong side of her. It was remarkable how much she reminded him of someone, but with more sweetness and vulnerability. He sprang to his feet as she emerged, a triumphant smile on her face.

'Hook, line and sinker,' she said, as they pulled away.

In Queen Anne's Gate, George's spirits were considerably lifted. He hadn't heard anything from his contacts about Gunn or Sylvia for a day or so, although he was confident they wouldn't get far. That idiot Meunier was useless and he didn't know what Edward was up to either, always hanging around. When the call had come through from Klara Schmidt, secretary to Mueller, with a strong Berlin accent (that man got through more secretaries than hot dinners, always had done, the old rogue), he had felt a palpable relief. He had some 'assets' being transferred from Cadiz later that evening, but he wanted confirmation about affairs in Rome and the safe house there, in the back streets near the Vatican.

Mueller was meant to be looking after that side of things.

'Klara' had told him that the English assets had returned to Paris and were staying near the Eiffel Tower. They would be back in England, under 'close supervision,' in two days. Yes, all was well with 'Operation Crown Jewels' from his side, he told her. She in turn assured him that arrangements in Rome were secure and could be 'activated' at any time, should anyone need such assistance.

'Fraulein Schmidt,' he interrupted her. 'Please make sure the female asset is brought straight to me in London. And pass on my thanks and regards to Herr Mueller.'

Wishing her a pleasant evening, he put the telephone down and allowed himself a delicious quarter of an hour, thinking about how much he would enjoy having some time alone with that little strumpet. From memory, she was more of an ice maiden than a strumpet, but he would soon sort that out. He walked along the corridor to see Louis, still deeply ensconced in his litigation, getting the discovery process done before the courts opened again. They walked downstairs together and parted company at the door, George to hail a cab and Louis to take a bus over to the Polish Officers' Club.

In Cadiz, later that evening, it was cold and the wind insistent, rattling windows and keeping most people off the streets. Two men, brims snapped down low, and with one case each at their feet, waited at a table in a bar just a short stroll from the waters that promised safe passage to the south and west. A blonde man, military in bearing, walked in and ordered a coffee in succinct, clipped Spanish. He drank without ceremony and flicked the coins onto the counter top. He turned on his heels and left, with the merest hint of a nod at the two men. They waited a minute and then followed.

'Nice knowing you,' he said, as he led them towards a small fishing boat. Just before they got on board, he said 'Herr Brand has done you proud.' He handed them a bundle each of papers and money, which they put carefully away. 'Good luck' and with that, he turned and left them.

Neither Otto Neumann nor Wilhelm Beck spoke as the boat put out to sea. Both were wrapped in thoughts of their own. It had been a long journey so far, and there was a lot more of it to come. Some might say that to travel together, when they were wanted together, was foolhardy. Others might describe it as hiding in plain sight and the very best way to evade capture.

Chapter 8

As the Citroen took them closer to the port, Sylvia told Gunn what George had said about 'Operation Crown Jewels' and Rome, and the confirmation of Mueller's involvement.

'After the épuration and everything,' Gunn marvelled. 'Shows how thorough they are. Yes, Rome definitely sounds like a safe house to me. Anyway, sounds as if you have done a good job and he is convinced we are within grasp. He does seem to have special plans for you. I expect it will be a bullet in the back of the head for me.'

Eventually, they drew to a halt on the run-off on the road above Marseille. The Vieux Port was busy below them, ships being shepherded in and out by busy, officious tugs. The old fortresses of Fort Saint Nicholas on the south side and Fort Saint Jean on the north flanked the entrance, keeping permanent vigil. Across and above the Vieux Port, Notre Dame de la Garde kept a more spiritual watch over the city below as she sat back on the big sky.

Gunn stepped out of the Citroen and leaned back on the bonnet as the engine ticked down. He handed Sylvia a cigarette and began singing 'La Marseillaise' in a ragged tenor. Behind them was a memorial with four names on, and the legend 'morts pour la France.' Sylvia sighed. With the pretext call out of the way, and some sunshine, she had planned a picnic on Le Puce's rug.

'Not if he is in this mood,' she thought. She gave him a hug, and, echoing his language, said: 'Come on. Let's see about that buggering boat.'

The Citroen slid easily through the streets of Marseille as they narrowed down towards the Vieux Port. Gunn patted the steering wheel. He would be sorry to see it go, but they would make some money on it and that was one less bread crumb on the trail. Keeping the Parc Longchamp on their right, they headed down the Rue Consolat, just about managed to squeeze through the Allée Leon Gambetta, took a left at a prompt from Sylvia and a right onto La Canebière. They made their way down to the waterfront, which was low-slung, back-lit and, to Gunn, stimulating. She noticed the look in his eyes and pursed her lips. They slowed to a halt on the Rue Paradis. Gunn let the engine wind down.

'We can walk the rest,' he said.

They soon found the ticket office for the Haifa boat. Unfortunately, a teeming mass of humanity, clutching their worldly goods, had found it too.

'I'm not standing in that sodding queue. Go and talk to that nice gentleman over there, Sylv.' Gunn pointed to a young French official behind a desk, away from the main queue.

'Wait a sec,' said Sylvia. She dashed into a little bar for a citron presse (she was parched) and emerged wearing a green number, one of the summery dresses she had packed. They took up virtually no space. She was wearing lipstick, Gunn noticed and the dress suited her, with those olive tones in her skin and that tawny hair. Despite the cut-glass accent, she wasn't your typical English rose.

'Could I have some of the money, please?' she asked.

About fifteen minutes later, after a conversation which had started with 'Impossible' and ended in 'Bien sur' (with a promise of a drink on the way back through Marseille), Sylvia returned with two first class tickets.

'Christ, Sylv, how much did you pay for these?' Gunn grumbled. He was secretly impressed that she had got them at all; it hadn't looked hopeful. He did like to keep her on her toes though, and to tease her. She always rose to it.

'Well, we got the very last cabin. I told them we were married. We should get it to ourselves, but it can be a bit of a scrum, apparently. We need to have a word with the purser when we get on.'

'Probably shouldn't leave it too late then,' said Gunn. 'Shall we get some lunch? You look every inch the officer's wife, by the way.'

'A compliment or part of their cover?' Sylvia wondered. At least the dresses she had packed would allow her to pass muster in first class.

'Only one thing to eat around here' Gunn commented, propelling her towards a waterfront bistro, Marcel Le Grand, all ill-matched tables and old linen tablecloths. A kitten played with the remains of a shrimp. Good pickings. A waiter showed them a table, brought them Pastis, and agreed with Gunn that bouillabaisse was just what was required. Le Grand's did the best bouillabaisse in the street and indeed the whole of Marseille. Gunn nodded his agreement and, having come to terms, turned to Sylvia and smiled. He poured cold, clear water into their glasses, raised his and said: 'Cheers, nice work, Sylv.'

He then allowed his gaze to scan the bistro and its diners; the usual motley crew of waterfront workers, sailors, spivs, whores and policemen. Then something caught and held his attention. He set down his glass and leaned in to Sylvia, looking for all the world as though he was going to kiss her.

'Say nothing, just smile as I speak, but I have spotted an old sidekick of Le Puce, a small time low life smuggler. He's called Jean Le Mec, because he is everyone's mate until it comes to doing a deal. A smile like a crocodile with toothache and eyes deader than a shark. He's over by the telephone, fishing in his pocket for change. I will have to stop him, just in case.'

'Agreed' said Sylvia.

Gunn wiped his mouth on his napkin and put his glass down. For a tall man, he could move very quickly. He glided between the tables. The first that Le Mec was aware of his presence was a hand on his shoulder and a whispered 'I would like a word with an old friend.'

He shot the shorter man through the kitchen, despite the chef's protestations, and out into the narrow rat run behind Le Grand's. He flung him face first into the brickwork opposite. Le Mec shook his head and spat out a tooth. He dropped his shoulder and reached down to his ankle for a sheath knife. Gunn spotted this, and, swinging an efficient shoe, flicked the Frenchman on his back and kicked him in the ribs. Sitting back on his haunches, he removed the knife from the ankle sheath and let it swing idly from his left hand. 'Been a while, Jean.'

'I wish it had been a little while longer.'

'Of course' Gunn smiled but the smile did not reach his eyes. 'Who were you about to call?'

'Alexandre.'

'Why?'

'Business.'

'What business?'

'Our business.' Le Mec spat another gobbet of blood into the rat run. 'That is all you need to know.'

'Does it involve me?' Gunn let the sunlight play on the blade. The reflection danced in Le Mec's eyes.

'No.'

'Sure? Because if you are lying, I will hurt you a little more. And I will keep hurting you until I learn the truth and then I will cut your throat. Just enough to scar, not to kill.'

'Nothing to do with you.' Le Mec shaded his eyes against the reflection. 'I swear on my mother's grave.'

'You don't know who your mother is. For all you know, you could have fucked her in one of the brothels around here.' Gunn laughed, and hauled Le Mec to his feet. 'I still don't believe you, but my time is precious and my lunch is spoiling. Don't do anything to make me come back here and discuss this further. Agreed?'

'Agreed.' Le Mec dusted himself down. 'You are a bastard.'

'Yes, I am. But I did save your life in '43, and stopped you getting taken away on Operation Tiger. Show some gratitude. See you around.'

'I sincerely hope not.'

Gunn walked casually back to the table. The waiter was just arriving with their bouillabaisse.

'Good timing. Sorry about that.' he said.

They were both ravenous. They agreed that the bouillabaisse, after years of rationing and ghastly English food, was out of this world. They mopped their plates with some bread and had another glass of pastis, followed by a coffee each. For the first time, they began to feel a little more relaxed.

'I could stay here forever' said Sylvia. 'But we should think about getting on the boat soon. What shall we do about the car?'

'Excuse me again.' Gunn wandered over to the patron, returning five minutes later with more cash, which he put away carefully. 'Two birds with one stone. I also got him to keep an eye on Le Mec. I don't trust that bastard any further than I can throw him. Shame about that car though.'

Soon, they were aboard the SS Sidonia. Waving their first class tickets, they managed to get through customs reasonably quickly and headed straight to the purser's office. A few others had the same idea but Sylvia and Gunn were first in the queue.

'Right, Mrs G. You can deploy those skills you learnt at school when you were skiving off gym. Pretend you are sick.'

Sylvia duly put on a virtuoso performance for the purser.

'La pauvre,' he said. 'Elle est enceinte, votre femme?'

Trying to contain his glee, Gunn kept a protective arm round Sylvia as they followed the purser to their cabin. It was tiny, with two narrow bunks and an even smaller bathroom, but it did have a small balcony.

'Luxury accommodation, mon cul' Gunn grumbled. 'Never mind. Alone at last.'

They stretched out luxuriously on their bunks for a nap before unpacking. A few people knocked on the door – several families and, bizarrely, a group of nuns. Gunn fended them all off, explaining about Sylvia's delicate condition.

'You'll have to keep this up now. All the way to Haifa. Eating for two. Best cut down on the snifters and fags. I suppose I could bring some secret supplies to you. If you behave yourself.'

'Do I look fat then?' Sylvia was alarmed.

'No' he laughed. 'You're not nearly at that stage yet. You look radiant.'

'How does he know so much about it?' Sylvia wondered as he took her arm again.

'Come on, Mrs Gunn. Let's go and explore.'

The Sidonia was a typical Mediterranean freighter. It had plied the routes between Marseille and Porto Vecchio, then Naples and Crete, and Haifa and Tangiers or Casablanca for more than twenty five years. It had been used during the war for people smuggling out to North Africa and running guns back into Corsica or down the coast from Marseille. There were perhaps fifteen cabins, Sylvia thought, and a lot of deck space now shaded by deck awnings pulled tight. There were far too many people on board, and both Sylvia and Gunn knew it as they picked their

88

way along the deck, treading on blankets and suitcases.

Becoming exasperated, Gunn whispered:

'You are meant to be pregnant so I suggest you find a nice old Jewish lady to sit beside and see what you can glean from her. I'll wander on.'

Sylvia could see he was relishing this pregnancy business. It was going to become somewhat tedious if he kept fussing over her like an old hen. But she had to admit she liked the way his arm was now tightly around her most of the time, and there was logic in his suggestion. For the benefit of the crowds around them, who were smiling benevolently, he said more loudly:

'Put your feet up, sweetheart, and I'll see you in a little while. Rest those ankles in this heat. Do you want me to bring you anything? Not feeling sick again?'

Tempted to send him off with a flea in his ear, Sylvia replied:

'No thank you, darling. That's sweet of you.' She drew him to her and gave him a kiss on the cheek. 'See you in a bit.'

She settled herself down by a slightly creaky lifeboat. Gunn spread his jacket out on the deck so she could sit down. He smiled, ruffled her hair and began to circulate. They were making their way along the coast towards Toulon, although Naples would be the first stop, then on to Haifa. The coastline was beautiful. It looked red in the late afternoon sun, with the sea a sparkling blue. If she could close her eyes to the conditions around her, she decided, it would be like being on a cruise.

A voice broke into her reverie. It felt slightly incongruous to hear London inflections in these foreign surroundings.

'He's a looker, isn't he, your husband? First baby, is it?'

The voice belonged to Joyce Hoffman, as Sylvia soon discovered. Within a few minutes, Sylvia had her life story; born in the East End and grew up there, widowed, and now on her way to start a new life in Haifa with her sister. Not a moment too soon, Joyce declared. Having lost Sammy, this would be a fresh start from her and she still felt young enough to want to be 'part of something new.'

Sylvia ventured some of her story and Gunn's. The strange thing was, she realised, she believed it. This was not the same as her other hair-brained pretext stories. It seemed completely right; a young bride, accompanying her husband on business but just pregnant and feeling a little lost. She could very easily lose all track of reality. In a way, she wished it was true.

'Get a grip' she told herself sternly. 'This is Gunn you are talking about.'

'Have you got anywhere to stay in Haifa?' asked Joyce. 'My Vanessa tells me it's still a little rough. But you're welcome to come and stay with us. We'll look after you while he goes off and does his work.'

Sylvia had just written Joyce's name and address down in her address book when a smiling Gunn appeared before her.

'Guess who is having dinner with the Captain this evening? Better go and get our glad rags on.'

They said goodbye to Joyce and he led her back to the cabin.

'You must be desperate for a wee now,' he said, seriously. 'With the baby pressing on your bladder.'

Luckily, nobody was about. Sylvia almost fell down the stairs, laughing.

'Gunn, stop it. You really are the absolute end sometimes. You sound like some awful medical text book. Come on, what are you going to wear this evening?'

'I haven't got a clue. I shall go and beg, borrow or, more likely, steal something.' He scratched his chin. 'And I'm not sure how we have ended up at the Captain's Table. I suppose the English officer façade comes in useful.'

'It is a façade, isn't it?'

'Pretty much.' Gunn sat down on his bunk. 'I am half-English, half-French, and just a poorish boy. Though not from a poor family.'

He stood up. 'Time for a wander and a forage. Back in a while.'

'He really is an enigma' Sylvia thought to herself, as she got ready. She tried to piece together what she knew about him, but gave up after a while, concentrating on making herself look presentable for dinner. She decided upon one of her favourite dresses, quite low cut, with pink and blue flowers on a white background, and a white collar. She had caught the sun on deck. It suited her. As she sat at the dressing table (a luxury after the fleapit and their nights on the road), looking in the mirror while she put some

91

lipstick on, she became aware of Gunn, standing in the doorway.

'You look beautiful, Mrs Gunn. I've never seen you in anything like that before. Shall I do you up at the back?'

'I'd like nothing better,' she thought to herself. 'He can be so sweet sometimes but at other times so infuriating. And he seems to be quite accustomed to living with a woman. That's strange.'

She would have to try and draw him out, she resolved. Gunn did her zip up and fastened the clasp on her pearl necklace. It was the only item of jewellery Mother had left behind, after her flight from Daddy, she explained.

She looked at Gunn appreciatively. He was wearing a dinner suit, purloined from the purser. Putting her arm through his, they sallied forth. The Captain had drawn his guests from both the first class cabins and from those camping out on the decks - World War 2 veterans and Holocaust survivors; a fascinating mix.

Gunn introduced Sylvia and then himself. He shook the Captain's hand and then let the stories unfold. He had resolved not to say much. His story was not relevant to these people or their experiences. As the first course, a rough potage, arrived with bread and a more than useful white wine, tongues began to loosen and scraps of lives began to float around the table like rags on barbed wire.

Next to Sylvia was Manny Kaltz, a scholar from Warsaw. He had survived Auschwitz by luck and no judgment. His family were dead. He had a cousin in Jerusalem. They did not get on, but there was a hope in their blood. Across from Gunn, and next to the captain, was Sarah Rosen. She ate sparingly, as if afraid she would not eat again. In Vienna, she had been a dancer. Her ankles had been broken with hammers. She could walk now, but she would not dance. She hoped to teach in Israel, in a place where olives grew, somewhere over the horizon from Galilee.

Next to Gunn was Solomon Kalinsky, a Pole. He had fought at Monte Cassino, been captured by the Germans and beaten forensically on a daily basis. He had lost an eye and was deaf in one ear. He was twenty seven years old. Kalinsky had been rescued by New Zealanders and carried a silver fern in his pocket that one of them had given him for good luck. He and Gunn fell into natural comradeship.

Sylvia chatted to Manny for most of the meal. He knew London a little and had attended lectures there one summer. After coffee, as people began to make their excuses, Gunn stood up and made theirs.

'I feel totally humbled,' Sylvia commented, on the way back to the cabin. 'I really hope it all works out for them all now. I'm glad I met them.'

'Yes, me too,' replied Gunn vaguely. Back at the cabin, he unzipped her dress and unfastened her necklace. She turned to him, unsure, but he simply planted a tentative kiss on her shoulder. Her eyes opened wide, but he appeared not to notice, simply saying:

'I'm off for a snifter with Sol. You get yourself into bed, sweetheart. Look after our baby. Sleep tight and I'll see you in the morning.'

Seething with rage, Sylvia climbed into her bunk, pulling the scratchy sheet around her. Of course, they were deeply 'under cover,' but surely this was unnecessary. A snifter would have rounded the evening off properly. Then, thinking about the people she had just met, she felt ashamed of complaining about something so petty. Tomorrow was going to be an early start.

'Not quite Homer's wine dark sea, but it will do,' Solomon smiled as Gunn joined him on the forward deck. The breeze was fresh and the sea eager beneath them. 'I used to quote from Homer in my head when the Germans beat me.'

'You must know Achilles and Hector pretty well.' Gunn sat down and leaned back against a crate marked 'Capernaum.' He handed Solomon his hip flask. 'Whisky?'

'Don't mind if I do.' Solomon grinned. 'Yes, I got to know them very well. Especially Hector... Hector of the glinting helmet, the Master of Horses. He paused and took a shot, coughed and passed the flask back to the Englishman. 'I always wondered why he didn't just hand Paris over to the Achaeans or kill the irritating schmuck himself.'

'Oh, that is good,' Gunn laughed out loud. 'Chop the little bugger up and have him thrown from the topless towers of Ilium to land at Menelaus's feet?'

Their laughter rose, then faded away on the breeze. Their silence was companionable. Then Sol shifted slightly and observed:

'Of course, it would have made no difference. The Achaeans would still have launched their war on Troy and Hector would have lost a brother for nothing.'

'You know there is a legend that Aeneas fled Troy and founded Britain.' Gunn took a sip from the flask and passed it back. 'Not well-known, but accepted as fact for a long time.'

'So you lot are descended from those who lived on the windy plains?'

'Explains a lot, doesn't it?'

'Of course. No wonder you are such a cold and awkward people.' Sol's expression darkened a little, as clouds obscured the moon. 'In the end, Hector was bonded by the deep ties of blood. That is something I see on this ship, and in what is happening in Israel. Ties of blood and memory kept us going for two thousand years from the day the Romans burned the temple and we began to wander again, and through everything such things kept us alive. Even in the camps they kept us alive.'

'And now you are going home.'

'Yes, home, a place I have never seen other than in stories or my imagination.'

'Make it a good one then.'

'Oh, I will, my friend. I will grow lemons and oranges and, when I grow old, I will sit on the porch and watch the sun set on Galilee.'

'Good plan.'

'First of all, I will be heading for Jerusalem just to see it.' Solomon brought himself up short. 'Listen to me, I talk too much.'

'Don't all soldiers, given the chance?' Gunn grinned and clapped him on the shoulder. 'We have to.'

'True.' Sol turned and looked at Gunn. 'So, why are you going to Israel, you and your 'wife'?'

Gunn noted the quotation marks in Sol's tone.

'Long story short, to bring a family a legacy and to save their lives.'

'That is quite a thing.' Solomon pursed his lips and gave a nod of appreciation. 'And do you know this family?'

'No,' replied Gunn.

'So why do this? It's just another Jewish family. Would their loss make that much difference?'

'It would to me.' Gunn folded his arms and closed his eyes for a moment. 'It matters to me.'

'I see.' Sol pressed no further. He reached into his pocket and pulled out a journal bound with string. He tore off a strip of paper and scribbled an address, using a stub of pencil he retrieved from behind his ear. 'Take this. You can reach me care of this address if you ever need me.'

'I will.' Gunn nodded and stood up. 'I will bid you good night. I will come and sit with you on that porch one day.'

'Good.' Solomon laughed and handed Gunn his hip flask.

Gunn shook his head. 'Keep it, and remember Hector every time you drink from it.'

'You and Hector.'

Gunn crept into the cabin, trying not to wake Sylvia. He stood watching her for a moment, then pulled the sheet back over her gently, gave her a kiss and climbed into his bunk.

Chapter 9

Next morning, Gunn was surprised to find Sylvia already up, sitting on the balcony with several large sheets of paper which the purser had given her. Jones's papers were spread out on the table, starting with the letters Marta, Louise's sister, had sent through about Mueller and his work. As his secretary, she had access to everything. Sylvia knew from working at the trials how meticulously the Nazis had documented things. Marta's material was no exception. Mueller, who had qualified as a doctor, had been involved in the early stages of a programme of sterilisation and euthanasia. After a while, he was moved to High Command, where his influence burgeoned and became more general. Then, in 1940, he was sent to France, near Chartrettes. That was around when Marta's letters stopped. It was almost as if Mueller had 'dropped off the radar.' However, he had certainly been a prolific correspondent. Sylvia recognised some, though not all, of the names mentioned from her time in Nuremberg. As she skimmed through the letters, she made notes in colour on her chart and drew a diagram, which resembled a slightly mad spider's web.

Something stopped her in her tracks. 'Gunn, come and have a look at this.'

'Explain it to me, Sylv. My brain is all fogged up with wine and whisky.'

'You're just impossible,' she said crossly.

'Probably. But that's not relevant.'

She glared at him. 'Right, it seems that Marta has given the names of various men who would be

98

involved in a pipeline in the unlikely event that the German regime were to fall. Odd really, because at the time she was working for Mueller, they all still thought the Reich would last a thousand years. Anyway, it's as we thought.' She paused and took a sip of water. Gunn did not react, beyond a grunt of acknowledgement. 'One of those named, and quite high up in the command structure, is one Lothar Kaltenbrunner.'

'Nothing remarkable about that name, except I get an image of a severe haircut and rolls of fat over the back of an SS collar. German by Central Casting.'

Sylvia laughed, despite herself. 'In parentheses, it gives an alias for Kaltenbrunner.'

'George Cumberland?'

'In one.'

'That could be awkward at Whites and the British Motor Racing Club.'

'Extremely. We've got him bang to rights now. Kaltenbrunner was on that scrap of paper of Joneses.' She pulled it out again to show him. 'I suppose we just stick to our original plan, and get all of this safely to Israel. But what happens when we don't show up in London, as George expects? Won't he smell a rat?'

'Sylv, he won't know where to start,' Gunn reassured her. 'France is a big place. I know Le Mec clocked us in Marseille, but I reckon I put the frighteners on him sufficiently. I think we've got a few days and that will get us well on the way to Haifa. I'll go and see about some coffee and breakfast. We can't have you wasting away. The baby needs to eat.'

He was off again, she thought. Well, it kept him amused. When he got back, he could damn well make himself useful, help her to tidy up the diagram and put a report together to hand over in Israel. Putting Marta's papers carefully away, she started on Jonathan and Louise's story. As she had predicted, it felt almost voyeuristic. Their letters, and every single one had been kept, from the time they first met, revealed that Jonathan had been something of a black sheep in his youth. He was sent down from university. His family had to bail him out of a few debts. Then, his father cut him out of his will. He was reinstated to the Jones family fortune when Clarence was killed at Loos.

The Paris trip, where he met Louise, was financed by some birthday money from his mother. Louise's family were extremely wealthy. Their origins were in Austria but they had been settled in France for some years. They did not practice Judaism, and in fact Jonathan and Louise were married in the little church at Chartrettes, in a quiet ceremony. Sylvia remembered passing it. They had decided to settle there simply because an opportunity came up to buy the house and the land. It had appeared in a newspaper advertisement. They didn't know the area before but fell in love with it. It was the ideal compromise between town and country, with Paris an easy train journey away. That answers that question, Sylvia thought.

They enjoyed working on the property together. Their one sadness had been that they were unable to have children. They enjoyed entertaining friends and extended family at Chartrettes though. Marguerite and her husband were frequent visitors from Paris; Marta less so. The youngest of the Vogel girls, almost an afterthought for their parents, she had attended university in Berlin in the twenties and had fallen in love with it. For Marta, these years really were 'the Golden Twenties.'

Marta had stayed on in Berlin afterwards and found secretarial work. There was some talk of her becoming an actress. Movies with sound were being produced by then. Marta was a stunningly attractive girl, with blonde hair and blue eyes and spoke German like a native. Nothing much came of those plans; they were shared by many other girls. However, one evening, Marta had met Dr Mueller at a party, a married man with four young children. The attraction between them was electrifying, like a moth to a flame, as Marta herself had described it. She always portrayed him, even in those early days, as rather a dangerous man.

For the sake of propriety, he had taken her on as his secretary and had installed her in a small apartment not far from the Zoo. After Hitler came to power, Marguerite and Louise implored her to come back to France. She refused. It was as if she was in denial; as if all the measures which were being taken did not and would never apply to her. Marguerite had described Marta in a letter to Louise as 'a bird in a gilded cage.' Then, in 1939, just before war broke out, Marta became pregnant.

At a stroke, she woke up to her situation. She had noticed that Mueller had become abstracted and distant, even sometimes looking at her with distaste.

101

Before, he had enjoyed going to parties with her on his arm. He was losing interest in her sexually. She could see for herself what the nature of his work had become and had charitably attributed his new attitudes to stress. However, her eyes were fully open now. As insurance, and in desperation, she began copying everything she could lay her hands on, and sending it to Chartrettes.

Her last letter was particularly poignant. One evening, Mueller had surprised her in the office with a sheaf of papers; her last batch, she had decided, before she tried to leave for France. It might of course already be too late. She was like a rabbit caught in headlamps.

'Working late?' Mueller had enquired, menacingly.

She had blurted out the news of her pregnancy, in a clumsy attempt to distract him from the papers. It didn't work. He tried to get her to tell him where she had been sending the copies. She refused. He was horrified about the pregnancy, called the baby a monster and an abomination, and kicked her hard in the stomach, repeatedly. He had to break off to take an urgent telephone call, whereupon Marta fled back to the apartment, where she miscarried the baby and would have bled to death, had her landlady not found her. Perhaps that would have been a mercy. Her letter was written from the hospital; someone kindly posted it for her. She was arrested there the next day. Jonathan's enquiries after the war had revealed that Marta had died whilst under interrogation at Gestapo Headquarters.

'I've got you some breakfast, sweetheart,' called Gunn, giving her a kiss on the cheek. 'Sorry I've been so long. Got chatting. Come on, let's get you inside. It's too chilly for you out here; the sun needs to come round a bit more.' He gathered her up, and all the papers. 'You've been crying' he observed, when they were back in the cabin.

Sylvia told him Marta's story. 'I suddenly felt all emotional. I even got upset about this ridiculous baby of ours, and I know that's absurd, when I read what Mueller had done. Fancy dragging that poor woman out of her hospital bed.'

'Not absurd. And it's not a ridiculous baby.' He held her gently for a moment and then said: 'Let's get some breakfast into you.'

'What I can't understand,' mused Sylvia, fortified by some bread and jam, 'is why, with all that evidence, Jonathan didn't turn everything over to the authorities.'

'Perhaps he had a cynical view of epuration,' commented Gunn. 'And he probably didn't speak German, so he wouldn't have been able to translate Louise's correspondence. He and Louise used to write in English, didn't they'?

'The other thing' ventured Sylvia 'is that Mueller's name has just been cleared. His ugly mug was in the paper only the other day. I wonder if he worked out though that Louise was in Chartrettes and took a special interest in her? Was it just fortuitous that he was transferred to France? We've still got to go through Jonathan's own papers of course. There are lots of them. I only had a quick look in the Tea Caddy the other afternoon but it's almost like a diary.

There are a few more letters too, from Cumberlands. Anyway, my head is spinning; so many questions.'

'I think we need to get you on deck for a little walk and some sunshine first. You look decidedly peaky' said Gunn firmly. 'Have a look at this amazing scenery and I'll help you properly later, I promise. You're doing a fantastic job.'

The breeze on deck was quickening, and the Sidonia was slipping through the waters like a hound let loose from the leash. They had passed Bonifaccio, on the southern tip of Corsica, and were heading out across open sea towards Naples. There was a cry from a child pointing at the starboard bow, and Gunn grinned at the dolphins racing ahead of the ship. He took a few shots with his camera.

'Like something from a Greek myth.'

'They do have a word or story for it,' Sylvia returned. 'But seriously, what about the papers?'

'I think it would be naïve to turn them over to the British authorities. They won't do anything to look after the family, and they won't arrest Cumberland either, as the father of a Spitfire pilot. Leaving him a free agent, with all that entails.'

Sylvia could see the muscles in Gunn's jaw tensing. He exhaled. 'The family will be inheriting some money; that will enable them to get protection, but I really think we should persuade them to speak to the Israelis. There's bound to be some way of getting close to whatever intelligence services they have in place. I would be quite prepared to take care of Cumberland.' He smiled, a sad little smile. 'Almost makes me feel sorry for Edward.'

'I'm getting cold out here. Let's go back to the cabin and work on our report. Can you believe we'll be waking up in Naples tomorrow? Have you ever been there before?' Arm in arm, and chatting happily about ideas for the next couple of days, while the ship was in dock, they went back to the cabin to continue their reading.

At Queen Anne's Gate, George Cumberland, who was becoming, it had to be said, somewhat lax with security, took a call from Dr Mueller himself. He didn't even bother to close the door to his office. Dr Mueller told him that a man and a woman answering the descriptions of the English assets had been seen boarding a boat for Naples. They would probably arrive in the morning. A little puzzled, Cumberland reiterated his instructions that the female asset was to be brought to him immediately, with the papers. The male asset should be liquidated. All was still well with Operation Crown Jewels in Rome; things were indeed 'moving into place' at high levels. Implementation had already begun; it could continue whenever required. They ended their chat with a few pleasantries and reminiscences about boyhood days. Then Cumberland complimented him on his new assistant, Klara Schmidt.
Mueller told him he didn't have an assistant called Klara. Cumberland made some excuse and ended the conversation in some confusion. Who the buggering hell, then, was that on the telephone the other day? He realised, and swore loudly in German, just as Louis walked past, and threw his cup of tea against the wall.

That little bitch was going to wish she had never been born.

'Good night, Mr Cumberland,' called Louis. 'Would you mind locking up, only I have an appointment this evening?'

'Idiot Pole,' thought Cumberland. 'Well, he won't have overheard anything. Or nothing he can decipher. Let's hope Mueller can arrange something quickly for tomorrow.'

On board the Sidonia, Sylvia and Gunn were startled to realise that the sun was setting already. They had scarcely looked up from the papers all afternoon. Jones had written a diary which carried on where Marta's letters left off. It was a very moving account. Because Louise's family had not practised their religion for many years, they did not consider at first that the measures which were coming in were of any relevance to them. However, they soon realised that they were. As 1941 wore on, life became more impossible. Going to their beloved Paris became unpleasant, as Louise was barred from certain shops, then cafes and, painfully, theatres and restaurants. She had to cram into the last carriage of the Metro. Jonathan would always squeeze in with her, of course, but they soon no longer saw the point in going. The radio was confiscated, and Louise's bicycle. Jonathan angrily handed his in at the same time, in solidarity.

Nonetheless, by comparison with Marguerite and her husband, who lived in Paris and had to endure the same measures on a daily basis, with open anti-Semitism all over the newspapers, in the streets and

106

on posters, and a constant fear of the 'round-ups,' they considered themselves fortunate. They hoped, by 'keeping their heads down,' that they might be able to see these dark days out. It became more and more apparent that this would not be the case. They heard that an official by the name of Mueller had moved into the area and had been making enquiries. This was, they figured, a relatively common German surname but as a precaution Jonathan put Marta's papers under what he described as 'secure lock and key.'

The only way to deal with the situation was to carry on as normally as possible. The knock on the door came in July 1942. Jonathan had been for a drink with his friend, seeing no particular reason to deviate from his routine. Louise was taken first to the local gendarmerie, and it was there that Jonathan lost track of her. Nobody could or would tell him anything, although they were unfailingly polite. In vain, he ran back and forth, all day, with their marriage certificate (theirs was a Christian marriage) and other pieces of identification that showed she had been educated in France, had worked there and was totally assimilated; all to no avail. He wrote to Louise every day, but his letters remained unanswered.

One evening, not long after Louise had been taken away, Jonathan received a visit from Dr Mueller, who introduced himself as an official with responsibility for ensuring the security of local residents. Jonathan did not believe it for one moment, but did his best to be civil, inviting Mueller inside. Mueller spoke of some papers that had gone missing while his French secretary was working for him. It was all very inconvenient. Looking searchingly at Jonathan, he requested that should the papers by any chance arrive at Chartrettes, Mr Jones was to hand them in immediately. He hoped this was understood and wished him a pleasant evening.

Jonathan received several more such visits. Mueller became less polite and more exasperated as Jonathan responded in a calm, measured and English fashion, to the effect that he knew nothing about any papers and perhaps Mueller could tell him what had happened to his wife, as nobody else seemed to be able to. Mueller's face went bright red and the veins stood out on his neck. On the last occasion, he brought along some 'ruffians' as Jonathan described them, who more or less tore the place apart and helped themselves to some valuable antiques which had belonged to the Vogels and the Dorset Westons for generations. They found nothing. Mueller promised Jonathan darkly that their next conversation would be at a different venue.

Just after the war, Jonathan began the process of uncovering the painful truth of Louise's fate. She had, along with thousands of others, been 'processed' through Drancy and then Auschwitz, where she had been killed in the gas chambers. She had never been strong. Jonathan had put his head in his hands and wept at this point. Marguerite and her husband had also ended up in Auschwitz, but they did not overlap with Louise. They had survived, although only just, and were in a Displaced Persons' Camp. A Red Cross official told him they were lucky to survive this long. The prognosis was not good. In a way, Jonathan thought, it was fortunate that the Vogel girls' parents had died relatively young, in the early thirties, when they were incredibly proud of their 'golden girl' in Berlin, blissfully unaware that she was Mueller's mistress and content to think of Marguerite and Louise being so happy and settled. He had always enjoyed entertaining them at the demeure.

Mueller had of course disappeared after Liberation. Assuming he was dead, Jonathan rather hoped that there was a special place in Hell reserved for him. He had stopped attending church years ago, having concluded bleakly that there was nobody up there. No rational and kindly deity would have allowed such wickedness and destruction to be unleashed upon the world. It was worse, and this was saying something, than anything he had seen in the trenches in 14-18. He was thinking of Clarence a lot now that he was to all intents and purposes alone in the world. Sometimes he found himself asking him aloud for advice. He could see his brother's face clearly, something he had been unable to do for years.

Soon, he began to receive strange silent telephone calls. The local gendarme would call round on his bicycle. Jonathan could see he thought this poor, affable old Englishman was going barmy. Nothing was done. Perhaps nothing could be done.

In 1947, he visited Cumberlands for the first time since the war. They had been the family firm for years, going back to Edwardian times (they were called something else then - the name escaped him now). He had tolerated, but never really liked Cumberland senior, with his clearly affected Englishness. He was rather pleased that Young Mr Cumberland had qualified and finished his articles after his war service, and made a special point of making the appointment with him.

Edward Cumberland was, Jonathan thought, a genuine and decent young man. Edward had urged him, tactfully, to make a new will (everything had of course been left to Louise but she was gone). There was a considerable amount of money involved. The demeure itself only formed a small part of it. Jonathan promised to think about it. He wasn't sure who to leave his estate to, if Marguerite and her husband didn't make it out of the Displaced Persons' Camp. He barely knew his distant cousin in Dorset. He and Edward were chatting about Jewish charities (Edward had seen an article about one in the Law Society Gazette, which might be worth looking at, as a residuary legatee), when Cumberland senior, who had been hovering at the door, came storming in. Calling his son an idiot, (why in God's name did he imagine that a fine, upstanding Englishman would want anything to do with a charity for vermin, he had said, under his breath), he had thrown Edward out of the room (even delivering a kick to his backside, Jonathan recalled) and then conducted a most bizarre conversation with Jonathan, almost fawning over him. Cumberland senior had raised the question of some significant documents which had been mislaid in Chartrettes and which 'the authorities' were anxious to retrieve.

This was when he put two and two together. His German was fairly non-existent, but he had seen something in Marta's documents, years ago, before they went into their hiding place, about a boyhood friend of Muller's in London. That had to be

Cumberland Senior, surely. He had denied all knowledge of any documents, in his usual calm and courteous manner, and then taken his leave. While he was downstairs, retrieving his hat and coat and chatting to Joan, he had heard Cathy say something about a call having come in for a 'Herr Mannfred Brand' and how she always put them through to Mr Cumberland Senior.

On an impulse, he had given Joan, who had always been a decent sort (Louise had loved her cups of English tea) his spare key, with instructions not to mention it to anyone. 'But just in case,' he had said to her. Thinking it through later, he wasn't sure what assistance Joan could have lent, but it had occurred to him that nobody had a spare set of keys.

Now, in the summer of 1948, he had made arrangements to visit Cumberlands again. He was booked in at Claridges, which always 'perked him up,' and was due to meet his bankers at Simpsons; a celebration of the Olympics. He and Louise had watched Eric Liddell run at the Stade de Colombes. He confessed to bafflement over the rapid passage of years. News had come from Marguerite and her husband; they were planning to start a new life in Haifa with Marguerite's cousin, Aaron Vogel. Jonathan's own health was deteriorating; he had recently suffered a small stroke. Clarence was putting in more and more appearances. The mysterious telephone calls were continuing. He was in fear for his life. He had made a new will and had it witnessed locally. The diary ended at that point.

'How long do you think it was between when he hid this diary in the wall and when whoever it was came to get him?' asked Sylvia. She was looking upset again.

'Well, I guess the French police are making enquiries to that effect right now' Gunn replied. 'Best leave them to it. Sweetheart, that was an excellent day's work. Only you could take a pile of ancient papers and coax a story like that out of them. My instinct is to carry on tidying up the diagram and the report when we are at sea again. For now, we should enjoy Naples. Let's go and see what there is to eat and have a snifter in the bar. Well, a snifter for me at any rate. Water for you.'

Chapter 10

That evening, as Gunn and Sylvia strolled around the deck, a car, a new model Packard Vignale Convertible, driven by a heavy set man in his thirties, left Rome and headed to Naples via the coast road through Aprilia and Formia. The driver did not exceed the speed limit, not that the Italian motorcycle cops could have caught him, but instructions were instructions, and he had an appointment in Naples and an asset to dispose of.

The driver, Guenter Voss, hummed an air from Bach as he drove in the warm evening sun. Life was good. Once this business was taken care of, he would return to Rome and his expensive and demanding mistress, to keep him amused and occupied until his next assignment. Voss was a specialist. He took out the trash and left everything looking nice and tidy. He was discreet and reassuringly loyal.

The Sidonia had to lay over in Naples for forty-eight hours. Some cargo needed to be overloaded and a few tractors taken on for delivery to Haifa. It would be a break for the passengers too, allowing them to stretch their legs for a last couple of days in Europe, before the final part of the journey to Israel. Wanting to take full advantage of this unexpected treat, Sylvia was rummaging through the holdall for some suitable shoes for sightseeing.

'Sylv, come out here,' came Gunn's voice from the balcony. 'We're in Naples.'

Naples was cradled in the arms of the bay, Vesuvius above the city, wisps of smoke from the eruption still twisting like minarets in the desert sun. Gunn laughed out loud. 'Not sure I would stick around here, considering the temper on that great lump.'

'Oh, I don't know.' Sylvia hugged herself. 'It's rather beautiful.'

'Yes, but potentially a fatal beauty.'

'Isn't all beauty?'

'Touché.'

'Gunn,' she asked. 'Can I have a break from this pregnancy malarkey?'

'Oh, you don't ever get a break from motherhood,' Gunn replied. 'Yes, but wait until we are well away from the ship. We'll lose this crowd and do some exploring of our own.'

There were some organised excursions planned, but Gunn and Sylvia disembarked happily, on their own, hand in hand. They wandered the narrow streets, enjoying some warm sunshine, watching the children playing and the sinuous cats darting in and out of the shadows. There was considerable bomb damage. Reconstruction was clearly going to be a challenge.

'Can you rig me something like that up for the cabin?'

Sylvia was looking in fascination at the washing suspended above the streets, between the houses.

'I'll give it a go,' said Gunn, steering her into a bar. They sat outside in the little piazza, with a cappuccino each. They had already decided to save Pompeii for the next day, to do it justice. Gunn's attention was drawn to a Packard Vignale, inching its way across the square. It looked large and somehow incongruous. The driver seemed to be a little lost. The car disappeared from view, into another labyrinth of streets.

'Nice car,' remarked Gunn. 'That's the new model. A joint Italian and American venture.'

Before he could launch into one of his lectures, Sylvia took his arm. 'You and your cars. Come on, let's go and look inside this little church.' Wandering happily around, as the fancy took them, they agreed this would be a day they would never forget. Clements kept them very busy and there had been little time for holidays.

Guenter Voss cursed roundly. There had not been so much a vestige of them so far. His mistress had said something about Naples, the car, madness and tiny, narrow streets but he never paid much attention to what she said. Now he wished he had. He was going to have to park the blasted thing somewhere and make street to street enquiries. There were hordes of tourists and the description he had from Mueller was pretty useless. If the stupid, patronising man had given him a photograph to work from, this could have been wrapped up in a fraction of the time. He sighed, and made his way towards the hotel where he was staying; it was one of the larger ones. That might be a good place to start; presumably they would need lunch at some point. He could leave the car there too.

He arrived at the hotel. Damn them; there was still no sign. He would, at least, have a decent long lunch, perhaps a siesta, and then continue his searching later. He wasn't entirely sure how long they would be staying in Naples; Mueller had been vague about that too. Rubbish intelligence; how was he meant to find two needles in a haystack? Mueller was normally a great deal more efficient, but perhaps this was second or third hand.

Gunn and Sylvia came round the corner into the Piazza Cavour. They were hungry but had decided to find somewhere less touristy to eat. The midday sun was becoming fierce.

'You know what they say about mad dogs,' Gunn observed. 'We'll hop on a bus in a moment, go up the coast a bit, find somewhere special. After what they've been serving us on board, we deserve to treat ourselves. There's the bus stop, shall we just check the times? They probably don't stick to them though.' Before Sylvia could answer, Gunn came to an abrupt halt. There was that Packard again; the driver was just parking it outside the modern hotel on the corner. That car was not something he would have expected to see in an ant heap like Naples and he would wager a fortune that somebody would want to lay a finger on it. Maybe the old sixth sense was working overtime, but there was no harm in paying a little attention to it. He came to a decision, noting that they were opposite an English bookshop, more of an alcove really. He leaned into Sylvia.

'Have a browse in here for a quarter of an hour. I'm going to take a look at that car.'

'That car?'

'Yes, I know, I like cars but I suspect something is not right. I want to clock the cove driving the damn thing.'

Gunn wandered over to the hotel, pretending to look at the menu on the window. He managed to take a look at the driver. Quite heavily built, and he looked a bit of a thug, although one shouldn't necessarily judge on appearances. He obviously had money and it seemed he was planning to eat in the restaurant at the side.

'Buongiorno, Signor,' said the waiter. Gunn noticed that the response came in English, with a heavy German accent.

Lunch in there would keep him out of harm's way for a bit, Gunn reasoned. Thinking it best to keep a safe distance, he took Sylvia's hand and led her straight onto a bus which happened to be bound for Posillippo. He'd never heard of the place, but that was where the bus was going. He told her it was 'serendipity;' rather like the games he used to play on the metro as a youngster.

The tall, handsome Englishman had not escaped Voss's notice. He could always discern them, from his time with Rommel. This one had a military bearing. You couldn't mistake that. Voss wondered idly what theatre of war he had been in. Of course, his specific instructions were to look for two people, not one. What had Mueller said - a bullet for the male asset and the female to be delivered to London? He was looking forward to that leg of the assignment tremendously. His view was partially obscured by a large vine growing over a trellis (this really was a lovely restaurant) but he thought he could see the

117

Englishman getting on a bus. Probably lives in Naples, he thought, dismissively. The waiter was coming over with a Campari and soda. Fritta del mare, Voss decided, would go down a treat. Then, after a siesta, he might just check out those buses and perhaps take a drive up the coast.

Posillippo turned out to be a beautiful neighbourhood. Gunn and Sylvia enjoyed exploring and choosing a restaurant. A few contenders were vying for their trade so they took their time before settling down for a long, leisurely lunch. They were in the best place in the world for pizza, Gunn commented. It was also safe for Sylvia to have some wine and a cigarette now, he announced magnanimously, away from the prying eyes of the Jewish grandmas. They had a bottle of Chianti in a 'fiasco' (Sylvia loved that word), chatting about Pompeii tomorrow, somewhere Sylvia had always wanted to go, and what the next leg of the journey to Haifa was going to be like.

'Extremely emotional, I should think,' Gunn remarked. He resolved to carry on with his networking when they were back at sea, to try and discern the authorities in Israel who would be best placed to help with the documents. For now, he was bloody well on holiday.

'Want to push the boat out and have some pudding?' he asked. 'Shall we try some cassata?'

When it arrived, both agreed it was the most divine thing they had ever tasted. Back home, rationing was still in place. To be eating a concoction made of candied peel and nuts, steeped in liqueur, was the height of decadence, but they decided they could swiftly get used to this lifestyle.

'I think we should set up Clements International,' ventured Gunn, only half-joking.

'Better not run before we can walk,' said the ever-cautious Sylvia.

After two small espressos, she pushed back her chair.

'I am stuffed,' she declared. 'I am going to have to walk that off.'

'Thought you were eating for two' quipped Gunn, signalling to the waiter. 'Il conto, prego.'

It was an unaccustomed feeling for both of them to have 'all the time in the world.' They wandered up to Virgil's tomb, and stood amongst the laurel and the bay, overlooking Vesuvius.

'Mantua gave me birth, Calabria took me away, and now Parthenope holds me.
I sang of pastures, farms and leaders,' quoted Gunn.

Sylvia looked at him. He had never spoken about his schooling, just the fact that he had hated it. Obviously a classical education had stuck. She crushed a bay leaf between her fingers.

'A lovely spot for a tomb.' She took his arm and they continued with their walk.

'We must have been hours over lunch.' she said 'It's getting quite dark.'

'We were. Dusk falls quickly here. Like a curtain coming down. Shall we have a wander down to the beach? It probably isn't very far. And it doesn't matter what time we get back to the boat.'

They made their way back down the hillside, stopping at a little shop for some cigarettes. Sylvia

119

noticed Gunn buying a half bottle of brandy. 'Snifters on the beach,' he explained, taking a swig. 'Would you like some?'

She shook her head. 'Not just now.'

By the time they got to the beach, it was pitch dark. There was nobody around.

'Fancy a swim?' asked Gunn.

'I haven't got my swimming costume.'

'Swimming costume? Where the hell do you think you are? Tooting buggering Lido? Live a little, Sylv.'

In no time, Gunn had peeled off his clothes and was in the water. 'Last one in is a…prissydrawers,' he said, giving her a splash as she joined him. She reciprocated, and they swam out to sea. This is a new experience, Sylvia thought. She liked the sensation of the water against her bare skin. They lay on their backs companionably, looking at the stars. Gunn named some of them for her.

'Where did you learn all this?'

'Oh, here and there. I paid attention, unlike certain people round here.' Gunn trickled some water over her.

Back in Naples, Voss had woken from his slumbers with a start. He had gone to have a lie-down in his hotel room, but, having imbibed a whole bottle of red wine and a cognac on top of his Campari and his fritta del mare, he had fallen properly asleep and now it was pitch black. On balance, he felt all right to drive, so he picked up his car keys and asked the sleepy clerk on the reception desk where the buses ran to, at the front of the hotel.

'Posillipo, signor.'

Posillipo it was, then. There was no harm in making enquiries about this 'Tommy.' He knew better than to return to Mueller with nothing and it would give him something to put in his report. He searched in his pocket for some gettoni so that he could ring him with a quick update. He laid it on thick, explaining that the investigation might take a little time but that he was getting somewhere. Mueller seemed unusually genial, merely asking if he was all right for funds. Voss replied that he was.

The sea was calm and warm, like a bath.

'I was always in the water, as a child,' Sylvia commented. 'Daddy used to call me the Little Mermaid.'

'Hmm, yes, la petite sirène. I can see that.' He turned to her. 'Stay in the water for a bit. Don't come out until I say. Try and keep still. Say nothing.'

Sylvia turned onto her stomach and swam away quietly, further out to sea. Gunn sculled slowly back towards the shoreline, his head low. He had heard an engine, a Packard engine. Something was up. He drifted into the shallows and crawled up the beach. He paused, his cheek close to the pebbles. He could no longer hear the Packard; the engine had been switched off. He dabbed his hand softly on the pebbles, and found one that would sit comfortably in his hand. That would do.

The scrub at the back of the beach shifted. Someone was pushing through it, heading straight towards Gunn. He waited for the moment when the scrub stopped shifting, reared up, drew his arm back and let fly. The pebble was wet and slipped out of his grasp fractionally too early. It shot away, pinged off a rock at the back of the beach and cracked into Voss's cheekbone. Gunn heard the crack and was up and sprinting low, looking to hit Voss hard. But his quarry had gone, not waiting to field the follow-up. Gunn heard the Packard cranking up and spinning away.

'Bugger!'

'What the hell was that?' thought Voss. It seemed as if it was just the Englishman on his own; unfortunately he didn't get a chance for a second look with that scrub on the beach. Strange behaviour and rather odd to go swimming on your own at this hour but Englishmen, as he knew, were quite mad. His priority now was to get some medical attention. That was going to scar. Scheiss! He headed for the hospital he had passed on the outskirts of town. Mueller was going to have to pay him danger money at this rate.

'So,' mused Gunn. 'What is this cove up to?'

The Packard was long gone, at any rate, and he wagered that the creep wouldn't come back in a hurry. They would be safe for a while. Gunn pulled his clothes on, opened the bottle of brandy, took several swigs and lay back to savour the moment. It went straight to his head. What did they put in this cut throat, buggering stuff?

Sylvia had heard the car too, and, after a while, took advantage of Gunn lying down, seemingly with his eyes closed, to come out of the sea and creep past him to retrieve her clothes. Actually, he had missed nothing. She really did have a delicious body, he thought. Ah, wait for it…here's trouble.

'Gunn,' she called. 'Where are my knickers? Gunn?'

For answer, he patted his top pocket.

'Give them to me now. Bastard.'

Gunn raised an eyebrow.

'Ask nicely. Such language. Anyway, mermaids don't wear knickers. At least, not in the type of picture books I used to read.'

'Gunn, I mean it.'

'I didn't hear a 'please.' You could just go without,' he suggested, rather unhelpfully. 'Nobody would know, except me. You could walk in front of me to the boat. Maybe get a bit drier first though. That dress is quite clingy.'

He suddenly realised that she was walking towards him purposefully, without a stitch on. It was a shame he had got quite so drunk, he thought, ruefully.

'Or,' he ventured, looking her up and down 'You could wrestle me for them. I wouldn't fancy your chances though.'

Giving him a vicious kick, Sylvia removed her knickers from his pocket and got dressed behind a rock.

'Sylv,' Gunn called. 'You're going to have to help me out with this brandy.'

He fell back onto the sand, laughing, and then closed his eyes. Sylvia thought for a moment about leaving him there, but decided instead to haul him to his feet and start the unsteady walk back to the bus stop. Back on the boat, she managed to get him to stand up properly as they passed the nuns, who were having an impromptu service on deck, and around the corner towards the cabins.

Just when she thought it was safe, he said:

'Sweetheart, have you been doing your pelvic floor exercises? You know, for when we've had the baby and we want to resume our conjugal relations? I want you in tip-top shape down there…'

He was in line for a damn good clout, she thought. A few people were staring at them, but she didn't think anyone had heard. She hoped not, anyway. She pushed him into the cabin and into his bunk. After a while, he enquired:

'Sylv, how about coming for a bunk-up? In my bunk? 'He seemed to find this hilarious. She told him in no uncertain terms that he wouldn't be able to perform in that state and to shut up and go to sleep.

'What am I meant to do? Lie here and decorate the ceiling?'

Sylvia decided against going over to him and giving him another kick. He appeared to be properly asleep now, anyway. He made her laugh, although he could be incredibly coarse sometimes. She was beginning to think that he might not find her very attractive. Maybe there was no mystique. They'd spent every waking moment in each other's company. They'd even been doing washing together yesterday. Perhaps he just thought of her as, well, someone like Sol. For once, she was the one lying awake with her thoughts, not Gunn.

Voss, suitably patched up by an attractive nurse in the Casualty Department, was back in the Packard. On an impulse, he decided not to head straight back to the hotel. He turned back towards Posillipo, and drove towards the beach. It was deserted. Maybe that Tommy just lived around here and was something of an eccentric. He remembered something his father had told him about the fearsome Black Watch - the Ladies from Hell. Could this madman on the beach be a Scotsman? In some ways, it was a relief not to have to confront him. Not until he had time to think. He might not be connected with the enquiry at all.

He called in at a restaurant nearby and got chatting to the waiter. He told him about a mad Englishman he had encountered on the beach, without giving anything away, of course. He bought the man a drink and was interested to learn that there wasn't an Englishman, as far as the man knew, living in Posillippo, but that an English couple had been in for lunch today. A couple. That was worth noting. The waiter seemed to think they were staying round here, maybe on a ship. Yes, tourists, doing the usual rounds. Voss couldn't believe his luck. He took his leave, and drove thoughtfully back into town.

Chapter 11

Gunn woke with a real throbbing at his temples. He raised himself up on his elbows. He could sense it was going to be a hot day, warmer than a pizza oven at full tilt. At least that would help with his head. He rolled out of bed, ran the sink full of cold water and ducked his head in once and then twice. He rubbed his hair dry, or tousled dryish, and got dressed.

He put some cold water in a tooth glass and threw it over Sylvia. She was soon wide awake. He was pushing it, she thought angrily.

'Come on madam, if we are going to Pompeii, we might as well get on with it.'

A seething mass of humanity was waiting to disembark. The loading of the tractors was causing chaos. They decided to let the crowds die down and have a quick coffee on board. It was easy enough to get to Pompeii.

'Where did you learn to fight like that, Sylv? You gave me quite a kick last night.'

'In the army. And Edward and I used to fight when we were children and Daddy and I were visiting. He was always a bit of a cry baby though. And a tell-tale.' She wondered what else Gunn remembered from the night before.

'Wouldn't want to come across you on a dark night,' Gunn laughed. Then, with his arm tightly around her waist, and to the accompaniment of beatific grins from the grandmas, many of whom were setting up camp on board in case anybody else got on and stole their coveted spot, they walked off the boat.

'There's an organised trip over there. Shall we investigate?' Sylvia asked. 'Then you get your admission paid and a guide too.'

Gunn, none too impressed with the idea of playing the gawping tourist on a coach, suggested instead that they take the Circumvesuviana train.

'Then we just get off at Pompeii and stroll up to the City. We'll pick up a decent guide book on the way.'

'He seems to know what he's doing,' thought Sylvia, following him into a taxi bound for the railway station. Voss was waiting for them at the docks. He set off in pursuit of their taxi. He was feeling a little under the weather this morning. He hoped it would be relatively easy to overpower the assets. He was in no mood for any 'antics' from that Tommy. Mueller had mentioned in his instructions that the female was pretty. He had to agree. This Brand chap who wanted her back in London so badly was in for a special treat.

'Don't look out of the window, Sylv, but you know that chap from the beach yesterday? The Kraut with the Packard? He's following us.'

'How are we going to shake him off?'

'We're not. He's coming with us, all the way to Pompeii. He'll enjoy a bit of sightseeing. Now, here's the plan and you'll have to do exactly as I say. Don't worry. I'll be with you every step of the way.'

Gunn bought their tickets, making sure that Voss could see them lingering on the platform. He

127

was amused to see the German try and duck behind a stout, black-clad peasant woman. The train stopped at every little halt, and every local, complete with mud, goats and farm implements, got on and off. It was a working train. Sylvia was less than impressed with Gunn's choice. She sank back on the hard bench, feeling a small knot of wood digging into her back as she did so, and glanced at her companion. He seemed cheerful enough on the surface, but she could detect a certain tension in his shoulders and back.

'Is he on the train?'

'Hmm.' Gunn grinned at her, although to Sylvia it seemed more like a grimace than anything resembling humour. 'I'm pretty sure he is. I get the feeling he is what is known as a 'clean-up man.' He is a professional; and I reckon he is ex-military'

'Clean-up man?' she probed.

'Oh, cleans up problems. You and I are a problem to somebody. Probably Cumberland's handlers and thus to Cumberland himself.'

'I suppose 'clean up' is a euphemism?'

'Naturally. I am sure he would expect to see me kissing daisy roots by the time the first snifter of the day is poured in Cumberland's drawing room.'

'Really?'

'Well, I am not going along with such a proposition.' Gunn laughed out loud, disturbing the young student snoring on the bench beside him. Sylvia was surprised that there was genuine humour in his laugh. 'I am awkward like that.'

Sylvia wished she felt reassured. Despite her surroundings, the oppressive heat and smell and the knot digging into her back, she began to wish they didn't ever have to get off the train. All too soon, the Circumvesuviana was pulling into Pompeii Scavi. They bought a guidebook on the way in.

'Look normal,' Gunn murmured, drawing her close to him. 'I know it's difficult, sweetheart, but you can do it. Don't look round.' In more normal tones, he continued: 'Amazing to think the whole place was discovered by accident two hundred years ago.'

'I've always wanted to come here.'

Sylvia told him about her Latin teacher, one of the few she had got on with, the scholarly Miss Venables. She had taken Sylvia and some of the other girls to a talk on new discoveries at Pompeii, at the local Town Hall. The story of the city preserved under the ash had captivated her ever since.

'Once upon a time, there were three little 'wheres.' Ubi, unde and quo.' That was one of her sayings. Another was 'I shall drown and nobody will save me.' And you never said 'Can you mark my book please,' because she'd always say 'Yes, I can. But whether I choose to do so is a different matter. The correct word is 'may.' She was a real stickler for grammar..'

'What are you on about, Sylv?' asked Gunn, absently. 'Why don't we have a wander up to the House of the Tragic Poet? I'm never one for following itineraries, and that has rather a nice ring to it. Something else will probably catch our fancy on the way though.'

He could see Voss, sidling along, trying to look unobtrusive but looking very uncomfortable. He

129

was not dressed in light summer attire like most of the tourists. He was wearing a heavy black jacket. Not surprisingly, he seemed to be sweating heavily and finding it difficult to keep up.

'Serves him right,' thought Gunn. 'I wonder what he's concealing under that jacket.'

Voss was delighted to note that Gunn and Sylvia were peeling off from the hordes and starting to look at individual buildings. He thought perhaps Gunn might have spotted him. He wasn't entirely sure. Anyway, as soon as the coast was clear, he could make his move. Inside his jacket pocket he had a decent cosh, a souvenir from his father, who had been a Brownshirt in the late 1920s. Having recovered from his fright at the hands of the Black Watch, he had graduated to frightening other people. He had survived the Night of the Long Knives and been one of the few absorbed into the SS. He was crucified by Russian peasants in 1943. Voss remembered him fondly, and always made a point of using the old man's cosh. He also carried a Tokarev TT-33 pistol in a holster under his jacket. Nicknamed the 'Tula,' it was actually a Soviet weapon. Voss, despite his general lack of imagination, enjoyed the twist.

Following nonchalantly in their wake, he took stock of his opposition. The Tommy was taller and lighter on his feet. He was younger too. It was hard to say whether he was particularly strong. Hopefully, it would not come to a fist-fight. The man had already proved himself to be quite insane. Voss rubbed his cheek angrily. The girl he could deal with easily, he thought, recalling his instructions that she was to be

130

delivered unharmed to London. He too had bought a guide book, and he stopped every so often, pretending to consult it.

Three elderly American ladies accosted him and asked him to take their photograph by a crumbling statue. With impeccable politeness, he did so, but then excused himself rather abruptly, as he could see the Tommy and the girl disappearing around a corner. With a curse, he began lumbering after them. 'What a strange man,' twittered the old ladies.

Voss turned the corner and caught the flick of fabric; the hem of the girl's skirt heading towards one of the brothels, which was some distance from the rest. Usually, he enjoyed a visit to a house of ill repute, but this one needed to be effective and profitable. These two were beginning to get on his nerves. He strolled on, muscles tensing, aware of a bead of sweat rolling slowly between his shoulder blades. He stopped and, despite himself, shook himself down. He wasn't used to being so tense. He generally approached each assignment with the ease of a man choosing the next course at Maxim's. This was very different indeed. He felt in his pocket for the cosh. Its weight gave him comfort.

He saw the female ahead, absorbed in her guidebook and seemingly alone. That was what threw him. Voss thought momentarily that she was actually just another tourist and that he was on the wrong track. He turned to retrace his footsteps. He didn't see the punch coming but he felt it in his kidneys. He stumbled forward and dropped to his knees. Sylvia turned and brought the back of a very serviceable

Beretta down on the back of his neck. The lights went out.

The salty tang of blood began to wake Voss. He eased his eyes open by will, and found that his back was against an erotic fresco and his hands tied. Gunn sat back on his haunches and slapped Voss's face hard, twice.

'Wakey wakey, old chum. Time for a little chat before you go'

'Go?' Voss was dazed. 'Where? Where did that mad Tommy appear from?'

To add to his confusion, the girl began to speak, in German. He detected a Berlin accent. How had this happened?

'Good morning, Sir. We shan't be disturbed here. Perhaps you wouldn't mind helping us with one or two queries.'

Voss had no time to gather his thoughts, as Sylvia questioned him. Gunn couldn't follow what she was saying, but clearly, she was determined to find out more than the man's rank and serial number. Gunn had tossed Voss's wallet aside and it lay across the floor, open. He was casting an expert eye over 'Tula,' pausing every so often to hit Voss if he failed to answer any of Sylvia's questions.

Sylvia turned to Gunn.

'You were right,' she said. 'Guenter Voss is a clean-up man. We are simply assets. You were to be killed, and I was to be taken back to London. Cumberland is in this up to his neck. That was pretty clear from Jones's papers and yes, Voss knew him as Mannfred Brand. He doesn't know much else about him. They both answer to a chap named Mueller in

132

Bavaria; the one who put the frighteners on Jones. The material in Jones's papers, which Voss was meant to bring back with me, could put a lot of people away for good. That would mean the end of the pipeline which, as well as being ideological, is profitable for many people. Again, he doesn't have too much detail on the pipeline, probably for operational reasons. He's starting to drift off, isn't he? '

She sighed. She felt dirty, all of a sudden. 'What will we do with him?'

'I think you know the answer to that,' Gunn observed. 'He's an asset. All assets come to the end of their usefulness eventually. It's time for him to go. In fact…here we go, chum, on your way.'

Gunn held Voss's head still and slid the commando blade between the German's widening eyes, just at the weak point of the skull. The blade met resistance at first, and then slipped free with a crackling of steel against bone and then the sucking sound of air and brain. Voss died upon the instant.

'I think I'm going to be sick,' said Sylvia.

'Well, don't be sick in here.' Gunn wiped the blade on the German's jacket. 'I'll get rid of him, stash him somewhere quiet.

Sylvia looked at the guidebook. It was a new edition, for the two hundredth anniversary, with a detailed map as an insert.

'I think we're in what's called the House of the Seven Women. There are some outbuildings a short step away which were part of it; I noticed them as we came in. They're marked on here but not

133

named and I don't think anyone would ever go and look in them. I only stumbled across this building by chance; most people go to the main brothel.'

'It was an excellent choice. We're well off the beaten track. Most people seem to go round on a fixed itinerary or with a guide. I think you're right about those outbuildings. The one on the end might even have been bombed. It looks even more dilapidated than the others.' Gunn put his knife back carefully in its ankle sheath. 'If we put him in there, I don't think anybody will find him for days. Eventually, the flies and the smell might give him away, assuming anyone makes it this far, but we'll be long gone. I don't think anyone is going to be reporting him as a missing person, just looked through the wallet quickly. Pop that in your handbag and we'll dispose of it in Naples.'

While Sylvia kept watch to ensure the coast was clear, Gunn dragged Voss out of the brothel and into the outbuilding. He placed him on his side and, after a swift scout and forage, placed some planks and hard core over the body. Brushing the dust and detritus from his hands, he stood over Voss and considered for a moment. He saluted, turned on his heel and did not look back.

Sylvia, meanwhile, had worked out a way of getting out of there without anybody noticing, using a path which was not overlooked and via which they could eventually get back onto the main drag by seeming to have come from a different direction altogether. Beside the erotic fresco, Gunn drew her close and checked her over, pausing to wipe something off her face.

134

'Lead the way,' he said. 'We'll just make our way slowly back to the exit now. Well done.'

Back amongst the crowds, Sylvia said:

'I need a cigarette.'

Her tone was terse. Gunn passed one over. She took it gratefully, surprised to find her hand shaking a little. Gunn held it still as he applied a match to her cigarette. It flared, briefly.

'That tastes good.' She inhaled, and then blew, and the smoke drifted away towards Vesuvius. They made their way back to the station. The train was even more oppressive and uncomfortable. At the railway station in Naples, Sylvia headed for the nearest dustbin and was spectacularly sick. Gunn, she noted, held her hair out of the way. He could be incredibly sweet sometimes and at other times, well...

He broke into her reverie.

'Back to the boat for a wash and brush up?' he suggested.

The taxi dropped them at the docks. They walked up the gangplank hand in hand, chatting to the grandmas and the little group of nuns, who were going to an order in Jerusalem. Gunn and Sylvia were very welcome to come for tea, they said, if they were in the area. Gunn rather liked the idea of being invited for tea in a convent. He helped her wash her hair when they got back to the cabin and they sat on the balcony with a cup of tea, which he had nabbed from a passing steward. She was very pale.

'You're shivering. You should lie down, get some rest. I'm popping back into town for a while. Got some business to take care of. Won't be long.'

He tucked her in, under the scratchy sheets, and planted a kiss on her forehead. 'You were amazing today, sweetheart. Couldn't have done it without you.'

Sylvia was awoken from uneasy slumbers and a bizarre dream by a knock on the door. She opened the cabin door a fraction.

'Yes?'

'Madam, can you come to the car deck please? Your husband requires your presence.' The young cabin boy turned and returned to his duties which would consist for the next hour of cleaning the heads, followed by a stint in the kitchen.

Sylvia wrapped her dress around her, tying it with an irritated flourish. She made her way to the car deck, wondering what on earth Gunn had been up to. Then she spotted him, leaning against the bonnet of the Packard. It had been winched on board, despite grumbling from the captain, with just a few bumps, dents and a long scratch down the side to show for its travails. It had been placed next to the tractors, which Gunn thought strangely appropriate. Sylvia inched past the tractors to reach him.

'Found this. Thought we could take it with us.'

Sylvia went pale. 'Gunn, what the hell have you done?'

'No need to worry. Found the keys in the wallet earlier. The registration documents were in the glove compartment. It's in his name. Guenter Voss. He won't be needing it any more. Oh, and he checked out of his hotel this morning after breakfast. That was something else I found in the wallet; the receipt, it was charged to a Dr Mueller. So, apart from Mueller himself, there won't be anyone expecting him back.'

'Give us a hand with these, will you, Sylv?' He handed her several bags. 'I got us some lunch. Some pizza and some fruit. I'm famished. We can have a picnic on our balcony. Oh, and I got you a dress. To wear when we get back to Paris; I'll take you somewhere really nice.'

'How did you know what size to get?' Back in the cabin, Sylvia was twirling in front of the mirror. The dress, a red polka dot number, fitted perfectly.

'I got a pretty good look at you the other night on the beach, ma petite sirène,' Gunn grinned. 'I was drunk, but not that drunk. And I wanted to apologise. I was very unprofessional.'

'You're just impossible,' she told him happily, as they finished their picnic and contemplated the evening ahead. 'How about a stroll on deck? We'll be sailing soon.'

The Sidonia was already inching its way out of port as Gunn and Sylvia came up on deck, beginning its journey to Haifa. They had already got to know so many people that a circuit of the deck had become a lengthy undertaking. A few new passengers had got on, joining the canvas encampment. Sol was chatting to some of the new arrivals. He gave them a wave. Gunn wandered over to join them.

Sylvia continued with her walk. Gunn found her, about an hour later, standing on her own looking back at the land. She was in a world of her own.

'Penny for them.'

'Oh, I was just thinking Richard died on one of those beaches over there. It's awful, but I feel I'm forgetting him. I owe his parents a letter, actually. We were hardly together at all. We were so young. Sometimes, I wonder if it would have worked out between us, if he'd made it. We scarcely knew each other. If it hadn't been for the war, we wouldn't ever have met.'

Gunn stood quietly beside her, absorbed in his own thoughts of landing in Italy.

'Destiny is a strange thing,' he remarked, after a while. 'Now, I think it might be time for a ceremonial funeral for a wallet.'

He threw Voss's wallet into the sea. It was weighted down with a few pebbles, Sylvia noted, and it sank straightaway.

'Nice of him to get you a dress, wasn't it? He'd probably have approved. There was quite a bit of cash in there, which I've kept, along with the hotel receipt with Mueller's name on it. Mueller's clearly not afraid to splash the cash.'

He didn't mention the photograph of Voss with comrades from the AfrikaKorps or the funeral card for a Frau Voss (a widow) from last year. Both were now inside the wallet, heading to the bottom of the sea.

'Meant to say, Sylv. You were quite ruthless in your interrogation. I mean, all I had to do was give the guy the occasional slap. Where did you learn that?'

'British War Crimes Tribunal,' she replied. 'I...well, I observed certain things. My boss was a lawyer, back in civil life. Frightened the life out of the

138

prisoners. Made one man crawl out of the room on his hands and knees like an animal after he had given his evidence. The guy had been some sort of hangman, I think. My boss had an almost uncanny way of getting information out of people, without them realising where his questioning was taking them.'

'I think you got everything you could out of that cove today. Incidentally, I just had an interesting chat with Sol.'

'Define interesting.' muttered Sylvia. She couldn't quite decide whether she liked Sol. He never seemed to take much notice of her, although, logically, why should he?

'Honestly, Gunn, you duck and weave like a boxer on the ropes.'

'Nothing too exotic,' replied Gunn. 'It's just Sol wants me to meet some friends of his in Tel Aviv. If time allows, of course.'

'Of course.' Sylvia folded her arms in a defensive gesture. 'What kind of friends? Drinking buddies?'

'Er, no, I don't think so. Something possibly more official.' Gunn let his gaze drift beyond the deck and out towards the horizon. 'Once we've met the family, of course.'

'Sounds intriguing'

Sylvia looked over towards a group of children who were playing a game of hide and seek, in and out of the canvas awnings. They were drawn from all over Europe. Language wasn't an issue. They were having a wonderful time. She wondered what life would be like for them in Israel, and thought how incredibly resilient children were.

139

Chapter 12

Back in London, Edward had just finished another call with Meunier. Early evening was not always the best time to catch Meunier. He seemed slightly impatient. Apart from the telegram, several days ago, Meunier repeated, there had been no contact. Of course he would let him know straightaway if there were any developments.

Edward sat at his desk, sipping a cup of tepid weak tea. It reminded him of being in the nursery with Nanny. That new receptionist would have to go. He grimaced. He was not a man given to much reflection; not that his father had ever given him much of a chance to reflect. He reacted, hence his skills as a fighter pilot. He was finding post-war life chafing and restrictive. Many others felt the same way. That didn't make it easier.

Not for the first time, he was wondering what sort of research commission he had sent Sylvia on. It was beginning to dawn on him that he might have been 'set up.' Had she not mentioned something about being followed, before they even left London? He could not approach his father, who would dismiss him with scorn, as he always had. They had never been close and Sylvia had driven a wedge between them deeper than a man of his imagination could have contemplated. A brief report had appeared in the papers about Jonathan Jones. Not much detail, but it troubled him to think of Sylvia finding a scene like that. What were they doing for money? He had given them a reasonable budget, but how could they access funds, if they hadn't been to see Meunier? Edward didn't think the man was lying. He would have no reason to.

Deciding rebelliously not to spend another tedious evening with Caroline and her ghastly parents, and resigning himself to the fact that he would be in for it the next day, he wandered down to Louis's office.

'Fancy a pint at the Two Chairmen, old boy?' Louis never turned down a pint.   'We'll lock up then and wander over there,' said Edward. They turned onto Birdcage Walk. Edward had always liked that as a name for a street. He told Louis that James I had once kept aviaries of exotic birds there. The Two Chairmen was their local. Carrying their pints, Edward sat down opposite Louis in the dark interior, and began to voice his fears.

Louis agreed that it was a little odd that there had been so little contact, but then again, they were on a mission. You wouldn't put that mission in jeopardy by talking about it and, if Edward thought about it, when Clements worked for them under normal circumstances, they did just tend to 'get on with it.' Gunn was an extremely experienced operative. He didn't think there was much cause for concern. They would soon shake off any 'goons' who were following them. The police were involved now in France. He had a feeling the pair of them would turn up at Queen Anne's Gate soon, full of beans and in their usual inimitable style, to tell them all about it.

'But supposing they don't?' Edward burst out. 'What if that clown has ditched her and gone off with what's left of the money? Why didn't they just come

142

back when they found Jones, as they were meant to? Supposing he has had his way with her?'

Louis clapped him on the back.

'You old devil. That's what's upsetting you. You're jealous, aren't you?'

Louis reassured Edward that Gunn and Sylvia were adults. They ran a business together; there would have been ample opportunity for that sort of thing before now. Why should he worry about it happening now? Why was he so bothered about Sylvia anyway? He couldn't resist mentioning Caroline at this point, with a smirk. Edward should just be patient. He reminded him that Sylvia was quite adept at looking after herself. She had lived in France as a child. She might even have her own contacts over there if anything untoward happened. Gunn was not, in his view, a chancer. He persuaded Edward that they should give them at least another week. Having talked it through, Edward had to admit that he felt a little happier.

It was Louis's round; they would just stay for one more, they decided. The talk turned to Edward's father. A little banter about him was always enjoyable.

'Where in Germany is he from originally?' Louis asked. 'He was speaking German loudly the other day; I could hear him from the conference room. I couldn't quite place the accent.'

Edward was surprised. He very rarely heard his father speaking German. There was the very occasional, carefully-selected German-speaking client but there weren't many of them. He had never really discussed his father's origins, but the world was moving on and there was probably no harm in it.

'Southern Bavaria,' he said, vaguely. 'Beautiful place. My grandparents had an estate. We went there a few times when I was young. Mummy didn't like going so if he did go and see the family, he often went alone. But you know he came to school over here when he was thirteen. Went to Wellington, like me.'

'And did you learn to speak German as a child?'

'No,' said Edward. 'Dad was always more English than the English. Shame really. I'm always quite envious of Sylvia and the way she switches between languages. Makes her good at what she does, I suppose.'

'More English than the English,' Louis murmured, almost imperceptibly. 'Or hidden in plain sight?'

'Whatever do you mean?' Edward did not mean to be obtuse; it was a natural talent, or so Louis had long ago decided. 'Now look here. Are you saying that my father is not loyal?'

'That is exactly what I am saying.' Louis had finally had enough. A long, fraying thread had given way. 'I think your father is a Nazi, remains a Nazi and is in fact involved in something up to the top of his jackboots.'

'You can't be serious.' Edward's brain began to crank up a gear, very slowly. Louis was serious, and the fact he had said it meant there had to be something in it.

'I can be serious and I am serious.'

With uncharacteristic generosity, it being Edward's round, Louis slipped to the bar and bought two more pints and two brandies. His old friend was as white as a ghost.

'Down the hatch.'

Edward turned to him. His world was falling apart. He thought angrily of his days with the squadron and how proud his parents had been. Surely that was genuine? Had there been some terrible mistake? Then he remembered, with dawning horror, the Jones Confidential file, which he had been unable to make head or tail of, but which was full of names and talked of 'assets.' It was now annoyingly firmly back under lock and key. His father seemed to be in the office more these days.

'Don't worry,' Louis reassured him. 'He'll slip up again. Tell me something, does the name Friedrich Mueller mean anything to you?'

Edward thought for a moment.

'Oh yes, Uncle Friedrich. Now, he was a boyhood friend of Dad's. A doctor. He came and visited us once or twice. Got involved in something rather unpleasant. I'm not sure we've heard from him since the war. Why do you ask?'

Louis explained that on his way past George's office on a couple of occasions, he had heard him asking for a Dr Friedrich Mueller.

Edward's brow was furrowed. His head was spinning, not assisted by three pints and a brandy. Louis put a hand on his shoulder.

'Fetch us another pint, and we'll work out what to do.'

Watching his friend's unsteady progress towards the bar, Louis turned a tattered beermat over in his hand, wondering not for the first time where his impulsiveness would lead him next.

When Edward staggered through the door of Chepstow Villas just before midnight, having eventually been thrown out of the pub at closing time, his father was lying in wait for him.

'Where the hell have you been?' his father shouted, his face close to Edward's. 'Your mother and I have had the Andrews on the telephone twice, wanting to know where you were. Caroline was terribly upset. And you reek of drink. How dare you behave in this way? If the Andrews call it off between you, I will....'

Edward ducked away and gave his father a hard shove against the wall. Get away from me,' he shouted. 'Piss off. Leave me alone.' For once, his father was slack-jawed and lost for words. Edward had never dared speak to him like that before.

Edward went up to his room, slammed the door and lay down on the narrow bed, which was still his from childhood days. His logbooks were in the drawers, his pilot's uniform hanging in the wardrobe. Several cricket trophies were arranged on the shelf. His battered teddy bear was on the pillow beside him, along with clean, ironed pyjamas. Edward threw both to the floor with an oath. The room seemed to be rotating. His feeling of being off-kilter was not assisted at all by the stars his mother had painted on the ceiling for him when he was a little boy and afraid of the dark. However, he thought, in his befuddled

146

way, at least he and Louis had decided on a course of action.

Both had agreed that it was pointless involving the authorities, without evidence. George had successfully got himself off the Isle of Man in double quick time (using me, no doubt, Edward thought, with unusual bitterness). Louis, who followed these things carefully, had seen in the press that Mueller had been exonerated by a tribunal in Munich only last week. Convincing the authorities of their culpability, before they even had a clear idea of what they had actually done, or who else might be involved, would not assist at this stage. They would be laughed out of court. It would be better if they could see what Gunn and Sylvia brought back from France, before making a decision.

The next morning, feeling rough, Edward tried to creep out of the house early, straightening his tie in the hall mirror downstairs. His father was waiting for him again. Trying to disguise his loathing, Edward called cheerfully:

'Must dash; got a couple of exchanges to set up and some new instructions to read through.'

He sprinted down the garden path, pausing to close the gate carefully behind him. George shook his head. What had got into the boy? He needed to be taught a lesson. That could wait; more important fish to fry. He went back inside to finish his breakfast, resolving to place a call to Mueller in a day or so. Surely there must be some news about that little bitch and those papers soon. Still, he was off for lunch at the Athenaum with His Honour Judge Arnold Peters,

147

an old friend from Wellington. He wasn't going to let anything spoil that.

Edward and Louis were also out for a 'hair of the dog' lunch, leaving the secretaries to a busy few hours holding the fort. They were at the Agrippa Club, in a little street near the Ritz. A comfortable stroll there and back across St James's Park, and it was one of their favourite haunts. It could be a little 'school dinner-ish' sometimes, although that bothered Edward less than Louis. Louis could never understand how anybody could refer to food as 'fodder.'

The Jones assignment was still troubling Edward. He was in complete shock about his father although certain pennies were finally beginning to drop. As far as he was concerned, everything was on Sylvia's shoulders. He discounted Gunn as a beast of burden, nothing more. He said as much to Louis. Louis set down his fork and laughed out loud, disturbing the other diners in the club, who expressed their displeasure with long looks over glasses and several 'harrumphings.' Louis ignored them. He was starting to get too stiff in the bones to worry about the rules of the game anymore.

'Gunn is a fine soldier,' he growled. 'He fought with Stirling in the Long Range Desert group. He fought Vichy in Syria and he spent '43 and '44 prior to D Day in and out of Europe, making a beautiful mess of things.'

'I see.' Edward's temples were throbbing, the glass of wine at his fingertips seeming more of a threat than a balm, and his response was suitably stiff.

'No, I don't think you see at all.' Louis jabbed a fork, heavy with fish, in Edward's direction for emphasis. 'He damn near got pinched by the Germans in Paris. He was wounded in Italy, took a bayonet in the shoulder and a bullet in the hip and landed in France on 5th June. Louis sighed. 'I think you owe Gunn a little more respect, at least as a fellow officer.'

They would have to differ on that score, Edward thought. Anyway, more people were starting to stare. If they got thrown out of here, his father was bound to hear about it and there would be hell to pay. He checked himself; he needed to stop being terrified of his father but old habits died hard. He changed the subject abruptly. Louis looked at him rather strangely but allowed himself to be steered into a discussion about the forthcoming squadron reunion.

In Rome, Natalia Buonsignore took one last look at the empty flat on the Via dei Serpenti, where she had, until recently, been maintained by Guenter Voss. She had done well out of him. He had bought her some very expensive furs and jewellery. Truth be told, though, she was tired of him. She had taken advantage of his absence to start a new life in Toronto, or just nearby (her knowledge of Canada was scanty) to live with her sister who had settled there with her husband. The contents of the flat, some of which actually belonged to Voss, were now in her capacious suitcases, which she carried downstairs and into the waiting taxi. The landlord could whistle for the rest of the rent; she was only a week or so behind.

In Bad Kaltenbrun, in Southern Bavaria, Friedrich Mueller took off his brown felt hat,

149

arranging the feather carefully. He had just been to Mass, which he never missed, with his wife and some of their little grandchildren. It was a patronal feast day for one of the local saints, and an unofficial holiday in this part of Bavaria. He smiled at them all fondly. Lunch would be ready soon, and they would be joined by some friends and colleagues. Drinks were being served outside, overlooking the lake. The champagne was cooling, to celebrate his exoneration at the Tribunal. Life was good.

He excused himself, and went upstairs to his study to use the telephone in peace. He thought he might make a quick call to Voss at the hotel in Naples. He frowned slightly when they told him that Voss had checked out yesterday. He wasn't overly concerned; Voss had told him briefly the other night that he had the assets in his sights, although it might be tricky and they were evasive. Perhaps his enquiries had taken him further down the coast. He could always ring the number he had for him in Rome if he didn't hear anything. He was off to the mountains tomorrow with his wife for a week. Things could wait until they were back. Lothar (he would never get used to 'George') would not, thank goodness, be able to contact them where they were going. Only a few trusted people (and the emphasis was on the word trusted) had the number. He went downstairs again to join his family and friends and sat with them, a veritable pillar of society and *pater familias*. His expression was that of a man at the centre of his own universe. He was in charge, and all deferred to him. Indeed, when he pulled an over-stuffed Havana cigar from his inside pocket, no less than three men stepped forward to do the honours. He chuckled. He could safely celebrate getting away with it. He was home and dry.

Mueller had no compunction when it came to issues, a term he used so lightly, with the indifference of familiarity. If someone or something had become an issue, said issue would be removed and all connection severed and cauterised. Voss was the ideal tool for the job. His loyalty could not be questioned, he was deadly in action, and he had never been bested yet. Inevitably, he would be bested one day, but when that day came, he would be replaced.

Now was not the time to dwell on 'issues.' Muller smiled indulgently instead, accepting the congratulations of his family, friends, his peers and those he knew loathed him but needed his approval and patronage. He enjoyed the champagne, a bottle from a case or two he had brought back from France in 1944. He also enjoyed the view of his niece's cleavage as she poured him another glass.

His mind drifted back to his boyhood, and Lothar's, in Bad Kaltenbrun. The name said it all really. Lothar's family had owned the small country estate that dominated the little village for thousands of years. Mueller's mother was a servant at the big house. He never knew who his father was, although he had had his suspicions. Mueller was the name his mother had been born with. She never married or had more children.

He and Lothar were exactly the same age. They were inseparable. Mueller let his mind run over idyllic, hot summers bathing in the cool lakes on the estate. Everything changed when Lothar was sent to

151

boarding school in England. Lothar had been decidedly 'distant,' when he came home for his holidays, talking about things Mueller could barely comprehend. Really, they went their separate ways. He brought some ghastly boys over with him later in the summer, who had bullied Mueller unmercifully.

Things never really come to a head; the boys simply went their separate ways. Lothar had gone to Cambridge and then taken solicitors' exams, becoming articled to a firm in the City of London. He had completed his education just before the war broke out and, with things becoming rather 'sticky' over there, had arrived back in Bad Kaltenbrun. Mueller himself was in the middle of qualifying as a doctor; he had finished the hospital training and now needed to specialise. Recently he had wondered idly who had paid for his education and why a small cottage had been purchased for his mother when she became too old to work.

The boys drifted apart again when the war started. Lothar was signed off as an asthma sufferer and given a desk job. 'Trust him,' Mueller had thought at the time. Mueller himself had joined up; the 16th Bavarian Reserve Infantry regiment, no less. One of his fellow recruits had been the Fuhrer. Mueller had not come across him; the great man had been a message-runner while Mueller had been assigned to medical duties. He had heard a few disparaging remarks about his dear Fuhrer's war service and had always been quick to put them down. Nobody was qualified to comment unless they had been in the thick of it.

Lothar had returned to England after the war and married an English girl. He had then managed, through the old public school and Cambridge network, to buy his way into Cumberlands, a small, moribund practice in central London. He took its name for his own. Lothar's wife did not like Bad Kaltenbrun or her in-laws, and the feeling was mutual. It was on a sunny evening in the late 1920s, just before Mueller set off to take up a new post in Berlin and when Lothar was on a flying visit to his family, that they had met and talked at length by the lake, as they had not done for many years. They had realised how many opinions they shared. That evening, it was as if they had never been apart. They had swum in this very lake, where dinner was being served now. The old Lothar had returned.

Still, there was no point in being sentimental, thought Mueller. Sentimentality was too costly an emotion. It had cost Germany the recent war and her place in the world. Mueller was bitter. He was a believer. He had been a disciple since the beer halls and brawls of Munich. He hid his faith, had packed it away deep inside him, but he held fast to it. He had reached the conclusion that Lothar was a dabbler, not a true believer. He loved the British Establishment too much, although it was true he had done some good work for the pipeline. Anyway, he had made up his mind. Voss could deal with Lothar in London once he had cleared things up in Naples. There was no immediate rush. He had every confidence in Voss. He had this lovely party to enjoy, and the mountains tomorrow. He smiled at the assembled guests, who had just risen to their feet to toast his health. He stood

153

to offer his thanks in a carefully-scripted speech. One had to be so careful nowadays.

At the Athenaum, George Cumberland and His Honour Judge Arnold Peters had just finished a second vintage brandy. It had been a superb lunch, George thought; though not necessarily from the food perspective. He and Arnold went back a long way, to that terrible day when his parents had dropped him at Wellington. He had found the place incomprehensible, even though he had been learning English with his tutor at home, and brutal. Peters had been new too and, like George, slightly 'lost,' having not been through the preparatory school system either. His father had been an administrator on the North West frontier. For various reasons, he had never got around to sending Arnold to England to school before then. Arnold and George had immediately become firm friends and had remained so over the years.

'Keep our discussions strictly *entre nous* for now, old boy,' Arnold advised, as they went their separate ways.

George was deep in thought as he walked across St James's Park, occasionally aiming a vicious kick at a pigeon that came too close. Usually, he liked to watch the girls sunbathing, but not today. Over lunch, Arnold had suggested that the Presidency of the Law Society could be up for grabs and that George's hat could be in the ring. A curious expression, George thought. He laughed out loud. He was in line for one of the finest prizes in the British Establishment, and he had played them like a dime a dozen piano player in a New Orleans cathouse. It was absurd and yet perfect at the same time.

Flicking a pebble with an exquisitely shod foot, he considered further. Perhaps Edward should have an 'accident.' Nothing that could in any way be attributable to him, but a terminal event for a young man who had fought so bravely in the Battle of Britain. He could almost read the headlines now; grieving family and grieving fiancée. Think of the weight that would add to his candidacy. It would take some time to arrange, of course and would require some thought. He needed to find the little bastard meanwhile, place a well-aimed boot up his backside and make sure he proposed to Caroline. Provided, of course, Edward's little stunt last night had not ruined things. Hopefully, that was not the case; his wife had made rather heavy weather of Edward having been taken poorly on the way home.

His other priority was to get those Jones papers back. He would make sure Gunn was dead and then, having taken Sylvia across the desk, he would kill her as well. His fantasies about that little trollop were becoming darker and more and more graphic by the minute as he arrived back at Queen Anne's Gate. This time, he would make sure nobody was around to hear her scream, he reflected, as he made his way unsteadily across the room to the cabinet. He stopped dead in his tracks. It was open and the drawers were completely empty. He screamed for his secretary, who arrived at the double.

'Anything the matter, Mr Cumberland?' she asked, rather unnecessarily. The corded veins sticking out of his neck and his bright red face were a giveaway. He asked, in a strange squeaky voice, what had happened to the files in the top drawer.

'Oh, they're here.' She indicated a neat stack of files on the floor. 'The electrician came in, to mend the switch by the window and we had to move everything. I was just typing that completion statement up for Young Mr Cumberland and then I was going to put everything back. It needed tidying, anyway. Are you all right, Mr Cumberland? Can I get you anything?'

George just about managed to be civil; yes, please, a glass of water would be 'just the ticket.' That was it. The files were coming out of that cabinet now. These girls really were idiots. Did Edward and Louis recruit them especially? And why was she doing Edward's work? She was meant to give his work top priority. He had conveniently forgotten, in his puffed-up vanity, that he produced so little actual work nowadays, that Edward sometimes borrowed his girl, as he called her, to help with the conveyancing,. He locked the Jones file carefully in his desk, where he kept certain photographs that he would rather nobody else saw, along with some magazines and membership cards to the type of 'gentlemen's club' his wife would have been aghast at, and went down to the conference room to get a glass of brandy.

He barely noticed the secretary coming back in with his water; he was deep in thought. He placed a call to Meunier in Paris. Still no word, apparently. He then had a call put through to Bad Kaltenbrun, but was told that Dr Mueller and his wife had left for a week's holiday. No, Dr Mueller had not left any messages for him.

George tapped a pencil on his desk, pensively. It did seem a little odd, given that the last he had heard was that the 'assets' were in Naples. He trusted Mueller's judgment implicitly in this matter; he had never let him down before. Nonetheless, with the narrow shave this afternoon, he could not afford to take any chances. Nobody else had a key to his desk but it could probably be smashed open with relative ease. It was nearly five anyway. Louis had gone to Lincolns Inn for a conference with one of the few members of the Bar still in town, and Edward had gone over to Great St Peter's Street to take some instructions from a little old lady about her will. He planned to go straight to the Tennis Club from there, according to the secretary. Idiot boy, George snorted; made far too much fuss of his clients. Why hadn't he got the silly old bat to come to the office? Anyway, just as well he hadn't.

He shooed everyone off the premises. The secretaries were only too glad of an early finish. Mr Roper, the old boy who was their Conveyancing Clerk and part-time book-keeper, took some shifting. He had lost half a leg at Gallipoli and wasn't one for moving fast. He liked a chat. George was beginning to find it hard to be polite, but eventually the wretched man shuffled off towards the underground station. Finally, with a sigh of relief, George turned the key in the lock and set off for the taxi rank with a set of files in two decent-sized suitcases.

Soon, he was on his way to Wardour Street. He had a friend, a tailor, an Austrian who had a shop in St Anne's Court, with a cat that drank good Scotch.

157

For a reasonable fee, the tailor's spare safe at the back of the shop could be hired for a time, which would give him some breathing space. After the afternoon he had had, he could do with some of the cat's scotch too. The cat, nicknamed Galland, was a contrary bugger but George got on with him as well as anybody did. He was quite sure Galland would share the Scotch. In fact, he would make sure he did. The taxi drew to a halt on Wardour Street.

'Three shillings please, guv.'

George unbuckled with his usual poor grace, giving the man the right change exactly and no tip.

'Tight old bastard' called the taxi driver. Fortunately for him, George was already halfway down St Annes Court, with his cases in his arms and other things on his mind. The door of the tailor's shop was shut. He tapped it with a highly polished shoe. He was not in the mood for being kept waiting. The street was deserted; it seemed to have battened down its hatches early, as London streets often do.

'Juncker, open this blasted door,' he shouted in German. 'Otherwise I will rip your head off.'

'All right, all right,' came the response. 'Give me a chance.'

The bolts were drawn back. Galland came rushing outside as if pursued by the hounds of hell and then careened to the kind of halt that generally results in a feline indulging in a kind of 'nothing to see here' wash and brush-up. Dignity fully restored, he gave Cumberland a good, hard stare and then stalked back into the shop to resume his post on the worktop not far from his habitual saucer of Scotch. George's gaze followed him.

'I hope he can spare some of his Scotch.'

Juncker nodded his agreement.

'He always shares with a gentleman.'

The tailor opened the door wide and George slid in, his decent coat, which he had worn for lunch at the Athenaum, brushing Juncker's grubby brushed velvet waistcoat. George managed to suppress a grimace, turning it instead into a smile of something approaching thanks.

Juncker looked him up and down with a practiced eye.

'So, why have you come to see me at this hour? Need me to let that suit out? I don't think there's much more 'give' in that seam. Too many lunches at the Club, my friend. You need to cut down a bit.'

George tried hard to suppress his irritation. Juncker was an excellent tailor, but he could do without the personal remarks. Who the hell did the man think he was? Too familiar by half, but at least here he could let his guard down and be himself, and talk about plans for a new world order. There were precious few places where he could do that. Nobody took much notice of an Austrian in a street full of Jewish tailors.

They had met on the Isle of Man, a time in George's life over which he preferred to draw a veil. He still seethed with rage, when he thought of the indignity of it all. He had had to appear before an Enemy Alien Tribunal when war was declared; the upshot was that he was deemed to be a risk to national security. That had been bad enough. But then, a few months later, during one of his weekly bridge nights, and in full view of the neighbours, the police had arrived. They had been courteous; he had struggled to keep a civil tongue in his head. They had left his wife at home; she simply had to continue reporting to the police each week.

In a strange sort of way, the Spartan conditions at the camp to which he was taken reminded him of Wellington. The food wasn't that bad. He hadn't even minded being shepherded along towards the camp, when they first arrived, by men from the Royal Welch Fusiliers. It had been something of a shock that he had had to carry his own belongings, although as he had still been feeling a little under the weather from the sea crossing, he hadn't protested. What he had really objected to were all the Jewish internees, and being constantly lumped in with them. All that rubbish they were spouting about conditions in the Fatherland. Somebody really should have put a stop to it there and then. He had been sorely tempted on more than one occasion. A group of British fascists had arrived soon afterwards, but they tended to keep themselves to themselves.

George had been quite surprised to find that, as detainees, they were relatively free. Not to leave the island, of course, but there was plenty to occupy them all. There were football matches, plays, concerts and even a makeshift university. He had started up a chess club, to give himself something to do and to try to keep his mind active, otherwise he found he just dwelt on things. To his surprise, as he had never been a patient man, he found himself rather enjoying the aspect of teaching the game to people who had never played before. Most of them picked it up very quickly It was a game of 'outwitting,' which he had always enjoyed, and always refreshing to have a different view on the game. His efforts at teaching Edward the game had not been a great success.

An early member of George's Chess Club was Franz Juncker, who had been born in Austria, not far from the border and Bad Kaltenbrun. By coincidence, Juncker had served with Mueller in 14-18. What a small world! Of course, in civilian life, he would never have struck up a friendship with somebody like Juncker, but those few months on the Isle of Man had been quite bizarre. They soon found themselves sharing confidences, and found they had more in common than they would ever have imagined. Juncker had trained as a tailor in Austria, and was soon operating a small business within the camp.

As well as running the Chess Club, George had busied himself with trying to get himself off the island. He had written to every Member of Parliament he could think of, and to various judges and Home Office officials. Some had been his contemporaries at Wellington and at Cambridge. For once, Edward had done something useful, by joining the RAF and flying Spitfires. He was never quite sure actually whether this had done the trick. Many other internees had sons serving in the Forces, he thought to himself, including those confounded Jews. It must have helped somehow though, as he was out long before Juncker, who had also eventually made it back to London where he set up as a tailor.

He turned to Juncker.

'My suit does not need altering,' he said, with as much dignity as he could muster. 'Thank you. Just pour me some of that blasted animal's Scotch, will you?'

Juncker poured a measure each into two rather dubious-looking glasses. Suppressing an urge to wipe the rim of his glass, George took a sip of the Scotch. He had expected a glass of gut-rot, not something of the first class quality he was sipping now. It was as smooth as silk on a lady's thigh. He looked at Juncker.

'This is good stuff.'

'Galland is most particular.'

'I am impressed.' Noticing Juncker's eyes sliding to the suitcases, George set his glass down and said:

'I have £20 for you here if you will lock these away for a few days. You will get another £20 when I collect them safely.'

'Must be important.' Juncker pursed his lips in thought.

'You don't need to know.'

'Of course, I was merely musing.' Juncker smiled. 'Agreed. I will do as you ask.'

'You will do as I am paying for.'

'You know you can trust me.'

'As far as I can throw you,' thought George, as he took his leave. 'But what's the alternative?'

He hailed a cab to take him to Chepstow Villas. As he walked up the garden path, he spotted Edward walking up the road from the underground. This time, he lay in wait quietly. His son did not evade his grasp. At the end of this painful encounter,

Edward comprehended fully, or so he said, that he was to propose to Caroline tomorrow. He could have some time off to buy a ring if he wished.

Having at last managed to flee upstairs, not daring to slam the door this time, Edward aimed a vicious kick at his teddy bear, sending it soaring to the ceiling and back down again. He desperately wanted to say something to his father, who now disgusted him even more. He knew he could not. Sylvia was all he cared about. He felt sick to the core. Tomorrow, he would ring Meunier again and perhaps call in on Joan. He could not believe, either, that he had just agreed to propose to somebody he did not find remotely attractive or even like very much, just so that his father could become President of the Law Society.

He was trapped, no two ways about it. He could not see at the moment how he could ever walk away from the life that had been imposed on him. He understood duty to his very bones and he understood honour too. The irony was that he had only ever been free when flying his Spitfire with the Squadron out of Biggin Hill. He lay on his bed and smoked a couple of cigarettes, remembering his younger days when, despite everything, he knew what it meant to be alive. Now, he knew nothing.

Chapter 13

'I think we deserve a break after all this,' said Gunn, looking at the diagram they had completed over several large sheets of paper and the report, which Sylvia had copied out neatly.

'I'm pleased with it,' Sylvia conceded, always something of a perfectionist. 'I reckon the authorities will be able to do something with this. The narrative flows quite smoothly. Thanks for helping me with that. Have you had any further thoughts about what we do when we get to Haifa?'

'A few.' Gunn was away with his own thoughts again. Last night, Sylvia had found him on the forward deck standing near a group of ladies having an animated conversation in French.

'What was all that about?' She had been only half listening.

'They were talking about little children who were thrown by their parents off the trains transporting them to the death camps. In some cases, they were found and looked after by Christian families but their identities were completely changed.'

Sylvia rather wished she hadn't asked. She didn't want to seem heartless, but she had watched endless footage of atrocities at the trials. It hadn't hardened her to the accounts by any means but had instilled in her a huge sadness about man's inhumanity to man. She changed the subject to more pressing issues. Gunn had managed a brief call to Joan in Naples, in between collecting the Packard and buying Sylvia's dress. All was well, Joan had assured him; nothing to worry about. She had received a visit or two from Old Man Cumberland but had sent him packing, with a flea in his ear.

On deck now, they could feel the excitement in the air. It was electric. Everyone on board had a story; for the most part, a terrible one. Their new lives were not far away now. Gunn noticed the smudge of grey smoke on the horizon and tapped Sylvia on the wrist.

'Haifa,' he said.

'What's that smoke?'

'Oh, probably a firefight or two between Israelis and Arabs. There was a battle here in April. The Israelis call it Operation Bi'urHametz.'

'Meaning?'

'Passover Cleansing.' Gunn shrugged. 'The British had left by the 20th, having informed the Israelis, and it all kicked off on the 21st.'

'Why Haifa?'

'It's a deep water port. Strategic location. And the area had been allocated to Israel. Simple as that. It was pretty much wrapped up by the 22nd.'

Now he mentioned it, Sylvia did recall seeing something about it in the newspapers. It all seemed very different; like nowhere else she had ever been.

'So have you ever been here before, Gunn?' she asked. One of her pet hates was not having a clear strategy in place but she could see this was going to be difficult to achieve, and she was open to a challenge.

'Me? Haifa? No, of course I haven't.'

Gunn turned to address an inconsequential civility to one of his ladies. Sylvia filed that away for future reference. He was not being wholly open, but that was not his way. He would dig his heels in like a mule at the plough if she tried to push him. She knew better than that. Instead, she took his arm.

'Well, darling, I suppose we had better start packing. It almost feels like home after all this time aboard.'

Their route back to the cabin was thronged with people wishing them luck with the baby.

'I feel a bit of a fraud,' she observed, when they were inside. 'I know it's our profession and I don't normally give it a second's thought. I will miss it though.'

'It's the nature of the beast,' Gunn shrugged. 'If you leave an implication twisting in the air, people latch onto it and it becomes the truth. Strange, really.'

He sniffed the air. It was heavy with heat. He was beginning to wonder if the Packard was such a good idea. Still, needs must; he wandered off to see it unloaded. It was already attracting attention from the dockworkers down below. Sylvia finished tidying the cabin, and took their holdall and camera equipment onto the balcony. She took out her notebook and started sketching out a basic modus operandi. One of us needs to, she thought. The first thing they needed to do was contact Marguerite's cousin, and see which way the land lay. With all this fighting going on, though, how easy was that going to be? She got out the street map which the purser had given her, and studied it carefully.

Gunn appeared beside her at the railings. 'Your carriage awaits, madam,' he announced. For

166

the benefit of their 'fan club,' he drew her close to him and gave her a long, lingering kiss.

'Right, Mrs G., that's your lot for now. Let's get off this buggering boat.'

The taste of the kiss lingered on Sylvia's lips. She felt weak at the knees. This was something very different. She had never felt that way before

'Ridiculous. Pull yourself together. Every sodding cliché in the book,' she scolded herself, subconsciously echoing Gunn's language, as she turned to wave to those she knew on the boat. She spotted Sol. He turned with a sardonic salute and disappeared from view.

'Pretty girl,' Sol thought to himself. 'Gunn is a lucky man. Hope she doesn't get in the way though.'

Sylvia resolved to ask Gunn about Sol. There was more to him than met the eye. She wanted to know how much more and in what direction. She found Gunn throwing the bags into the back of the Packard. He looked irritable and cross with himself.

'Bringing this bloody car was probably one of the dumbest moves I have ever made. Knowing our luck, the family will be two streets from here and we could walk it in five minutes.'

'I think it's a bit further than that,' Sylvia commented. 'I've got a map here.'

'Sooner we get rid of this beast the better.' Gunn held the door open for her. 'I'll drive, you navigate.'

Navigation, thought Sylvia, was going to be interesting. The purser had asked her if she knew where she was going, explaining somewhat patronisingly that it wasn't your average tourist port, especially in light of recent events. Not wishing to be drawn about their plans, Sylvia had said something suitably vague about relatives, thanked him and walked off with the map. It was indeed fairly basic; street names were already starting to change. Still, she could discern a rough layout of the city and where they should go.

'Turn left onto that big road,' she began. 'That should put us on the right course to start with. I think it's quite some way though. Not really walking distance.'

As they pulled out of the docks, Gunn stole a glance at her. He had enjoyed that kiss too. It hadn't just been for the benefit of the crowds. He had wanted to take her back inside the cabin to develop things further but had reminded himself, just in time, that they were on what could be an extremely dangerous mission. He was under no illusions about that. Right now, he could see people turning to look at them and the Packard. This took hiding in plain sight a step too far.

'I wish I had painted the blasted thing olive green.' He laughed at the absurd nature of their excursion. 'Still, it adds to the adventure. Which way now?'

'South, or rather south west. It looks as if they live the other side of Mount Carmel. Not far from a place called Nehalim, on Ha-Tamar Street. I think we can skirt around the mountain and take our luck from there. Oh look, Gunn, it's beautiful.' She turned to him. 'I feel as if I'm inside one of the pictures in the bible.'

Gunn slowed down for a moment, feeling a little calmer now that they knew the way.

'So, Gunn,' Sylvia gave him a direct hazel gaze. 'What are we going to say? How do we broach it? My instinct would be to start with a fairly pleasant but guarded conversation with Aaron. We need to find out whether Marguerite actually managed to get here. Because if she didn't, what happens then?'

'Nobody else named in the will?'

'No, nobody else. Let's hope she made it.'

'Hmm, so really we are bringing a modern day miracle to the land of miracles.' Gunn's tone was laced with an acidic humour. He considered for a moment as they passed a flock of sheep minding its own business on the road. He shook his head. 'Lunch on the hoof.'

'You are terrible.'

'No, it would have been terrible if I had mentioned mint sauce.'

Gunn shifted gear and let the Packard stretch its muscles on the curves of the mountain road.

'You know, Sylv, I'm not sure there's much point in being guarded. The bush telegraph will have the entire district primed. In fact, I wouldn't be surprised if they were expecting us.'

'Whatever makes you say that?' Sylvia was startled. She was in a place with no familiar reference points, she decided. The modus operandi she had sketched out in her notebook on the Sidonia was about to go right out of the window.

169

'Instinct.' Gunn bit his lip and opened up a little. 'Sol knows of the family. I bet he has been on the nearest available blower to them already.'

'But Gunn,' she began, 'how do you know we can trust Sol?'

This wasn't how they normally operated. She wondered how much he had divulged to Sol. However, this was very far from being a normal mission.

'I suppose we have no choice,' she murmured, almost to herself. 'Our turning is coming up on the left.'

'And you're right,' she said, moments later. 'I think there is a reception committee.'

Sol was standing on the worn steps of a stone-built house. The windows were set deep, and olive trees flanked the front door, providing shelter. Sol waved, a big, knowing grin on his face. He stepped forward as the Packard drew to a halt, and bowed slightly as he assisted Sylvia from the car. She shook her head.

'I should have known.'

'Gunn knew.'

Sol kissed her hand and then reached into the boot for the bags.

'Come on in, I have some people for you to meet.'

The interior of the house was simply furnished; the walls were thick, keeping it cool. Sol dumped the bags by the stairs and, inviting her to follow, stepped through the house, past a dining area with a long wooden table, into a kitchen and out onto the terrace of a courtyard which was fringed with orange trees.

Adjusting her eyes to the light, Sylvia did a double take. Here was one of the Vogel girls, all right, she thought, as Marguerite Werner stepped forward to take her hand. The unimaginable horrors she had undergone were etched on her face, but Sylvia could still discern the girl who had smiled into the camera for Jonathan at Chartrettes, her arm around her sister. Lev Werner, her husband, must once have been a tall man; he was now stooped. He moved slowly, as if each step hurt him. Like a living ghost, thought Sylvia, as she shook his hand. Aaron, Marguerite's cousin, was quiet and watchful, although quite welcoming. His part of the family, he explained, had been settled here for some years.

Sylvia noticed straightaway that Sol had introduced her as Sylvia Fordred of Clements Investigations of London. He had either done his homework well, or Gunn (where had he got to?) had divulged more than he had let on to her. On the Sidonia, she had been Mrs Gunn. Well, it probably didn't matter, she reasoned.

'I expect you want a wash and spruce-up after that journey,' said Marguerite, showing her towards the bathroom. 'We'll talk properly after lunch. Sol has told us a little. You have to understand that Lev is a very sick man, and Aaron, well, he is kindness itself, but he doesn't really like to hear about what we went through. He never says anything, but I can tell and I understand.'

Sylvia smiled her thanks. She was looking forward to talking to Marguerite at length. She could tell they were going to get on.

'Sol, where is Gunn?' she called back over her shoulder. She followed her hostess and was soon grateful for a splash of cool water across her face and wrists.

Gunn had decided that leaving the Packard out front was a risk too far. He manoeuvred the car along to the end of the block, counting as he did so, took a left down a scrap line alley and then another left, the car protesting as its flanks nuzzled up against stone walls. He counted again and stopped the Packard in the scrappy shade of a worn down olive tree, underneath a wall which was topped with the heads of orange trees. He switched the engine off and stepped onto the bonnet. He hoisted himself up via a creaking olive branch and onto the wall of the courtyard. His count had been good, he thought, as he looked down. He could see Sol. He jumped down and landed like a tired cat. He grinned at Sol, who handed him a drink. Vodka, with a dash of freshly squeezed orange. It hit the spot.

Sylvia appeared at his side. Sol gave her a vodka and orange too, with a 'L'chaim.'

'So, are you two going to bring me up to speed?' asked Sylvia. Aaron, Lev and Marguerite were having an animated discussion over by the table, she noticed, so this would be a perfect opportunity.

'Polish,' Sol observed, as he sat down in the shade of the orange trees.

'Of course,' Gunn grinned. 'Though I prefer the Swedish as a rule.'

172

'The Polish does not bruise as easily.' Sol helped himself to an orange, peeling it with a commando knife, British army issue. 'So, we will eat and relax a little, drink a little more and talk business.'

Sylvia could see she was going to get very little sense out of these two. Cryptic utterances, in-jokes and meaningful looks were going to be the order of the afternoon. She couldn't help feeling a little jealous, but she decided that it was simply because she had had Gunn all to herself. That kiss had perturbed her. Everything would be fine when they started to present their findings to the assembled company. 'Get a grip,' she told herself. 'We're a professional team.' Drink in hand, she wandered over to talk to the others.

In Pompeii, in a corner of Ancient Rome that would forever be the Fatherland, Voss lay undisturbed in his makeshift grave. There was nothing on his body to identify him, even if somebody found him. He was, as Sylvia and Gunn had surmised, in what had been a grain store for the House of the Seven Women, one of the lesser-known and rougher brothels. The grain store and the other outbuildings had suffered some bomb damage. Nobody really had cause to go there.

Two enterprising Belgian schoolboys had read about the 'dirty frescoes' and had made it their mission to visit every whorehouse in Pompeii, something which was not on the itinerary that had been so carefully planned for them and their classmates. The House of the Seven Women, after a

173

most enjoyable afternoon, was the last whorehouse on their agenda. It was not to be. Their outraged schoolmaster, sweating profusely and brushing two flies fastidiously away from his forehead, had eventually caught up with them at the foot of the hill, given them a good clout each and dragged them back to the rest of the group.

In the Bavarian mountains, Mueller had woken up early. Although officially on holiday, he was never one to switch off altogether. That went against the grain and all good sense. He had a small office set up, with a ticker tape machine that kept him abreast of events in the fields that concerned him. He wandered in, cup of coffee in hand, his velvet robe shifting uncomfortably where it touched skin red from the thrashing his wife had so kindly administered the night before. Tender, loving abuse, as Mueller termed it.

The early morning sun was creeping in through the windows and the ticker tape machine was chuntering merrily away to itself. Mueller set down his cup and padded over to see what the chatter was about. He frowned. This seemed to be from an old Abwehr contact of his, who, with the help of an agent with the code name Alaikum, provided a daily briefing on the Middle East. They had an office in Cairo. What they provided was quite often generic. Frankly, he sometimes rather resented having to pay for it. Their intelligence didn't normally come through until the afternoon. Mueller decided on balance to read it now, as he and his wife had planned a long walk to the lake at the top, which would require an early start. The restaurant up there was excellent and the forecast was good.

Checking there was sufficient ink in the drum, as there seemed to be a lot coming through today, Mueller settled down to decipher the long strips of paper. Amongst the usual chat and gossip was a note from one of their contacts in Israel, to the effect that an English couple had been seen disembarking from the SS Sidonia in Haifa that morning, in a red Packard Vignale Convertible. Mueller put the strip of paper down carefully and considered.

Wait. A Packard? Hadn't that cretin Voss been boasting about a new Packard recently, after a particularly dirty piece of work he had given him to do? Well, it was his business what he spent his money on, but where the devil was he now? Why was somebody else driving his car? It could only be the two assets.

He ran to the telephone and, trying hard to keep his voice very calm, asked the operator to put him through to Rome. Sofort. He would make that verminous, pox-ridden Italian whore of Voss's tell him exactly where he was. The number had been disconnected, he was told. Scheiss. He slammed his fist down hard on the desk. Voss had almost certainly taken the advance money and 'cut and run.' In retrospect, he should have paid 'on delivery.' The Packard was a puzzle. How had the assets got hold of it? It was a distinctive car. Was it simply a coincidence or had Voss sold it to fund his escape? That was probably irrelevant at this stage, Mueller decided. He would hunt Voss down and kill him, slowly and painfully, and would relish every moment.

For now, he needed to focus on Israel, the worst possible place for the assets to be. They needed to be apprehended, fast; hopefully, it wasn't already too late. He asked the operator to place another call, this time to Cairo. He needed somebody, he told Alaikum in no uncertain terms, who was not an amateur.

In Haifa, several hours later, Omar Bin Saladin sipped a coffee so strong he could have stood a spoon upright in it. It shot through his system. It felt good. He stretched out his legs and leaned back in his chair. He unfolded the note again, and memorised the address and instructions. They were clear and specific. Getting up, he threw a coin on the table, adjusted his jacket to conceal the 9mm Browning under his arm, and, with a wave, joined the others in the run-down Citroen in the street outside.

There were four men in the Citroen; well-dressed, businessmen to all intents and purposes, and well-armed too. Each had a 9mm Browning and they had two Sten guns between them. That should be more than adequate, Bin Saladin thought, checking the note again. The Englishwoman was to be spared and brought to London, with a set of papers. The papers were vital; if she said she didn't have them, she was to be made to reveal their whereabouts by whatever means necessary, although she was not to be injured and was to be kept alive. The man was to be dispensed with.

Chapter 14

Lunch in Marguerite and Lev's courtyard was simple but good. A Polish meatloaf, plenty of salad and fruit, and a wine that had Sylvia and Gunn reaching for the vodka bottle after the first sip. The rhythm of food allowed awkwardness to slip away. Sylvia found that explaining the reasons behind their presence in Israel came more easily than imagined. Gunn sat back and let her do most of the talking. Sol listened carefully too. She spoke eloquently. He was starting to change his opinion of her. He could see what Gunn saw in her.

There were plenty of tears during the course of the afternoon, but laughter as well. Marguerite of course knew the story of Jonathan and Louise better than anyone. She described idyllic summers in Chartrettes, swimming in the lake and helping with the farm. She had been told about Louise being taken (it had actually happened just before she and Lev were betrayed by their landlady) and put on a train going east. Later, they had been told about her death by the Red Cross, and then Jonathan had managed to trace them.

They had been in a bad state. 'Living dead,' as Lev described it. The Red Army's arrival at that point had saved them. They hadn't heard about Jonathan's death. They were a little out of the way here, and tended not to read the foreign newspapers much, finding it more therapeutic to tend their orange trees instead. They knew, because he had mentioned it

177

briefly, about Jonathan's small stroke. But for him to die like that, and then not to be found for days…

'That will be Mueller's doing,' was Marguerite's immediate response. She had plenty to say about Marta and Mueller.

'Do you remember when we went to Berlin, Lev?' She turned to her husband. 'When Marta had just taken that job with him?'

'If you can call it a job,' responded Lev. 'I didn't like Berlin very much.'

Sylvia had been there once with Jutta, and stayed with her parents. They had been kind to her and Jutta had taken her to the Zoo. Jutta had bought them both ice creams. They had both decided that Bobby the Gorilla was their favourite. She had been sad to learn that the zoo animals had to a great extent survived the war but not the Russians. She decided not to share her reminiscences. It was strange how memories came back, almost unbidden.

'There was almost a forced atmosphere then,' Marguerite went on, thoughtfully. 'As if it was one great party before the end of the world. And you had no choice but to enjoy it.'

'Live fast, die young,' chipped in Lev.

Mueller had been almost embarrassingly infatuated with Marta at that point. He had taken them to the best restaurants and nightclubs, insisting flamboyantly on paying for everything. It was in one such establishment that they had met a friend of his, Lothar, who had been to school in England, now a solicitor in England and over on a visit.

'A most unpleasant, rude man,' Marguerite said. 'So was Mueller, although he disguised it better.'

Sylvia and Gunn exchanged amused glances. Rude and unpleasant? Surely not.

'Where was it they were working, can you remember, Lev?'

Lev said that the last place he could think of, although of course they never actually went there, was along the Tiergartenstrasse, something Mueller was working on, but that came much later. Again Sylvia and Gunn exchanged glances; that was the headquarters of the euthanasia programme, for people who were 'incurable.' What a euphemism. Marta had sent some of the papers back just before she was killed. It was all in the report. Not the type of thing Mueller, after his recent exoneration, would want bandied about.

Sylvia took another sip of vodka, which was going down a treat with the lovely orange juice, and cleared her throat. She brought the subject back again to Chartrettes, and the will, going through it briefly with them and explaining that Marguerite was the sole beneficiary. She understood from her client that there was a lot of money involved.

'I see,' said Marguerite, thoughtfully.

She and Lev had of course lost everything in Paris, even the clothes they stood up in. From the enquiries they had made, it seemed that their landlady had sold all of their possessions as soon as they were rounded up. She had been there, watching, her arms folded and an avaricious smile playing across her lips when they were dragged downstairs. Luckily,

179

Marguerite's father had made some very shrewd investments in Palestine in the 1930s, with the assistance of Aaron's father, her uncle, who was already there. Consequently, they wanted for nothing out here, and never would. Like Louise and Jonathan, they had not been blessed with children. They lived quite simply. They were lucky to live at all. Each new day that dawned was a special one to them now.

Thinking it best to keep the atmosphere light before they moved to the inevitable and most tricky topic, Sylvia got out the photographs and the letters Jonathan had written to Louise. Marguerite clutched the letters to her for a moment, then excused herself and went inside. Gunn, who was sitting next to her, pulled her gently towards him.

'You're doing brilliantly, sweetheart. I love how you're doing this, letting the story tell itself. You're a star.'

Marguerite, coming back to the table with some cups, gave them both a knowing look and smiled. They looked at the photographs together over coffee, with a running commentary from Marguerite. Aaron had been to Chartrettes too as a boy and had fallen under its spell. The pictures of the interior were exclaimed over. Louise and Jonathan had done a lot of work on the demeure when they first bought it, and had thoroughly enjoyed doing this.

'Oh, look, that's them,' commented Marguerite. 'Mueller and that Lothar. Loathsome creatures. How alike they look.'

This was one of Marta's pictures; they hadn't paid much heed to it. All agreed there was a striking likeness between them. Sol leaned forward to take a

180

closer look, as if he wanted to commit their features to memory.

'Now, that brings me to Marta's papers,' Sylvia said, softly. 'Were you aware that she was sending Mueller's correspondence back to Chartrettes?'

They were not altogether surprised to hear about this. Sylvia went on to explain how the papers clearly documented Mueller's involvement with the euthanasia programme and incriminated several others. In addition, and this was very unusual for 1939, when the future seemed golden for the Third Reich, the rudiments of a pipeline had been put in place, so that key people could be removed to safety if needs be, with Lothar and Mueller at the centre of it. Again, there were some high profile names on there, including two who had been sentenced *in absentia* by the War Crimes Tribunal.

'Maybe it would also have been useful at the point when Britain was to be invaded?' suggested Gunn. 'With Lothar already on the ground, gathering sympathisers around him?'

He and Sylvia unfurled the diagram they had made from several sheets of the purser's paper, detailing the network. Marguerite marvelled at the amount of work that must have gone into it.

'If I may interrupt at this stage,' said Sol. 'I represent SherutBitachon. I have told Mr Gunn a little about it already. Aaron, Lev, you of course know more, and we've already had discussions about my *bona fides*. I think you are satisfied, yes? In short, we would be very interested in these papers.'

181

'It's Marguerite's decision of course,' volunteered Sylvia, who had decided that they could probably trust Sol. She usually had a decent instinct, having had to survive alone from a young age, for this type of thing. She had never been convinced by the 'porch in Gallilee' story.

'But Mr Gunn and I both thought all along that it was futile to hand these papers to the British or French authorities. That's why we brought them to you here. Frankly, you are going to need close protection now, whatever you decide. And fast.'

'Which SherutBitachon will give.' Sol smiled reassuringly. 'I can have my men here in ten minutes. Less, even.'

Marguerite looked dazed. She took Lev on one side for a few minutes and they conferred. They called Aaron over. He lived with them; he had to be part of the decision.

Then, speaking very slowly, as if deep in thought, she thanked Miss Fordred and Mr. Gunn from the depths of her heart for bringing the documents and photographs to her, and of course Jonathan's will and diary. It meant a lot to her. Provided Mr. Kalinsky could guarantee them protection, and if there was anything he could do to bring these filthy creatures to justice, then she would gladly hand him the papers. Although it would never bring Louise and Marta back (she angrily wiped away a tear at this point) it might save others, especially if they were planning to re-group in South America. So all those rumours were true! All she and Lev wanted now, all they had ever wanted, was a quiet life. While Mueller and his ilk remained on this planet, they would be denied one.

'So, Mr. Kalinsky, please take them now, with my blessing. I don't want to look at them again. Do what you have to do.'

She moved the papers up the table in front of Sol and turned to Sylvia and Gunn. Still speaking slowly and deliberately, she took from the bundle of photographs the key which Joan had given them.

'I have no desire ever to set foot in France again. Chartrettes turned from a place of happiness, tranquillity and love into a place of horror and fear. It is the last place on earth I would wish to visit. I think the demeure is a relatively small part of Jonathan's estate. Lev and I already have more than enough money to live out our days in comfort and peace. With the rest of Jonathan's money, we can enjoy life; even spoil Aaron here a little. Perhaps buy more land nearby.'

Handing Gunn the key, she said:

'I want you both to have the demeure.'

Sylvia was shaking her head:

'We can't possibly…you mustn't…'

'No arguments,' Marguerite said, firmly. She turned to Gunn.

'Take this beautiful, clever girl home and marry her. You remind me and Lev so much of us at your age. And with your children, turn Chartrettes into a place where love can flourish again. Do it for me, and for Jonathan and Louise.'

Gunn took the key and kissed Marguerite's hand.

183

'Thank you,' he said. 'That is precisely what I intend to do. All of it.'

Sylvia was lost for words. Her head was spinning. What was he playing at? Was this one of his cover stories or did he mean it? She didn't know what to think. This was Gunn, who had challenged her to a wrestling match on the beach and who usually woke her with a playful slap or a dash of cold water to the face. All the same, the thought of that kiss this morning made her shiver in a delicious way. And Chartrettes would be theirs? It was far too much to take in and far too generous.

She excused herself, deciding to have a moment alone in the olive trees at the front of the house. She closed her eyes and fanned herself with a newspaper she had found in the kitchen. She could hear the murmur of conversation from the courtyard, a murmur that soon succumbed to the cough of an engine. She opened her eyes. A Citroen was drawing up, with a man on each running board. She stood up, shouted, and turned to run. The man closest to her leapt from the car and tackled her into a dusty heap at the foot of the steps into the house. He had knocked the wind out of her and she had banged her head. Out for the count. Good. He picked her up and bundled her into the Citroen, while the man on the opposite running board hosed the front of the house with a magazine from the Sten gun. He followed it up by tossing a grenade through the open front door. It bobbed and rolled along the tiled corridor before blowing up. The Citroen raced away with its cargo and Bin Saladin fingering the worry beads in his pocket, hoping his client would be happy with the decision he had made. The adrenaline and the coffee had been keeping him going. He frowned. There was something not quite right. At the turn of the street, he came to a decision.

'Go back,' he said. 'We have papers to get, people to kill. Leaving a job half done looks sloppy.'

The driver, an old school friend of his, who had fought with the Muslim SS Division in the Balkans, nodded his agreement, threw the Citroen round with no ceremony and hit the floor. Then, he braked hard and switched the engine off. Bin Saladin nodded. 'Time to go.'

Leaving a groggy Sylvia in the Citroen, Mueller's four recruits, weapons cocked and loaded, entered the house. They knew who they were looking for. Alaikum's 'intelligence' had been thorough and accurate, which had made a refreshing change.

Sol was waiting in the hall, in the shadow of a coat-rack. He allowed the first three men in before stepping out. With a back-handed swing, he took out the throat of Bin Saladin's old friend. He folded to his knees, eyes glazing, drowning in his bubbling blood. His last sight in this world was a one-eyed Jewish soldier raising a 9mm to his head and slowly squeezing the trigger. 'Go and find paradise.'

Gunn took down one of his targets with a double tap into the head, and then stuck his blade through the eye socket of the next, twisting as he did so. The man screamed, from a world beyond pain, and Gunn shot him in the heart for the sake of something approaching mercy.

Bin Saladin was in the courtyard, alone and with no leverage, as Lev, Marguerite and Aaron were safely in the storm cellar and Sylvia was still in the car. He swore and turned as Sol and Gunn entered the courtyard, blood on their hands, faces and shirts, and their shoes tapping out a rhythm on the brass littering the corridor and entrance to the courtyard. Bin Saladin raised his 9mm, but Gunn shot it out of his hand. Sol shot the Arab in the knees and they put him on the deck.

Sol looked at him and shook his head.

'Time to talk.'

He squatted down beside Bin Saladin, whose face was contorted with agony.

'Who is paying you?'

Silence.

Gunn slapped him hard across the face.

'Perhaps this will help you to remember?'

'Alaikum,' spat Bin Saladin.

Sol looked interested. 'Someone must be spending some serious money on this. It's got to be our German friend, hasn't it?'

'And he isn't about to go away in a hurry. I would imagine there are more where this one came from,' replied Gunn.

' Well, let's see what we can do to address that,' said Sol.

Gunn nodded in agreement. He worked the snout of the Tula into Bin Saladin's wounded knee. He twisted it each time he asked a question. Sol winced.

'What did you want here? Tell me, and we will ease your passage into paradise'

Sylvia appeared in the courtyard at that moment, looking dazed and pale, crunching over the debris in the corridor. She swayed slightly, holding the door frame for support. There was a small cut on her cheek.

'What's going on?'

Uttering a silent prayer of thanks, Gunn said firmly:

'Sylv, go in the cellar, sweetheart. Now. Do you hear me? Don't come out until we say.'

Sylvia didn't argue. She made it to the cellar just in time. Lev opened the door a crack, let her in and locked it, whereupon she promptly passed out again.

Bin Saladin closed his eyes and gritted his teeth against the pain. The worst part was waiting for the point when Gunn excavated the wound a little more. Another deep thrust and turn (for hurting Sylvia, thought Gunn) and he cried out loud and began to talk. He was spilling the world, things that Gunn didn't even care about, although Sol made a note of some of them. Bin Saladin took five minutes and then stopped.

'There is nothing more.'

Gunn smiled. He cradled Bin Saladin's head in one hand and with the other dribbled some cold water into his prisoner's bloody and puffed-up mouth. It tasted as good as any other water Bin Saladin had ever known. Gunn cocked the Tula.

'I promised you mercy.'

The shot rang around the courtyard. Sol smiled, and murmured:

'Top C. Impressive.'

Gunn had to agree. He let Bin Saladin's head drop. Sol looked over their handiwork.

'We'd better get this over to the café he mentioned. Make a point. But first things first.'

A quick telephone call brought Sol's 'team,' as he called it, to the door; six of them, a mixture of veterans of the British army and others who had honed their skills in the Warsaw Ghetto. One was a doctor. Sylvia was back on her feet now and he checked her over. Looking at the cut, he commented: 'That won't leave a scar. 'Just surface. Put a dressing on it.' He turned to Marguerite, who had trained as a nurse. 'She might have a bit of concussion; keep an eye on that, especially if she's sick. Make her rest.'

They fanned out around the house, checking for reinforcements. Marguerite was in her element, fussing over Sylvia. Nothing on earth was going to get anywhere near the house.

'While these guys clean up, you and I are going to pay a visit.'

Sol grinned at Gunn and patted the box under his arm.

'We have a delivery to make.'

'We'll take their Citroen,' Gunn suggested. 'I'll drive, you navigate and hold on tight.'

'Agreed.' Sol threw the box onto the back seat. Something inside rumbled against its sides before settling. Checking his Browning was fully loaded, he got in. Gunn turned the ignition key and put the Citroen into gear.

'Tell me about this Alaikum character.'

Throwing out the odd instruction, every few minutes, as they drove through the dark, Sol explained that 'Alaikum' (he didn't know his real name) had been part of Operation Salam.

'Heard of it? You know, getting German spies into Egypt?'

Gunn nodded thoughtfully. In his days with the Long Range Desert group, he had heard many stories about Laszlo Almasy, the desert explorer who had headed up Operation Salam. A while ago, Alaikum and a colleague, formerly of the Abwehr, had set up their own Middle East intelligence business, out of Cairo.

'It's funny, all sorts of people use them, from all sides of the spectrum,' Sol said, 'Although you would be foolish to trust them. That aside, their intelligence isn't bad. They produce a daily briefing. You have to subscribe to it. Not cheap, but then I guess why should they be?'

'Damn good idea' thought Gunn. He had the germ of an idea himself. He hadn't been joking when he had thrown out the idea of Clements International to Sylv over that fabulous lunch in Posillipo. It would take some thinking through, expansion, extra staff, and the right investors on board. Still, they had plenty of other fish to fry for now. He would talk to Sylv again. She was bound to have some ideas. He turned to Sol.

'So Mueller is one of their subscribers and he paid them to introduce him to someone who could dispatch me and deliver Sylvia and the papers to London. That's the gist of what that cove said, wasn't it? Well, the last bit, anyway.'

'In one,' laughed Sol. 'Pull up here, we've arrived.'

The Citroen idled down to a halt, its wheels gently scraping the rough kerbstones. Nobody in the café or in the street paid it the remotest attention. It was nothing out of the ordinary. That was good.

Gunn peered into the café. Five or six men, for the most part with the comfortable air of men of the world, chatting and drinking coffee and drawing on Turkish cigarettes. He turned again to Sol.

'Right then, subtle or in like Flynn?'

'In like Flynn?'

'You know, the film star, straight in, no mucking about.'

'Oh, in like Flynn,' Sol chuckled. 'You really are quite mad.'

'Of course. I am an Englishman.'

The customers in the café looked up idly, as Sol and Gunn strolled in, for all the world as if they were about to order a coffee. They looked up again, sharply this time. Most café customers were not splattered from head to toe with blood.

'Evening, gentlemen,' said Gunn pleasantly, as Sol walked up to the counter. Taking the grisly head of Bin Saladin out of the box, its lips drawn back in a grimace, he set it down carefully so that it looked as if it was surveying the scene.

'A warning for you,' Sol remarked casually. He turned on his heel and walked out with Gunn.

The customers recoiled in horror, too shocked even to attempt to remonstrate or give chase. One of them, slightly younger than the rest, looked thoughtful and went to the café door for a moment as the Citroen tore away, his hand reaching into his pocket for his worry beads. Bin Saladin was his cousin.

They abandoned the Citroen a couple of streets away, Sol adding a flourish by tossing the ignition key to a pastry seller on the corner. The man could not believe his luck. Sol nudged Gunn in the ribs.

'Now they'll follow that car. They'll get confused, because neither of us are in it, and probably write it off.'

Sol predicted, with local knowledge, that there would be a taxi rank around the next corner. There was. He rousted a driver from his nap and offered a more than decent fare, which was accepted with alacrity.

'I don't think we will have any trouble for a little while,' ventured Sol, as the taxi ground its way up Mount Carmel.

'Yes, but Mueller isn't going to give up, is he?'

'Not until we make him,' smiled Sol. 'If you catch my drift.'

'I do indeed' said Gunn. 'Let's talk about it in the morning.'

Back at the house, while Sol talked to his team, Gunn took over from Marguerite, keeping watch over Sylvia. She said she wanted to go to sleep. Marguerite, ever the experienced nurse, thought this would be fine, as it was the time when she would normally sleep, but that he should keep an eye on her. There was a small spare bedroom. Gunn made

191

himself comfortable on the floor with a pile of cushions. After a while, he went over to the narrow bed, climbed onto it and held Sylvia close for a few moments, feeling her heart beating against his. With a sigh, he tucked her up and gave her a kiss. This time, he wanted to do things properly. There was something he wanted to tell her, which had been on his mind for a while; meanwhile, though, he and Sol had work to do.

On the floor, more comfortable than the fleapit and cleaner too, he started to think about Mueller. That article in Le Figaro, which they had cut out and kept, said he was living in southern Bavaria. It shouldn't be beyond the wit of man to track him down. However, he was unlikely, even at the age of, what, late fifties, to go down without a fight. He might even have security. He and Sol would talk it over tomorrow. That bastard had to be taken out.

Chapter 15

In the morning, Gunn sat with Sol and Sylvia, trying to piece as much together as possible on Mueller. Marguerite had already given them the photograph of him with George. He was relieved to find that Sol's German was excellent. Sylvia had offered to go with them to interpret. That idea had been firmly ruled out.

'So, as we thought then, late fifties, married with four grown up children and some grandchildren. Wife is called Elise. About the same age.'

Marguerite came past with some orange juice for them.

'I remember Marta saying she wore the pants in the relationship. Fearsome lady. Probably made a change for him to be a bully in the workplace.'

Sylvia got the article out again.

'Here we are. Bad Kaltenbrun is where he lives now. Wonder if that is anything to do with George or Lothar or whatever he calls himself?'

'Quite possibly. Maybe a shared joke or reference to their joint situation.'

Gunn considered further and started to turn an idea over in his mind.

'Look, we can fly from here to Limassol. There are RAF bases in Cyprus. I'm sure we could cadge a lift from one of those into Germany. We'd have to drive in to Bavaria, as it's under US administration, but I'm sure we could liberate a motor somewhere along the line. Play the part of a couple of officers on leave, exploring. We'll hide in plain sight and try and track him.'

193

'What will you do once you have tracked him?' asked Lev.

'Bury him,' came the response.

By lunchtime, Sol had tickets to Limassol and the name of a contact at RAF Akrotiri. The plan was coming together; only the very last part was up in the air but that was not uncommon. Sylvia had no concerns. She hugged Gunn to her.

'I'm going to miss you.'

'I know, sweetheart. I'll miss you too. But we'll be back before you know it. You look after yourself, plenty of rest and sunshine. And don't fret. You're in the safest possible place.'

He folded himself into the back of a jeep with Sol, driven by one of the security team guarding the house night and day and started the drive to the airport. Sylvia felt Marguerite's hand on her shoulder.

'Don't you worry about him. He'll be back. That one would walk through the gates of hell for you. I can tell.'

'And I'd do the same for him,' thought Sylvia, watching the jeep disappear round the corner.

In his little office, high in the mountains of Bavaria, Mueller inched his way gingerly towards the ticker tape machine. Elise had been, perhaps, a little too over-exuberant with the riding crop last night. He swore when he caught sight of what was coming through, and swore again as he dropped into a chair to berate Alaikum over the telephone.

'Dummkopf!' He almost screamed the word. 'What the hell is going on? You are telling me that Bin Saladin's head was delivered to a café? What sort

194

of madman are we dealing with? Now the assets are at large? And they have protection? This is unacceptable. Is this how you treat your clients? Find them both now. I don't care how much it costs.'

Squirming a little, he tried to gather his thoughts. Bin Saladin had been, he was assured, one of the most skilful and deadliest operatives in the area. Why then in God's name had he bungled this operation? The intelligence had been clear. How difficult was it to capture one girl and to kill one man? Then again, he reasoned, it wasn't just them now. They had reinforcements. Where the hell were those papers? His number could be up.

A sense of foreboding began to creep over him, as if a stitch in his tapestry had been snagged and was unravelling. He tried to think clearly. He was not, as that in-bred idiot Lothar had led him to believe, dealing with two amateurish academics from London. The message they had delivered about Bin Saladin was loud and clear. They were prepared to kill, in the detached manner of the professional. Perhaps he should speak to Alaikum again, in a more conciliatory fashion. And maybe the time was coming when Operation Crown Jewels would have to be put into operation for him and Elise, although it had always been his dearest wish to live out his days in the Fatherland. Grimacing in pain as he moved, he picked up the telephone again.

In Cairo, Alaikum took a sip of water and smiled at his colleague, Otto Eppler, formerly of the Abwehr. Life was good. Money was rolling in. They were about to move to larger premises although both

195

rather liked it where they were. He was turning over a note the boy from the bank had delivered by hand, notifying them of a large payment that had come in, drawn on a bank in Tel Aviv. 'Large' was putting it mildly.

'Well, my friend,' said Otto. 'That's put the cat among the pigeons, as the British say. What are you going to do now, Mr Duplicity?'

Alaikum thought for a moment. Mueller had subscribed to their services for some time, and had always paid without a murmur. Clients like that had their value. However, he had been damn rude. He had insulted their professionalism and integrity. That was too much. He could go to hell in a hand basket.

Wait. That was him on the telephone now. He smiled at Otto.

'Just watch me.'

'Yes, hallo, Dr Mueller. No, please don't apologise. I do understand. What a terrible shock it must have been. Yes, we have another operative in mind. Fought alongside the SS Handschar. 13[th]Waffen Mountain Division. Ha! Thought you would appreciate that. Now, this could be a little tricky. He will need to assemble a team. It may take a day or two but we need to get this absolutely right. Yes, an advance payment would be very helpful. You have the bank details. Thank you, Dr Mueller. Do enjoy the rest of your holiday.'

'You utter bastard. Otto shook his head. 'What are you going to do when Mueller realises his assets have evaded him? And that won't take him long.'

'Oh, we'll cross that bridge when we come to it.' Alaikum smiled reassuringly. 'Anything could happen between now and then.'

'Anything indeed,' laughed Otto. 'For instance, we could lose one of our best clients. Is this sensible?'

'Oh, there will be others.' Alaikum took a long toot on one of the finest cigarettes Egypt had to offer. 'And the cleaner we look to the right people, the better for future business.'

In Queen Anne's Gate, George was in a thoughtful mood. He had just taken a very odd telephone call from Mueller, to the effect that the assets were at large 'somewhere in the Middle East.' Mueller had screamed at him, asking why he had not seen fit to divulge that they were deadly assassins. He had said something about somebody's head being cut off and that now the game would have to be 'upped.' Considerably. And yes, before he asked, the plan still was that the male asset would be killed and the female asset (with papers) would be returned to London. It sounded for all the world as if his dear old friend had been imbibing too much schnapps although surely it was far too early in the morning.

George did not feel altogether reassured, but his only option was to trust Mueller's judgment in this matter. He sat looking at his magazines. My God, the things people thought of nowadays. He resolved to pay a visit to the shops down Charing Cross Road to make some 'preparations' for Sylvia's return. He began to feel quite excited; the adrenaline took away the nagging worry a little. That little whore would not be able to move once he had finished with her. Then again, she wouldn't need to. On the way to his shopping trip, he would call in on Juncker and that ridiculous cat. He did not trust that slippery, grubby little man one iota.

'Get out, you idiot. Before I kick you across the room' he shouted at Edward, who was standing beside him with a sheaf of conveyancing paperwork for signing. His attention had been caught by a particularly graphic picture, which had given him even more ideas. Edward turned on his heel and walked out without a word, slamming the door behind him in disgust. He hoped fervently that he would not be reduced to having to read such literature once he was married off to Caroline. He had hoped for another chat with Louis, but his friend was deep in conversation on the telephone. Maybe a pint at the Two Chairmen would be in order later.

At Ha-Tamar Street, Sylvia was hard at work, notebook in hand. One of Sol's team had already driven to Tel Aviv with the papers. The others were fanned out around the house. It was a relief to have the papers out of the way, although she was under no illusions as to the danger she herself could be in. Gunn had given her Voss's money, just in case, and had taken his Stavisky gold (she still didn't profess to understand this). Sol had mentioned further payments from SherutBitachon.

Nonetheless, Clements Investigations still had to be kept on the road. She had almost lost track of how long they had been away and had no idea when they would be back. She had arranged use of the telephone with Lev and Marguerite, and had just been talking to Joan. No, she still couldn't say where they were. New instructions were coming in thick and fast, including another request from Vera, whose divorce case was now going through. She reckoned her 'ex' was lying through her teeth about his assets. She was prepared to pay well, if they could find out what his true position was.

Sometimes, when they were very busy, she and Gunn used the services of a New Zealander named, rather unoriginally, Kiwi. He worked freelance, and lived with his English girlfriend in London. He had served with Gunn in the Long Range Desert Force days. She had no idea what his real name was. Gunn had told her though that Ralph Bagnold, who had set up the Force, had had the idea of recruiting New Zealanders because he thought they were energetic, self-reliant, physically and mentally tough and able to live and fight in seclusion in the Libyan Desert. Kiwi certainly possessed all those attributes and more, and he didn't charge the earth. He might as well make a start on some of these cases and Vera's. Having chatted to him over the telephone, she took a sip of orange juice and began to prepare some budgets and costings. It felt good to be taking control again, after the madness of the past few days.

At the airforce base in Akrotiri, Sol and Gunn were having a beer before the next stage of their journey.

'Blimey, Sol,' Gunn dug his Israeli friend in the ribs on his blind side. 'We should be honoured. The RAF boys have laid us on one of their new transport numbers. Handley Page Hastings. Not exactly the Ritz on wings but not bad either.'

'Do you think it has parachute lines on board?'

'I suppose so, why?'

'You were trained, and I know a little. We could do a static line jump over Bavaria. Saves us driving back from the British zone and the crew of the plane can deny our existence.'

'That rather appeals,' Gunn scratched his chin. 'How do we get out?'

'Oh, that's when we liberate a car. We could even take a train.'

Mueller put his head around the door of the dining room, where his wife was eating breakfast.

'Good morning, liebchen,' he said, obsequiously.

He suggested that they try their walk up to the top lake again. Perhaps they could stay at the cottage which the restaurant hired out, just around the lake? They had stayed there before; it was beautifully secluded. The silence was ominous and the clock ticked impassively. To his surprise (she wasn't keen on walking these days), Elise agreed. Telling their young man (butler was far too grand for their mountain hideaway; more of a 'factotum' really) what their plans were, they set out happily along the path. Mueller was a vain man, and he thought he cut quite a dash, in his new lederhosen and hiking boots. The sun was set to shine all day and there was a slight but pleasant breeze. He had thought over what

200

Alaikum had said. It sounded quite satisfactory. He had no reason to doubt his word.

Elise was indeed a little resentful of the walk, although she had to admit it was worth it, to get to the top. If the truth be told, she had struck quite an interest in Mueller's 'factotum' (what a silly puffed-up man her husband had become). He was actually called Hans. What was wrong with that? Anyway, maybe he could assist her on their return.

Mueller had met Elise in Berlin, at a party in the early twenties, some years before he had taken up with Marte Vogel. Elise had been legendary in certain circles in the Party for her ability with a riding crop, her biting wit…and her bite. They had married quickly, and children had followed in regimented succession, every two years. She had of course known about Marta. Mueller had suffered for that. It was Elise who had made quite sure at the end that Marta had been dragged, bleeding, from her hospital bed to Gestapo Headquarters. Ordering Mueller to stay at home, she had gone round to that bitch's apartment and had beaten the truth out of her landlady, as to which hospital she was at.

At the headquarters, the Gestapo had been more than delighted to assist Elise in the prosecution of an enemy of the Reich. Even some of their officers, however, had winced at her enthusiasm and indeed expertise at bringing pain out of Marta. For three days and nights, with only the merest respite, she had gone to work on Marta, who was weak anyway from the miscarriage. By the end, Elise had been stripped to the waist, and shining with spittle, water and blood. It didn't matter. She always relished her work and especially relished snuffing out Marta's life. This ghastly Valkyrie was the last vision Marta had, as she drifted out of the world, beyond pain with a tear in the corner of her eye. And after all that, Marta still hadn't said where the papers were. Mueller (ungrateful worm) had said something about it being perfectly obvious where they were anyway and now everyone knew their business. As if they hadn't already, with him flaunting that woman on his arm.

Almost ten years later, few in the outside world would have credited that this large, rather silent lady with thick blonde plaits and that snarling, gory monster were one and the same. Except Mueller, and, truth be told, he was still terrified of her, although he revered her. Nonetheless, there were a few rumours circulating about her past. Mueller's spies had mentioned it. Elise would have as much cause, possibly more, to be spirited away on Operation Crown Jewels as he did, when the time came. For now, they were savouring their day in the mountains, where, they both thought, there was just the faintest hint of autumn.

'Gruss Gott,' they chorused cheerfully, to some fellow hikers.

On board the Handley Page Hastings, Gunn was in his element. They could scarcely hear themselves talk over the noise of the engines. He was running through some procedures with the RAF boys.

'I take it you've done this before,' one of them ventured to ask.

'More than once.' Gunn grinned and buckled the harness. 'Mostly over France and Italy. Got a little arse-tightening at times.'

'Not much has changed.' The RAF man returned the grin. 'We will be over your drop zone around 7, so landing just as dusk closes in.'

Gunn shrugged and relayed the information to Sol, who smiled and mouthed:

'So what?'

'Makes a change from a midnight run,' Gunn observed. 'Never easy but got to be done.'

He paused, and looked the RAF man full in the eye. 'Look, you haven't seen us, and you know nothing. Understood? Rest assured, we are doing this for a damn good reason. The piper is calling and a real bastard will be footing the bill.'

'Understood. Go and get him.'

The RAF man extended his hand. Gunn took it, and they knew where they stood.

'We will.'

He was quite right, nothing had changed, thought Gunn, as the wind rushed past him and the ground came up to meet him. Soon he and Sol were extricating themselves from their parachutes and checking themselves over. Sol had landed slightly awkwardly on his ankle but was otherwise fine. They were in a field of cows. There was a bull in with them. It started sauntering nonchalantly towards them.

'Right, let's get out of this buggering field,' said Gunn, stowing the parachutes neatly in a patch of nettles at the corner of the field 'and find somewhere

where we can look at the map. We're lucky there's a full moon. Are you all right on that ankle?'

'Oh, I've had worse to contend with' replied Sol.

Their drop zone, it transpired, had been accurate both in terms of time and place. Dusk was just falling and they were about half an hour's walk from Bad Kaltenbrun. They seemed to be skirting along the edge of the grounds of some sort of small castle. There was nobody about, but as they walked down a gentle slope into the village, they immediately spotted a brightly-lit building. Everywhere else seemed to be in darkness.

'Looks like the local bier keller,' said Sol. 'Fancy a pint?'

'A couple, actually,' Gunn responded. 'And of course there's nothing surprising about a couple of officers on leave, hiking and exploring.'

'Naturally.'

'Of course, they will loathe us, and their courtesy will be a study in poison, but they won't realise how well you speak German.'

'Just for once, I am glad that I do,' sighed Sol.

The two men straightened their shoulders, adjusted their packs and walked into the Bier Keller as if they were nothing more than a couple of British officers on leave, on a hiking tour of Bavaria. There was a large group of men seated at a round table, each with a large beer stein in front of them, decorated in ornate patterns. A wrought iron sign above their table bore the legend 'Stammtisch.' A few other customers were grouped around the bar.

Conversation stopped and gazes followed them as they found a table out of the way, but with a clear eye line to the door and to the counter. They sat down, stowing their packs under their chairs. Gunn cleared his throat and spoke, a little too loudly:

'I say old chap, what a charming place!'

Sol nodded his head in agreement, and laughed, as the atmosphere around them changed and the conversation began once more. Gunn ordered them a beer each from the young waitress, flirting a little and exchanging stilted pleasantries in English. Sol looked across at Gunn when she had gone back to the bar.

'Bingo.'

They had, by pure coincidence, stumbled upon an informal meeting that took place each week.

'I'll listen to them and pretend to be listening to you. I wouldn't be surprised if Mueller was amongst them; can't spot him though. Just chat. Prost!' said Sol, in an appalling accent, raising his stein. 'Tell me about your family.'

It was quite odd, a little like talking to himself, Gunn thought. Looking round to make sure nobody was listening, and he could see nobody was, he spoke about his mother, who was French and had died when he was thirteen (which had led to him being sent to boarding school in England), how his father had been a policeman before the Great War, and an NCO during it. After he had met Gunn's mother in Paris, just after the end of the war, they had lived in London and he was promoted to the rank of Inspector. Gunn was born in London. Then, his father had landed a job in security at the British Embassy in Paris.

'So, that's where I grew up, but Dad lives in Brighton now. He has a little hotel, just off the front' finished Gunn. Sotto voce, he asked 'Is Mueller here?'

Sol looked thoughtful.

'Actually, no, but I think I have found out where he is. On holiday in the mountains with his wife; not far away. There's more but I will save that for later.' In a louder voice, he suggested:

'Ready for another beer, old boy? Shall we have a look at the map in a minute and plan our day tomorrow?'

The waitress, all heavy thighs and milk braids, and in her early twenties, returned with their beer and some bread and sausage, a complimentary snack for hikers. She looked over Gunn's shoulder, moving in as close as she was decently able. Sol suppressed a smirk. The waitress pointed at the map and suggested they should walk around Meerjungfrausee, a lake surrounded by only a very few houses, used mostly by business people from Munich and beyond.

Gunn exchanged glances with Sol and then smiled his thanks to the waitress and introduced himself. She smiled shyly and shook his hand and said her name was Ute and that she was working for her father for the summer. She left, rather reluctantly, to take other orders and Gunn and Sol returned to the map. The latter observed:

'I think she wants you to tug her braids'

'All in the line of duty, old chap,' Gunn responded. 'Anyway, this lake, what do you reckon?'

'Meerjungfrausee, Mermaid Lake..,' began Sol.

'Oh, not more sodding mermaids,' said Gunn.

In low tones, Sol said that he had overheard the Stammtisch table commenting that Mueller and his wife were staying up in the mountains for ten days and that they had decamped from there to Meerjungfrausee for a few days.

'Nothing seems to go unnoticed here. Probably including us. What is it with you and mermaids, anyway?'

'Never mind,' said Gunn, absently. He had been trying to keep his mind firmly on the task in hand. Now he had visions of Sylvia, without a stitch of clothing, on that beach in Naples. 'Reckon we could hike it in a morning?'

'If we make an early start, yes, I think so.'

'This place looks as if it's closing. Excuse me for a moment. I'll try and get us a billet for the night.'

Gunn disappeared for a 'private word' with Ute, at the back of the kitchen. He came back, with a key, looking triumphant.

'A room above the stables. Might smell a bit but we'll be making an early start.'

It didn't smell especially pleasant but it was reasonably comfortable. There were two single beds; it was hardly ever used apparently.

'I'm meant to meet her behind the shed at midnight,' said Gunn, getting into bed.

'Are you going?' asked Sol.

'No. A bit too broad in the beam for my taste. I like them with legs that go all the way up. If you catch my drift.'

'I know exactly who you are thinking about. You old devil, Gunn.'

'Yes, I know I am.'

'You will disappoint her.' Sol picked up his pack and put it under his pillow. Gunn raised an eyebrow.

'I like a bit more ballast under the pillow,' Sol explained.

'Like them broad in the beam too?' Gunn returned.

'Not as much as you do.'

'Seriously,' Gunn remarked. 'If I tupped that one, we'd have Daddy raising a posse wielding pitchforks and torches before you know it. I have my moments, but this is not one of them.' Gunn stretched luxuriously. 'Anyway, I'm getting some shuteye. Could be a tidy step tomorrow.'

Chapter 16

Next morning, Gunn was awoken from a deep sleep shortly before dawn by a cock crowing. It sounded as if it was right underneath him. More of them started up. Having spent most of his life in the city, he didn't always appreciate animals very much. His days helping out in the racing stables seemed light years away.

'Bugger it,' he said. 'Come on Sol, let's get on our way.'

Soon, they were striding along a path that would lead them up into the mountains to the lake. It wasn't quite light. Nobody was about yet. The dawn chorus was in full swing. From the map, the route looked direct, in a different direction from the path they had taken from the cow field where they landed. It could presently be described as a 'gentle incline,' although there was a tough part coming up, Gunn calculated, in an hour or so. He hoped Sol's ankle would hold out; he had no idea of the man's level of fitness. A short rest might be in order, in a while, to go through their plan. Sylvia was always a stickler for that. They had some Israeli 'iron rations' in their packs to tuck into later.

One or two questions were taxing him. They both expected that Mueller would not be a pushover. Now, it seemed they would have to deal with his wife too. Hadn't Marguerite described her as a fearsome woman? Well, it was just something they would have to factor in. And this cottage seemed very remote. What would the escape routes be like? Gunn was not unduly worried but a couple of years working with

209

Sylvia and his army experience had reinforced the old adage: 'prior preparation and planning prevents piss poor performance.'

In a small clearing, just before the gentle incline turned into a steep ascent, Gunn shrugged his pack off and let it slip to the ground. He stretched his hamstrings whilst pressing against the trunk of a pine and then took a mouthful of water. He passed the canteen to Sol, who took a long draught and handed it back. Gunn peered up the trail. It was barely a deer track, twisting and fading up the incline.

'You know, we should probably decide how we approach this.'

'We don't know if they'll be in the cottage. We don't know where they'll be.' Sol shook his head. 'Basically, we are going in blind. Why don't we knock on the door and pretend to be two hikers who cannot make head or tail of their map? At worst, we get no answer. At best, Mueller or his wife will come to the door. Then we are in.'

It was as good a strategy as any. They walked in silence up the steep track for almost an hour, stopping occasionally for a cigarette. They were making good time. It was getting quite warm. Eventually, the track took them onto a gentle downward incline. Mermaid Lake was now visible, between the tall, brooding conifers. Gunn appreciated its beauty; he would have enjoyed this hike under normal circumstances.

'Well, here we are,' said Sol, a few minutes later. On the opposite side of the lake there was a restaurant. It was popular with walkers, and they were already setting tables for lunch. There was a mooring for boats. There were a few little houses beside it, which looked like cuckoo clocks, well-tended, with pots of red geraniums outside. They, and the restaurant, looked rather inviting.

Gunn got out a pair of binoculars. Whoever had assembled this pack had done them proud.

'I don't think it's one of those. I think it's that building, over to the right.'

The cottage was on the same side of the lake as them, probably about twenty minutes on foot. It didn't look as though it got much sun. He noted that there wasn't really a path between them and the cottage. Obviously, most people came and went by boat. They would have to strike off, away from the side of the lake and back through the trees. Still, that would afford them good cover. A boat was moored neatly outside.

It was harder going through the forest than they had imagined. At times, it was quite dark, with slippery moss underfoot. Just as they were both feeling despondent and irritable, they emerged beside the cottage. 'Well, no time like the present,' said Sol, as they walked up the path. Gunn was reminded, strangely, of Hansel and Gretel, except there were no sweets on this cottage. It was whitewashed, low and austere.

'Maybe we should have left a trail of crumbs, so we could find our way back,' Gunn suggested. Sol gave him a quizzical look, and knocked on the door. There was no response. Both almost felt relieved. Then Sol led the way through a gate in a high wall, which led to a bend in the lake. He stopped dead. Gunn almost fell on top of him.

211

'I think that's what you call a sight for sore eyes,' murmured Sol.

It was indeed a ghastly apparition. Mueller and Elise, were about to take a dip in the lake, thinking, perfectly reasonably, that there was nobody about. Elise was a vast square of solid, white flesh, any trace of a distinction between her mountainous breasts and her waist having disappeared years ago. Beside her, Mueller looked small, although he was probably of average height and stature. Apart from having lost much of his hair, he had changed very little since the photograph Sol and Gunn had seen. That was them all right.

'I just pray she doesn't turn round,' breathed Sol 'In case she turns us both to stone, or causes a tidal wave in the lake. Some mermaid, anyway.'

'It's not funny, Sol. Jesus Christ, what's that all over his back?'

'Scars,' Sol grimaced. 'I would guess the gorgon beats him. He gets his jollies that way. Some of them look fresh.'

They watched in horrified fascination from their vantage point as Mueller lowered himself gingerly into the water, braced for the bite against his wounds. His back was a network of scars, old and new, fading and freshly scabbed. Gunn thought quickly. They would probably have to let them get them out of the lake and then take them by surprise as they got dressed. The woman was built like a brick outhouse. It would take some doing. He relayed his thoughts quietly to Sol.

Mueller and Elise made little noise in the water. Their frolic seemed formulaic and bored, lacking any primal joy. They were trapped in a world of their own creation, sealed off and bitter but unwilling or unable to do anything about it.

Sol and Gunn hit them just as they applied towels to their heads to dry off. Sol cracked Elise across the back of her skull with the butt of his Browning. She went straight down, as if felled, landing in the soft lakeside soil. He bent and checked her pulse; she was still alive. He covered her lack of dignity with a towel and her dress, and turned her head to the side to free her airways. 'We won't hear much from her for a while,' he observed.

Gunn hit Mueller in the ribs and brought him to his knees. Glassy-eyed, the German stared up at him. Gunn smiled.

'Dr Mueller, it's time for a little chat.'

Sol came over to join them, introducing himself as Lieutenant Solomon Kalinsky; formerly of the British Army and now with the Israeli forces. Mueller stared at him with an expression of absolute disgust.

'We'd like to find out more about your distinguished career, after you finished murdering defenceless women and babies in the womb,' said Sol, companionably. 'Including your own, we believe.'

There was no response. Sol walked round and slapped Mueller on his bare back. Mueller winced. His teeth ground together.

'Of course, my friend here is a little irritated with your efforts to kill him in Pompeii and in Haifa.'

Sol leaned in, his fingertips pressed into one of Mueller's fresher scars.

'Remember, he is an Englishman, and you know what cold bastards they can be, under that polite façade. He really doesn't like the cut of your jib, old boy. Now, are you going to talk to us nicely?'

Raking his fingernail across Mueller's back, he continued:

'Perhaps this might help to remind you. Tell us about Lothar Kaltenbrunner. And the little operation you have been running together. Crown Jewels, I believe it is called. No marks for originality.'

Mueller looked at Sol and Gunn hopelessly. He was in agony. They must have found the papers and been through them. There was nobody about. Even if he screamed for help and someone from the restaurant heard him, he would be taken straight into custody. The evidence was damning. He was going to die, either at the hands of these two or at the end of a rope in a military prison. He had read about what those bastards had done in Nuremberg. The game was up. Unless perhaps...

Gunn looked at him. He could almost see the cogs turning over. He shook his head.

'Turn it in, old man, tell us what we wish to know and you will have an honourable way out. That is as good as it gets.'

Out of the corner of his eye, he could see something. Jesus, Mary and Joseph, as his father used to say.

'Sol, watch out. Hold on, I've got you covered.'

Elise had risen to her feet and was standing naked in front of them.

214

'If I might make a suggestion, gentlemen,' she said, in perfect English, 'I may be able to assist.'

Their jaws dropped.

'I have wanted rid of the disgusting little worm for years.'

'Elise,' protested Mueller, weakly.

She turned to Gunn. 'I would prefer to negotiate with you rather than this filthy Bolshevik.'

'Charmed, I'm sure,' muttered Sol. He had been called worse. The 'filthy' part was almost more offensive. He shrugged, and stood aside.

She turned to Gunn.

'Mr…'

'Captain Gunn,' he replied.

'I know something of his activities. He did not make me aware of them but I heard enough to know what was going on.'

Elise, despite her precarious situation, was cold and aloof. Gunn almost admired her for it.

'I suggest you make him write a confession and let me see it. I will confirm, as far as I can, what he has written. You then make him write a suicide note and hang him.'

'Elegant,' Gunn grinned. 'Well, practical if not elegant.'

'My silence is guaranteed. I know you will come after me if I say a word.' She accepted Gunn's offer of a cigarette. 'I am, for my part, glad of a way out.'

'Cold, isn't she?' Sol observed, his Browning cradled in his hand in case Mueller made one false move.

'I'm not cold,' Elise snorted. 'I just hate him. Nothing cold about that.'

The scene became almost surreal, Sol and Gunn agreed later, as they set to work. Elise got dressed and went inside with Gunn to find some paper and a pen. He came out with some rope under his arm.

'That tree over there will probably do, he remarked to Sol.

'Where did you learn your English, Frau Mueller?' he asked.

'I was a nanny for a family in Hereford, before I met Friedrich,' she replied. 'They had an estate. Lots of hunting and riding.'

That explains a lot, thought Gunn. He turned to Mueller:

'How are you doing, old chum? Best not to drag proceedings out unduly. Better make a start on your confession and your suicide note. Take your time over them.'

Patting him on the shoulder, he commented:

'We will forgive a certain slapdash penmanship but we will not forgive lack of clarity. Crack on.'

Sol sat on a rock and took a slug of water from his canteen, amused at the situation. It was bleak, but funny. Mueller was getting a rich reward for all his efforts and was being shown a consideration he had probably never shown anybody else. Mueller began to write but his hand was shaking. He stopped for a moment and looked up at Gunn with hate in his eyes. He reminded him in some ways of those boys Lothar had brought over from

Wellington, but there was a difference. With this one, there was a hardness underneath that civilised veneer. As if he could read his mind, Gunn gave him one of his thoughtful stares.

After a few minutes, Mueller had written both notes. The confession was brief, summarising his career in racial purity and the work he had pioneered in Berlin before his transfer to France. He made no mention of Marta. It was, after all, Elise who had finished her off. She could have that on her conscience, if she possessed such a thing. It gave some sketchy details of Operation Crown Jewels and the way it worked, between Germany and 'points west,' arranged by Manfred Brand, otherwise known as Lothar Kaltenbrunner, or George Cumberland, solicitor of London. The suicide note paid tribute to his children and grandchildren and ended with a simple statement that life had become intolerable and he was killing himself 'fur Heimat und Vaterland.'

Gunn passed the note over to Elise and to Sol for their approval.

'Usual self-serving guff, but some material I'm sure we can use,' was his verdict. Turning to Mueller, he said, almost conversationally, 'You, sir, are a shit of the first order. However, even a shit deserves some consideration.'

'What do you mean?' Mueller looked up, and was surprised to find Gunn handing him a hip flask. He took a sip; it was brandy, and a decent one too. Gunn indicated that he could take another sip before he took his final step towards the tree.

'I don't think we need to hear any more from you now, mate,' said Gunn.

217

Mueller's last, disordered thought was that this 'Tommy,' as Voss had referred to him, was indeed totally insane and ruthless with it. Gunn tied the rope in an expert noose around his neck.

'That should do the trick,' he said. 'Not that the bastard deserves it, but we may as well make this humane.'

Elise shifted her vast bulk behind him and delivered a hard kick to Mueller's backside, to send him on his way.

'You've done this before then,' remarked Sol.

'A few times,' replied Gunn. 'But never for a fellow who deserved it quite this much.'

Mueller kicked and gurgled, and then Elise pulled on his ankles. Her weight broke his neck. Shit and piss ran down the legs of the pride of the party, and his tongue lolled out like something on a poorly maintained butcher's slab. Sol spat his disgust both at Mueller and the task they had to perform. He sent a thought into the universe to the effect that the next man to marry Elise should keep a gun under his pillow.

'Right, that's it I reckon' said Gunn. 'I wouldn't exactly say it's been nice knowing you, Frau Mueller, but I must say your assistance this afternoon has been invaluable.'

'Likewise, Captain Gunn.' She contorted her features into a lascivious grin. 'You are a very good-looking young man.' Gunn recoiled a little.

'Now, what I propose is that you take our car, while I sort things out here.' She placed the notes neatly amongst Mueller's folded clothes and then led them to an outbuilding. 'By the time I have done that, and walked down the track, you will have had a good three hours start. I don't walk fast now.'

'It was going to be my getaway,' she continued. 'I had planned to leave him. Maybe I will start up a brothel back in Berlin one day, when things have settled down there.'

The car was a silver 1938 Horch 853a, top of the range. Gunn was, as usual, in his element.

'Enjoy it, Captain Gunn,' Elise said, as she waved them off down the track 'Friedrich was given it as a reward for his work on the mental defectives. I think it came from a member of the party who had displeased the Fuhrer.'

'Thank you. Good luck with the brothel.'

As Gunn drove off, with Sol beside him, he tried not to let that image and other equally vile ones spoil his enjoyment of the Horch. Watching a man dangle at the end of a rope was never pleasant. Instead, he filled his mind with thoughts of Sylvia. Not just on the beach at Posillipo, although that was probably his favourite, but at other times. That red polka dot number, for instance, or the one she wore to dinner with the Captain, which he had zipped her into. Her face when he had had the Packard winched on board (a picture, with every emotion crossing it). That kiss on the balcony when they docked at Haifa. He told himself that every mile was taking him closer to her. At least, he hoped that was the case.

He turned to Sol.

'Where to next?'

'Perhaps Italy,' Sol considered. 'Urbe. About twenty miles north west of Genoa.'

'Why there?'

'Our new air force has a training course there. Sol leaned back in the seat. It felt good. 'Chap called Harry Fredkens has 'borrowed' a few aeroplanes. Used to be one of your lot. We could cadge a lift back to Israel, I'm sure. And no buggering parachutes, to use one of your phrases. I will have to get this ankle checked out when we get back.'

'No buggering parachutes then,' echoed Gunn. 'Well, that sounds like a good plan. Shall we see what this beast can do?'

'Good idea.'

As Gunn put the Horch through its paces, they discussed how things were going to unfold. Gunn reckoned, and Sol agreed, that George would be like a rabbit caught in the headlamps without Mueller. It would take him a while to realise what had happened, and now that they had details of Operation Crown Jewels, that escape route would be closed to him. His world would start to disintegrate around him. However, he was no pushover, and he was vicious.

'My guys would like you to take him out,' said Sol. 'And I've been watching how you have performed over the past few days. We'd like to offer you a job. Maybe for a year, while we get things up and running in Israel?'

'I've got a job,' replied Gunn. 'I'm a partner in Clements Investigations in London with Sylvia. Remember?'

Sol dug him in the ribs. 'You love that girl, don't you?'

'Yes,' said Gunn firmly. 'That's the one thing in this mad life of mine I am absolutely sure about. Although I haven't actually told her that yet.'

'Well, just think about it, all right? The money will be good. But you don't have to decide anything straightaway. '

The Horch rode the mountain roads and passes on rails, low slung, and it swept like a raven's wing. Gunn bit his lip in thought as the night came down and they raced towards it. He had to admit that he was intrigued by and attracted to the prospect of working with Sol and the Israelis. It appealed to his personal sense of justice. More than nineteen hundred years to get back home again, and to have to lose millions for that to come to pass. It would be a good and fine thing to be part of that, although he wondered why it had to happen right now. There was so much to consider. Still, a more pressing concern right now was removing that evil excuse for a man, George Cumberland, from the planet. He needed to work out how to do that.

Chapter 17

Edward Cumberland was pacing around Cumberlands' conference room like a caged tiger. His father was now turning up at the office every day, which meant he no longer had free run of the office; just a desk in the corner like some office boy. The atmosphere could be cut with a knife. His father wanted to know where he was and what he was doing at every moment of the day. He had had to come in here to ring Meunier. It was probably pointless anyway; Meunier was struggling to be civil to him now. In a moment, he would walk over to Clements and talk to Joan. Now that the Olympics were over, it was easier to get around town. He could not stop thinking about Sylvia. He had, reluctantly, asked Caroline to marry him. The engagement had been announced in The Times. Wedding plans were under way. He was caught in a trap and could see no way out. He poured himself a large measure from the brandy decanter – if he got into trouble about that, he really didn't care - and sat, with his head in his hands, at the conference table.

Louis kicked open the door of Juncker's shop in St Anne's Court. His arms were full of files from an old litigation case. He had just collected them all from the High Court. It was the type of thing he would normally have got the articled clerk to do but they were 'in between' at the moment. He and Edward felt it unfair to get one now that George had reappeared in the office; whoever they got wouldn't last five minutes. They all used Juncker's back room for what they called 'interim storage' while they waited for space in other, larger archives to become available.

'Usual deal, Franz,' said Louis. 'And then I'll have some of that cat's whisky if I may.'

'Oh yes, put them in the back room.' Juncker seemed rather distracted. Truth be told, Cumberland's suitcases had gone right out of his mind. 'Go on through.'

Louis immediately spotted George's suitcases in the corner; he had seen him in the office with them and thought it strange. They weren't locked. He had a quick look inside while Juncker continued to write up his ledger book in the next room. Just as he thought; full of confidential files. They might as well stay here. He concealed them carefully amongst his own files, which he scattered all over the place, and then wandered through for a drink with Juncker and Galland. He never quite knew what to make of Juncker. Still, the whisky was superb.

Nothing much escaped Louis's notice. He had eyes and ears everywhere, including Haifa, where his cousins had just settled. He had heard all about the nice young English couple they had met on the boat, staying with Aaron Vogel out towards Mount Carmel. Well, they clearly weren't there for a holiday at Cumberlands' expense. He recognised that he needed to sit tight and let them do what they had to do. The crucial thing was to keep Edward under control. What was the expression the English used, loose cannon? That was Edward down to the ground. He drained his glass and set off back for the office, just in time to whisk Edward off for a liquid lunch at The Two Chairmen.

The duplicitous Alaikum had kept his word to his Israeli paymasters. No harm would come to the English girl. He was a little surprised not to have had a reaction from Mueller to the completely fabricated and carefully crafted report ('You're terrible,' Otto had said, shaking his head) he had sent through earlier but Mueller had said something about being away for a few days.

Out of breath from her walk down the mountains, Elise had taken one look at the pile of paper by the ticker tape machine, gathered it all up and thrown it in the bin. It could rot in hell now, along with Friedrich. Feeling strangely liberated, she began packing her case for her new life back in Berlin, her riding crops at the top. She had already been on the telephone to Trudl, her old school friend, who had been 'on the fringes' of the party. Trudl, seeing an interesting opportunity in four power Berlin, was opening a brothel and was delighted to find Elise was available to come and help. She would ask no questions; everyone had secrets nowadays.

In Haifa, Sylvia was in the garden with a cool drink. Things seemed to be running smoothly at Clements (she resolved to take Kiwi and Joan out for lunch somewhere decent as a thank you) and she had had a brief but cryptic call from Gunn, to the effect that 'everything was fine' and that they would be back soon. He seemed to have acquired yet another

224

car. They would have to open a garage at this rate. The young Israeli doctor who was part of the security team and who had checked her over had taken a shine to her and had taken her out for a 'spin' with a couple of the 'lads,' as they were designated, in the back of the jeep. It made a refreshing change to be out for the day without having to kill someone. She had also become firm friends with Marguerite, Lev and Aaron, who seemed totally unfazed about having her staying with them and the whole security team. The 'lads' were billeted in the storm cellar.

She was perfectly aware that this was a false idyll. The time was approaching when they would have to return to London and face Cumberland. She knew that Gunn would prefer to 'deal' with him himself, believing that the authorities would be indifferent to the whole business. There was probably a certain merit in such an assumption but she had to admit she was worried about their constant stepping outside the law. An idea was beginning to form in the back of her mind. For now, she returned to the moment, the sea shining blue and gold in the late evening sun, and the simple fact of being in a place where history was stamped in every stone.

Sol and Gunn were on the edge of Lake Konstanz, with a sandwich each. It looked for all the world like a picture from the top of a chocolate box. Sol threw some of his bread to a family of swans which had been watching them hopefully.

'I keep expecting Elise to rise up out of the water.'

'Like a German Lady of Shalott? What a ghastly image.' Gunn shuddered. They smoked a cigarette each and watched the mother swan expertly marshalling her brood of cygnets into a line.

'This place of yours in France, this demeure,' began Sol.

'Well, we'll have to see about that,' said Gunn. 'From what Sylv tells me, probate needs to go through in three different jurisdictions. We're not putting money on it happening any time soon. We're expanding the business in London so I think the emphasis will be on that for a while. Tell me about this work you want me to do.'

Sol chewed on his sandwich and then took a sip of brandy from what had become the communal hip flask. He considered for a moment, and then, assessing Gunn as being someone who wouldn't appreciate a lack of directness, plunged on:

'Well, as I mentioned earlier, you have a talent for the kind of work we are undertaking. We have people to pay back, a reformed country to protect, and we would appreciate someone like you. You have brains, you can handle yourself, you're not afraid to kill although you can show mercy.'

He looked at Gunn.

'Are you sure you're not Jewish, somewhere along the line?'

Gunn thought about this. 'I'm a real mixture. There's some Irish on Dad's side; he was raised a Catholic. Had me baptised as such; family pressure more than anything else. Rest of his side as English as they come. I think my grandmother on Mum's side was Jewish, although we didn't talk about it. I'll have to ask Dad. I can't remember Mum's family very well; she was an only child and her parents died when I was young. Mum died when I was thirteen. A late pregnancy killed her. Fairly horrendous.'

He fell silent for a moment, reached for the hipflask and said

'Your good health. Sante. Slainte. And l'chaim. Sums me up really. Ready for the off? We'll find somewhere for a kip when we get over the border.'

They drove on through the darkness into Switzerland, the Horch eating up the miles. Their papers passed muster at the border, along with their cover stories.

'This Clements Investigations of yours,' Sol asked. 'Are you the boss?'

'No, Sylvia is,' replied Gunn. 'Absolutely. I wouldn't dare. Seriously,' he explained 'We're equal partners. Always have been. She tends to be a little better than me at the detail; I go out on the ops. But she goes out on a few too. She's brilliant at her pretext calls. She'd be a good poker player, I reckon. And we talk about everything.'

'Quite a girl.'

After a while, they pulled off.

'Let's see what that fat old Frau kept in the boot,' suggested Sol. 'Something horrific, I should think. Maybe a whip and some handcuffs?'

Actually, there were two very serviceable travel rugs, which they spread out across the grass. Gunn looked up at the stars before he drifted off, identifying constellations again, and thought back to when he had done that for Sylvia, in the sea. He also resolved he was not going to part with the Horch. That was going back to London, one way or another. He had always wanted a decent car. The liberated Packard had been useful but did not fall into that category. He wanted something rakish but piratical, engineered to within an inch of its life. The Horch made the grade. The irony of a British Army officer of questionable background owning a car beloved of the fat clerks of the master race merely added to the appeal. Mueller would certainly not have appreciated the irony.

They were back on the road again at first light. Sol reckoned they might 'have to hang around a bit' to get their lift back to Israel; the sooner they got to Urbe, the better. The questions began again. Gunn didn't mind really; it helped to pass the time.

'Where did you meet Sylvia?'

'Oh, when I was back on leave. She was in a bookshop in the Charing Cross Road. I'd come in out of the rain. She was completely engrossed in a book. Scarcely noticed me, but I noticed her all right. She reminded me of...well, for me it was like seeing a ghost. A devastatingly pretty one.'

'Ghost?'

'Oh, someone I once knew.' Gunn turned to Sol. 'What about you, you old devil? Anyone in tow?'

'There was.' Sol was suddenly pensive. 'Sarah. I know, I know, a bit of a cliché. But, she really was called Sarah. We grew up on the same street. We were at school together. Everyone assumed we would always be together. Then the Germans came. I got out before they arrived. Sarah stayed, with

228

her family. I have a pretty good notion of what became of them.'

Gunn didn't know what to say; anything he could think of almost seemed banal. He steered the conversation onto more neutral ground for a while. Sol, who seemed fascinated by Sylvia, asked why they were only just getting together now. Gunn paused for a moment.

'Actually, I can't really explain that. Irrelevant now, anyway. But, you know what it was like back then. I needed to forget, well, never mind, I won't go into that. I went back out to France for Liberation. She was off somewhere with the army, then she went out to Nuremberg to the War Crimes Trials. She had a German nanny when she was a child, hence she speaks the lingo. She was married before, you know, to a Canadian. Not for very long. He died in Italy. We were both, and probably still are, fragile in a way. And then we started up Clements Investigations.'

'Why Clements?'

Gunn told him about the building, their office, which they called the bunker, and Joan and her legendary tea. That led on to Cumberlands, and Edward and George, and the best way to take him out.

'You could use Sylvia to lure him' suggested Sol. 'That would probably be the most effective way of catching him off-guard.'

'Not an option, old boy,' said Gunn firmly, remembering what Sylvia had told him about George's previous advances. 'I'll think of something.'

At the Italian border, a sleepy official gave their documentation the most cursory of glances, for

229

midday. After a stop for coffee and cigarettes, they decided to press on to Urbe, check the situation with the air force, and then if they had to hang around, to go into Genoa for something to eat. Sol watched Gunn changing up through the gears as they negotiated more mountains.

'You love this car, don't you?'

'However did you guess?'

'Oh, just the way you seem to wear it as opposed to drive it.' Sol laughed aloud. 'Wild horses would have their work cut out, dragging you out from behind that wheel.'

'Possibly.' Gunn changed up, and the Horch slipped faster out of the traces like a hound at the chase. 'So, this Urbe place – I have heard of an Urbe near Rome?'

'That's why we chose it.' Sol tapped his nose. 'There's a smaller one near Genoa. Local airfield, nobody pays much attention to it. Good training area. We have a flying club in there now.'

'Clever.'

'We like to think so.'

Urbe was, exactly as Sol had described, more of a flying club from the outside. Sol got Gunn to wait outside the perimeter gate. Gunn lit a cigarette and walked around a bit, to stretch. It was warm and he could hear crickets. He watched a pair of lizards chasing each other in and out of a stone wall. Sol emerged smiling about twenty minutes later.

'Eight thirty tonight,' he said. 'No buggering parachutes. And I may have found a way to get your precious car to London. If you want.'

'Landing on Mount Carmel could get spiky,' commented Gunn, drawing on his second cigarette.

'We're not going to Haifa. Well, I suppose we could, but we'd have to wait for a couple of days. We're flying into Sde Dov, outside Tel Aviv.

'Righto.'

'The British built it.' Sol cadged one of Gunn's cigarettes. 'The evil British.'

'We are evil,' agreed Gunn. 'But we're good at it.' He grinned and passed Sol his lighter.

'So, from Sde Dov, how do we get back to Haifa?'

'Drive, I guess, though it won't be the same standard as the Horch.'

'Pity. Now, tell me about the plan for getting this beast to London.'

Sol had spoken to an airman who was off to England with his Italian girlfriend for a holiday. For £20, he would drive the car there (he jumped at the chance) and park it at a location of Gunn's choosing. They drove into town for a long lunch, which they both agreed they had earned and then Gunn said his farewells to the Horch, giving the steering wheel a fond pat. He handed it over to the young man, wondering if he would ever see it again. He was to park it in Oriental Place, Brighton, at the hotel, and leave the keys with his father. Gunn watched his beloved car roar away, with the speed of a tumbling angel.

He turned to Sol. 'If I don't see that car again, somebody is going to get a severe beating.'

'Oh, don't worry about that,' Sol smiled. 'I told him a partial truth. Said you were a member of

231

the unit, just in. A fine soldier and a cold-hearted killer.' Sol winked at a raven-haired lady as she walked past. 'You'll see it again.'

'I hope you're right,' said Gunn.

In Cairo, Alaikum could hear the muezzin man in his minaret, calling the faithful to prayer. He had long since ceased to be among their number, but sometimes, on a lovely evening like this, he found himself moved by the austere beauty of the call. After their usual siesta, he and Otto had been sifting through the reports that were coming through from across the Middle East. The news from their woman in Haifa was interesting. She didn't always report in every day; since April, her situation had changed, although she hadn't gone into much detail about that. However, the intelligence, when it came, was unerringly accurate - frighteningly so, sometimes. Male asset left on civilian aircraft to Limassol two days ago; destination after that not yet known. Ha-Tamar Street surrounded by a cordon of security.

The boy from the bank had called earlier with a further draft from Israel.

'You're not going to meddle then?' asked Otto, amused.

'I could have a lot of fun but no, I'll leave well alone.'

'You're a terror,' Otto said affectionately.

Much later, Gunn and Sol were trudging across the runway. Sol was limping noticeably now.

'Where to now?' asked Gunn.

'Sleep,' came the response. 'Got us in at the barracks. Busy day tomorrow. Lots of people for you to meet.'

Dawn was a rose wash over Mount Carmel. Sylvia was up to see it. She sat in the courtyard, eating orange segments and drinking coffee. Everything was in hand now in London. There little more she could do until Gunn got back with Sol. She hated the thought of going back to Tufnell Park but she was troubled by what lay ahead, knowing that it was not going to be all crustless sandwiches and tea at the Ritz. She took out her notebook and made a few notes, but her mind was on other matters and had been since the kiss on the balcony. Absently, she wrote Gunn's initials and hers in an ornate loop inside a heart.

'For God's sake,' she said to herself angrily. 'Like a teenager.'

As if on cue, the telephone rang.

'Hallo sweetheart,' said Gunn. Sol was watching him, shaking his head and smiling. 'I miss you too. Can't talk now; got meetings to go to. I'll be back tonight, I expect. Lots to tell you. Can't wait.'

Uttering what had become his catchphrase, 'you and that girl,' Sol led him firmly towards the canteen.

'Come on. Let's get some breakfast before the first meeting.'

Breakfast turned out to be surprisingly good; apricot jam, decent butter, orange juice and tea. It was so good that Gunn started to feel resentful. Sol noticed his expression darken, like passing clouds on a summer's day.

'What's up?'

'This.' Gunn tore off a heel of bread and smeared a good coating of butter over it. 'We won the fucking war, and here we are, still on rations. The French and the Italian have plenty and we're giving up food and goods to feed the fucking Germans.'

'Isn't that proof positive, despite what people say, that the British are a little above the rest of us, morally?' Sol patted his colleague on the shoulder. 'I can understand your anger. Maybe working with us will be something positive.'

'Not entirely sure I see the relevance,' growled Gunn. 'I just don't see why the British, who stood alone in Europe in 1940, and I sodding well know all about that, who kept fighting on so many fronts, who sent supplies to the Russians, somehow have to keep digging in. Despite winning.'

'Well, come and meet your new colleagues,' Sol said.

The day turned out to be a busy one, with many questions to field about his war service, family and life in general. His new colleagues, as he had expected, were a complete mix; some had lived under the British Mandate, some were British forces veterans. He would, if he accepted the assignment, be reporting to Sol. He had half expected this; he had suspected for some time that Sol was more senior than he let on.

He spoke at length about the discoveries he and Sylvia had made, emphasising the contribution she had made, and how it had led to the report and paperwork they had before him. They wanted to know all about Sylvia too. They were impressed with

234

Mueller's downfall, commenting that it was a fitting end. Operation Crown Jewels was well under way. Two assets, sentenced *in absentia* by the War Crimes Trials, were already in Argentina. Many more were waiting in Italy and in Cadiz. George was a major player, but there were others. Even so, he and Mueller had been controlling the logistics, so once Cumberland was out of the way too, that would be a major coup. To facilitate and speed up matters, Sol would arrange transport for Gunn and Sylvia back to England the next day. A large payment would be forthcoming once Cumberland was dispatched.

With his head spinning, Gunn emerged into the sunlight in the late afternoon. Sol was outside with a jeep and a driver.

'Sightseeing now, my friend. Show you round a bit. And a bite to eat.'

In the small hours, the jeep pulled up at Ha-Tamar Street. Marguerite had 'billeted' Gunn and Sol with the lads in the cellar, on camp beds.

'Won't be a minute,' Gunn said to Sol, with a smile. He was used to prowling around buildings like a cat. He didn't wait for the inevitable catchphrase.

'Budge up, Sylv.' He climbed onto the narrow bed and took her into his arms. He buried his face in her hair. That perfume again. The cut on her face seemed to have healed. 'I won't stay long, sweetheart. I don't want to disturb you. This bed is bloody uncomfortable and I don't want to cause a major security incident. I'll tell you all about it tomorrow though. I've just, well, I've missed you.'

She tightened her arms around him and murmured something which he couldn't quite catch. He had a smile on his face when he re-joined Sol in the cellar.

'What are you going to tell her?' Sol asked curiously.

'Oh, probably best not to say anything until I hear formally from you guys. Until I've been through the agreement and all that. I agreed with that last guy I saw that it would be under contract through Clements. He said he'd get it all drafted. And we need to focus on Cumberland now. '

Next morning, Gunn and Sylvia were out in the courtyard early. She had been telling him all about Clements, the work she had managed to do and her sightseeing trip with the lads. The sunshine had lightened her hair and had turned her skin golden brown. Sol wandered through to join them, with Marguerite, Lev and Aaron.

'Come on then, said Lev. 'Tell us how that monster met his end. I hope it was painful.'

Gunn stretched out his legs and leaned back in his chair, one arm draped round Sylvia. He reached up behind him, plucked an orange from a tree and began to peel it.

'Let's just say that he died slowly, and not as a man should. And his wife helped finish him off, which says a good deal about him.'

He swallowed a segment and spat a pip into his empty cup. It rattled around in the dregs.

'And Cumberland's passing will make Mueller's seem quite civilised.'

'What assurance can you give us that you will be able to kill him?' asked Lev. 'We must congratulate you on getting rid of Mueller, but you must understand that we still won't feel safe until Cumberland is dead.'

'It's a valid question' observed Sol. 'He is unlikely to go down without a fight.'

'I think surprise will be key,' said Sylvia. 'I was thinking of doing something he really won't expect, but which seems on the surface quite normal; maybe if I made an appointment with him to discuss Jones's will?'

'Absolutely not' began Gunn. 'I won't…'

'Since when did you become my boss?' Sylvia thought, angrily. Shooting him a furious glance, she cut across him and carried on:

'Around now, Cumberlands have a day when they close their offices altogether and go to Lords for the cricket with some clients. They don't even have anyone on reception. George has always hated cricket and goes along under sufferance. He might jump at the chance of an excuse to get away.'

She realised Gunn was looking at the picture in her notebook, of their initials entwined in a heart. He gave her an amused smile. Turning the page firmly, she said, in her best professional manner:

'Of course, Mr. Gunn and I still have to discuss the *modus operandi* in full. But rest assured that we will have this matter in hand immediately on our return to London. For everyone's safety.'

'And what about Mueller's wife,' asked Marguerite. 'How come she helped finish him off? Isn't she a danger now?'

237

'She won't say a word,' said Sol.

'Can you be sure?' Marguerite's fingers kneaded the hem of her skirt in her anxiety. Sol leaned across and placed a hand on hers. He smiled.

'Mueller's wife has every interest in keeping quiet. She also saw at first hand what we are capable of. One word out of place and she will pay the piper.'

Sylvia and Gunn were having a quiet word under the orange trees.

'Sylv, I'm sorry about earlier. I didn't mean to…It's just, well, these guys are animals. We need to mull it over carefully.'

'We'll talk about it later. I've been a busy girl while you were away; writing ideas down.'

'So I see,' he commented, with a smile. 'I liked the picture with the heart.'

She chased him back into the courtyard, to join the others.

In the city of a thousand minarets, Alaikum and Otto were winding down for lunch, which was going to occupy much of the afternoon. They had commissioned a new house in Heliopolis and were meeting the architect, to go through the plans. Alaikum reflected on how far he had come. Here he was, a boy from the bazaar, about to move into the place of his dreams. He and Otto already had their names down for the Heliopolis Club. They were going up in the world, fast.

'New client,' said Alaikum, putting the telephone down. 'Solicitor from London but I reckon he's one of your lot. Said Mueller had recommended us.'

'Interesting,' said Otto. 'Wonder what he wants.'

'Put him on the mailing list.' Alaikum was staring thoughtfully out of the window. 'Try him on the generic stuff first. Usual old flannel. He won't know the difference, anyway.'

George had had a busy morning at Queen Anne's Gate. Having thrown Edward out of the room, with a satisfying boot up the backside, he had started his morning with a most peculiar telephone call to Bad Kaltenbrun. They had no idea of Dr Mueller's whereabouts or when he was likely to return.

'Am I talking to a complete idiot?' he had screamed down the telephone, to one of Mueller's staff. Listening in on the conference room telephone, a pile of files in front of him, Louis winced at the tone and the language. Eventually, George had got through to Hans, in the mountains, and berated him soundly. Hans's family had worked for George's parents for generations. Hans remembered George's parents with affection, particularly his mother, as well-bred courteous people. George was just a shit. He did confirm, though, that Mueller was still at the top lake, on his own. He did not mention, because George did not ask him, that he had seen a strangely elated Elise off in a taxi two days ago. She had not, in any case, said where she was going.

What the hell was Mueller playing at, wondered George? Probably up at the lake with some little tart; Elise was rather a battle axe these days. Oblivious, clearly, to the fact that some people had work to do, and that they had 'assets' waiting to move to Cadiz and points west, who would not be able to

239

remain *in situ* for much longer. He was going to have to take up the reins for a while, as if he didn't have enough to do already. He made a few more calls to his contact in Rome and gave the man some false reassurance. He wasn't sure it was very plausible, but it would buy time.

Then he frowned. Until he had those papers back, had made sure Gunn was dead and had dispensed with Sylvia, the whole operation could be blown sky high. Hadn't Mueller mentioned something about the Middle East? Didn't he have a contact out there, that effeminate creature from the Abwehr? He rang Hans back, in a more conciliatory tone, and got the number for Alaikum. A very odd man, he reflected, after their conversation. Still, there wasn't much else he could do on that front at this stage, and it might prove useful. To take his mind off things, he got out his magazines, along with the riding crop and handcuffs he had bought on his recent shopping trip.

Cumberland could lose himself for some time in his fantasies. In some ways, he shared his predilections with Mueller. In others, they were very different. At Wellington, a matron had taken him under her wing. She was Austrian. He still remembered her fondly. She had taken mothering to a whole different world, where rules seemed to be a matter of negotiation, not fixed in the firmament. He had often wondered what had happened to her; apparently, she had left England in the thirties, at the time of the *Anschluss*, and was last heard of running a field brothel on the Eastern front. No woman had ever quite measured up to her. George now regarded most women as creatures that required domination, of the most severe nature.

The telephone rang loudly, disturbing his thoughts. He scowled. It was that fat old mare, Joan. What the hell did she want? Then he smiled. She was ringing on behalf of Miss Fordred, to make an appointment for tomorrow. She had some papers that she wanted to deliver in person? Yes, two o'clock would be fine. Edward and Louis would be at the cricket but he was certainly available. Thank God for that, he thought. He had hated cricket with a vengeance, ever since Wellington.

He wondered whether this was some sort of trick. His instinct was that it was not. Of course, better to be safe than sorry. As Mueller was clearly totally inept, he was going to have to factor in Gunn's demise, and fast. He thought for a moment and then picked up the telephone again. He knew just the person.

Stanley Garner let the receiver drop into the cradle, where it rocked itself to stillness. He lit another cigarette and looked out of the window onto Wapping waterfront. He grinned at the prospect of some real money, some real action, the first in a long time since the Blitz, although the Olympics had provided some easy meat, foreign mugs to be ripped off and kicked to the kerb.

He turned to his sidekick, a long-time draughtsman named Alex Hughes, generally called Trip because of his two left feet. He was clumsier than a drunken bovine in Whiteleys china department, but he was a skilled operator.

'Trip, put the word out, we should gather the boys at the Prospect tonight. Bit of a board meeting.'

'Nice one, skip.'

Chapter 18

'Well, we're on the way.' Gunn smiled at Sylvia. They were in the back of the jeep, on their way to the airport.

Their route back to England was to be one Cumberland would never have credited. Haifa to Cyprus, Cyprus to Northolt with the RAF. A telephone call to Joan had revealed that the Cumberland Client Cricket Day was indeed tomorrow. They had got her to make the appointment for two o'clock. George had accepted with alacrity.

'In like Flynn?' said Sol from the front.

'Pretty much,' they replied.

Saying goodbye to Marguerite, Lev and Aaron had been emotional. Marguerite had taken them on one side just before they left, to sign some documentation on Chartrettes. 'Come back and see us with the family,' she had said. 'And…thank you.' She had broken down in tears at this point.

There were hugs and kisses for Sylvia, promises to write, and handshakes for Gunn from the security team.

'Took quite a shine to you, didn't they?' he commented.

He handed Sol the keys to the Packard.

'Could be useful, old boy,' he said.

'See you in a few weeks,' Sol responded, with a smile.

Sylvia gave him a quizzical look but decided not to ask Gunn about it; he could be a secretive so and so sometimes. She followed him into the hangar. He turned to her, now that they were alone.

243

'Now, you are all right about this, aren't you, sweetheart? If you're not, just tell me and I'll go to the appointment with Kiwi.'

'I'll be fine.'

'That's my girl.' He gave her a hug. 'Oh, and by the way, Sylv. You're not going back to that sodding mausoleum in Tufnell Park. You're coming home with me. No arguments.'

Sylvia shot him one of her direct glances. Normally, she would have objected vociferously to being told what to do. Actually, she liked Gunn's idea, but she wasn't going to let on, or not straightaway.

Gunn paused. 'I've overstepped the mark again. I keep doing that. It's just you had that goon following you before we left, remember? And I don't trust Cumberland. But seriously, Mrs O always has a room going – if you want, of course.'

Sylvia had been to Gunn's place once, after a raucous evening in the pub with Kiwi, his girlfriend and the Free French crowd. They had played records on the gramophone and started dancing, and been summarily thrown out onto the pavement by an outraged Mrs O.

'Well, it can't be any worse than Tufnell Park,' she said, happily. 'It might even be warmer!'

'I'll smuggle you in tonight then. I reckon it could be quite late by the time we get back.'

Much later, after lunch with their architect and a siesta, Otto and Alaikum let themselves into their office.

'What a day,' said Otto happily. 'Oh, whatever's all this?'

The ticker tape machine had been working overtime.

'It's from Scheherezade. In Haifa or wherever she bases herself now. Says the English couple have left Ha-Tamar Street in a jeep.'

'Wonder where the man went on his own the other day,' mused Alaikum. 'She never said. Oh well. You could mention it in tomorrow's briefing if you can be bothered.'

Garner sat out on one of the verandas at the Prospect of Whitby, half a brandy at his elbow. He sipped, he never supped deep. He was watching the boats moving up and down the Thames while he waited for Trip and the others. There was Coop, a gunman whose real love was the knife; Irish, a prize fighter and horse doper; Bill Gladwin, a driver, fast and safe, one who could be relied on to get a team out of the tightest of holes; Mendelson, who had trained as a tailor but preferred breaking the law. He was handy with pliers, mostly on teeth and knuckles. He had, however, popped a policeman's eyeball in the winter of 1941. They filed in, one after the other, and were soon ordering pints.

Garner was a natural leader. He had been, ever since he left school at twelve, ducking and weaving for local villains. That's where he had learnt the ropes. He kept it nice and clean, kept his own counsel and had risen up the ranks, with the war giving him a boost. He was doing all right. Cumberland had put him on commission a couple of times already.

This new one looked good, he reflected. Sounded easy enough; just the one bloke. Late twenties, ex-military, and he had a description, which he read out to the assembled gang. Had to be out of the way by lunchtime.

'What I reckon,' he said 'is we go over to his gaffe now, this Clements Inn, turn it over, leave a calling card as it were, and lure him out here. Onto our territory.'

Gunn and Sylvia arrived at his digs at midnight. It had started to rain, and there was a chill in the air. The house was in pitch darkness and locked up. Sylvia climbed onto his shoulders and up the drainpipe onto the porch. He passed the bags up to her and then climbed up himself.

'Home, sweet home,' he said.

The room was sparsely furnished. A double bed, a sofa and a sagging wardrobe; not much in the way of possessions, Sylvia reflected. More or less the same as she had in Tufnell Park, although Gunn also had an open fire place. He reached under the bed and brought out a bucket with some coal in it.

'We're not supposed to have fires but I'm bloody well going to light one. Are you hungry?'

'Starving.'

'Won't be a minute then. If you need the loo, it's just down the corridor. Just make sure nobody sees you.'

He came back with two mugs of tea and some buttered toast. Goodness knows who the bread belonged to, or the milk. No doubt there would be hell to pay in the morning, but he was past caring.

They sat by the fire, warming themselves, both deep in thought.

'I'll sleep on the sofa tonight,' offered Sylvia. She tucked his army greatcoat round her and tried to sleep.

'Gunn? Are you still awake?' she whispered, after half an hour.

'Yes. Wish I sodding well wasn't.'

'Fire's lovely though,' she remarked. 'I just stoked it up a bit.'

They both agreed there was something really luxurious about having a fire in the bedroom. It reminded them of childhood illnesses; something not normally allowed.

'I' think we should have a fire in the bedroom at Chartrettes,' she ventured, daringly.

'Gunn, can I ask you something? Did you mean what you said the other day to Marguerite?'

'I did, Sylv. Every single word. Did you mean what you said the other night when I got back?'

'Yes.'

'Ha. Got you. You weren't really asleep, were you? Miss Fordred.'

She ignored that. 'Can I ask you something else?'

'Go on then.'

'In your sleep, you mention this girl's name sometimes. Josephine. Who is she?'

Gunn sighed.

'Her name is Josephine Amelie Gunn. And she is…was my daughter. And there's something else. Her mother's real name was Madeleine Billet. I knew her first as Sandrine.'

Sylvia moved across and sat on the edge of his bed.

'Billet was the name of the cognac house where my mother went. I remember that now. My God. What happened?'

'It was when I was in the SOE,' Gunn continued. 'Madeleine – Sandrine and I – were in the same unit, you know, going round causing mayhem. We fell for each other. Not the idea, really.'

'What was she like?' Sylvia breathed. 'I mean, I don't remember her at all.'

'A lot like you. Those cheekbones. Same colouring. Her hair was a little darker. Not quite as tall. Bit fuller up top. Bottom might have been slightly bigger.'

'That's something,' Sylvia thought, cattily.

'But her smile didn't reach her eyes. And Sylv, she was an absolute bitch. I don't know and I couldn't care less what happened to her in the end. All I know is, she damn nearly got me pinched by the Germans. And I think she killed our baby. Don't ask me about that part, please. I really can't...'

Her arms were round him, tightly.

'Just tell me whatever you want, darling,' she soothed him.

He told her that the last time he had seen his daughter was in a room above a café. Madeleine had been feeding her. She looked like a Madonna, he had thought, bathed in candle light. She had handed him the baby and was buttoning her dress and doing her hair in the mirror. Josephine was replete with milk and very content. She was like a doll, as light as a feather in his arms, a tiny finger hooked around his. Then she smiled.

'She's beautiful. Look at that smile, Maddie.'

The words which had come out of her mother's mouth could not have been a bigger contrast.

'It's wind. And you can take her. For good. I can't do this anymore. '

'But Maddie, don't you dare...you know I can't...You don't mean that.'

'Watch me,' she had said. Horrified, he pleaded with her. He would get them out somehow, to his father in Brighton. They'd already discussed this, she had to be patient. She told him she wasn't interested; she was ready to walk out and leave the baby. He had managed to persuade her to take the baby again, telling her that she was exhausted, and that he would be back as soon as he could.

'I think I convinced myself, not her. And I left them, Sylv. I had no choice. And I have had to live with that. I'm pretty sure Josie died. I hope she didn't suffer. I hope she didn't lock her in a drawer or smother her. Some of the grannies on the Sidonia were talking about children who survived, whose identities were completely changed. Do you remember?

'And this is the really strange thing. Dad received an envelope, after the war was over. It had an *acte de naissance* inside, and my name as the father. Mark Gunn, Captain, HM Army. Looks official but I doubt very much that it was...And a lock of hair.'

He got them out of a side table to show her. 'Postmarked Cognac.'

'I did try to find them, Sylv. I went back, but the café had shut down. The cognac house was all locked up. It was as if the whole town was closed. Nobody would talk. Not even the parish priest. I had him in a choke hold against the church wall. But I drew a total blank. The only conclusion I could reach was that Maddie was dead, Josephine was dead, and I had to try to forget. She'd be nearly five now.'

'And you never told me?'

'I only ever told Dad.'

'We'll find out what happened.' Sylvia was determined. 'And we'll bring Josephine home. I'm glad you told me. We'll kill that bastard tomorrow and then, well, we can talk about everything, can't we?'

Giving him another hug, she went back to the sofa. It still felt strange to be talking in such a matter of fact way about 'killing someone the next day,' and the revelations about her family were unsettling. She had, she supposed, become acclimatised to having no family. Just before she left for Nuremburg, she had received a short letter from Cumberlands, to the effect that they had 'received information' that her mother and her sister were dead. She had torn the letter into small pieces. It meant nothing. Now she wondered how Cumberlands knew – and what else they knew. As the firelight flickered, making patterns on the ceiling, and the coal sizzled and spat, she drifted into an uneasy sleep.

Gunn skirted around the edges of sleep, drifting in and out. He hadn't told Sylvia the full

250

story, but their conversation had taken him back to territory which he had tried to put firmly behind him. As he had said, he was pretty sure Maddie was responsible for his almost getting his collar felt at the Gare de Lyon. There had been a Gestapo-approved Citroen outside the local station. He had only glanced at it in passing but he thought he had caught a glimpse of her in the back seat, smoking a cigarette and laughing. She had not been a prisoner. He had feared the worst for Josephine after that and his momentary lapse in concentration had almost been his downfall.

He put those images out of his head and looked across at Sylvia, under his greatcoat on the sofa, and started going over the plans again and again. He had a feeling there was something they had missed, but could not for the life of him think what it was. After a while, he dozed off.

Both he and Sylvia were awake with the dawn. He chatted to her as he shaved, thinking how much he liked having her around.

'I'll pop down and make us a cuppa in a minute. Then I'll have to smuggle you out before the old battle axe spots us.'

'Is this your usual routine with your conquests?' asked Sylvia.

Gunn decided to ignore this. His 'conquests,' as she called them, were irrelevant; in the past. There hadn't been that many, contrary to what she imagined. More recently, there had been that Sophie girl who hung round with the Free French crowd but she was history now.

'And then I'll smuggle you back in so we can ask her about the room,' he continued. 'I'm sure the one next door is empty. It's not as big as this but it's quite nice, it catches the sun in the mornings'

In the end, there was no need for subterfuge. Mrs. O caught him on his way back upstairs with two mugs of tea.

'What have I told you, Mr Gunn? About young ladies in your room? And fires?'

She didn't miss a trick, he thought. Sometimes, he thought she plugged herself into an electric socket so that she could avoid sleep altogether.

'Sorry, Mrs O,' Gunn said contritely. With a smile that would have charmed the birds out of the trees, and which never failed to work on Mrs. O, he explained that his friend needed somewhere to live and that she would be interested in renting the room next to him if it were available. Hearing them talking, Sylvia came downstairs. It was settled in minutes and Sylvia was given a key from a huge bunch in the cupboard.

'And I don't want any goings on up there. This is a respectable household,' she called after them. 'Nice girl,' she thought. 'Classy. What he needs. Much better than that last little piece he brought back. Now, if I was thirty years younger…'

'No goings on' and 'respectable household' kept them highly amused over their tea. Gunn regaled Sylvia with Mrs O stories on the bus all the way to Clements Inn. They were going in early because Joan had the day off and Kiwi was in Blackpool on an adultery case.

252

They stopped in their tracks as they went up the stairs to the bunker. The door was hanging off its hinges. Desks were turned over. A telephone had been half buried in the soil of a rubber plant. A set of reference books had been arranged on the floor and then urinated upon. A new packet of coffee had been opened and poured over every available surface. Panes of glass had been punched out. Gunn stepped into the room and then turned to Sylvia.

'Somebody is panicking.'

'I'm bloody well panicking at the moment,' Sylvia responded, trying to think whether she had renewed the insurance. 'Don't touch anything until the police get here. I'll call them. Thank goodness we took most of the camera stuff with us.'

'Just a shame there isn't much of a dark room left,' said Gunn. 'Wait a minute, what is this?'

He sat back on his haunches and picked up a note from the floor. It was doggerel, the sign of a mordant wit, but it was a message nonetheless. He stood up and recited:

'Where prospects are grim and the wall is dark, come and meet those who have made this mark.'

Sylvia wasn't paying attention; the reference books had belonged to her father. She had very little else of his.

'Very funny,' commented Gunn. 'Prospect of Whitby. Has to be. Sylv, don't bother with the police. The excess on the insurance would probably be more than this lot's worth. We can get some new reference books. I know they were your Dad's.'

He came over and gave her a hug.

'I'll go over there and sort this as soon as it's open. It'll be one of Cumberland's stupid goons. I'll put the door back on its hinges while you start cleaning up. Make us a cuppa in a minute, would you, sweetheart? I'll go and get the toolkit out of the props cupboard. '

Sylvia poked at the sodden mess disdainfully, wondering whether she had, at a stroke, been relegated to making tea and clearing up. Feeling rather resentful, she began clearing up the broken glass which seemed to have got everywhere and then set to with a mop and disinfectant. It would take all morning to get this shipshape.

'Right, that should hold up now,' said Gunn, as they drank their tea and inspected his handiwork. 'Keep it locked until I get back; don't let anybody in. I'll take the spare key. Shame Kiwi and Joan aren't here, but I think the accountants are in downstairs if you're worried. We need to leave here at half past one for Cumberland's. I should be back in plenty of time but if by any chance I'm not, I'll see you there.'

Shortly after opening time, Gunn walked into the Prospect of Whitby. It was almost empty. The landlord rated him a passing glance and nodded to a snug to the left of the bar. Garner and his mob were sitting waiting. Garner raised a glass to him in mock salute.

'Mr Gunn. Join us for a snifter before the games begin.'

Gunn walked over slowly, his right hand unclipping the catch on the sheath of his army issue knife, which he kept sewn into the right hand pocket of his jacket.

'Don't mind if I do.'

At Lord's, George, Edward and Louis were already on their second glass of champagne. Their guests had started to arrive. Edward was looking forward tremendously to the day's play. Louis did not profess to understand cricket but never turned his nose up at champagne. George was doing his best to be civil to the boring little bank manager who had almost become surgically attached to his side. His thoughts were elsewhere. There were 'assets' who needed removing from Cadiz this evening, as a matter of urgency.

He had spoken briefly to Garner late last night at home. He had pushed his wife into the bedroom upstairs and slammed the door on her while he took the call. Usually, he made sure that her bruises were not visible; last night he had perhaps been a little careless. At least, from what he could make out, the first part of the mission had been successful. Hopefully Gunn would take the bait and that would be him out of the way. Then he would handcuff that little bitch, and, after he had enjoyed her, she would be out of the way too.

He turned to the bank manager.

'Do excuse me,' he said.

'Going back to the office,' he told Louis shortly.

'What's he up to?' Louis wondered idly. George did normally slope off on these occasions, but not until after lunch. Play was only just starting.

Probably one of his 'assets,' he told himself. He watched thoughtfully as George disappeared into the distance.

At the Prospect, Gunn turned to Garner and the assembled crowd.

'To what do I owe this pleasure?' he enquired.

'To a very short acquaintance and a very profitable transaction, both for myself and for my associates'

'I will drink to the first part of the toast.' Gunn sipped the brandy and lit a cigarette. He let a match burn a little, allowing the others to be transfixed by the flame. Then he threw the rest of his brandy across the room and into Trip's lap. He dropped the match. While Trip screamed and ran round, with the others trying to put him out, Gunn put his blade to Garner's throat and dragged him out of the pub and down a dark alleyway. The landlord did not bat an eyelid.

With one hand round Garner's throat and the other holding the blade, perilously close, he said: 'I suggest you start spilling the beans, mate. Who are you working for?'

Garner struggled in Gunn's grip. He cursed his useless team silently. He was either going to end up strangled or sliced, at this rate. Neither, if he could help it. He growled 'Cumberland' and then head-butted Gunn full in the face. Gunn wheeled back, his grip lost and his nose split.

Garner took his chance and went for the Webley in his waistband. Gunn swung his arm, his blade a cold extension of his grip. Garner ducked, and the tip of Gunn's blade scored across the brickwork, snapping the tip. Garner laughed and pulled his Webley clear. Gunn, gobbets of blood lacing the air, volleyed Garner's hand. The gun kicked and barked out a shot which rang off the opposite wall as Garner's knuckles gave way under the blow and Gunn raced in hard and low, his shoulder hitting Garner under the ribcage. Gunn returned the head butt with interest, smashing Garner's already off kilter nose.

Garner, screaming in anger and pain, laced his arms around Gunn's chest in a bear hug and squeezed, lifting Gunn clear off his feet. Gunn leaned in and bit Garner's right ear, twisting it in his teeth. The gangster loosened his grip. That was all Gunn needed; he brought his knees up into Garner's belly, knocked the breath out of him and dropped him flat across his knee, breaking his back. Garner was a bundle of rags on the newly washed cobbles. Gunn, short of breath, dropped to his knees and finished Garner off with his broken blade. 'Bastard!'

Inside the pub, Gladwin had managed to roll Trip up in his coat and put the flames out. Trip was grilled like a seven day steak. Gladwin's hands were charred at the edges. He looked up at Mendelson, Coop and Irish.

'Make yourselves fucking useful. Get out there and give that guy a twice over. Beat him so hard that he'll need lessons from Lazarus to come back.'

As they tumbled out of the pub and arrayed themselves across the street, Gunn heard them coming. He wiped his mouth down. He had Garner's Webley in one hand and a razor in the other.

Mendelson came at him first, pliers at the ready, looking for eyes to pop and teeth to break. Seeing the others were coming up close behind, Gunn rolled forward and past Mendelson and nicked the man's hamstrings. Mendelson went down as Gunn rolled up and swayed, as Coop's bayonet nearly took his throat out. He shot Coop full in the face.

Irish was not armed. Gunn considered for a moment, then, thinking 'this is not tea at the Ritz,' he shot him in the shoulder and the knee. Irish went down. Gunn stood over him. 'Come near me again and you are in the river.'

Gunn turned away and went over to Mendelson.

'Nasty little shit, aren't you?'

Mendelson said nothing. He just glowered at Gunn with eyes as angry as the weals on Mueller's back. He spat.

'Save it,' Gunn laughed. 'Step out of this part of town, assuming you can ever walk again, and I will kill you.'

Gunn left them and walked into the Prospect. He strolled up to the bar and gave the landlord a couple of guineas for his trouble. He looked at the clock over the bar. Bugger. It was nearly 2 o'clock. Hoping fervently that Sylvia had not decided to go to the appointment alone, he rushed downstairs to the gents to make himself presentable and then gave a taxi driver outside a fistful of notes to take him to Queen Anne's Gate as quickly as possible.

258

Chapter 19

In the bunker, Sylvia had been working tirelessly. The glass would have to be mended, and the dark room re-assembled, otherwise the office was almost back to normal. She had managed to collar a telephone engineer, using the accountants' telephone downstairs, and had sweet-talked him into reconnecting them. She settled down to read through the ledgers and the post. Joan had done an impressive job, as had Kiwi. He had left her a set of photos for one of the cases, which she turned into a report.

As she put it into an envelope for the client, along with an invoice, she was startled to see that it was already 12.45. Where was Gunn? She picked up the note he had discarded. She knew the Prospect; it was in Wapping. A notorious meeting place for villains; she had never been there. Well, he needed to get a move on. She had a bad feeling about this. It looked as if she might have to tackle Cumberland on her own.

She opened the props cupboard and got out the navy jacket she always wore when seeing solicitors or going to the City and some matching court shoes. She pulled out a briefcase and put the set of papers she had made up inside. Every inch the partner in Clements Investigations, she told herself proudly, applying some lipstick in the cramped loo they shared with the accountants downstairs. The problem was that her part in the plan they had sketched out in Marguerite's courtyard extended to getting inside George's office and talking to him about the papers. Gunn was meant to be there for the next part.

Praying that he would be, she checked her handbag for her Beretta, locked up carefully and set off towards St James's. Gunn had taught her in the past how to spot and shake off a goon; so far, so good, nobody about. She went over the plans again in her head, trying to work out how she was going to get a confession out of George and then 'take him out,' to use Gunn's terminology. She was surprised to find herself already by the pelicans. Normally, she liked to stop and watch them. Edward had told her once that they were a gift from the Russian Ambassador to King Charles II and that they had been in the park ever since.

She was early, so she sat on one of the benches, watching a mother and her little girl feeding the ducks. Josephine would be about that age now. She thought about what Gunn had told her. The fact that he had been in love with her sister did not bother her. It was just bizarre coincidence. What had shocked her to the core was the cruelty. In spite of the statements she had typed up at the trials, she found it difficult to believe that of anybody, let alone her own flesh and blood.

Watching carefully for goons, she crossed the rest of the park, arriving on the corner of Birdcage Walk. She headed down an alley and lit a cigarette. She had five minutes to make her decision. There was no sign of Gunn. While George still walked this earth, she and Gunn were dead men walking and so were Marguerite and Lev. But what was it Gunn always told her? 'Don't go that extra mile if it is going to put you in danger.' That wasn't a piece of advice he tended to apply to himself. In these circumstances, would Gunn want her to pull out? What if he was already there, concealed, ready to implement the next stage of the plan? If he wasn't, and she would have a surreptitious scout round shortly, it would probably be better if she cancelled the appointment.

She put her cigarette out and took a deep breath. Her decision was already made for her. George suddenly appeared in front of her.

'Good afternoon, Miss Fordred,' he said, in unctuous tones.

Sylvia had never noticed that one of the conference room windows looked out onto the alleyway. By pure coincidence, George had been in there, to pour himself a large glass of brandy. He had taken a sip, and decided to put it on one side. He wanted to be able to enjoy her. Rather irritatingly, he had recently started to experience a few problems 'in the bedroom department.' He wasn't sure if it was alcohol that exacerbated the difficulty or his ugly old trout of a wife, but he wasn't going to take any chances.

Scarcely able to contain his excitement, he took Sylvia by the arm and led her firmly inside, through the side entrance. The front door was probably locked, she thought, as there was nobody on reception. He led her up the back staircase to an office she recognised as Edward's.

'Take a seat.' He ushered her to an armchair by the window. 'Can I offer you a drink of water or perhaps a brandy?

'No thank you,' she replied politely.

He sat down in the armchair opposite her. They were separated by a small table with a leather top. After a few pleasantries about the weather, she got out the bundle of papers she had made up and began talking about the sad discovery they had made in Chartrettes. He seemed distracted and was fidgeting.

'But Miss Fordred,' he commented. 'You and Mr Gunn have been away for over two weeks. I don't see why my firm is paying you for information which appeared in the press the day after your departure. And I believe we have paid you considerable sums already.'

Sylvia explained, patiently, that this 'information' had only appeared in the press at all because of the discovery that she and Mr Gunn had made but George did not appear to be listening. Perhaps this was just as well, because the papers she had made up were a complete fabrication. She had used the time-old trick of staining paper with tea to make it look old; a bundle of scrap paper of Marguerite's. This was the point at which Gunn was meant to appear, help her incapacitate Cumberland, extract a confession and take him out.

'You look very nice today, Miss Fordred.'

'Thank you,' she replied absently.

Something had happened to Gunn. She could sense it. He had been set against the idea from the start of her being used as a 'lure.' He would not have left her alone. Deciding she ought to make a bolt for it, she stood up.

'Thank you for agreeing to see me today, Mr Cumberland. I think on reflection it would be better if we adjourned this meeting until Edward and Louis can join us.'

He was ready for her.

'Miss Fordred,' he murmured. 'I believe you and I have unfinished business. I have always thought you needed a firm hand. We were interrupted last time. Now, where were we?'

Seizing her arm and pinioning her arm behind her back, he led her over to the desk. Squirming in his grasp, she managed to free herself and to kick him hard in the groin with her heel. He doubled over with pain, at which point she smashed him over the head with a heavy paperweight. He fell to the ground. He was unconscious, but for how long?

Sylvia went over to the table, got the Beretta out of her handbag and kept it trained on George while she tried to think what to do and how to do it all by herself. She noticed the paraphernalia on the desk; the riding crop and handcuffs placed tidily on a pile of magazines and felt sick to the stomach.

'Those will do,' she thought, deftly slipping the handcuffs on George.

He began to stir. He shook his head, clearing the fog. He looked up at Sylvia and then at his cuffed hands. A vein throbbed in his temple, pulsing like a sick cobra. Sylvia could feel the bile rising in her throat.

'You little bitch. Wait till I get my hands on you!'

'I'm afraid you might find that a little difficult,' replied Sylvia brightly. 'Incidentally, don't even think of moving. I'm not afraid to use this.' She began to wonder wildly how long she could keep this up. The Beretta was loaded (she had checked). She glanced down at it again. It was an MI934, generally issued to the Royal Italian Army, chambered for the 9mm Corto cartridge. It was reliable. Not heavy on the stopping power. It could do serious damage to George if she felt inclined. She had to admit that at the moment, she did.

There was a sound outside, a tread. The door opened. It was Edward.

He surveyed the scene in front of him, confused.

'Father, what's going on?' Edward edged into the room, trying to avoid the covering arc of the Beretta. 'What's happened?'

'This woman has gone mad.' Cumberland senior had gone puce in his anger. 'Now, stop these damn fool questions, sort this bitch out and help me out of these confounded things.'

'Bitch?' queried the younger man. This was Sylvia he was talking about, the girl he had idolised for so long. George shook with frustration. His handcuffs jingled.

'Why do you have to question everything, you tedious little shit? It was just a game that went wrong.'

'What do you mean, a game?' echoed Edward. He was clutching at straws. Perhaps what Louis had said was all lies after all. He really did not know what to think.

Sylvia couldn't believe the brass front of it. 'I don't think I would ever be so desperate as to want to play games with the likes of you,' she replied, with bitter amusement.

To Edward's combined shock and enjoyment, Sylvia pressed the Beretta into the folds of the old man's neck.

'How about this for a game?' she suggested, mischievously.

She was playing for time. She could not trust Edward. When they were children, and the families were friends, he had been a cry baby and a tell-tale. He used to encourage her to do more and more audacious things and then go and tell, seeming to relish getting her into trouble. She had got wise to it after a while. All these years later, he hadn't changed but the stakes had.

Gunn made his way carefully upstairs. He could hear voices, raised and high. He was pretty sure one of them was Edward's. He avoided the third stair from the top, which he remembered always creaked, wincing as he did so. He was somewhat battered, but he had a job to do. Edward being there muddied the waters somewhat; if needs be, he would have to go too.

He opened the door a crack, very cautiously. Sylvia saw him straightaway, but didn't react.

He gave her an encouraging smile and remained on the landing. Keeping the Beretta trained on George, she suggested: 'I think you have some explaining to do, Mr Cumberland. I'm sure Edward would love to hear what you have been up to. After those years he spent, risking his life and defending his country.'

Cumberland spat.

'Defending his country? He hasn't got the imagination to see beyond his Spitfires, pints of beer and darts at the White Hart. And the job I created for him. He is nothing but a disappointment. And I don't have to explain myself to anyone. How dare you insinuate such things? I should have dealt with you years ago, you little trollop.'

'That last remark of yours rather spoilt things, Mr Cumberland? Dealt with me?' Sylvia began. But Edward had crossed the room and was at her side.

'I know all about you,' he said, to Sylvia's surprise. 'You and Uncle Friedrich and your 'assets.' You make me sick to the stomach. Give me the gun, Sylvia.'

Cumberland laughed out loud at his son.

'You haven't got the courage to do that. It was easy enough, wasn't it, shooting down a hero of the Reich from behind your gun sights, but this? No.'

'Sylvia, give me the gun. I'll take it from here,' Edward repeated.

'Let me handle this, Edward.'

Sylvia turned again to Cumberland senior, still purple with rage and muttering about giving them both a damn good thrashing.

'Mr Cumberland,' she said. 'You have a choice. Not an especially palatable one, I grant you…'

Before she could outline the choice, however, Edward was upon her, trying to get the gun.

'For God's sake, Edward,' she shouted. 'It's loaded.'

He was stronger than she remembered, although the last time they had fought, she had been about thirteen. That day had not ended well. A shot cracked away. It took Cumberland senior in the shoulder and sent him spinning to the floor. The back of his head cracked on the edge of the small grate. He would not be getting up from that.

Edward went over to his father. He backed away. He turned on Sylvia, his face white. He grabbed her by the shoulders and shook her.

'What have you done?' he yelled.

Sylvia, her face taut with shock, slapped Edward so hard across the face that the blow left a reddened print.

'You did that, you idiot. You did exactly what you wanted to do, what you've always wanted to do. And now you're blaming me, like you've always done. You always went and sneaked on me. Well, I'm not having it.'

Edward was upon her, pushing her to the floor, with his full weight upon her.

'Get OFF me, Edward,' she screamed, trying to push him away. 'What the hell are you doing? I can't breathe.'

Gunn took a deep breath and kicked the office door wide open. This was his cue. He pulled Edward's jacket up over his head, disorientating him, marched him across the office and launched him, face first into the grate.

Edward tumbled over in worried confusion, his head ringing. He had no idea of who his assailant was. He shook his head, ripped his jacket clear and stood up and turned. He saw Gunn before him, looking like someone who had just received something for which he had been waiting a long time. Gunn smiled, a slow baring of the teeth.

'Come on then.'

Edward's sangfroid and dapper appearance were now things of memory. Gunn standing before him was a provocation too far. He left science behind and came high at Gunn, who twisted and ducked about on his waist. Gunn slapped him across the ear, as if he were a naughty school boy caught with his fingers in the tuck kitty.

Edward cracked his shoulder on the door frame and held onto it for a moment, catching his breath. He turned and went at Gunn again and again. Gunn swerved, and flicked him across his left ear. This was humiliation and they both knew it, with Gunn determined to add more to Edward's creaking morale.

'Come again, old son,' Gunn grinned. 'This has been a long time in the brew. I reckon you want to make the most of it.'

Edward leaned against the mantel over the grate to give himself some purchase and smiled back. He reached over to his right and picked up a fire poker.

'Going to even the odds up, old boy.'

Gunn shrugged at Edward's choice of weapon and invited him on. Edward did not need a second invitation and launched himself at Gunn, raising the poker as he did so. Gunn smiled.

'Got that wrong, chum.'

Edward's poker tangled in the light fitting in the centre of the office and Gunn was in on him, landing punches in tight combinations into Edward's midriff, groin and head. Edward could not let go of the poker and his body danced like a marionette with the strings snapping as his blood sprayed across the desk, his father's body and his expensive suit. His head twisted back, and a molar described a lazy arc up and out of his mouth before rattling into the grate. He had not landed a single blow. He was desperate. He dropped his hands and went for Gunn's eyes. Gunn rolled back with Edward's momentum, placed a foot on Edward's belly

and threw him on his head, through the open door and onto the landing.

Gunn got up. Edward staggered to his feet, gobbets of blood lacing his shirt and face. He leaned on the banister. He reached into his pocket. He had nothing. He shrugged and came back at Gunn, who danced in on boxer's feet, avoiding Edward's flailing arms, landing a first-class upper cut on the younger Cumberland's jaw. Edward's eyes rolled back. Lights dimmed. He hit the floor.

Sylvia stood up and dusted herself down. She was relieved to see Gunn, but her mind was racing ahead. She was worried that Edward, when he woke up, might pull some sort of stunt and call the police; as, in the past, he had gone running to Nanny. She walked over to Cumberland senior and removed the handcuffs. The keys were on top of the magazines, by the riding crop. She scooped them into her handbag.

Gunn propped Edward up in a corner of the office. He patted him on the cheek. Nothing, just a dull murmur. He sat down at the desk, rooted around in the drawers and found a decent bottle of Scotch. He did not bother with a glass; he took a long, neat swallow. He said nothing to Sylvia. He did not look at her. He was calculating.

The Cumberland situation could be explained, so long as Sylvia could persuade Edward to get the story straight with enough fraying at the edges so as to make it not so cast iron that the police would get nervous. However, the Wapping connection would probably come to light once the wheels were in motion, so he had to make a move and a good one too. He had to make it quickly.

He crossed over to Sylvia and held her close. She flinched slightly.

'Are you all right, sweetheart? They didn't hurt you, did they?'

'I'll live.' Her arm still hurt, where George had grabbed her.

'Sylv, I've got to go,' he said gently. 'I hate leaving you with all this, but they'll link Wapping to Cumberland and that will come back to me. I didn't leave many standing at the Prospect of Whitby.'

He rubbed his jaw.

'So I suggest you and Master Edward get a story straight, get Louis in on the act and go down to the police station.'

'Where will you go?'

'Back to France. Change of clothes first and a shave and go down to Brighton. I'll leave in the small hours and take the back roads to Dover. I'll see you there tomorrow. I'll meet the two o'clock boat train. Make sure you're on it.'

He kissed her, and then he was gone. Sylvia realised she was shaking. She needed to pull herself together. Edward was already stirring. She took a deep breath and sat beside him on the floor. She said nothing; just let him take in the scene of devastation around them.

'My father...' he began.

'Edward,' she said gently. 'Do you remember what happened?'

'He's dead?'

It was more of a statement than a question.

'I'm afraid so, Edward. It was a terrible accident. I came here to tell him about our findings. But then he started abusing me, you know, like he used to abuse you, and you pulled the trigger, remember?'

He was sobbing uncontrollably now. She put her arms round him and drew him to her.

'I'm so sorry, Edward.'

They sat like this for about twenty minutes. After a while, he said:

'I do remember. And I'm glad he's dead. Louis told me he was a fucking Nazi. I hate him. Hated him. But, Sylvia, what do we do now? What about Mummy?'

Edward's mother had been unkind to Sylvia as a child. She could not bring herself to feel much sympathy. Now she was the least of their problems.

There was a noise downstairs. They both started up.

'Hallo?' called Louis, as he came upstairs. 'Are you up there, Mr Cumberland? Rain stopped play. I left that tedious little bank manager fast asleep on a bench, can't hold his drink…Oh God…'

He looked at Edward.

'You've been in the wars, haven't you?'

Sylvia didn't want Edward thinking about Gunn, although she imagined he would want to draw a veil over whatever he remembered about his pasting. She explained to Louis that she had come to report on her findings, not realising it was the Cumberland Cricket day, and that George had started to abuse her. She gestured towards the magazines and the riding crop.

'And thank goodness Edward came along.'

Louis sat on the edge of the desk as Sylvia continued to explain the situation as succinctly and as swiftly as possible, without skimping on the details. He had a good sense of the reality behind George's chosen mask and grasped things quickly.

The Beretta was still on the floor. Edward was on the floor too, with his head in his hands. Louis and Sylvia exchanged glances. Louis said gently:

'You know, Edward, you mustn't think you did anything wrong. There isn't a court in the land that would say otherwise. You understand that, don't you? It was an accident, nothing more. Things just got out of hand.'

Edward nodded, miserably. He winced as he tried to move. Sylvia put a hand on his arm.

'Look, we simply have to get this straight between us, go to the police, make our statements and then get on with our lives as best we can.'

'How?'

'Muddling through usually seems to work.'

272

Over a brandy each, they went through the story, meticulously, until they knew it off by heart.

'He must have had the gun in his desk and kept it loaded and got it out to try and frighten you, Sylvia,' Edward reflected. 'Mind you, he had all sorts of things in there. Kept it locked most of the time. I thought it was just for all that…filth of his.'

'Edward, I think we should try and give him a dignified exit, don't you,' she said, gently. 'Not for his sake, but for yours and for the firm? Reckon we're ready now?'

With his canvas holdall over his shoulder, Gunn was making his way through the back streets of Brighton towards Oriental Place, in a zigzag. Seagulls were circling raucously overhead. He was beginning to feel tired and he ached all over. He was thinking about the day's events, and Sylvia. If anyone could sort all this out, it was Sylv, but he hated having to leave her like that.

In no time at all, he found himself outside the Gunn House Hotel, a tall Regency building in need of some renovation. The cream paintwork looked grubby in the early evening light. His father had picked the building up for a song when he came back from Paris in the thirties. The Gunns came from a line of East End publicans and his father had inherited some money on the death of his parents. His father always maintained that the building's proximity to the Pavilion had spared it from the Luftwaffe and would regale anyone who cared to listen with the theory that Adolf Hitler had intended to base himself there after the invasion.

Inspector Gunn, an older version of Gunn (the first thing anyone remarked on) was propping up the bar. He shook his head as Gunn limped in.

'There's a sight for sore eyes,' he commented. 'What on earth have you been up to, son?'

'Let me have a wash and spruce-up, Dad,' said Gunn wearily, 'And then I'll tell you all about it.'

'Your room's all ready,' came the reply 'and I'll have a snifter lined up for you.'

Gunn's room was in the attic, at the top of the building, up four flights of rickety stairs. There was a sad-looking pot of maidenhair ferns on each landing. They needed a good watering and some fresh air but Gunn walked straight past. His room was huge, with fantastic views, a real vantage point. The floor sloped away at an angle because of the subsidence. Gunn liked it like that; it added to the character. A box in the corner contained toys and books from his childhood and his sister's. They had been close in age, but she had died of complications from measles when they were small. A little holy water font was attached to the wall, passed down to him from his Irish grandmother. It was empty, 'for ornamental purposes only,' but it reminded him of France, so he had kept it. Nobody ever stayed in Gunn's room, even if the hotel was jam-packed. His father was meticulous about that.

Back in the bar, where it was still a little early for the regular crowd, his father passed him a pint. Gunn sipped it appreciatively, enjoying the hoppy taste.

'We're trying out one of the Lewes breweries for a change. Now,' said Inspector Gunn, who missed nothing, even after a tipple or two. 'Young Israeli cove was in the other day, brought your car from Italy. Nice motor. So come on, spill the beans.'

'It is a nice motor.' Gunn agreed. 'Well, it all started as a research case that got a little out of hand.'

'Meaning?'

'Imagine kicking a pebble off a mountain peak and the resulting situation when it reaches the bottom.'

'I see. Mayhem, chaos and thunder.'

'Not to mention blood and guts.'

He recounted the story from the beginning; there was no end in sight yet, he reflected. His father listened carefully, putting in the occasional aside. He got them another pint each.

'This Sylvia girl, she's the one I speak to on the phone sometimes? Your partner at Clements?'

'That's the one.'

His father nudged him in the ribs. 'You've fallen for her, haven't you?'

'Well, yes.'

'I can tell. You look...different. Like you did before, you know...that little French piece.'

'But life has a habit of getting in the way. Always does, with me,' remarked Gunn, deciding not to mention Maddie further at this stage.

He told his father about the prospect of a year in Israel working with Sol. He remembered Sol's question, about whether he had Jewish ancestors, somewhere along the line.

'Yes' Inspector Gunn replied. 'Your grandma

275

on your Mum's side. She loved you, but you probably won't remember her; she died not long after your Mum and I went back to Paris. I've got some photos upstairs; I'll show you some time.'

'I really want to do it, Dad. But...'

His father considered this for a moment.

'If she's worth it, and it sounds to me as if she is, she'll wait for you,' he advised. 'But more immediately, this predicament you're in...you're right to get out for a while, let the dust settle. Get your head down for a few hours, then get on your way while the roads are quiet. I'll come and wake you.'

Inspector Gunn was as good as his word. Just before two, with some sandwiches in the glove compartment, a flask of coffee with a tot of whisky, and a whispered 'look after yourself, son,' Gunn was driving the Horch towards Lewes. The chalk cliffs shone white above the little town, a dramatic contrast against the night sky. There was a hunter's moon. The roads were clear.

He headed on towards Polegate and then took the back roads towards Herstmonceux and Battle, enjoying putting the Horch through its paces. He followed the narrow roads that ribboned across the green fields, through Westfield and Cock Marling, before leaving Rye in his wake. The Horch dropped down the spiral onto the Folkestone Road and onto the labyrinth of the Romney Marsh. He had heard it called the Fifth Continent. Its remoteness would suit him fine.

He pulled into St Mary in the Marsh, crossed the stone bridge and parked in the lee of the church, taking shelter beneath the weight of its ragstone tower. He turned the engine off and it ticked down and cooled. He was tired. He had fallen into a heavy sleep in his old room. It had been one hell of a day. The Horch was heavy on the concentration and his ribs were aching. He lay back, looking at the wild skies above and began counting stars. Soon, he fell into the deep sleep of the just and utterly spent. A cockerel woke him again - another of these sodding things, he thought, drifting back to the night in the inn at Bad Kaltenbrun. The rain was pattering against the windscreen. He looked at his watch. Still early; bags of time before he had to be in Dover.

He got out of the car and locked the door. The rain would pass soon enough. He needed to empty his mind and stretch his legs. He went inside the church to shelter for a moment. It smelt faintly damp. He studied the plaque to Edith Nesbit, 'who delighted the hearts of so many children by her books.' The Railway Children, that was the one; he still had his copy in Brighton.

After a swig of coffee and a sandwich, he drove on through the Marsh. The rain had stopped and he was enjoying the strange beauty of the landscape. He wasn't exactly sure where he was going; he was really following his nose. Apart from a flock of sheep and a tractor, there was nobody about. He remembered a poem they had made him learn at school about the rolling English drunkard making the rolling English road. The poet must have been here, he thought.

He sat by the canal for a while. Built to keep out Napoleon, the sign said. Gunn thought Napoleon would have made short work of it. There were a few people around now, so he inched the Horch up into the hills, coming to a stop by another Norman church with a pub opposite. Beside it was a sign:

'The highest Church and the lowest Steeple;
The richest Parish and the poorest People.'

Sylvia would love all this, he thought. The pub looked decent. It was just opening. A snifter and a bite to eat would be in order. He was in Battle of Britain country. He sipped his drink and reflected on his experiences with the people of Kent. They had always been somewhat contrary, awkward sometimes; independent-minded and even prepared to have a divide within the county. What was it, Man of Kent or Kentish Man? He could never remember which way round. Such things mattered though. They could certainly give Yorkshire folk a run for their brass farthing in the awkward stakes. His East End publican forebears originated from somewhere round here, he recalled, and were fiercely proud of that. He would ask Dad about that next time, he resolved, and decided to order something decent to eat, a proper ploughman's lunch.

The previous day had been quite surreal for Sylvia. She went with Louis and Edward to the Cannon Row police station, where the station clerk had made rather a meal of booking them in. They seemed to have to spell every second word for him. They were all interviewed separately. Sylvia was questioned by two rather obtuse sergeants, a male and a female. She explained briefly about Mr Jones, not going into too much detail (it was in the newspapers after all) and then described her meeting with George. They seemed to be satisfied with her account and the

278

way she answered all their questions. They let her out at the same time as Louis and he took her round the corner to the Two Chairmen to wait for Edward. They sat in a secluded alcove with a brandy each. They spoke frankly and at length about George and his affiliations, Jones's will and the lawyer in Haifa Marguerite had instructed. Cumberlands were of course still the administrators of the Jones family trust.

'In it up to his neck,' Louis said. 'Stupid, arrogant man. He had no regard for the fact that I speak German. Operation Crown Jewels indeed. But I fear there are more where he came from.'

Louis told her about the files that George had hidden at Junckers, and the cat that drank whisky from a saucer. Sylvia was fascinated. Louis shared her views and Gunn's about the British authorities. What was important now was for George to have a dignified send-off. That way, Edward and his mother (old hag, thought Sylvia viciously) could have some sort of peace and he and Edward could just carry on with Cumberlands. Louis suggested the files should be handed over to the Israelis as soon as possible, but they would probably be all right at Juncker's for now.

They returned to the police station an hour later, just as Edward was coming out. He looked exhausted; his hands were in his pockets and his hair flopping across his brow. The police had already been round to Queen Anne's Gate; what they had found seemed to coincide with everyone's recounting of events. He smiled, without much in the way of humour.

'I could do with a drink.' He paused and considered, flicking a pebble off the pavement and down into the gutter with the point of his shoe. 'Probably more than one.'

They went straight back to the Two Chairmen, in time for last orders, and then over to the Agrippa Club where they managed to get more drinks and some sandwiches. Nobody really felt like eating. While Louis was at the bar, Edward took Sylvia on one side.

'Sylvia, I am so sorry about forcing myself on you earlier. It was unforgiveable. I suppose I deserved that beating I got from your boyfriend.'

'Boyfriend.' Sylvia turned that word over in her mind.

'Be careful of him,' he warned. 'That's all I am going to say on the subject.'

After even more drinks for Edward and Louis and coffee for Sylvia, who simply could not keep up, they dropped her off at Mrs O's.

'You're living with him now?' Edward queried.

'No, I just have a room here,' she replied, amused despite herself. 'I couldn't stay at Tufnell Park any longer. But the landlady's locked me out. Help me up this drainpipe.'

Waving goodbye to Louis and Edward, Sylvia almost fell into Gunn's bed, draped his greatcoat over her and drifted off to sleep.

She was up early, wanting to be in the office before Kiwi and Joan, so that she could explain about the break-in and the forthcoming trip and sort out the wages and a few invoices.

Louis telephoned, as promised. Sylvia was concerned, and remained concerned, that Edward would go to pieces when confronted by his mother and retract his statement. Louis assured her that this was not the case so far; funeral arrangements were going ahead, with a small family service and cremation in a week's time and a memorial service to be arranged at a later date. An obituary had already been prepared for the papers.

Sylvia was at Victoria in good time for the boat train, scanning the menu outside the café and deciding against the unappetising fare on offer, opting for a simple cup of tea. She picked up her canvas holdall with her good arm and headed for the train.

Gunn was on the platform at Dover. Sylvia jumped off the train, straight into his arms.

'Missed you, sweetheart' he said, giving her a kiss. 'Come and have a look at our new motor.'

He took her hand and put her bag over his shoulder.

'Bloody hell, it's heavy. What have you got in there? The crown jewels?'

'In a manner of speaking,' she replied.

The Inspector at Cannon Row put down the telephone after a brief conversation with a colleague at Wapping. He had said something about this Cumberland fellow having hired a gang of thugs to beat someone up. It sounded as if they had come off worse. The Wapping Constabulary were, truth be told, quite relieved to have this gang out of commission; Garner in particular had been a nasty little thorn in their side for years. They wouldn't be taking any action their end. For his part, he had already received a note from the Home Office on Cumberland, stating 'no further investigation required on this matter.' Strange, but he had encountered stranger over his long career. Putting on his jacket, he headed for the underground and home.

Down at Wapping, Detective Inspector Collins let the receiver drop. It was late. He had missed dinner and would be in trouble with the missus. After a few moments consideration, he came to a decision. He would head down to the Prospect for a pie and a pint and get the lowdown on the Garner incident; no harm in having the full starting price on this one. Just in case. It was, after all, on his 'patch.'

Gunn watched as the Horch was lowered onto the car deck. It should be all right there, he thought. It had better be. He smiled at Sylvia.

'Come on, time for an exceptionally large snifter.'

The Channel was in one of its more capricious moods, which became apparent after the ferry cleared Dover's embracing sea wall. Gunn peered out of the brass ringed port hole close to their pew at the bar.

He took a sip of brandy and looked again.

'It may slow us down a little. Still, paws crossed, nobody is following on behind.'

'Excuse me a second,' said Sylvia, as if on cue. He found her outside, watching the sea rushing past. She took the handcuffs from her handbag, threw them in and watched them sink.

'I can't believe I walked into the bloody police station with these. Supposing I had been searched?'

'You'll get cold out here, come back in and tell me what happened. I felt awful, leaving you to sort all that out.'

Back in the bar, over a brandy, she told Gunn the whole story and about how she had, with Louis's help, convinced Edward that he had pulled the trigger but that it was a terrible accident. 'I think he'll stick with it,' she concluded. 'In a way, it was a relief for him.'

'What happened to your nose?' she asked.

'Oh, got into a scuffle with those lowlifes at the Prospect. I'd broken it before actually, playing rugby at school.'

'So what happened at the Prospect?' Sylvia asked. 'You did say you hadn't left many standing.'

'I certainly didn't. One or two won't be playing in the gang again. That's the way it goes. It was a decent scrap though.'

'My Beretta is now 'Exhibit whatever,' I suppose,' Sylvia said, sadly. 'Mind you, I dread to think what would have happened if I had had to fire it. It's been a while.'

'We can practice if you like; good idea to get your confidence back. But you were a star, sweetheart. All the same, I'd rather you left the dangerous stuff to me and Kiwi.'

'I'd love some practice.' She always enjoyed Gunn's training sessions. Most of them ended up in the pub. 'So what happens now? Where are we going?'

'Fleapit first,' he smiled. 'And then, well, over the next few days, wherever you want. I can show you round Paris. I'd like that. I reckon we should give

283

the Cumberlands time to bury their dead and for the dust to settle.'

'I might have to go shopping,' Sylvia considered. 'I haven't brought all that much in the way of clothes.'

'Boulevard Haussmann tomorrow then. I'm awash with cash at the moment.'

Sylvia decided not to enquire why. She had her suspicions. Despite the enormity of what they had done, she was feeling happier than she had done for some time. She settled luxuriously into the crook of his arm and watched France approaching. They seemed to be making up for lost time now. Gunn felt her relax against him.

'We'll be in Paris for dinner at this rate, sweetheart.'

Chapter 20

A casual salute from a tired gendarme at Calais and Gunn put the Horch into gear, pointed its nose towards Paris and swung onto the long straight Route 1 framed by Lombardy poplars. Sylvia thought about the story he had told her, about those poplars and Napoleon. It seemed a lifetime ago. They drove in companionable silence; they were at ease with each other and didn't have to fill gaps.

'Oh, incidentally, Sylv, I'm not sleeping on that buggering floor tonight at the fleapit. Bloody uncomfortable. I was camped out under the stars last night, absolutely frigging freezing. Woken at dawn by a chorus of sodding cockerels.'

Gunn's choice of language made her laugh. She had no intention of either of them being on the floor. However, his seduction techniques needed improvement. She smiled mischievously, suggesting they could toss a coin.

'I mean it, Sylv,' he grumbled.

'I can drive if you're tired,' she offered. 'I'd love a go with this beast.'

'I am absolutely not letting you loose on this gearbox.'

They went on in this vein, sparring happily as the Horch swallowed up the miles.

In Israel, Sol picked up the telephone. He leaned back, his one eye narrowed in thought as the fan swung overhead with little effect. It was on days like these that he missed the sharp cold of Warsaw in winter. He thanked the caller and put the receiver back on its handset. He got up, moved across the office and rapped sharply on his boss's desk.

'David, they're on the way to Paris. Just had a call from a friend in Calais.'

'Get on a flight, get yourself over to Paris. You need to bring them in close to us.'

'On my way.' Sol grinned, amused at the prospect.

Sylvia carried their bags up the steps to their room at the fleapit while Gunn went to find somewhere to park the Horch. La patronne was delighted to see her honeymooners back. Sylvia was in her element, settling back into that role. She ran herself a bath. Somebody had actually cleaned it in their absence. She had the window open onto an amazing view out over the rooftops and luxuriated in plenty of hot water, admiring herself in the mirror. She wasn't usually vain, but those days in Israel had done her a power of good.

She dressed carefully, in one of the only decent sets of lingerie she had and put on the red polka dot dress he had bought her in Naples. Gunn did a double take.

'I'll do you up at the back,' he said. Had the fleapit been a classier establishment, he would have ordered room service, but he had promised himself to do things properly this time. 'I've got somewhere in mind. It's not far.'

'Good, I can't remember when I last had something to eat.'

Hand in hand, they walked through the Marais to a brasserie Gunn knew in the Rue de la Bastille.

286

Sylvia looked in awe at the glass dome that spread over most of the dining room. As they sat on velvet banquettes, studying the menu, a bottle of champagne arrived at their table.

'From Monsieur and Madame over there,' the waiter gestured.

Their benefactors were a French couple celebrating their fiftieth anniversary. Somebody had bought them a bottle of champagne when they were on honeymoon. They had been looking for 'un joli couple,' so they could return the favour. Sylvia and Gunn chatted for a while, then thanked them and returned to their table. They only had eyes for each other. In years to come, when they talked about the evening, they would remember the champagne but not what they ate.

'You realise we'll have to do the same,' said Gunn. 'We'll be in our seventies. Imagine that.'

They considered this, contemplating what the Golden Wedding couple must have gone through, staying together and surviving two terrible European conflagrations. Neither of them could imagine living to that age. Both felt as if they had nine lives. They didn't keep count.

'And you, Miss Fordred,' said Gunn, leaning towards her 'haven't stopped smiling since we left Dover.'

Sylvia excused herself and returned a few minutes later. She handed him her knickers under the table.

'Your trophy, I believe, Captain Gunn.'

'I'll get the bill,' he said quietly.

Outside, he leaned her against a wall for a lingering kiss and, checking there was nobody about, a surreptitious feel.

'Fleapit, now' he managed to say.

They half ran through the streets, slipping over the cobbled stones. At the fleapit, she stopped on the final ascent, slipped his jacket off and undid his shirt. Pressing the light to keep it on, she leaned in for another kiss.

'Two can play at that game, madam,' was his response, deftly unzipping her dress. 'I think I might win though.'

At the top, he struggled with all the hooks on her bra.

'How am I supposed to undo this buggering thing?' he complained.

They fell through the door in a tangle of limbs. Gunn kicked it shut behind them. He scooped her up and carried her over to the bed, which was already sagging alarmingly in the middle. Paris had woven its spell around them, as she had woven her spell around countless couples in the past, and would do in the future.

Afterwards, she lay back in his arms. They shared a cigarette.

'Thank you,' she said shyly.

'For what?' he asked.

'For…showing me what all the fuss is about. I mean, Richard and I had so little time together. We only managed it a couple of times. I didn't quite realise it could be like this. I thought I was destined to be a dried up old bag like Aunt Hortense.'

'You're far too pretty for that, ma petite sirène. Not that I ever had the pleasure of meeting your aunt, but I can't imagine her in any of those positions. Or making all that noise,' he said, in reproving tones.

'Definitely not,' she replied. 'Talking about positions…where were we?' she said, climbing on top of him.

'You little minx.'

As they drifted off to sleep, he said:

'I love you, Sylv.'

She tightened her arms round him.

'I love you too.'

On the flight, Sol sat back with a couple of decent vodkas, reading through files various, thinking about where he might find them in Paris. The Horch would be easy to find; Gunn was unlikely to let it out of his sight. He would let them have a couple of days, he thought, and then engineer a chance meeting in a decent café somewhere in the Marais.

Gunn was up early, on the forage and prowl for cigarettes and coffee. Their clothes from the night before had been placed in a neat bundle outside their door. Sylvia's bra was on the top. Her knickers were still in his jacket pocket.

'Don't you dare lose them,' she had told him, on the way back from the restaurant.

'Bonjour, Madame,' he said politely to the femme de ménage on the way down. He felt as if he was walking on air. He had told Sylvia that he loved her. He had said this before to other women. This time, he meant it. She entranced him mentally, physically, emotionally and sexually. He had only ever come close to experiencing that combination once before. The difference was that Sylvia loved him, unconditionally.

On the way out of the tabac, he thought he saw Sol disappearing around a corner. He shook his head, and decided it was a figment of his imagination. What would he be doing in Paris? He went back up to their room with two coffees. Sylvia was asleep, lying on her stomach. He got undressed again and pulled the covers over them both.

'I got us some coffee, sweetheart,' he murmured, pulling her towards him. 'Drink it while it's hot.'

One thing led, inevitably, to another.

'Where did I learn what?' Gunn leaned back on the bolster, eyes closed, a smile ghosting about his lips, knowing full well what she meant.

'To do what you just did.'

'Ever read Proust's biography?' Gunn opened one eye. 'If you had, you would know that he had been sent by his father, as is traditional, to a courtesan, to learn how to pleasure a lady.'

'Really?'

'Yes.' Gunn closed his eye again and settled back into the bolster, wincing slightly. 'Bloody uncomfortable thing, this. Anyway, as I was saying, the same thing happened to me. All part of a rounded education.'

'How old were you?'

'Not sure it matters,' Gunn quickly tired of questions which he deemed irrelevant. 'But I was thirteen, I think.'

290

'That seems very young,' Sylvia was fascinated. 'But I don't have any complaints. In fact, would you mind just showing me again...'

They fell asleep again afterwards, wrapped around each other tightly. The Angelus bell from the church opposite woke them at midday. It sounded as if it was right outside their window.

'I've worked up an appetite,' said Gunn. 'Let's go and get a sandwich and then have a wander down the Boulevard Haussmann.'

Gunn absolutely drew the line at lingerie shops, and wandered off to get himself some new shirts. He caught up with Sylvia in a dress shop.

'I like the ones I zip you into and out of' he said, watching her trying a handful of them on.

They walked the streets of Paris for miles, hand in hand. She dragged him up to Montmartre, although he complained about 'every buggering cliché in the book' and 'this sodding great hill' and how there were much better places to go. She leaned in for a kiss on the steps of the Sacre Coeur, where they watched the sun go down.

'Back to the fleapit so I can show you my new lingerie?' asked Sylvia.

'Definitely. And next time, we're staying at the Georges V. You've broken the bed, Miss Fordred. We'll be on the bloody floor tonight at this rate, both of us.'

'We could go down to Chartrettes tomorrow,' she said, mischievously. 'You've got the key. We've signed all the documentation. What do you think?'

Gunn considered. 'Well, I did wonder if we should try anyone connected with Jones back in England. The whole thing seems slightly unsporting.'

'It does almost seem unprofessional,' Sylvia ventured 'Deriving a benefit from the investigation. There was only really that distant cousin of Jones's in Dorset but he died this summer, not long after Edward spoke to him. He was getting on, and he never had children. So, it looks as if it's ours. I spoke to Louis while you were away.'

'Oh well. It's obviously meant to be then. I'll believe it when I see it though. God knows how we are going to do it up.'

'Well, I can't quite believe it either,' Sylvia admitted. 'As for doing it up, we'll cross that bridge when we come to it. It might just be fun to go and have a look though. Now, if we do go down tomorrow, can I have a go at driving the Horch?'

'Out of the question.'

'Spoilsport. Right, back to the fleapit for that fashion parade.'

Not far from the fleapit, Sol was enjoying some late afternoon sunshine, a gentler heat than he was used to these days. He was ensconced with a beer at a café with zinc tables outside, engrossed in the London Daily Telegraph. Tucked away on the inside pages was a column detailing the death of George Cumberland, respected London solicitor and a rising star on the London legal circuit. His hands shook. They had done it. Cumberland was dead. This called for another beer.

In a military prison camp in Bavaria, Joachim Mecklenburg was pacing up and down in the exercise yard. He made no protest when a small group of men in American military police uniform grabbed him and manhandled him into a jeep. The young clerk on the front desk simply waved them through; he was busy reading a long letter from his girlfriend and barely listened to the explanation one of them gave to the effect that Mecklenburg was being taken for further questioning regarding his forthcoming trial.

Mecklenburg had been deputy Commandant at a small camp where Jewish prisoners had been set to work on making weapons. Many had starved. His senior officer had recently been convicted of war crimes and hanged. It had taken a while for them to catch up with him; being a man of slight build, he had 'hidden' in concentration camp uniform and been processed through a Displaced Persons Camp under a different identity. One of his fellow inmates had recognised him and let the authorities know about his previous incarnation.

'Thank God for that,' said Mecklenburg, when they were safely out of hearing. 'And thank you, gentlemen. Where are we going now? When do I leave for Argentina?'

'Not yet,' came the reply. 'There's been a slight hitch. Our man in London is dead and Mueller has disappeared.'

'What the...' began Mecklenburg. 'Who is running the show then?'

'Nobody yet. And that's a problem.' One of the fake police turned round to him. 'We're taking you to a safe house in Bavaria for a few days, until someone has replaced them.'

Mecklenburg had never been one to let things happen around him. He fell silent, uneasy about this so-called safe house. Still, it would be good to get out of these damn prison clothes and have a proper wash. Argentina could wait for a while.

Sol had found his way to a bar on the Rue Vielle du Temple which he had discovered many years ago. He always appreciated the curving zinc counter top. As he had once observed to a friend, it had more curves than Betty Grable.

He could not trust himself to sit still; he could not walk any distance. He needed another drink, something to aid his digestion. He ordered a whisky and then another. Both hit the spot. His attention was caught by Sylvia and Gunn, walking along holding hands, carrying shopping bags. They looked radiant, immersed in each other. His mind drifted back to Sarah. He remembered moments like that. He would give them another night. They deserved it, after what they had pulled off. He sat behind his paper, looking at Cumberland's obituary again.

At the fleapit, the fashion parade collapsed into disarray.

'Show me more of what that courtesan taught you,' urged Sylvia.

'Minx. Come on then.' He reached down to give her bottom a playful slap.

There was a little patch of sunlight which they were basking in, like two cats. They had given up with the bed and pulled the mattress onto the floor. Sylvia was listening to Gunn's stories of his childhood in Paris. Things had fallen to pieces when his mother died, and his father had hit the bottle, leaving Gunn to run wild. Eventually, his father came to his senses but had dealt with the situation by sending his son to a Jesuit establishment in the north of England.

'Imagine that, Sylv. I was thirteen. I missed my mum. I missed Paris. And it was brutal. I stayed for some exams. I should have stayed for more, but I ran away before they could expel me. I made a home run to Brighton though, on the train, dodging the ticket inspectors all the way. Dad's face when I turned up at the hotel was a picture.'

'I would have done the same, if I'd had anywhere to go,' Sylvia told him.

They agreed they weren't ever going to send their children away to school. Gunn, smoking a cigarette with Sylvia in the crook of his arm, decided that if this was loss of freedom, he rather liked it. He would have to broach the subject of Israel at some point but for now, he didn't care about anything except the girl beside him. Curling a strand of her hair round a finger, he fell into the deepest sleep he had had for a long time.

Sylvia gave him a gentle kiss and, as Gunn had taught her during one of their training sessions at the bunker, crept downstairs without making a sound. She rang Marguerite from the cabine téléphonique, to let her know they were going to Chartrettes. Marguerite was overjoyed that they were going. She called in at the pharmacie for some perfume and bath oil. On her way back with her purchases, she did a double take and stopped dead outside a café with zinc tables. Sliding into a seat, she enquired:

'To what do we owe this pleasure, Lieutenant Kalinsky?'

'Oh, a combination of business and pleasure,' Sol responded. 'Always a pleasure to do business in Paris with two friends.'

He looked over at the girl in the green dress, and thought, not for the first time, that Gunn was a lucky sod. The pair of them must have been at it nonstop. Something had put that smile on her face, anyway.

'You and I both know that isn't why you are here. Come on,' she leaned forward. 'Tell me what you have planned for Gunn in Israel.'

He stiffened. This wasn't what he had expected. He motioned the garçon over and ordered her a whisky and another for himself.

'It's all right,' she told him, giving him a captivating smile, which was meant to be reassuring. He found it anything but. 'We haven't discussed it yet. But I know. I heard Lev and Aaron talking one night. The thing is, if I'm going to lose him for the best part of a year, I want assurance he is getting the best deal possible. It does affect me. I'm his business partner. And Sol, I love him. I want to understand something of what he is getting himself into. I'm sure you can understand that.'

She took a sip of whisky and gave him one of her level glances.

Sol shrugged.

'Well, he has sympathy for Israel and he and I work together well. We need good men and women on our side. Gunn is someone we need. He will be well paid. Not that he is that motivated by money.'

Sylvia gave him another level glance. He hadn't really answered her question. That was Sol all over. It would test her to her limits, but she recognised she had to let Gunn do this. She decided to try another question, remarking:

'It's no coincidence that you are here, is it?'

Despite the amount of beer and whisky he had already imbibed, Sol recognised Sylvia was not going to be fobbed off. He sighed.

'All right. We heard about the death of Cumberland and although we are certain the pipeline will recruit new 'engineers' to keep it going, Cumberland being removed from the game is highly satisfactory.' His tone was level and neutral. 'Others will require a similar fate. We know that someone like Gunn is an asset we need on board as a matter of urgency.'

'And you came all the way here to tell us that,' Sylvia observed. 'By the way, I managed Cumberland's exit myself. Gunn was unavoidably detained.' She filled him in on the details.

'Impressive,' he remarked. He was genuinely impressed.

'I'm assuming you want to take Gunn back with you to Israel,' Sylvia continued. 'Can you give us another week together, to let the dust settle back in London? We'll have a lot to discuss if I'm to run the business on my own for a year. And we need to check over our house in Chartrettes.'

She gave him another of her looks. Sol was, in spite of himself, captivated. Against his better judgment, he agreed on a compromise. He had some family members who had settled back in Paris to look up. He could spin David out for a few more days.

'I will give you until Wednesday,' he said. 'Then I want you both back here for one o'clock for lunch'

Sylvia went round to his side of the table and gave him a hug. 'You don't know what this means to me,' she said. He shook his head as he watched her running back towards the hotel.

In Cairo, while Alaikum was out shopping, Otto was reading the London Daily Telegraph. He liked to try his hand at the crosswords; often fiendish but they helped keep his mind razor sharp. Today his attention was caught by a small paragraph about the death of their new London client, the German solicitor. Mueller's subscription had also just been cancelled earlier that day, without so much as a by your leave, by his bank. He tapped his pen against the desk. There was a connection somewhere and he needed to find it

Chapter 21

Dieter Fischer perched on a sofa in what he took to be the salon of a hunting lodge in Bavaria. The walls were heavily panelled and trophies were mounted at various points along the walls. A set of 1923 Purdey Hammer guns crossed barrels over the mantelpiece. The young lawyer sipped his brandy and awaited developments in surroundings he imagined Goering would have approved of. Originally from the Sudetenland, he thought to himself how much he still had a lot to learn about this part of the world.

A door opened, with a slight creak of protest. Fischer set his drink down and stood up, shooting his cuffs as he did so. He turned and faced a tall, saturnine man of middle years, of military bearing, hair cut high above the ears in the Prussian manner. His suit was sharply cut, expensive and his shoes were handmade, Fischer assumed, in London. The handshake was brief and hard.

'I am Major Ernst Wirth, late of the Ahnenerbe, dealing with the origins of the German people. Now,' Wirth's expression softened a little, 'I am a humble curator of a two-bit museum out in the forests.'

In Wapping, Inspector Collins reached for his coat. It had been another long night in the Prospect, and he would have some grovelling to do with his missus. He had finally got hold of that little shit, Mendelson, and got some sense out of him. It seemed, (Mendelson was hazy on the details because Garner had always operated on a 'need to know' basis), that a

West End law firm had indeed commissioned the gang to take out a guy called Gunn, a private investigator. Gunn had apparently set Trip on fire (nice touch, Collins thought) and then turned the tables on them, taking out several gang members, including Garner, and giving the others a severe beating.

Mark Gunn. He chewed the name over a few times. Years ago, before World War 1, when he was a police constable, he had worked in Paddington with a Dominic Gunn. He remembered him well. Good bloke. Might have liked the odd tipple but he was a damn good policeman. When he returned from war service, Dominic had a French wife in tow. He did recall a little boy called Mark. They had lost touch when Dom went to Paris to do diplomatic protection work. Didn't someone say something about a hotel in Brighton? He filed the information on the fight away in his prodigious memory, deciding on balance Wapping was probably safer without Garner and his ilk.

'I still can't believe this is happening,' Gunn remarked, parking the Horch outside the mairie in Chartrettes. The old men were still playing pétanque under the plane trees. 'This lot don't seem to have moved since the day we found poor old Jones.'

'I don't suppose they have. And I can't believe it either,' Sylvia replied. 'Let's see what the Mayor has to say. You'd better do the honours.'

The Mayor was intrigued to meet the young couple who had discovered Monsieur Jones. He had always had a high regard for the old chap. It had been a sad business about his wife, he agreed. Gunn could tell straightaway that the Mayor had 'looked the other way' and had it on his conscience. He liked to play the patriotic Frenchman. Well, he had met plenty like that. He would play this to his advantage. Make him squirm.

'So you're telling me that Mrs Jones's sister has signed the house over to you.'

He pursed his lips.

'Yes' said Gunn.

'Most irregular,' commented the Mayor.

Gunn fixed him with a thoughtful stare.

'The way Mrs Jones was treated, and the way her sister and her husband were treated,' Gunn observed 'almost make me ashamed to be a Frenchman. And how some people have the audacity to present themselves in the public eye,' he added softly 'Well, it beggars belief.' There was an uncomfortable pause.

Finally, the Mayor sighed and said 'Go and see Monsieur Ricard. He's our local notaire. He's only in the next village. I will telephone him now, and he will prepare some documentation for you to sign. That's all we'll need for now. Welcome to Chartrettes.'

They soon found their way to Maître Ricard's office, where the paperwork was signed in triplicate. Ricard was almost overwhelmingly helpful, explaining that they now had a licence to occupy the demeure pending the grant of probate.

'It's really happening.'

Sylvia was dancing on air. Gunn was enjoying being back behind the wheel of the Horch and looking forward to a night in a decent bed. He reached over and stroked Sylvia's thigh.

'Gunn,' she went on, thoughtfully. 'Guess who I ran into last night, at that bar round the corner?'

'No idea.'

'Sol.'

'What the hell is Sol doing in France? Didn't he want to speak to me?' Gunn frowned.

'I'm not sure, he wouldn't say. He has some family in Paris he wants to look up. We're to meet him on Wednesday for lunch'

'So, why didn't you come and wake me?' asked Gunn, suspiciously.

'You were tired, darling. And he was as drunk as a lord. Anyway, as I said, we're meeting him on Wednesday. So that gives us a good few days in Chartrettes. I reckon we'll need them.'

'And you didn't think to mention Sol this morning?'

'Oh, we had other things to do this morning,' Sylvia replied. She blushed faintly at the memory. 'I'd imagine he'll want you to go straight back to Israel with him,' she added sadly. 'He didn't tell me much, but I reckon you've got a lot of work to do out there.'

'I'm not sure about this' said Gunn. 'I don't want to lose you, Sylv. I've only just found you.'

'You won't lose me. I'll be in London, running the business. I'll wait for you, you know that.' She tried to brush away a tear, hoping he wouldn't notice. He did.

'We'll talk it over when we get to the house,' he said gently. 'Not too much further to go now. Been quite a caper across the countryside this morning.'

'Can I drive?' Sylvia asked hopefully, trying to change the subject.

'Out of the question. I need a cigarette though, after all that. Don't know about you? Shall I pull in here for a moment?'

They leant against the bonnet, smoking. A long way down, sparkling silver, the river ran past. The Horch was parked on the bluff, screened by trees.

'You, Miss Fordred, are an incredibly naughty girl,' Gunn told her, reprovingly. 'You just wanted an extra few days with me, didn't you? And you got me down here so that we could secure the house. I can read you like a book. Go on, admit it.'

'Certainly not,' she replied primly, trying to sound like the consummate professional. The smile gave her away. 'We have a lot of business to discuss. And yes, of course, we do have our new property to look at.'

For answer, Gunn bent her over the cooling bonnet of the Horch. Her cheek was pressed against the cooling metal and she could sense the ticking down of the engine. He ran his fingers down her back, down her bottom and up under the hem of her dress. He flicked her dress up, to expose her stockings and knickers. He softly stroked her flesh where it met the material of her stockings. He could tell from her response that she enjoyed that, so he continued up her legs, slowly, gently, with an increase in pressure as he did so, drawing an even more fervent response. He reached her knickers and simply pulled them down.

303

He unbuckled his belt, and began to stroke her with the shaft and head of his erection. He waited as she wiggled, and he knew, and he entered her hard and fast. His thighs were pressed up against her buttocks and he drove in deep, his shaft wrapped by her. He paused and withdrew. She bit her lip in frustration and then exhaled as he drove in again. Each thrust lifted her higher up on the bonnet of the car. She gripped, her nails flaking against the metal as Gunn fucked her in a way she had never experienced before. It was primal and raw, as was her orgasm. Still, he did not stop, bringing her back and taking her over and over again. A long time afterwards, they lay lazily in the sun, on Elise's picnic rugs.

'I can't move' said Sylvia. 'I'm still shaking, look.'

'You did want to know what else I had learned with the courtesan,' Gunn pointed out, reasonably.

Sylvia closed her eyes. He propped himself up on one elbow and looked at her. He found it difficult to take his eyes off her; a few more images to keep in his heart now, he thought.

'Well, madam,' he said eventually. 'I could lie here with you all day, but shall we go and have a look at our house? We can always carry on where we left off.'

'I'd like that,' she murmured.

They stopped at the next village for provisions and were soon driving through the gates of the demeure. Someone had done a good job of tidying up downstairs. They found Jones's cocktail cabinet, got

304

out two glasses and poured themselves a glass of wine each, to carry round on their tour.

'We could make love in each room,' suggested Sylvia.

'Better start soon then,' Gunn replied.

He was already looking round with a trained eye. After he ran away from school, his father had resigned himself to the fact that, despite entreaties, blandishments and eventually a damn good clout, Gunn was never going back.

'Fucking well make yourself useful then,' he had told him, and had set him to work on the Gunn House Hotel. Gunn had learned fast, that year before the war. He had been glad to join up straightaway, but all the same, it had been useful experience. For a house of its age, he had to admit it was in surprisingly good nick inside. There didn't seem to be any damp. The roof would need some attention, as would some of the masonry outside, but there was nothing pressing. For now, the house just needed painting and airing. He went down to the cellar and turned the electricity and water back on, checking over the wines in the wine rack carefully - something else his father had taught him.

'Up and running, sweetheart,' he called. Sylvia was already on the top floor.

'I've found our room,' she called. It was huge, made more so by the fact that it just contained a double bed, a washstand and a dressing table. Most importantly of all, it had a fireplace with a blue and white tiled surround.

Gunn came up behind her and kissed the back of her neck.

'Do you reckon it was Jonathan and Louise's?' he asked.

'No, I think they were down the corridor.' She noted a small room off this one, with a wardrobe in it.

'I'll make the bed up,' she called, already off down the corridor to Louise's linen cupboard. She came back with an armful of sheets, still faintly scented with lavender.

'I was just thinking of Le Grand Meaulnes again. Have you read it?'

'Alain Fournier. Yes, I have. Only wrote one book. Got killed in the woods near Verdun, not long after the Great War started. Poor bastard.'

'I've always wanted a house like this.' Sylvia explained how daydreams like that had sustained her through the winter in Tufnell Park and Christmas on her own.

'Well, now you've got one. And you're not having Christmas on your own again, ever. 'He smiled down at her. 'It's just, well, there's nothing major structurally wrong that I can see, and I love it, but houses like this don't maintain themselves.'

'We could get a tenant,' she suggested. 'While you're in Israel. And don't forget I come into my trust fund in a couple of years. I haven't a clue how much that is, mind. After George attacked me that first time, I never asked. Anyway, the business is doing well, isn't it?'

'Brilliantly. You're a clever girl, sweetheart. You could ask Louis about the trust, next time you see him,' Gunn said. 'Wonder how all that's going, back in London?'

In the drawing room at Chepstow Villas, Edward was aghast and lost for words. Caroline sat lumpenly opposite him, fiddling nervously with her engagement ring.

'For Christ's sake, Caroline,' he said eventually. 'What a time to tell me.' His head was all over the place. Thankfully, Mummy was upstairs nursing a migraine. They had just returned from the crematorium. It had gone off reasonably well. Louis had been an absolute brick, getting George's body released and making all the arrangements. His mother had of course questioned the cremation, as they were a Catholic family. He himself had no particular views on the matter. He suggested to his mother that he could in due course scatter George's ashes at the estate in Bad Kaltenbrun and erect a small memorial.

'How far along are you?'

'A couple of months,' she replied. He groaned. With creeping horror, he recalled the occasion. He had been rather drunk at a tennis club party and she had lured him into the bushes. He had sobered up quickly but too late.

'What's the matter, Eddy?' she asked. Edward scowled. He hated being called Eddy. 'Don't you love me?'

'Love?' he echoed. 'There is only one girl I have ever loved. You don't even hold a candle to her. And you never will.' He was going to say something a lot more brutal but Caroline burst into noisy tears at this point.

'That's it, turn on the waterworks,' thought Edward sullenly. Mummy appeared as if on cue. Caroline told her the situation and what Edward had said. He would be in trouble later. He didn't give a damn. He thought to himself randomly that no matter how vile he had been to Sylvia when they were growing up, he had never managed to make her cry

'I expect he is a bit upset, dear' said Mrs Cumberland. 'It's been quite a day. But you can bring the wedding forward, can't you?' She glared at her son. Leaving them to make plans, Edward made an excuse and went back to the office. It was the first time he had been there since that fateful afternoon. Mechanically, he began to go through the post. He was quite looking forward to getting back to work.

New conveyancing instructions were arriving. It would be good not to have his father breathing down his neck. A thick envelope with a Cairo postmark lay on the desk, addressed to George Cumberland. He settled down with a cup of tea to read it but soon put it aside. It was full of gossip about the Middle East. He couldn't make head or tail of it or see the relevance. He would ask Louis; he could perhaps shed a little light on any contacts in Egypt. He did recall his father alluding to a trip there once; the usual see the sights and patronise the locals type of thing. He sat back in his chair, wondering not for the first time why he, an RAF veteran, was so malleable when it came to his family. It was embarrassing. His old comrades would have been ribbing him until daylight. Now he was trapped, good and proper. He shuddered at the thought. Maybe he would make that trip to Germany after all. Apart from one or two trips as a child, he had only ever seen his father's homeland from a great height. As far as he knew, they still owned Bad Kaltenbrun. That would have to be sorted out, somehow. He reached into his father's cabinet and took out a file containing his late grandparents' wills.

'*Shukran*' said Otto, absently, handing a few coins to the boy from the bank. It was a scorching hot day. He would love to have gone home for a siesta. Another large bank draft had arrived from Israel. More specific instructions would follow.

'Something big is about to happen,' said Alaikum pensively. 'Not that I feel like rocking the boat with all this money coming in. Did you find out about Mueller?

'Suicide,' said Otto briefly. 'Or so it said in the papers. Don't believe a word of it.'

'Well, I suppose that explains why he stopped subscribing to our briefings. Someone else will take the reins though, and whoever it is will have to pay us an awful lot.'

At the restaurant at the Meerjungfrausee, Dieter Fischer sat with his weissbier, looking over his notes. He had relished the hike up to the lake, in gentle autumn sunshine, starting at the crack of dawn.

It reminded him of his early days in the army, before he was sent to the Eastern front. He had been so young; too young for all that. Dieter had read the brief notice in the *SuddeutscheZeitung*, about Dr Friedrich Mueller and his unfortunate suicide at the Meerjungfrausee. It had paid tribute to his distinguished medical career, and made mention of his wife, Elise and their four children. None of them were available for comment at the time of going to press and attempts at contacting Elise had proved fruitless. She was not at the family home in Bad Kaltenbrun. Nobody knew her whereabouts. He would describe the responses of those he had spoken to as 'polite but guarded.' Hans at their little country retreat had been equally guarded. Dieter thought he was almost trying to play the role of village idiot too well.

'Gruss Gott!' said the landlord, appearing in front of him with another weissbier and some snacks. 'I believe you wanted a word, Herr Fischer.'

The two men spoke at length. It seemed that Mueller had come up to the cottage with his wife but she had left alone. That was when he must have killed himself. No, he hadn't seen anybody else around, just the two of them. Yes, they always kept to themselves, on that side of the lake. It was known locally that they had 'strange predilections.' Would Herr Fischer like to borrow one of the boats and go and look at the cottage?

Dieter rowed himself across, thoughtfully; the key in his pocket. It had rained in recent days. The makeshift gibbet was still there, but there was not a lot else to be seen. The police had shown him the suicide note. The writing was terrible, but weren't doctors renowned for having poor handwriting? The landlord had mentioned that the couple had a Horch; Frau Mueller wasn't very keen on the walk these days, it played havoc with her knees on the way down. No sign of a car here, Dieter thought, peering into the ramshackle garage. He rowed back, took his leave and started the hike downhill. Something else troubled him. He had read about Mueller's recent exoneration. There was no reason, surely, why the man should have been driven to despair, unless his past had caught up with him. Yet the police had found no evidence of foul play. Perhaps then the death, only days later, of this English solicitor was mere coincidence. There was clearly a lot more to this assignment than met the eye. It could be highly lucrative, but he was under no illusions about what the future held.

Relegated again to the uncomfortable sofa in his Victorian semi overlooking Wanstead Flats, Inspector Collins had slept fitfully. He and the trouble and strife had been married far too long, he mused. In his pocket, he had a chitty for a trip to the seaside, and he wasn't planning on taking the miserable old cow. Time to look up an old friend, he thought. In no time at all, he was alighting at Brighton, raincoat slung over his shoulder. The sea air tasted good, salty and brisk. He coughed. Wapping was deep in his lungs. As a rule, he wasn't a man for leaving London, but there was no harm in bending the rules occasionally. He headed straight for the taxi rank, seeking an older driver, one not averse to a few shillings and imparting information and he was soon outside the Gunn House Hotel. Needed a lick of paint, he thought, but a nice place. Dom had done well for himself. He'd probably be in the bar, knowing him. He carried on up the steps, intrigued to find out what Dom's young lad was doing on his 'manor.'

At the demeure, Sylvia had made spaghetti bolognese. They had dressed for dinner and had eaten in the dining room, overlooking the garden; the table

311

set with Jonathan and Louise's glassware and cutlery. Marguerite had told her on the telephone that the contents were theirs. Mueller's thugs had emptied the house of much that was valuable but they had missed a few things and Sylvia was enjoying 'pla1ying house.'

'This is one of the few things I know how to cook' she told him after the meal, washed down with a decent red from the cellar. She drew the heavy brocade curtains across.

'Never thought you were just a pretty face, Sylv,' he replied, unzipping her dress.
'You know the way to my heart anyway.'

Gunn was in a playful mood at the end of what, in years to come, they would   remember as a magical day. He had brought some champagne up from the cellar, which they
were drinking out of cut glass champagne saucers.

'It's not vintage,' he said. 'Won't keep forever. Needs drinking.'

'These are beautiful.' Sylvia ran a finger along the rim of her glass. Aunt Hortense had glasses of a similar pattern, locked away in a dusty cupboard. She looked at him.

'What's the matter, darling?'

'Just got a feeling, that's all. Something is brewing.'

'Do you often get feelings like that?'

'No, only when someone is making some kind of trouble.' Gunn was serious. 'Someone is stepping where they shouldn't.'

'Tell you what,' he added, zipping her back into her dress. 'We'll call Sol. He gave you the

312

number of where he was staying, didn't he? If I'm wrong, all well and good; best to be prepared though.'

'I'll come with you. We'll call him from the bar Jones used to go to. I fancy a walk.'

At the bar, Sylvia sipped a glass of wine while Gunn spoke to Sol. She thought about Jonathan and his daily visit here, with his newspaper. She wondered if the same people were running it.

Sol confirmed that the pipeline was operating; there had been an escape from an American prison camp in Bavaria a few days ago. There didn't seem to be an immediate link to them; at the moment the focus seemed to be on getting assets out. But Gunn was right in his suppositions; it was only a matter of time before the connection was made.

'They'll use someone reasonably smart, I think. Maybe someone young. You're all right for now, though,' he confirmed. 'They'll be some way behind; they'll have other fish to fry for now. Give me the address of the demeure, just in case. And I'll see you both on Wednesday. And you had better be fit for work. Give my regards to Sylvia. Lucky bastard.'

They walked back, hand in hand. Sylvia perched on the sofa with her champagne glass, bathed in soft lamplight.

'I'm glad we rang him,' she ventured.

'I am too, sweetheart,' he said. She didn't ever complain, he thought to himself. One of the reasons he loved her to distraction. 'Now, where were we?'

313

Sol set down the receiver and considered, and then went and stood at the entrance to the hotel. He lit a cigarette and watched the demi monde of the quartier wander past on their business of the night. He smiled to himself and murmured: 'the children of the night, how sweetly do they sing.'

He crushed the cigarette under his heel and went for a walk. His old injury ached. Fresh air and a clearing head seemed to be the only cure. Weighing up the logic, it seemed wise to assume that someone was taking Mueller's place or at least being primed to do so. He had read other articles about Mueller's suicide and distinguished medical career. His face darkened. Today, he had visited his aunt and uncle. They had settled back in the Marais, although he was trying to persuade them to come out to Israel. They had been lucky to survive. The stories they had told him were all too familiar. It would be good to have Gunn on board.

At the Gunn House Hotel, Inspector Gunn put another pint carefully down in front of his old colleague. They had been happily reminiscing about their days on the beat on the streets of Paddington in the twenties. Both could have written a book.

'Been a while,' he remarked. 'A lot of water under the bridge.'

'Certainly has,' Collins responded. 'So what happened to the nippers? And Annette?'

'We lost Genevieve, back in Paris. She was five. Complications from measles. Annette never got over it. That's why she wanted to go for another baby.

314

Not a good idea at her age. Lost the baby and it killed her.'

'Sorry to hear that, Dom.' Collins paused. 'What about Mark?'

'You've got a good memory,' Inspector Gunn narrowed his eyes. 'Mark's a partner in a firm of enquiry agents in the West End. Doing well for himself. Saw him the other day.'

His instincts were kicking in, fast. Why would a serving police officer come all the way to Brighton, just to look him up? It had to be something to do with what Mark and this girl had got themselves into. Mark had said he was picking her up off the boat train. He hoped they were somewhere safe. Something had changed in Mark; he seemed happy and at peace with himself for the first time in years. He was glad about that. Well, Collins was going to be disappointed. He would get nothing out of him.

'Whatever happened,' he asked, selecting a bottle of whisky from behind the bar and steering the conversation into less controversial waters 'to DCI Crawford? He was a tartar, wasn't he? Had us working day and night.'

At the demeure, Sylvia wandered back into the bedroom and slid under the sheets. Gunn was sitting up in bed, reading something. She saw, to her horror, that it was her notebook. She dived for it, but he was too quick.

'No you don't, madam,' he told her firmly, grinning broadly. 'Don't even think about it.'

Sylvia was never one to turn down a challenge.

'Why didn't we get together before, Sylv?' he asked afterwards, holding her close.

'I didn't know you thought about me in that way.'

'For such a clever girl, you are remarkably unobservant sometimes. Mind you, first time I saw you, in the bookshop in Charing Cross Road, you were miles away. Took you ages to look up and notice me. You were going from shelf to shelf, looking for books.'

'Poetry, if I recall correctly' she said. 'We were both fragile. Probably just as well, we'd never have built the business up to this level. We're together now, darling. Nothing else matters.'

'Sylv, you know I won't go to Israel if you don't want me to,' he began.

'You've got to go, Gunn. I hate the thought of being without you. I'll get myself a calendar and cross the days off. But I think the contacts you're going to make are going to be great for us. They'll fit in with the long-term plans I was going to tell you about.'

'Oh yes, I was reading about those,' he smiled. 'I like what you've written. We'll work on all of it when I'm back. Let's see what Sol has to say when we meet him.'

Chapter 22

Dieter Fischer was cooling his heels in the Botanical Gardens just outside Munich, waiting for his appointment. It was quiet here on a week day; he supposed that was why this location had been chosen. He had discovered it himself soon after his arrival in the city. He had a lot of work to get on with in the office. Hopefully, Wirth would not be too much longer. As he studied a display of Alpine plants, Wirth appeared, dressed with expensive discretion. Once again, Dieter could not help wondering how the curator of a small country museum could afford such style, something out of his reach even as a lawyer. Wirth shook his hand, taking in his appraisal.

'Oh, I have other means which permit this little indulgence.' He indicated a small café down the path. 'Shall we adjourn in there? We have some significant matters to discuss.'

Wirth ordered them a coffee each, noting the little flirtation between the young lawyer, who was clearly not unaware of his attractiveness to women, and the waitress. 'I was the same at his age,' he thought, indulgently. He studied Dieter, observing the blonde hair and blue eyes. Good. He noted that Dieter's smile met his eyes. 'Wears his heart on his sleeve, this one; he's young, he'll learn. It's what is inside his head that matters.'

To Dieter's surprise, Wirth opened with a personal line of questioning.

'Tell me about your early life, your family. You are from the Sudetenland, yes?'

Somebody has done his research, thought Dieter. He probably already knows what I am going to say. He confirmed that he was born in a small village there in 1924. His parents ran a hotel. He was the youngest of three boys. His brothers and his father had ended up on the eastern front. He was the only one to survive. His mother had been thrown out of the area in 1945, where her family had lived for generations. A shadow crossed over his face. An old neighbour had told him that all their belongings had been loaded onto a cart. She seemed to have lost the will to live, with her husband and two of the boys gone and Dieter's whereabouts unknown. She had died while they were travelling through the forests.

'I don't suppose she even knew where she was going,' he told Wirth.

'A crime against humanity,' Wirth put in, sympathetically. 'And your family lost everything they had worked for.'

Dieter did not respond. He had been a member of Hitler Youth; he still remembered the excitement in 1938, when the Fuhrer had visited their town. Then he had joined the army. At the time when his mother had been cast out of their home town, he had been living in a cellar in a bombed-out house in Berlin with some other youngsters. The Red Army was outside the city. Bombs were falling everywhere. Their orders were to fight to the death.

He was still surprised today that he had survived. By some fluke, he had made his way to Munich and enrolled at the university to study Law. He preferred to draw a veil over his earlier years, he told Wirth, and look to the future. It was easier that way.

318

'Ah, my young friend, don't be so quick to draw a veil over such times when, with people such as I...' Wirth opened the door to his world. 'We have much in common and much to rebuild and fight for, by quiet means if necessary.'

Dieter was not convinced about what he and Wirth could have in common, but he was not that scrupulous. He came from a deeply religious background and did sometimes think back to the simple truths of his childhood. But a commission was a commission. For now, he would listen carefully and divulge as little as possible. Wirth would expect that of a lawyer.

In the bar in Chartrettes, Sylvia and Gunn had been talking over their plans for Clements. Attempts at their usual weekly briefing meeting had collapsed, back at the demeure.

'Good thing we're not on our own in the office any more,' said Sylvia.

'Yes, I'd be taking you across the desk all the time. The accountants downstairs would have something to say, I'm sure. Anyway, about staff...I think you're right. We need to bring Kiwi on board full time. I'll ring him. I don't think he has any plans to go back to New Zealand. I'd feel happier if he was around more.'

'Ask him if he's done that report for Vera yet. Just go through it with him; I'm sure it will be fine. Joan's very good. I had a look at the ledgers the other day. With all this work coming in, do we need to recruit? I mean we'd probably have to lease the middle floor as well.'

'You'll have to be the judge of that, sweetheart,' said Gunn.

His sixth sense was troubling him again. He worried about Sylvia on her own back in London, although it would be reassuring to have Kiwi in place. The report for Vera sounded fine, he told Kiwi to send it off with the invoice. He rang his father after he'd spoken to Kiwi, to tell him he and Sylvia were in their new house in France, (he couldn't resist that) and that he would be off to Israel soon.

'I'm glad about that, son,' came the response. That car and now a house; you had to hand it to the boy, he was ambitious. 'Got an old pal from my police days propping up the bar right now, asking about you. He's based in Wapping now. Inspector Collins.'

'Don't worry,' Inspector Gunn continued. 'He'll get nothing out of me. We go back a long way, when I was in Paddington and you were knee high to a grasshopper. What's that young lady of yours going to do now? Lie low for a while?'

'Everything all right?' Sylvia asked, as Gunn came back over, looking thoughtful.

'Everything's fine, sweetheart,' he said, with a smile. 'Sylv, if you need anything, you know, while I'm away, you can always talk to my Dad. I've told him about us.'

Dad was right, thought Gunn. Israel was the safer option for him. He was pretty sure that this Collins chap was simply marking Dad's card for old time's sake. That was decent of him but also carried weight and intent. He reached across the table for a cigarette. That tasted good, he considered and shrugged. There would be some good tobacco in Israel at least. Sol would see to that.

Sylvia was his main concern now. They were secure in their love for each other; separation would not be an issue. They were both used to that. But he needed to put a structure around her, to keep her safe. He thought about how calm and content she had been, since they left Dover. That was what he wanted for her. He took her hand.

'Let's go home. Do some more exploring.'

In the Botanical Gardens, Wirth leaned across the table towards Dieter, checking first that nobody was listening. Dieter noticed for the first time the duelling scars on his face.

'Can I take it then that you are interested in helping with our work?'

'If the price is right,' responded Dieter. He wondered whether Wirth was a little disappointed by his answer. His own feelings towards his country's past were ambivalent; he had no particular axe to grind. He was young, ambitious and his eye was to the future. He could see that from Wirth's perspective, this ambivalence could be an advantage. Nobody would be looking for somebody like him as a pipeline engineer.

'Come to the hunting lodge tomorrow,' Wirth said. 'There are a few people I would like you to meet.'

In Cairo, Alaikum stood at the office window, watching the faithful make their way to the mosque for lunchtime prayer.

'Who's this new client then?' he asked Otto. 'Yet another of your lot?

'Chap by the name of Ernst Wirth,' replied Otto. 'A museum curator in Bavaria apparently. What the hell would a museum curator want with our services? I'm sure I recognise that name. I'll ask around.'

'Stick him on the generic list for now,' advised Alaikum. 'Usual guff. See if you can find anything out about him. Someone will remember something. Now, how about a spot of lunch, old chap, and then a siesta?'

Sylvia and Gunn had made their way through the orchard, helping themselves to perfectly ripe greengages and plums, to the lake. After a glorious swim, they were sunning themselves on what they were already describing as 'their beach.' They recognised it straightaway from Jonathan's private photo collection of Louise.

'Now, this is what worries me slightly, Sylv. Gunn gestured towards a long, low branch. 'All this buggering vegetation. The roof is one thing, and the painting inside, but how will we cope with all these trees? And a lake as well. I mean...'

Sylvia was sitting astride him.

'Don't worry about that, darling.' She leaned forward to give him a kiss. 'I already told you, we'll get a tenant and then all that will be up to them while we are away. I can manage a few fruit trees. Aunt Hortense used to make me do the garden. I'll take care of everything, I promise. You concentrate on coming home safely and making lots of money for us.

Anyway,' she added. 'Mermaids need water. The lake will look after itself.'

'You,' Gunn sighed, 'are such a little minx.'

Back at the house, Gunn had started jotting down some questions to run through with Sol. He hadn't particularly thought about the financial side of the assignment in Israel; she was quite right to raise it. His attention was caught by Sylvia wearing nothing but a pair of knickers, making greengage jam. She had found a preserving pan in the scullery, some jars and a bag of sugar.

'Needs using up,' she explained. 'The wasps will eat all the fruit otherwise. Seems a terrible waste. I love making jam. It's therapeutic.'

'I don't want today to end,' he told her, drawing her onto his lap, when the jam had set and was inside the jars.

'We've still got lots of today left,' she pointed out. 'And more exploring to do.'

At an establishment in Berlin, known to cognoscenti simply as 'Trudl's,' Elise had just finished servicing a client, helping him to explore his darkest fantasies. She was already proving to be a great asset to her friend's team. Business was brisk, despite the blockade. Venereal disease was rife in the aftermath of the war, after various armies had swept through. Trudl's had a reputation for being scrupulously clean. It had been a particularly energetic session. She had already been through three riding crops; maybe they needed a new charging structure. After a shower, she went downstairs to the bar, for a cigarette and a break before her next appointment.

Her attention was caught by a conversation between two American servicemen. They paid no heed to her; few people realised how fluent her English was. They were talking about Joachim Mecklenburg, who had been 'sprung' a few days ago from a military prison in the American zone. Elise knew Mecklenburg; he had been a friend of Friedrich's. If he had been sprung within the last few days, somebody must already have taken up the reins at the pipeline. She knew Lothar, or Cumberland or whatever he called himself now was dead; she still kept in touch with Hans at Bad Kaltenbrun. She had read the obituary. She had never liked him; his family had always treated Friedrich like some sort of poor relation. She had always suspected that that was exactly what he was without the 'poor' part, though that was thanks to his endeavour.

She let her thoughts stray, as they often did, to the handsome young English Captain who had got rid of Friedrich for her. If only she had been younger! She had always had a thing for Englishmen, since she had lost her virginity to the young master of the house in Hereford where she had been a nanny. She wondered how he was enjoying the Horch. Reluctantly, she finished her cigarette and went to greet her next client.

With memories of her late husband freshly arisen to the surface, Elise put her weight into her work. Sweat beaded her shoulders and thighs as she raised weals on the quivering buttocks of the naked wife of the Police Chief. The woman whimpered her enjoyment. Elise laughed. She bent down and asked if the little mouse wanted something extra. The woman did. She was emphatic. She needed something else. Elise smiled, stripped herself of her corset and knickers, buckled on a phallus from what she called her 'toybox' and returned to her client. One never knew, she reflected, when it might be useful to have a contact within the highest echelons of the police. 'Keep the customer satisfied' was her mantra.

Edward was at Queen Anne's Gate, relieved to have escaped the clutches of Mummy and Caroline, who had formed an unholy alliance. He hated it. It seemed to have given Caroline an alarming new confidence. She was constantly at the house. The church was already booked for November, with a small reception to follow at Caroline's parents' house, on the basis that she would start to 'show' after that.

'You're fairly vast already,' he thought disdainfully. Edward was vain about his looks and could not bear to think about being seen out with this squat, lowering creature. He decided to keep busy by clearing out his father's old office, which he had taken over after a brief but good-humoured spat with Louis.

How many of these filthy magazines had his father possessed, he wondered, throwing another into the bin? He put the riding crop on one side, as a precaution. His mind drifted back to the afternoon when his father lay dead by the fire grate and Sylvia had sat with him on the floor, with her arms around him. 'Edward and Sylvia against the world,' as it always had been, he reflected, although he had usually managed to let her down. If only she would give him another chance. What did Gunn, that vicious upstart, possess that he didn't, he wondered bitterly? Perhaps he would give her this Bad Kaltenbrun probate file to look at, he thought. He couldn't fathom it out at all.

Sylvia and Gunn were wandering around the demeure, losing track of time. Their clothes were discarded in a heap in the hall. Jones's room was neat and tidy; nothing much in there. He had packed Louise's clothes and possessions in a suitcase. They looked at it silently. It seemed intrusive to open it. A few of the other doors along the next corridor were locked. Sylvia had found a key on a hook in the scullery which opened them all.

'It's like The Secret Garden all over again,' she called. 'Remember that?'

Gunn was examining a framed map on the wall, produced during the Revolution, showing the demeure, its boundaries and what it produced. This place could tell some stories, he thought. He caught up with Sylvia in the nursery. There was a doll's house on the floor, a cradle and a cupboard full of embroidered linen.

'This must be before Jonathan and Louise's time. They didn't have children.' she said. 'It's beautiful. A perfect room for a little girl. I wonder ...'

She caught herself in time and fell silent.

'Let's go back up to our room,' she suggested, holding him close.

Lying in the crook of his arm, listening to the wood pigeons outside, Sylvia talked about the way some houses gave her the creeps. This one didn't; it was as if it liked having them there. She told him how, alone in Tufnell Park the previous Christmas, she had put all the lights on and had stayed up until it was nearly light, half-frozen.

'You really are a silly girl sometimes,' Gunn told her, affectionately. He rested his hand against the curve of her hip as he drifted off to sleep. He woke with a start an hour later. Hearing her clattering around in the kitchen, he went downstairs. She was fiddling with the coffee percolator. Her face was wet with tears. She tried to turn away, but he was too quick for her. He led her firmly back upstairs with their coffee.

'What am I going to do with you, sweetheart? How can I leave you like this?'

He told her again that he loved her, and that most people never found love like this. They usually ended up with a relationship that was second best or worse. They were lucky to have found each other.

'I'll be fine,' she promised. 'Really, I will. And I know it's a really good opportunity for you; well, for both of us.'

She was a brilliant actress, but he could read her like a book. He told her that if he saw any more tears, even just one, he wouldn't go. She turned to him.

'Dinner by the lake tonight?' she suggested. 'I think this weather could be breaking up; one hell of a storm later.'

Sol replaced the receiver in the bar that had become his 'headquarters' in Le Marais, and bought another whisky. David in Tel Aviv had asked him what he knew about Ernst Wirth, late of the Ahnenerbe, a new subscriber to Alaikum and Otto's briefing. The Israeli subscription package, which Alaikum described as 'de luxe,' included occasional information as to the identity of other subscribers. Any such revelation usually constituted a precursor to a request for a hike in the fee.

Taking a sip of whisky, Sol cursed Alaikum and Otto roundly. Was there ever an end to their deviousness? The problem was that no matter how much you paid, and he kept trying to impress this on David, they were as trustworthy as the depth of the pockets of their paymasters. The name Ernst Wirth rang bells; he was another of those that had escaped in the confusion of 1945. David seemed to think he was back in Bavaria. It was only a matter of time. There was nothing for it; he needed to talk to Gunn and Sylvia sooner rather than later. A night in Chartrettes would also be rather pleasant; the heat had become oppressive and he could scarcely breathe. He went back to his hotel, packed his holdall and headed to the Gare de Lyon.

Gunn and Sylvia had just finished their dinner by the lake, watching the sun set and two swans, swimming around busily.

'Is it true that they mate for life?' he asked her.

'I think so,' she said.

Gunn was trying to remember the verses to a song with which his father often regaled the regulars at the Gunn House Hotel after a few drinks. He sang it to her. It finished with the line: 'it will not be long, love, till our wedding day.'

'That's beautiful,' Sylvia commented.

'It is, but from what I remember, the girl in it dies before they can get married.'

Sylvia shivered. A fat raindrop landed on her wrist.

'It's going to bucket down,' said Gunn. 'Reckon we can make it over to the hayloft before we get drenched?'

Sol bought his ticket and stepped onto the last train to Chartrettes. He had caught it by the skin of his teeth. He settled back into his seat, as the train slowly pulled out of the station on its way south. The clouds rolled in. Forked lightning hit the summit of the Tour Eiffel and the rain came in heavy gusts, driven by a hard wind. He peered out into the weather and prayed there would be a taxi at the railway station. He had remembered a little more about Wirth. It did not bode well.

Gunn and Sylvia had been listening to the storm, up in the loft. The ancient beams traced an arc above their bodies. The hay was dry and sweet. They made love slowly and easily, with the familiarity of new belonging. Sylvia drove her nails into Gunn's back, wrapping her legs around his hips as she did so. Her body rode with the rhythm of his drive. He bit her throat gently and she groaned, her groan adding weight to his thrust. He filled her up and she shook, her cries echoing to the roof.

Gunn rolled off her and lay panting beside her. He said nothing. Nothing needed to be said.

Sol made his way up the drive, his feet crunching over the gravel. The house was in darkness. The back door was open, but nobody was in. They had to be here somewhere, he thought; the Horch was in the drive. Leaving his holdall in the hall, he started to make his way methodically around the outbuildings.

The rhythmic crescendo of their lovemaking identified their whereabouts. He thought back to the few times he had had with Sarah, and felt rather sad.

'Best give them some privacy,' he thought, closing the door of the barn softly. Up in the loft, Gunn was in a deep sleep. Sylvia had noticed that he always fell asleep straight afterwards. That amused her. She wrapped her arms around him, luxuriating in the warmth.

'Gunn,' she whispered, after a while. 'There's somebody outside, can you hear?'

'There's nobody there, sweetheart,' he murmured.

'Listen!'

Gunn was instantly wide awake. He pulled on his trousers, rolled off the mezzanine and landed with a soft crump, kicking up dust on the floor below. He looked around. That old pitchfork would do. He flicked it up with his toe and hefted it. It had a lot of front end balance but that was all right. He brushed webs and dust from the wooden stave shaft and slowly, on the balls of his feet, moved across the floor.

To the left of the barn door was a window, with wooden shutters that opened outwards. He chose that as his exit, as the egress was wider and taller than the interior, fork first followed by a dive and roll out. He followed his plan to the letter, rolling up onto his feet to find Sol examining the pitchfork at his feet and smoking a decent cigarette.

'What the buggering hell are you doing here, Sol?'

'Judging by the noise you were making, I don't have to ask you the same question,' retorted Sol. 'There have been some developments. We need to talk. Can we go inside?'

Sylvia emerged, still pulling her dress round her. She had straw in her hair and looked faintly flushed. Gunn did her dress up for her and she accompanied them into the house, her arm through his; an instinctive gesture but one not lost on Gunn. He drew her close to him.

'Nice place,' said Sol. 'Secluded. You wouldn't think you were only an hour from Paris.' An idea was beginning to form in his mind. He examined his wine glass appreciatively; Gunn had been foraging in the cellars again. Sylvia was making a bed up for Sol upstairs.

She came back downstairs, having got rid of the rest of the straw, and sat next to Gunn. He poured her a glass of red wine and put his arm round her. He had lit a fire in the magnificent hearth. The room looked impressive.

'It should be all right; maybe a little smoky at first,' Gunn told him.

Sol looked across at them both. He remembered Marguerite's words in Haifa about Gunn and Sylvia. She was right; they belonged together.

331

They always looked every inch a couple; even more so in these surroundings.

Coming straight to the point, he said:

'The pipeline is starting up again.'

'Well, I think we all knew that, didn't we?' Gunn was a little bemused.

'The man behind it now,' Sol continued, 'makes Mueller and Cumberland look like a pair of clowns.'

He gave them an outline of what he knew about Wirth and the Ahnenerbe. His view was that Wirth wouldn't be content simply to get people out of hot water. With Mueller and Cumberland out of the way, he wanted to set up a Fourth Reich in Argentina, with a view to the world once again being ruled by Aryan peoples, in accordance with all the myths. They could expect more people to be spirited away, including those who were sympathisers but not necessarily on any current list. It would be quite easy to set up a sizeable population out there, and a dangerous one.

'This guy has money,' Sol told them. 'Both inherited and gleaned by nefarious means. It's no object. 'I'm not sure yet whether he has made the connection between you and Mueller and Cumberland. He has just subscribed to the Alaikum newsletter. Mr Duplicity and his sidekick. It's a matter of time, but he is some way behind.'

Sylvia suddenly remembered the paperwork Louis had given her; copies, he had explained, of a much larger set of information stored by Cumberland with an Austrian tailor named Juncker.

'With a cat that drinks excellent whisky,' she added.

'What a waste,' was Sol's comment. He hadn't heard of Juncker.

'We'll have a look at them tomorrow,' he said. 'It's late and we all need some sleep. We've got a lot of plans to make. And you two had better be fit for work in the morning.'

He took his leave and went up to his room. Sylvia and Gunn were curled up on the sofa together in front of the fire. Sylvia wondered what these plans would entail, and if they might involve her. She stretched, luxuriously, and manoeuvred herself onto Gunn's lap.

'I've always dreamt about making love in front of the fire.'

'Better keep the noise down then, sweetheart. Reckon you can?'

As the fire died down, they crept up to bed, hand in hand, still trying not to make a noise, wanting to make the most of every second they had together.

Sol could not sleep in any case. He had tried, but his furtive imagination and the heavy silence of a country house played on his mind. Eventually, he got up and dressed, and went and sat on the low wall at the edge of the property, looking towards the woods. He drank some coffee and smoked half a packet of cigarettes.

The isolation of the house was certainly useful but could represent a weakness. There was shelter for those inside, but also for anyone wishing to get up close and personal. Sol shrugged and tossed a silver

333

coin he kept in his pocket. It was one his father had given him many years ago. He kissed the coin and followed its glittering arc in the creeping light of dawn. Heads. It would do.

In his small but centrally located apartment in Munich, Dieter Fischer was awake early, preparing for the drive into the countryside, to the hunting lodge. He wondered who else would be at the meeting. Wirth had struck him yesterday as a rather menacing character, one not to get on the wrong side of. Not that he was in the habit of being afraid of anyone, but a little caution, nonetheless, would not go amiss. Wirth had told him to pack an overnight bag. He wondered whether he would see this museum. In spite of himself, he was intrigued. He had heard a little yesterday about Wirth's visits in the thirties to India, when he had been Professor of Archaeology at Gottingen. Dieter gave his girlfriend a farewell kiss; she scarcely stirred. Soon, he was on the road.

Gunn was awake early. He padded downstairs to make coffee, noting that Sol had been down earlier. He went upstairs again to find Sylvia, asleep in her usual pose. He ran a finger down her spine, addicted to the silkiness of her skin. She woke, turned over and gave him a kiss and a tentative smile.

'You should go down south,' he told her. 'Keep a distance from London for a bit. See how things pan out there. Work on that beautiful suntan of yours.'

'I wouldn't mind going back down south,' she said. 'Let's see what Sol has to say about the pipeline. It's still early, isn't it? We don't have to get up yet.'

Louis kicked the door of the storage room open at St Anne's Court, arms full of another set of litigation files for storage. Galland stalked in ahead of him, tail held high. He stopped suddenly, nearly tripping over the cat. The room, which was normally a complete tip, was empty. He had left the floor covered in files last time. Where the buggering hell were they?

'What files?' Juncker was maddeningly vague.

'You know full well.'

'Oh, those files,' Juncker said. 'I've stored them elsewhere for safe keeping, after Mr Cumberland's terrible accident. I'm sure that's all it was. All the same, you can't be too careful.'

'So where are they now?' asked Louis.

The tailor shrugged. He was indifferent, or presented himself thus. It was easier, a means of hiding himself in plain sight. Louis bent down and tickled Galland under the chin, being a polite man. Then he launched himself from his haunches and, with a twist of his waist, hit Juncker first with a right and then with a left for good measure.

'Those files matter. Mr Cumberland was in trouble.'

Juncker dabbed at his lip. It was split and raw. His glasses were askew. His hair was ruffled. He had a pistol in his work table drawer but Louis was standing in front of the table and Juncker did not

335

relish the idea of hanging from a rope. With all the dignity he could muster, he gestured towards a cupboard.

'In there,' he said. He toyed briefly with the idea of asking Louis for more money but decided against it. Louis was already looking inside the cupboard. The confidential files were stacked neatly on top of the others, with the two empty cases on top. Louis turned.

'I take it you've had a good look inside the files.'

'Me?' asked Juncker. 'I'm the soul of discretion.'

Louis did not trust him for one moment. The files did all seem to be present and correct, but he wasn't entirely sure what to do with them now. They needed to be handed over to the Israeli authorities, and fast. He hoped Sylvia would get in touch soon. He loaded them into George's cases and, taking an icy leave of Juncker, walked down St Anne's Court to hail a taxi. Juncker waited until Louis was around the corner and then shot off in the opposite direction, to the nearest telephone box, Galland leading the way.

Upstairs in the demeure, Gunn woke and stretched, disentangling himself from Sylvia. She was beautifully warm. She had asked him to show her another of the courtesan's tricks earlier. They had both particularly enjoyed that one. There were plenty more of them. Bugger. It was twenty past nine.

'Time to go downstairs and see Sol, sweetheart,' he said gently.

He watched the expressions flitting across her face; sheer happiness to total dismay to careful professionalism in seconds. She lay across the bed for a moment, watching him shave, drinking in every second.

'Come on then,' she said. 'Let's face the music.'

In a rather grubby telephone box in Soho, Juncker fished in his capacious wallet for coins of a realm he did not care for. He was becoming more indignant by the minute. He was finally connected and spoke briefly and succinctly, like a soldier making a field report, not a rather vague tailor acting as staff to an eccentric cat. He noted his instructions and returned to the shop. He divested himself of his glasses, shaved off his whiskers and soon, sharply dressed and leaving Galland to mind the shop, locked up. With a Walter PPK with the serial number chiselled out under his jacket. He was under orders to retrieve the files and take no prisoners.

Inspiration struck Louis just before the taxi reached Queen Anne's Gate.

'Would you mind waiting a minute?' he asked the driver 'And then taking me down to the Kent coast? And back?'

The taxi driver's eyes opened wide.

'No problem, guv,' he responded.

Louis rushed into Edward's office and, searching deep in the cabinet, pulled out an old deposit box marked 'Fordred Will Trust.' What he needed was safely inside, along with the address.

Time was of the essence. Edward, who had been to see a client in hospital, met him on the stairs.

'Off to a conference with Counsel,' Louis explained.

'Have fun, old boy,' came the response.

Louis hurled himself into the taxi. He heaved a sigh of relief as they crossed Westminster Bridge. This was probably the safest place of all for the files. Nobody, probably not even Sylvia, knew it existed. While Edward had been out of the office and busy with the funeral, he had undertaken a complete review of all George's cases. There seemed to have been a combination of plundering and total neglect.

Sylvia's family trust, after George's depredations, consisted of a mixture of shares (fortunately blue chip, which should have held their own quite nicely), monies in the bank (what was left now needed proper investment) and a cottage in the Kent countryside. It had once been in the family. It had a tenant; it was on agricultural land, but the house, and others nearby, had been requisitioned by the army in World War 2, when the country was on alert for an invasion from across the Channel. After the war, the army had returned the keys. The tenant had gone elsewhere and the house had been securely locked up ever since. A condition survey had been done; the army had looked after it well.

He would have to talk to Edward about the trust at some stage. That was Edward's field; his own speciality was litigation. Sylvia would be within her rights to sue the firm. For now, the house would do as a hiding place, until the Israeli authorities collected the files. He sat back to examine the rest of the contents of the box and soon became enthralled by a story that Charles Dickens would have killed for. What a family!

The taxi driver cleared his throat. 'We're here, guv.' Louis looked up, startled. That was quick. They were outside a pub on a bend in the road going out towards the Romney Marsh.

'Wait here for me please,' said Louis, watching the driver go inside.

Once the driver was out of sight, he trudged back, with his cases, towards a small detached cottage they had driven past. It was all locked up. Several sheep watched him inquisitively. Making sure there was nobody around, Louis slid the rusty key into the front door. It opened straight away.

Putting the post into his coat pocket, he made his way up the rickety stairs, a little unsure about the condition of the floorboards, and emptied the contents of the suitcases into an old oak chest. He locked it, pocketed the key, locked the house again and was back at the pub in five minutes, in time to join the driver for a pint.

'Just so you know,' Louis told the driver, putting a second pint on the bar for him 'Nobody gets to find out you have been here. Do you understand me? You will be hunted down and killed in a most unpleasant fashion if you so much as breathe a word.'

'Not a word, guv,' gasped the driver.

At Queen Anne's Gate, as Edward made his way up the stairs, a hand grabbed him.

'Where are the files?' asked a sinister voice.

'Fuck off, Juncker,' Edward whisked round. 'Why are you wearing that ridiculous disguise? I know it's you.'

'Where's Louis?' asked Juncker in his normal voice, beginning to feel slightly foolish.

'None of your business. What the hell are you doing here anyway? I don't know anything about any files. Get out before I kick you out. And close the door after you. '

Edward, since his beating by Gunn, had decided to become more assertive. He felt rather proud of himself. He stood by the door, watched Juncker walk through it, then returned upstairs. Juncker was furious at being spoken to like this by Cumberland's idiot son. He simply couldn't allow that to happen. That Pole could have gone anywhere with those blasted files. After a moment, he crept back into the building.

Edward did not look up at first, until he felt the touch of cold, brushed steel at his temple.

'You should have learnt some manners at your father's knee,' snarled Juncker. 'Now, where is Louis?'

'No idea.'

Juncker smacked him across the knuckles with the flat of the pistol. Edward's knuckles cracked under the strain.

'Not good enough. Try again.'

'He's out.'

Juncker went to bring down the flat of the pistol again.

'All right,' said Edward. 'He's at a conference with Counsel. Lincoln's Inn, I believe. But he won't be back until this evening; they never start until the barrister gets out of Court. What is all this about, anyway?'

'Family loyalty,' replied Juncker. 'Think about it. Now, I am going back to St Anne's Court. I suggest we have a further chat tomorrow, when you've had a chance to speak to Louis.'

Edward locked the door behind Juncker. He didn't want any more unwelcome visitors. Security in this place had deteriorated markedly since Joan's defection. He sat down in the reception area. First his father had bullied him, now Mummy. And he was going to have to marry that hideous creature. Actually, loyalty and duty had availed him nothing since the war. In fact, family loyalty meant nothing to him now.

He sketched out some calculations on a scrap of paper. He had around £150 in ready cash in the bank. The office safe contained around £75 in petty cash and sundries. Perhaps it was time to pocket what he had, stroll on and let the rest of the world go hang. He could get a flying job somewhere, perhaps fly through wind, sand and stars delivering post and other essentials across North Africa, out of Algiers or Tripoli. He could get himself a little house, work hard and play hard, the latter being something he had left to others. Sylvia might even find him attractive then.

He was meant to be going to Caroline's parents tonight, to sort out wedding arrangements. His mother was going too. He knew she was at the hairdresser's this afternoon. He had a small window of opportunity. He scrawled a note to Louis, the only person he felt the remotest compunction about.

Within half an hour, he was at Chepstow Villas, packing a holdall. He put in his pilot's log book and his passport, and, after some reflection, his teddy bear. With a great feeling of liberation, he closed the door and was walking briskly down the path when a bony hand seized him by the scruff of his neck.

'Where do you think you're going?'

'Mummy,' he thought, with a sense of dread. He would be in for it now. Pulling himself together just in time, he broke free, pushing her roughly head first into a bed of winter pansies.

'I'm going away,' he told her. 'And you can't stop me and you won't ever find me.'

Ignoring her outraged shrieking, he jumped aboard the number 11 towards Victoria Station and his new life, just as Louis was wending his way towards Queen Anne's Gate across St James Park, the deposit box under his arm. He had got the taxi driver to drop him by the Ritz, leaving him with an unusually generous tip and a repeat of his earlier warning.

Louis frowned. It was a strange time for the office to be locked up and in darkness. He let himself in with his key, put the deposit box back in the cabinet and locked the outer door. With a sense of foreboding, he sat at his desk, reading Edward's note. He could understand about the new life; he would have felt the same in those circumstances. It was the bit about Juncker that concerned him, nearly breaking Edward's knuckles and wandering around in disguise. He would have to be careful. Nobody would ever find the files, but he would have to find a way of getting them into the right hands.

The telephone rang, breaking into his thoughts.

'Gunn? Sylvia? How are you? Is everything all right? Yes, I'm fine. Edward? Oh well, his fiancée is pregnant and he's run away to North Africa with the office petty cash but otherwise he is in fine fettle. No, I'm not joking. The funeral? Oh, that was the other day, all went fine. Listen, it's a long story but Juncker has become very agitated about the files. So, I've hidden them in a house your family owns, Sylvia, on the Kent coast.'

Sylvia and Gunn were listening to him together, in the bar in Chartrettes. They had left Sol having a look round the house, while they went for cigarettes and to make a few calls.

'Not another sodding house, Sylv,' Gunn groaned.

'Oh, a house at the seaside; I like the sound of that,' she teased him. 'I do remember an ancient relative in Hythe. Funny little house, if it's the same one. Near the canal. Daddy's family had a farm down there. Perfect place for the files. Well done, Louis.'

'I was in Hythe the other day, before I picked you up,' Gunn told her. 'Dad's family were from that neck of the woods too. That's a coincidence.'

'Wonder who Juncker is taking his orders from now?' he mused, as they walked back, hand in hand. 'The same person Sol was describing?'

'Maybe. But I have a feeling there are more involved, at a higher level.' A frisson ran over her. 'Can you believe that about Edward?'

343

'Mummy will be going frantic. He won't be back for tea time,' Gunn chuckled. 'Whoever would have thought he would do anything like that?'

Chapter 23

Edward had caught the boat train to Dover. He was a long way south now. He did not care for Paris or Lyon or, indeed, anything much right now, other than putting the miles between himself and Mummy. He had his tickets, he had what he needed, and for only the second time in his life he felt free. The irony of feeling free during wartime had never quite escaped him and had probably informed his dealings with his parents and Caroline.

Caroline was an issue. She was pregnant. His name would be mud in all the right social circles. He had never especially enjoyed those circles; that did not bother him. He would wire her money on a monthly basis for the next eighteen years or until she married, which, with a sour humour, he estimated would be within six weeks. Her family would see to that.

He pulled a hip flask from his travelling bag. A few miles south of Lyon, as the sun was coming up, he raised it in salute.

'To wind, sand and stars.'

Winifred Cumberland pulled herself out of the flower bed, praying that none of the neighbours had seen the altercation between herself and Edward, just as Juncker slid round the corner into Chepstow Villas. She recognised him instantly; he had come to the house a few times after that awful business on the Isle of Man. Dreadful little man, she thought. Lothar, as she would always think of her late husband, had never really liked him. He looked different - He had lost his whiskers.

'Can I help you, Mrs Cumberland?' he asked obsequiously. 'You seem to be in a bit of a predicament.'

Juncker offered her his arm and they went inside the house. She would never have invited him in under normal circumstances but her head was spinning. She poured him a glass of whisky, struggling to follow what he was saying about her husband, Edward, Louis and incriminating files.

Juncker had staked out Queen Anne's Gate for a while but there was nothing doing, so he had decided to have another go at Edward. He listened incredulously as Winifred poured out a tale of Edward having got his fiancée pregnant and how he had left earlier on the bus, after pushing her into the flower bed.

'Needs a damn good thrashing,' she said, vindictively.

Juncker agreed. Winifred turned to him.

'I want him found. Immediately. Bring him straight back here. Then I might help you with your files.'

Having finally managed to push Juncker out of the door, Winifred embarked on a difficult telephone call to the Andrews with a feeble excuse as to why she and Edward would be unable to join them for supper that evening. She went upstairs and lay down in his room, looking up at the stars on his ceiling. Why had life panned out like this, she wondered? Her mind drifted back to that glorious summer, just before the Great War, when she had given herself to Tom Fordred in a funny little cottage his family owned at the coast. They weren't supposed to be there at all; it was being renovated to house an elderly maiden aunt who had found herself without lodgings. Tom, just down from University, was meant to be supervising the renovations. She could still picture the white walls inside, the rough floorboards and the coolness of the kitchen; their eyes had adjusted after a while from the brightness outside. They had rushed along the canal bank on the baked earth, stopping for kisses and watching the kingfishers.

The war had changed Tom and not in a good way. He had married Amelie, a nurse he met at the front. Half French. His family had withdrawn all his allowances. Winifred, half mad with grief, had married Lothar on the rebound (he had somehow inveigled his way into Tom's crowd). Looking back, Lothar had probably realised he was second best, and had taken out his frustrations on Edward. Winifred had been overjoyed when, some years later, Tom had rented the house next door, with a small daughter in tow, after Amelie had run off with the man from the cognac house. She had been cruelly disappointed to find that Tom did not want to carry on where they had left off. She supposed she had rather taken it out on Sylvia. No more than she deserved; Sylvia was probably the reason for Edward's present bizarre behaviour. Perhaps she should mention her to Juncker; no immediate rush; she would wait and see what he came up with.

Back in his shop in St Anne's Court, Juncker sat with the blinds half way down. He liked the dark. It allowed his mind to wander and cleanse itself. He patted Galland and poured his insistent feline a saucer of the finest. Leaning back in his chair, he began to wonder how to play things. He had started to dismiss Edward other than someone who could be used and then dropped; Louis was the real means of accessing the files. If he could somehow take Winifred along with him, and make her think he was close to finding Edward, then perhaps she could help. Her husband and son had been partners in the firm. Now they were gone, where did that leave her financially? Might she be susceptible to a 'sweetener' from his paymasters? He resolved to let the dust settle for a few days before calling on her again.

In a hunting lodge in Bavaria a few hours later, Dieter Fischer walked in on a telephone conversation. Wirth was finding it hard to suppress his fury; his voice was cold and hard.

'I am at a loss,' said Wirth, 'to know why I should have to deal with retarded people like you. Your orders were to catch that stupid Pole, get the files and kill him. Now you say he is alive but you don't know where the files are? Where is Cumberland? What do you mean, he has disappeared too? Sort this goddam mess out *sofort*. Otherwise, I will arrange a very gruesome death for you. I should probably have done it already.'

'Excuse me, my young friend,' he said to Dieter. 'I didn't see you there. An idiot in London, I'm afraid. Some rather incriminating files are on the

348

loose there. Compiled by Cumberland. Remember I told you about him? They are, shall we say, dynamite.'

Dieter was keen to make himself useful, or to be seen to be doing so.

'Cumberland was a solicitor, you say. Did he have a family?'

'Yes, an English wife and a son he referred to as 'the idiot.' Ex Spitfire pilot. Why?'

'And he was the heir to the Bad Kaltenbrun estate?'

'Well, yes, I suppose so, but he hasn't been able to visit for years.'

'Maybe – in a while - an approach to the family from me would help, as a Munich solicitor?'

'Let's go through and have some coffee,' said Wirth, clapping him on the back. 'I like your thinking. I have a feeling these files are safely hidden now. They can probably stay where they are a little longer, but I shan't tell that imbecile tailor that. First things first; we have some cargo that needs moving; been *in situ* for too long.'

Part of the 'cargo' to which Wirth referred was sitting in a café in Madrid, as he had every single morning for the previous month. He drank a coffee or two, but no more than two, and nibbled on bread dipped in olive oil. He paid and left and wandered the streets, keeping his head down and his brim way down low. He was waiting. He had been ready to leave but this was taking too long, and he was worried. He would leave it another forty-eight hours, he resolved, then he would leave Madrid and head for

349

somewhere like Tarifa on the south coast. A long way from anywhere and where nobody would pay him the slightest heed.

In the event, he would not have much longer to wait. Over coffee in the hunting lodge, Wirth was giving Dieter details of Father Alfonso Hoechst, who ministered to a German community which was beginning to form around a beach near Cadiz. Being half Spanish, Father Hoechst was able to come and go as he pleased. 'What we call hiding in plain sight, my young friend. I expect they told you about that in the military.'

Dieter nodded.

'Beautiful part of the world, if you are ever down that way,' Wirth continued. 'The asset we need to spring is in Madrid at the moment. There are lots of people after him so we decided, while we got things operational again, to keep him away from any centres of population, if you catch my drift, and to use someone we could trust implicitly. Hoechst will be saying Mass at the moment; best time to catch him will be this afternoon. Ring him from here, after lunch. Then he can make his way up to Madrid to pick our chap up. I can listen in, and it's a good opportunity to introduce yourself. Now, how about a chat with your new colleagues and a look round our museum?'

Dieter thought to himself how much Wirth reminded him, superficially, of some of his university professors. Of course, that was exactly what he had been. There the resemblance ended. He had seen a different side to him several times now. He tried to focus on the money he was going to earn, rather than what it was that he was doing, and who was being assisted, as he followed Wirth out of the lodge and into the grounds of a castle straight out of a tale by the Brothers Grimm.

The curtain wall of the castle ran some thirty feet high and eight feet thick. It was crenellated and had four spire-tipped towers at each point of weakness. The castle gate was iron-bound oak with supporting towers, a killing ground and an inner oak gate of similar craft led into the main courtyard of the castle. To the left, Dieter noted a stable yard and barracks. To the right, a bake house and a forge which was now a garage. Ahead was the castle proper, the citadel towering over them as if seeking to match itself with the surrounding mountains.

Wirth smiled at him. 'A little kingdom of our own.'

'Quite a place,' murmured Dieter.

'Thought you'd like it. The original plans were set out by Ludwig II, and then my family brought them to fruition.

DerMarchenkonig, also known as Mad King Ludwig. Appropriate for the insane world he now seemed to inhabit, thought Dieter, following Wirth inside.

'Our little museum is usually open by appointment only; it's just outside the castle walls,' explained Wirth. 'I'll take you round after I've made the introductions.'

The castle was staffed by men of military bearing, for the most part in their late twenties and early thirties, with a sprinkling of officer corps and the usual run of blonde milkmaids with regulation

351

braids and heavy thighs. Despite the lack of uniforms, and the addition of plastered-on smiles and cheerful faces, the Castle was clearly military or rather para-military (as in SS, Dieter thought).

He took it all in, his mind in a whirl, before finally asking Wirth when they were in a small courtyard where ivy crawled up the walls and leaded windows faced each other in a blank manner:

'Tell me, how does this escape the attention of the Allies?'

'They have enough to do in Berlin, worrying about each other. We keep our heads down and our noses clean, and the local people support us.' Wirth brushed an invisible speck of dust from his sleeve. 'Well, for the most part. There were a couple of accidents last year, before we got under way properly.'

'I see.'

Wirth added: 'By the same token, nothing much escapes our notice. We have intelligence coming in from everywhere. You're inside the nerve centre, my young friend. Exciting, isn't it?'

Dieter nodded, thinking privately that that was not the way he would have described it.

On the way to lunch in what Wirth described as 'the works canteen,' but which was one of the castle's ante-rooms, laid out as a formal dining room, Wirth stopped at one of the desks, frowning, and spoke to Karl Adler, a young man of around Dieter's age.

'Yes, this is utter garbage,' he agreed. 'Telephone those effete creatures in Cairo. Tell them we're not being fobbed off with it anymore.'

'Yes, sir,' said Adler, reaching for the telephone immediately.

In Cairo, Otto held the receiver away from his ear, wincing slightly.

'One of Wirth's minions,' he explained, as he replaced it. 'Not impressed with our bulletin. Didn't mince his words. Wants higher grade intelligence. But they're not paying for it.'

Alaikum frowned. 'Well, unless they pay, they can whistle for it. Although I do think it might be time for another meeting with our friends in Tel Aviv. Want to make the call?'

In the bar in Chartrettes, Sol replaced the receiver after a difficult conversation with David. Things were clearly heating up. Alaikum was stirring the pot. He was a little weasel. It was a great shame, Sol thought, that there was no competition. There was no choice but to use them, perfidious and unreliable as they were. There should be competition; he had had a few ideas about that. Maybe this was the time to talk them through with Gunn and Sylvia. He had come out to buy some cigarettes and to give the couple some time alone. They had had a productive couple of days, he thought, time well spent. Neither of them should be under any illusion now as to the road ahead.

Sylvia and Gunn had been taking advantage of Sol's absence to 'christen' the kitchen, the last room on their list. The attics, cellar and outhouses could wait. Gunn had just lifted her down from the counter when the door opened. He hastily zipped up her dress. Sol decided to be tactful, simply raising an eyebrow.

'A word,' he said to Gunn.

Sylvia wandered into the garden, to pick some fruit for pudding. She hadn't been required at all of their discussions, but had enjoyed contributing to those where she was needed. She could sense their idyll at the demeure was coming to an end for now. Her way of coping with that was to live for the moment. Gunn had negotiated leave at Christmas.

'Out of the question,' Sol had growled.

'Something of a *sine qua non,* old boy,' Gunn had told him. 'And I haven't imposed any other conditions, have I? You may have noticed that there are two things in my life to which I attach importance. Sylvia is the first. With the Horch a very close second.'

'You and that girl. You can have ten days. That's it.'

'So that's not so bad, is it, sweetheart? We'll have Christmas together. Breaks it up a bit,' Gunn had told Sylvia. 'We'll go to Dad's in Brighton. You'll love it. And then maybe you can come out to me at Easter, or we could meet somewhere in the middle. Somewhere neither of us has been.'

In the kitchen, Sol handed Gunn a cigarette and a light.

'You and I need to get busy. We have to deal with a situation in Damascus and then we have to kick the pants of a couple of nancy boy freelance agents in Cairo, who are getting a little above themselves.'

354

'Noted.' Gunn drew deep on his cigarette. 'Which comes first?'

'Damascus.' Sol seemed to see into the miles to the south and the east as if he could see the city. 'Nazis keep floating to the surface like pond life. Problem is, they seem to be in positions to do us damage by proxy. The Arabs don't like Jews. They never have, and they like us even less now we're home.'

'So, the Krauts are taking advantage of that to push a little.'

'Of course,' Sol grinned, a baring of the teeth. 'Every now and then we have to push back. David will have transport arrangements and another briefing for us this evening. We'll ring him from the bar later. Might be an idea to put a telephone line in here.'

'Chartrettes was once a Gestapo listening post,' Sylvia offered as she came back into the kitchen and started slicing up fruit. 'The outbuildings here could be used for something like that.'

'Not a bad idea,' Sol nodded, stealing a piece of apple. He winced at its sourness. 'Be good for security too. It would give the French the sense that we are being polite in our behaviour. I'll talk to David; we might get the quarter-master to have a look.'

'You'll have to sweet-talk the mayor, Sylv,' said Gunn. 'Try and keep him on side, if we're going to do something like that here.'

'Might be an idea, she agreed, vaguely. She was trying to keep busy, finishing the inventory for Marguerite, making the dinner and setting the table. She went down to the cellar and found a decent bottle of Bordeaux. Gunn looked over at her speculatively. She was putting an incredibly brave face on things. He loved her for that and so many other things. He couldn't deny though that he was excited about the scenarios Sol had outlined, having fought in Syria in the war. He was intrigued by the operation Alaikum and Otto were running in the Middle East. They had cornered the market. Clements International could do something similar with far more integrity and professionalism, he thought.

Sol asked Gunn, on the way to the café, whether he was going to let Sylvia have the Horch.

'Debatable,' Gunn replied. 'Not sure about letting her loose on that gear box.'

Inside the castle which King Ludwig had once envisaged as a base for hunting, Wirth and Dieter were continuing with their exploration after a light lunch. Wirth had been impressed by Dieter's call to Father Hoechst, in which he introduced himself as his new handler.

'Concise and clear, and you didn't overload him with information. You'll be an excellent addition to our team. Now, let's take a short stroll to our little museum. You'll like it.'

Dieter feigned interest in several cabinets of rings inscribed with runes. One looked much like another. The same applied to a collection of hunting horns. Wirth wasn't fooled. He put a hand on Dieter's shoulder and steered him casually into a room with a sign on the door saying 'Anthropology,' saying 'You'll find this fascinating.'

There was an overpowering smell of formaldehyde. Dieter struggled with rising nausea as he looked around.

'Everything we need to prove the superiority of the Aryan race,' Wirth told him. He explained that the 'specimens' had been obtained from a small camp in Poland. They were all Jews. They had been kept apart from the other prisoners, to avoid contamination, as there had been an outbreak of typhus in the camp. They had been gassed, then immediately preserved, and brought here so that research could be undertaken. The specimens had arrived with the Allies hard on their heels and were spirited away into underground vaults.

'There is much still to be done,' Wirth explained, nodding politely to a girl in a white coat.

Dieter excused himself and rushed outside for a cigarette. Wirth followed him.

'I do hope you are sympathetic to our philosophy, my young friend,' he said.

'Yes, yes,' Dieter managed to reassure him. 'Rather an early start this morning and I'm fighting off a cold. I'd very much like to go back in and see the rest of the museum.'

The last part of the museum was dedicated to the pre war expeditions to Tibet and India, in search of occult weaponry and ideas and evidence to support the racial theories of the regime. Dieter shook his head at the thought of Wirth measuring the head and noting the physical characteristics of a Tibetan guide. He decided he was not one for the up close and personal; he preferred a pristine sheet of crisp paper with numbers and ideas and theories set out in black ink. Nonetheless, he was careful to express a deep fascination for the flora and fauna Wirth and his colleagues had brought back.

Declining Wirth's offer to join him and some colleagues for a session of deep meditation in the castle, Dieter instead embarked on a brisk walk around the grounds. He wondered what he had let himself in for. There was no way out now, that was for sure.

Much later, after a sumptuous banquet in the castle keep, Dieter and Wirth were sitting in deep armchairs in front of a roaring fire, with a glass of vintage brandy each. Wirth looked across at him thoughtfully. He wasn't convinced Dieter was a 'believer.' He believed he had his measure; money was the motivation for this young man. He would do, for their purposes, and would be easy to eliminate should he no longer fit the bill.

Dieter was struggling to keep awake after his early start, so, having drained his glass, he bade his host good night and made his way to his room. It had been designed for one of the princes, Wirth had told him. The walls were decorated with frescoes depicting Teutonic knights. A fire was crackling in the grate and his bed had been turned down. He was confident that, if he had blotted his copybook with Wirth earlier, he had rectified the position. With that comforting thought, he fell into a deep sleep.

Chapter 24

Rainer Matthaus, a former member of the SS and now a resident of Damascus, sat in his apartment not far from the old citadel, sipping hibiscus tea and thinking of home. He was listening to German lieder song cycles on a gramophone a friend had given him before he had left Germany in early 1945. His loyalty had stopped dead with the failure of the winter offensive into the Ardennes. 'Nuts.' That expression still echoed in his memory.

He set down his tea cup, watching the fan above his head as it barely stirred the evening air. Damascus, as he had learned on arrival, derived from an old Aramaic name Darmesq, which apparently meant 'well-watered place.' He had not been well-watered of late. His supply of schnapps and wine were close to the heeltaps. He could not abide heeltaps and had few safe means of procuring further supplies. Money was not an issue, and his skills with a knife, a garrotte fashioned from a rosary and a gun were in well-rewarded demand from various government agencies. He was often sub-contracted out to Arab governments who appreciated the idea of a German killing Israelis.

His bones were getting weary; he could not last forever. His last job had been close – a farm in the hills overlooking Galilee, a young farmer of military age and his wife and child. He had taken a moment too long, only making the border by a fraying of his nerves and coat tails. He had a feeling somebody was coming for him. The sun was going down and the call to prayer echoed across his quarter.

He frowned. He rolled off his bed and went to shut the window. He looked down; there was barely anybody about. The air was still, as if expectant. He shut the window, and moved over towards his bureau. He took out a velvet cloth. He unwrapped it and took comfort in the weight of a Browning 9mm. It was in good condition with a full clip and three spare. Enough for a job and to get away. This time, it would have to be enough to get away.

In Cairo, Alaikum was putting together a report for Wirth; even if he said so himself, it was a work of genius. There was enough in there to make Wirth believe he was getting the inside story, but not enough to arouse any suspicions in his Israeli paymasters, who had upped their subscription a little. They could definitely do better.

'Not heard from old Matthaus in Damascus for a while,' Otto commented. 'Seems to have gone rather quiet.'

'That's not like him,' Alaikum agreed. 'Ask around, see if anyone knows anything.'

'Early start tomorrow from what David was saying,' Gunn remarked to Sol, on the way back to the demeure. Sylvia had told him earlier in bed that she would love to have gone with them. A step too far for Sol, Gunn thought. Anyway, he needed to keep his wits about him on assignments like this.

Whilst putting the finishing touches to the pudding, Sylvia was thinking about the coming weeks. Tomorrow she was meeting the mayor, and she was meeting Sol's quarter-master in a fortnight, to discuss plans for Chartrettes. That left her with ample time to get down to Cognac and back. Aunt Hortense had been so dismissive about her mother's family and she had scarcely known them. There were no other relatives on that side, as far as she knew, but perhaps someone was around who would remember them. She would have to go back to London after that. In some ways she was looking forward to getting back to Clements.

'Thought you said you couldn't cook, Sylv,' Gunn said, after pudding. 'That was lovely.'

'Oh, I just made it up.' Sylvia wandered back into the kitchen, to tidy up. She needed to keep busy.

Gunn was packing, lightly and efficiently, under Sol's approving watch. There would be no loitering in ancient ruins on this trip. They had checked out of the fleapit with their luggage and the camera equipment. Sylvia would have to take it all back to England with her.   He took the Tula apart, cleaning out any dust and debris. Probably imagined, as Sol observed, a little grumpily, but that was Gunn's way.

Sol passed over the flimsy file on Matthaus. Gun glanced over it once, and then read it properly on second glance. He looked over at Sol.

'Real charmer, isn't he?'

'A delight. A real low life schmuck.' Sol chewed on a finger, a sign of irritation. 'And the Syrians, amongst others, love him.'

'Sounds as if we'll have our work cut out then.'

361

Winifred Cumberland kicked the door open at St Anne's Court, almost tripping over Galland. Juncker woke with a start. Business had been quiet since the Olympics. He seemed to have a lot more competition too. Who on earth was this? Women rarely ventured into his establishment.

'I thought you might have had some news for me on Edward,' Winifred said testily. 'He and his wretched father have left me in a real mess.'

Juncker tried to think quickly; he had drunk far too much whisky. He had nothing for her on Edward. Louis had been over to see him again, to put the 'frighteners' on him, telling him he would kill him – he had already taken out a contract on him, apparently - if he ever saw him anywhere near his office again.

'His girlfriend is pregnant,' Winifred went on. 'Her family are contemplating a breach of promise case against us. That'll need money. And that idiot Pole won't let me anywhere near the firm. Says he has a lot to sort out first. I'm going to be destitute, on the streets.'

Juncker couldn't help feeling a degree of schadenfreude. After the camaraderie of chess club on the Isle of Man, Cumberland had dropped him with icy disdain. He owed the family nothing. Unless she was proposing to pay him, and to pay him well, he would leave matters in abeyance.

'It's possible,' Winifred told him, 'that he has gone off after that little piece he's always carried a torch for.'

Juncker was really losing interest now; he was going to have to make some excuse to extract this awful woman from his premises.

'Her name's Sylvia Fordred. Clements Investigations. Little bitch.'

Juncker did remember the name Clements; it had cropped up in some of the litigation files that Louis had deposited with him. He always read them diligently, just in case there was any material he could use against somebody. He had seen the name in another context recently although he could not remember where. He wrote the details down carefully in his notebook and then hustled Winifred out of his shop, closing the door firmly after her.

Once he had seen her safely down the street, he poured Galland a saucer of whisky to keep him quiet and, as he did not expect any customers that afternoon, sat down to think things through without that infernal woman jabbering away. He didn't believe for one moment that she was on her beam ends. George had been filtering money out of the practice for years, for nefarious purposes. He had admitted as much over a whisky too many. Juncker's natural inclination was to be lazy and to let sleeping dogs lie, but Wirth would not leave him alone indefinitely. Louis had to be dealt with, one way or another. Granted, a beating from some of the lads who had dished the Black Shirts nicely in Cable Street was not to be recommended. London's traffic was bad, the crowds were still pressing. Maybe Louis could fall under a bus. Provided he had told nobody else where the files were, nobody would know where they were.

Across the park, at Queen Anne's Gate, Louis was taking stock. In some ways, he envied Edward his new-found freedom. He missed his own flying days. However, the opportunity now before him was a God-given one. Old Cumberland had stitched him up like the proverbial kipper when he had bought into the partnership after the war. Louis had built up the litigation side of the practice, earning them a good reputation, to go with the decent name the firm had always had for conveyancing and probate. He thought George had been very unfair to Edward, who had the makings of an excellent solicitor.

For now, he was working tirelessly, going through every case they had on the books, including matters George was meant to have dealt with. Once he had finished that, he would schedule a meeting with Roper, their accounts clerk. He suspected things were not financially as they should have been. Mrs Cumberland had appeared twice at the office already this week, wanting money and news of her son's whereabouts. He had sent her packing on both occasions. He wasn't an unfair or dishonest man; she would get what was due to her, once he knew where the firm stood, although he would never reveal Edward's whereabouts. He had a feeling though that she would not be easily fobbed off. He was also not fooled by Juncker. That man was up to no good. He would have to watch his back.

Outside a bar in Marseille, along the Canebière, Edward was waiting for an old RAF chum, Yves Bonnard. Bonnard had flown Hurricanes in the north of England in a Free French Squadron, and had a brace to his credit. He had flown all through the war, been shot down once, over Amiens in August 1944. He had left the military in 1946 and had started a small private airline, one or two aircraft from an old fly-bitten aerodrome down the coast. Edward and Bonnard had been good friends for reasons of being opposites. The clock ticked round slowly. Edward sipped a pastis and waited, enjoying some early autumn sunshine and exalting in a huge sense of liberation.

Another glass of pastis arrived in front of him. Edward looked up and smiled at his old comrade.

'Well, you haven't changed a bit.' Bonnard looked at him curiously. 'But I thought you were working in your old man's law firm. What's brought this on?'

'Long story,' Edward told him, 'and I'll regale you with it one day. I'm in a bit of a fix, to be frank, old boy. I need to get away and stay under the radar for a while. And I believe you need experienced pilots'

Bonnard raised an eyebrow and sat down and considered.

'Trouble?'

'Well, yes' Edward leaned in and glanced around, discretion at all times. 'Not of my making, but I am the one left with my head above the parapet.

'Not the wisest position to be taking.' Bonnard laughed. 'You should learn to duck.'

'I will indeed. For the moment, however, I want a job where the call on me is limited to my boss, air traffic control and the vagaries of the weather,'

'I think we could manage that.' Bonnard finished his drink and looked over at Edward. 'We do need a good pilot and you were certainly good.'

'I still am.' Edward flexed his fingers. 'I've been flying regularly, out of Headcorn. Have to keep up.'

'Good.' Bonnard scribbled on a napkin and pushed it across the table, which wobbled slightly as he did so. 'Report to this aerodrome at 6, two days from now. Got a cargo that needs a decent pilot to take it across to Tangiers.'

'I'm going to bed,' said Sol, well to the north of Edward and Bonnard. He was downstairs at the demeure, draining a glass of Jones's excellent brandy. They had lit the fire again before dinner. The room looked spectacular; even in these few short days, they had started to make it home.

'Make sure you get some sleep, Gunn,' he added, shooting a meaningful glance at Sylvia.

'See you in the morning,' Gunn replied, amused. He was young, there would be time enough for sleep on the journey, and he wanted to make the most of the next few hours. He put the guard in front of the fire, helped Sylvia tidy up and then locked up for the night.

'Gunn,' she said thoughtfully.

'What?'

She was sitting astride him, while he played with her breasts. He was watchful; she got him to agree to all sorts of things when she had him at her mercy. Usually things that, he had to admit, he liked.

366

There were, however, limits. He sensed one such limit.

'Can I borrow the Horch, for my trip down south, before I meet the quarter master? Not to go back to England of course.'

'Not falling for that one, madam, he said, moving her dexterously over onto her front. 'That car is not moving one inch until I get back from Israel.'

'You're such a spoilsport.'

'Am I now, you little minx? We'll see about that!'

Eventually, he rolled off her, exhausted.

'That's your lot for now, Mrs G,' he said, giving her bottom a slap. 'I must get a couple of hours sleep now.'

Mrs G was Sylvia's favourite of all the names he called her. That's something at least, she thought. Gunn fell into a deep sleep at first, but woke before dawn. He pulled her closer to him.

'I've never loved anyone like this,' he whispered. Sylvia murmured something and put her arms round him. They both drifted back off to sleep.

Sylvia got up with him in the morning. She was a calm presence, making him a cup of tea, fetching him anything he needed for last-minute packing, chatting to him quietly. She gave him and Sol a jar of Chartrettes greengage jam and one for Marguerite.

'You will be all right, won't you, sweetheart?' he asked.

'Of course I will,' she told him.

'You'll be all right for money?'

He had pressed into her hand most of the money Sol had given them for taking out Cumberland.

'Sylv,' he said. 'I mean every word I've said to you. Every single one. When I'm back at Christmas, we'll...'

He traced a finger around her face. Sol was pacing around outside; the taxi would be there any moment.

'I won't come outside,' she told him. She was on the verge of breaking down. 'Take care of yourself, darling. I'll write as soon as I can. I love you so much.'

'I love you, sweetheart. I'll write too, I promise.'

After she heard the taxi disappear into the distance, Sylvia fled upstairs, lay on their bed and cried until she had no tears left. Then, reprimanding herself for being a sentimental fool, she got dressed, put on some lipstick and sallied forth to use her best persuasive powers on the mayor.

On the Paris train, Sol maintained a tactful silence for the first part of the journey.

'Cigarette, old boy?' he suggested gently, after a decent interval.

Reaching into his jacket pocket for a light (he hadn't worn it for a few days), Gunn pulled out Sylvia's lacy knickers, from the restaurant. He hastily stuffed them back in; perhaps they could be a talisman.

'You and that...' began Sol.

'Yes, me and that girl,' Gunn finished the sentence for him. He wondered what he would have done if Sylvia had broken down. That had been a tremendous gamble, but he knew deep down she wanted this for him. Life had a habit of getting in the way of his plans. There was nothing either of them could do about that; they were under no illusions about how difficult the year ahead would be. But she had his heart and he had hers. With that conviction to fortify him, he turned to Sol with a smile as they began to discuss their plans.

After a successful meeting with the mayor, and a certain amount of smoothing of ruffled feathers, Sylvia came away from the mairie with his permission for the demeure to be let 'to suitable tenants.' The tenants she had in mind were eminently suitable. Earlier, she had been to look at the Horch. As she had expected, Gunn had removed the keys and the distributor cap. He had probably taken them with him. She understood. It would make her a target and would anyway be quite safe where it was. At the garage, she negotiated a deal even Gunn would have been proud of on a 1937 Citroen 7c traction coupe, and drove it carefully through the gates of the demeure. Several hours later, having cleaned the house and changed the bedding, she locked the camera equipment carefully inside one of the rooms, put a holdall in the back of the Citroen and took the long road towards the south west, her past and her family's past.

Chapter 25

Sol and Gunn were met at Haifa airport by an official car, camouflaged in muddy desert sands. Fighting had been intense around the area in recent days. Any advantage to be gained via the paint can was useful. There were a couple of soldiers in the car.

Gunn nudged Sol.

'Bloody hell, this is going to be cosy.'

The ride to Tel Aviv was hot, dusty and uncomfortable. It felt interminable. Gunn and Sol were glad to get into the barracks for a wash and spruce-up; it was a few days since they had left Chartrettes. It felt even longer. They had been delayed in Vienna while they waited for transport. Gunn took a long draught from a water fountain and stretched as he followed Sol inside.

'Better get some rest,' Sol told him. 'You must be exhausted after your exertions over the past week. There's quite a reception committee planned for us. All sorts of big wigs. Including, rather curiously, one of your lot.'

In Cairo, Alaikum replaced the receiver thoughtfully.

'That was Scheherazade,' he told Otto. 'She really is lethal. I'd hate to come across her on a dark night. Says Kalinsky and Gunn just flew into Haifa.'

'Something big is about to kick off,' said Otto. 'You mark my words. We'll have to think how we package this for our briefings.'

'Yes, I can imagine your countrymen in 'Camelot' would love to hear about that' said Alaikum.

It hadn't taken much to find out about Wirth and his castle. The reference to Schloss Wewelsberg was not lost on Otto. Yet another instance of hiding in plain sight; it was a wonder the authorities tolerated it, Alaikum reflected, but everyone seemed to have so many fish to fry nowadays.

'But after that little shit was so disgracefully rude to us the other day,' he continued 'I'm not inclined to include it. Not yet. I think we might need a spot of research on Gunn and Kalinsky, don't you? Nothing from Matthaus yet?'

'Nothing from him,' Otto frowned. 'I spoke to his landlord; says he can hear him moving about, but he's keeping himself to himself.'

'Keep onto that landlord,' advised Alaikum. 'Up his payments, if necessary.'

At Trudl's in Berlin, Elise put her phallus and impressive selection of riding crops and vibrators back in the toy box, after her last client of the night, and looked around the room.

'Alles in Ordnung,' she thought approvingly, as she got ready for her shower, putting a clean corset, pair of knickers and towel at the ready. She had, just that week, bought into the business as a partner. Her reputation was reaching stratospheric levels, although nobody apart from Trudl knew her real identity. Few would recognise her now in any case. She had shed prodigious amounts of weight; she was renowned for putting all her might into servicing 'clients with special requirements.'

There was a knock at the door. It was Trudl, wanting to know if she could take just one more client. He was prepared to pay well above the odds. With a sigh, Elise nodded her assent, asking for just a few minutes to have a shower.

Trudl was back again within a minute. Elise was stark naked after her shower, but there were no airs and graces between the pair of them.

'Two of them, as it transpires; from some castle in Bavaria. Your old neck of the woods,' she told Elise. 'I'll stay outside in case you need me; they seem slightly drunk. Usual code word?'

Elise nodded gratefully. She put the fear of God into most of her clients, and, with the terrifying weapons at her disposition, had never had any trouble. Nonetheless, it was reassuring to have back-up. Trudl laced her corset for her at the back. Before she emerged into the room, Elise paused, as she always did when a double session had been booked, to listen to her clients talking. A male and a female; both sounded quite young. Not her normal clientele. She was instantly alert to their conversation. A young Munich lawyer, originally from the Sudetenland, had been recruited to the team at Wirth's castle. Elise knew all about Wirth; she had been to the castle for functions with Friedrich. He was one of the most menacing people she had ever met. That was saying something. She knew the young lawyer in question - Dieter Fischer. He was at law school with her youngest and had put a damn sight more effort into his studies, if she remembered rightly, having come to

Munich on some sort of scholarship set up by the Americans. What a small world. Perhaps the delectable Captain Gunn might be interested in this information, she thought.

The session collapsed shortly after Elise strutted into the room in her full regalia. No matter; they had paid in advance. They got all sorts here. Trudl was right, both were drunk. She mentioned Dieter, Captain Gunn and his Bolshevik friend to Trudl as they locked the brothel up carefully for the night.

'I have an old client in the British special forces,' Trudl told her. 'I'm meeting him for a drink in a minute. Fancy joining us?'

Raising their umbrellas gamely against a sudden squall of rain, Trudl and Elise sallied forth into the square outside. In a bar in one of the side streets, Major Howard Riordan was waiting, weissbier in hand. He always enjoyed a drink with Trudl when he was in town. They had become good friends. He wasn't so keen on the Valkyrie she hung out with now. He had no truck with the type of thing she indulged in. Never mind, each to his own.

'Oh God, there she is,' he thought. He gallantly bought the ladies a beer each. Thirsty work, their line of business.

'Captain Gunn.' He played with the name. 'I knew a Mark Gunn at school,' he said. 'Used to fag for me. Decent rugby player. Never comes to any of the reunions.'

'Well, if it's the same one and you come across him,' Elise leaned forward, 'Tell him I have information of the utmost importance.'

'How did you meet him?'

'In a forest,' replied Elise, mysteriously. 'With a Jew, Lieutenant Kalinsky.'

'Sol Kalinsky?' asked Riordan. 'One eye missing'?

'That's the one' replied Elise.

'I know him well. I'm meeting him in a couple of days. I can pass on a message if you like.'

'Make sure it gets to Captain Gunn,' Elise specified.

As Sol had predicted, the next few days were a whirlwind of briefing meetings. Lost in his thoughts, Gunn was just going into the canteen for lunch with Sol, when he stopped dead.

'Hallo, Gunn,' said Riordan.

'What the buggering hell are you doing here, Riordan?' Gunn asked stiffly. This was one of the last people on earth he wanted to run into. He had hated school, and sadistic prefects such as Riordan, with a vengeance.

'I could ask you the same thing,' replied Riordan. 'I'm about to go into the same meeting as you. Funnily enough, I ran into a friend of yours in Berlin. Elise. Sends her regards.'

'Wouldn't have put you down for that sort of thing,' Riordan continued. 'Anyway, she seems to have taken quite a shine to you. You always were a dark horse. She wanted me to pass on a message about some young chap who went to law school with her son. Seemed to think it was urgent.'

'Interesting,' said Sol, who had just appeared. 'Quite a character, was Elise. How are you, anyway, Riordan? Want to join us?'

It turned out the two of them went back a long way. There was some convoluted explanation as to why, but Gunn was really not interested in reminiscences of any kind.

'Oh, I've just remembered,' Riordan turned to Sol. 'We used to call him Tadpole when he first arrived at school. With his mother being French. '

'Hilarious,' remarked Gunn.

'Until he grew, of course. Now, didn't I hear some rumour about you and one of the maids? After my time of course.'

Gunn made an excuse and left them to it. He smouldered a little, his temper crackling like early embers. Riordan was one of the vilest people he had ever met but he was clearly a good soldier. Sol had respect for him. Maybe school day judgments should be set aside for the greater good. Despite all the ribbing, he was curious to hear what Elise had to say.

He sat outside in the sun, with a postcard from Sylv, which had just arrived for him.

She sounded all right; on her way south now. Smiling at the row of kisses, and feeling considerably calmer, he put the postcard carefully back into his pocket and went back inside for the meeting. These briefings were all well and good but he was anxious to get on with taking out Matthaus. Sol had told him they would have a final separate meeting with David on Damascus. This next meeting was about the pipeline.

Gunn summarised their findings so far, and filled them in on Cumberland and his death, and the fact that Edward had run away. He was glad of the notes Sylvia had helped him put together, at the demeure. He also told them about Juncker and the files which were safely stored in Sylvia's house in Kent.

'Done well for yourself, haven't you Gunn?' whispered Riordan. 'Considering your background. Is Sylvia a Valkyrie too?'

'Fuck off, Riordan,' Gunn replied, in quiet but murderous tones.

'The intelligence we have, gentlemen,' said David, 'is that Wirth is a far more formidable adversary. He won't put himself forward as a front man; that's not his style.'

'An old friend of Gunn's may have some inside information on that,' put in Riordan. 'Goes by the name of Elise. Partner in a brothel in Berlin. Specialises in clients with, er, specific requirements.' This raised a laugh.

'You're pushing it,' thought Gunn. He explained the connection, and how she had helped them to hang Mueller. 'Formidable lady. Not my type.'

'Well,' Riordan continued, 'According to your 'friend,' Gunn, Wirth has recruited a young Munich lawyer. Goes by the name of Dieter Fischer; comes from the Sudetenland originally. Came to Bavaria on a scholarship funded by the Yanks and did the Bar exams there. They also 'sprang' a guy called Joachim Mecklenburg recently, through Madrid. Ring any bells?'

It did. Glances were exchanged. The pipeline was an issue. Wirth's agenda was different from Mueller's and Cumberland's. He wasn't just a believer, he was a fanatic. He was trying to engineer a resurgence; that was clear. They would have expected operations of this nature to have started winding down by now. The very opposite was happening. Better intelligence was needed. The Alaikum/Otto operation was a joke. They needed dealing with. The new listening station in Chartrettes might assist matters. Sylvia's meeting with the quarter master two weeks hence was confirmed. Gunn told them that the way had already been paved with the mayor. Riordan raised a quizzical eyebrow; Gunn, a partner in a London investigation agency and with a house in France.

'Well, you two,' David turned to Sol and Gunn. 'Shall we adjourn so I can brief you on our immediate problem in Damascus?'

Riordan's parting shot, again sotto voce, was: 'I might just look up that young lady of yours next time I'm in London, Gunn. Sounds quite a girl.'

'She wouldn't touch you with a barge pole,' Gunn replied.

He followed Sol and David out to a waiting car. He had taken to David straightaway. Hard as nails, but clearly an intelligent man. He told Gunn on the journey how he had once had aspirations to become a concert pianist but in 1925, when he was ten and living near Capernaum, his Arab neighbours had killed his parents and broken his hands before destroying the ramshackle piano which had been his treasured possession. He had gone to live with relatives in London and had enlisted with the Green Howards in 1939. After demob, he had returned to Israel and joined the underground.

The three of them were in a barrel-vaulted stone office in Tiberias. The building was old, history virtually whispering from the stones. As they entered, Gunn had pressed his ears to the walls as if listening. He thought he could hear fragments of tales long since told and long since forgotten.

'Gentlemen,' David spread a map out on the wooden trestle table. Other than that, three chairs and a bureau, the vault was bare.

'Syria took the northern shore of the Sea of Galilee in May. It holds it still, but the situation there is chaotic and fluid, so that may be your best route into Syria and then on to Damascus.'

'How far is that?' Gunn asked.

'Around sixty miles,' David mused. 'Hilly country, rough, some half decent roads and the potential for trouble.'

'The usual recipe,' Sol smiled. 'My favourite. Any ideas as to a route?'

'All a bit ad hoc,' David shrugged. 'There are troops all over the area and let's face it, the locals will not be friendly. The fewest troops seem to be on the line between Al Harah and north towards Kanaker, skirting the latter to the east and entering Damascus via Darayya. Again, rough country but that is in your favour.'

Stubbing out a cigarette, Gunn leaned forward. 'How are we getting in?'

'Boat.'

378

'No chance of a low level drop, sort of thing we did in the LRDG?' David shook his head. 'Too much of a risk of broken bones. We couldn't come and get you.'

'Nice,' Gunn nodded. 'So, punting on the Cam?'

'With a few added extras,' David responded, drily.

'There is another option.' Sol leaned back in his chair and laughed. 'It is fairly suicidal but I could suggest it as long as it does not go beyond these walls.'

David folded his arms, keeping his hands carefully concealed. Some memories did not fade. 'This should be amusing.'

'Bugger amusing,' Gunn chimed in. 'Knowing this one, it will be wilder than a rhino on a ski slope.'

Sol spread his hands in a gesture of compliance.

'Since you insist, it occurs to me that if Gunn and I are dressed in British Army fatigues, dropped at the border at gunpoint as prisoners, with suitable documents, there is a fair chance the Syrians may take it easy on us and give us a ride into Damascus to any British diplomatic mission, and we jump ship at a moment of our choosing and then do what we have to do.'

'Might be less risky than the boat option and fighting our way for sixty miles,' Gunn observed.

'Possibly,' said David. 'And I suppose it would be simple to arrange. But you'd have to find yourselves some equipment, and quickly. You'd have nothing but your British Army papers.'

And when we get to Damascus,' Gunn went on. 'Is there anything else we should know about Matthaus? Other than what's in the file?'

'Funny you should mention that,' David commented. 'There is some material I didn't put in the file. Seems he was a deserter. Not common knowledge. Got out of Berlin a few weeks ahead of the Red Army and made his way to Damascus. But you shouldn't under-estimate him. He's a vicious thug. Now, this little jaunt of yours…'

Unaware that, only a matter of hours earlier, he had featured in Gunn's briefing to the Israeli forces, Edward was drinking mint tea in the souk in Tangiers. He had a few hours to kill before heading back to the aerodrome. He liked the city, and the bright colours of the spices and fabrics in the markets. He had stipulated to Bonnard the type of job he wanted. That's what he had got. The 'cargo' he had brought over earlier turned out to be two taciturn Germans. He had not enquired further.

Yesterday, he had spoken briefly to Louis. Mummy was becoming a nuisance. Louis was losing patience with her. Caroline's parents were bringing breach of promise proceedings. Well, in that case, he thought, she could whistle for any money from him. Juncker had been warned off, but Louis reckoned he wouldn't go down without a fight. He had left a God-awful mess behind him, he thought ruefully. Still, he was a long way from all of that now.

He threw a few coins on the table, placed his cap on his head and gave the brim a snap. Then, glancing at his watch and assessing, he took a stroll. He needed to clear his head and fill it anew. The hard, flat light of Tangiers framed by the wind off the sea and the sand to the south beneath a big sky would do just about right.

In Cairo, Otto had managed to speak at last to Matthaus. He never knew his compatriot had been a deserter. Had he done so, his opinion of him would have been quite different. As it was, he had built up quite a rapport in recent days.

'Sounds rather odd,' he said, frowning. 'Reckons there's somebody coming for him.'

'Probably been at the schnapps again,' said Alaikum, vaguely. 'You said he liked a tipple. Anyway, he's probably right. Had a few close shaves recently.'

'He has. Sounded different this time though.' Otto frowned.

'Lunch in Heliopolis?' suggested Alaikum.

'Weren't we going to go through that stuff from Scheherazade that came in earlier? There was a lot of it.'

'Oh, that can wait' Alaikum told him. 'I'm ravenous. I want to have a look at our new house.'

In Damascus, as Otto had surmised, Matthaus sensed that danger was imminent. A life built on staying ahead of a bullet had given him a certain sense that tipped over now and then into paranoia, which had resulted in one or two unfortunate

381

incidents in coffee houses, smoothed over with the exchange of cash. He had run out of alcohol altogether and was not in the best frame of mind. Still, he was ready for whoever it was.

Chapter 26

Gunn was studying the map quietly, while David and Sol spoke in hushed tones at the other end of the room. He was thinking about the campaign against the Vichy French he had participated in, during '41. He recalled an Arab proverb:

'Choose your neighbour before the house and your companion before the road.'

Gunn had no qualms about either. He and Sol worked well together. As David and Sol moved back towards his end of the room, he shifted in his seat, looking up from the map.

'You know, I've never been especially keen on mucking about on waterways. Fast cars, yes, Rivers, streams, seas, lakes, not really. Sol's prisoner wheeze gets my vote.'

Sol looked at Gunn and then at David, grinning.

'See, boss, I told you. Hand over the folding.'

David winced and fished in his trouser pocket, pulling out a roll of notes. He peeled off a couple and handed them to Sol.

'That should get you started.'

'When do we pick up the uniforms and fake documents?' asked Gunn, his mind already racing ahead to the subterfuge stage.

'Won't take long; our people are good at this.' David said.

'How about some fresh air and a stroll?' suggested Sol.

In Bavaria, Wirth was escorting Dieter to his car.

'So, my young friend,' he observed. 'You have some travelling to do. Are you quite clear about what you have to do?'

'Oh yes,' responded Dieter. He was trying not to think too deeply or too far ahead. He was looking forward to the weekend ahead with Ursula, which was shaping up to be the perfect mix of 'social' and 'quiet'; the past few days had been intense. They were meeting some old law school friends for dinner that evening, and her parents had invited them for lunch on Saturday. The forecast looked good.

As Wirth waved his young friend off, Karl Adler appeared at his elbow.

'Mind if I run something past you, Sir? Just been speaking to Otto in Cairo.'

'What did he have to say? Nothing useful, I don't suppose,' replied Wirth, in avuncular fashion. Adler was a real asset to the team; a true believer; Wirth would almost go as far as to describe him as a disciple. He had been a doctoral student of his at Gottingen; a promising one. Wirth liked to think he was fulfilling his academic potential now.

'Usual rubbish; rabbits on about nothing. He did ask in passing if we knew of anybody called Rainer Matthaus.'

Wirth paused. He knew Matthaus from boyhood. He had last seen him on a road south of Wurzburg in early 1945. Matthaus had been less than forthcoming. That had never been his style. Equally, he had been driving a Mercedes Benz rather than being driven. Wirth had supposed pressures of manpower and the general situation had allowed the normal niceties to slip. They had run into each other, on and off, for a decade up to that point, and more than once shared a beer and some stories. But on that cold spring morning, Matthaus had been lip-chewingly brief and spare and had dodged any questions as to his mission or destination. At the time, Wirth had applauded his colleague's discipline. Afterwards, he had wondered about him, when sipping a brandy and leafing through memories.

What about him?' he asked.

'Only that he may be in some sort of trouble,' said Adler. 'He's been in Damascus for a while, apparently, operating as a hitman. Lying low.'

Wirth's curiosity was well and truly piqued. The Matthaus he had known had never been one for lying low.

'You might just give these people a call,' he suggested, giving Adler a list of names. 'Old colleagues of mine. See if they know anything. And keep a close eye on the verbiage emanating from those two pansies in Cairo.'

As he made his way back into the castle, to see how the rest of his young acolytes were doing, he remembered that Matthaus had been born in Alexandria, to German parents, and had grown up speaking Arabic in the streets. Perhaps that explained why he had gravitated towards Damascus. Wirth had just finished his circuit, giving friendly advice here and there, when Adler came over to him, with the whole sorry tale of Matthaus's departure from Germany, through Austria, Romania and Greece. In

385

Greece, he had stolen a Fieseler Storch from the Luftwaffe and slipped over to Turkey. From there, it had been an easy run to Syria, to join old boyhood friends. Adler had pieced this together in half an hour.

'He's good,' thought Wirth. 'If everyone on my team was like this, we'd be up and running again in no time. My young friend Fischer from Munich is going to have to show his mettle – and soon.'

'I have to wonder, Sir,' mused Adler, 'who else could be interested in an enemy of the Reich.'

'Get back on the telephone to Alaikum,' Wirth advised. 'They know more than they are letting on.'

In Tiberias, Gunn was going through the fake documents with a practised eye, thinking over his cover story again. Sylv was always brilliant at this, but he had to admit, he was impressed by what had been put together for them here. He looked up at a pat on the shoulder from David.

'So, Englishman, what do you think?

'A stroll in the park before tea,' Gunn replied lightly, seeing the veiled concern in David's eyes. 'That reminds me, I could do with a cuppa.'

'You people are incorrigible,' David laughed, the tension cracking like a spoon on a crème brûlée. 'Nothing much bothers you, does it?'

'Au contraire.' Gunn shook his head. 'We just don't want to let our mates down.'

'I see.'

'As you'll remember from your days with the Green Howards, that's how the regimental system works' Gunn amplified. 'King and Country is all very well, but what matters is your mate to the left and to the right. You stand and get on with it.'

'You'll do' said David.

In Munich, Dieter looked up appreciatively at Ursula, who had brought him a stack of letters to sign and a coffee. She was one of the best secretaries he had ever had. He had barely registered the drive home from Wirth's castle; his head was spinning. The reunion with the law school crowd had been fun, in a smart restaurant. They were all beginning to flourish in their careers, in their different ways. Erwin Mueller had been there, and, wondering why he hadn't made the connection before, Dieter had made a beeline for him.

He and Erwin had moved in different social circles. It was time for that to change. It seemed the Bad Kaltenbrun estate needed sorting out. A small part of it had been left to Friedrich in the thirties, in recognition of his late mother's 'services' to the household. The lion's share devolved upon Edward Cumberland in London. Friedrich's share now belonged to Elise, who had vanished off the face of the earth. Erwin didn't seem too bothered about it or hi mother; his life was in Munich now. The estate as a whole was being run by loyal retainers, but that situation would not continue indefinitely. His blasé attitude both perplexed and irritated Dieter.

Turning all this information over in his mind, Dieter signed the last letter with a flourish, and picked up the receiver to take another call from Adler at the castle. The pipeline was keeping him busy. At least, he thought, arrangements were running smoothly.

Bonnard down in the south of France had taken on new staff, including a former Spitfire pilot. Dieter had been amused about that. He had heard good reports of the new pilot.

As the dawn eased itself up and across the Sea of Galilee, an Israeli army truck, with a white flag pinned to its radiator, drove slowly up to Syrian positions on the north shore. Around one hundred yards from the border, David applied the brakes and the truck came to a halt. He turned, looked over his shoulder and nodded, and troops pushed two men in British army fatigues out of the truck. At gunpoint, they invited them to march slowly towards Syria. They were dusty, bruised, one had lost an eye and they had clearly taken more than one beating. In a raised hand, one of them clutched a white rag. David muttered a prayer of good fortune, started the truck up and reversed it back towards the Israeli position.

Winifred Cumberland lay on Edward's bed at Chepstow Villas, looking once again at the stars on the ceiling. Lothar had been livid about them, accusing her of turning their son into a fairy. She had, upon reflection, made a terrible mess of things; Lothar had treated Edward appallingly. She had done nothing; transfixed for all those years by her own deep unhappiness. Venting her spleen on Sylvia had felt good at the time but it had driven Tom away. If only the Great War hadn't intervened, all those years ago, and ruined things between them.

Lothar was dead; that was a blessed relief. She could admit that now. But Edward was gone for good.

Taking his teddy had been the ultimate gesture. She had been 'blackballed' at the Tennis Club. Caroline was refusing to marry anybody else – Eddy was the only one for her, she lamented, to anybody who cared to listen. She had told her parents that she was keeping the baby no matter what. They were now pressing for money. Caroline's father had told Winifred that if she wasn't forthcoming with the 'readies,' they were quite prepared to put the baby out for adoption. They might just do that anyway.

Winifred could not and would not allow her grandchild to be put up for adoption, although she did not much care what happened to Caroline. It might be her only chance to make amends. Louis had told her that she could expect little financially from the firm; George had been plundering it systematically, almost running it into the ground. He had been suitably vague. That dreadful little tailor, Juncker, had come up with nothing on Edward. A few letters had arrived from Germany which she did not profess to understand. Other letters were beginning to arrive, from closer to home; untutored and menacing.

Pensively, she threaded through her fingers a card Edward had dropped on the floor of his room, advertising the services of Yves Bonnard, commercial airlines. An hour later, she had packed a holdall, locked the house and set off for the boat train. Edward would damn well have to sort out Bad Kaltenbrun; she was certainly not going there. Lothar's parents had taken a dislike to her immediately; their icy froideur had been most hurtful to a young bride. In a rare moment of kindness, Lothar had taken her hiking, so they could have some time on their own. It had been one of their nicest times together; Edward had been conceived somewhere up a mountain, on the way to a lake. Sipping her gin and tonic on the deck of the ferry, and feeling alive for the first time in years, she leafed through her Baedeker, planning her route.

Edward flew in low over the North African coast. He glanced through the port glass of his cockpit. He could see sheet lightning over the Nile Delta. His instruments would not take kindly to that. He would have to skirt south some distance before turning north again, heading for the small airfield at Hawara, the city that in Pharaonic times had been named Avaris. He was looking forward to having a look round. He had wanted to study Ancient History at university, to the derision of his father. The war had put paid to any such plans.

The airframe began to shake and tumble as the ride became rougher. The plane could kick like a mule, but he was experienced enough. He would bring her down. He glanced over his shoulder into the cabin at his passengers, two soberly-dressed Germans. They were bringing their last meal up. Edward found this entertaining momentarily, but then remembered he was part of a commercial enterprise; Bonnard had impressed on him from the outset the distinction to be drawn between wartime derring -do and transporting passengers.

'All right back there, chaps?' he called.

Many miles away, Sol and Gunn were approaching the Syrian border slowly, as befitted the injuries both were sporting.

'More like a mile than a hundred yards,' commented Gunn. 'My father often said that about being in the trenches.'

Sol dug him in the ribs.

'Hello, who's this? Looks as if they have sent out a reception committee.'

'Oh God,' muttered Gunn, through thinly compressed lips. 'In no man's land, unarmed, with twenty tooled-up Syrians heading our way. Not sure today could get any better.'

They came to a halt. It seemed prudent. There was no cover. They waited. As Sol observed, leaning in a little:

'A couple of bullets and we won't feel a damn thing anyhow.'

Gunn smirked and then blanked off a smile as the Syrians came close. An officer stepped forward, narrow eyed and shrewd of expression. He said nothing, but rifled through their pockets and found their warrant cards and their passports. British. He nodded to himself and with a drop of the head indicated that they should follow him. They had no option.

In Cairo, Alaikum was idly watching a brawl in the market in the street below their office. This neighbourhood really was getting a little rough. Heliopolis would be so much more civilised.

'Get hold of Scheherazade on the telephone, would you, Otto dearest?' he asked. 'I want to talk to her about her report. It says Gunn and Kalinsky have been in meetings in Tiberias. I think we can guess who with, don't you? And 'activity at the Syrian positions.' I think we can surmise what that is too. Even so…?'

'Of course,' smiled Otto. 'And then what will you do?'

He held up the slip of paper the boy had brought from the bank; another large payment from Israel.

'What wouldn't that little shit Adler give for this information?' He had had a call from Adler earlier.

'He's not getting anything' said Alaikum, 'If he's not prepared to pay. His attitude stinks. Maybe you should speak to the organ grinder and not the monkey. See if you can tempt him with the material we have found about Gunn and Kalinsky. Dangerous game, though. Make that call to Scheherazade and we'll think about it.'

'You're terrible,' Otto told him fondly.

In the Syrian camp, Gunn shifted round in his chair. His wrists ached from their bonds. His ankles felt as if they were going to swell. He was hungry and thirsty. His lips were cracked. One eye was closed and he was fairly certain a back molar was somewhat looser than it had been yesterday. Still he stuck to the script.

'I am a British soldier. That is my warrant card. I was captured by the Irgun or whatever the Jewish Underground called itself and now they have Israel, they don't need me or my colleague.'

The Syrian officer leaned forward on his desk and sipped his coffee. It was good and thick. He allowed it to filter through to his teeth.

'Well, you are fortunate, my friend.'

'Fortunate?' Gunn allowed himself a laugh. 'How so?'

'They could have stretched your necks like those two British sergeants in 47.'

'Oh, good point.' Gunn spat out some blood and decided that enough was enough. 'So, are you going to beat me again? It won't change what I tell you.'

'I am aware of that,' the officer grinned. 'I simply don't like the British very much.'

He stood up, and was at Gunn's chair in three strides. He punched him full in the face. Gunn's loose molar popped out in a capsule of blood and flesh.

'But you are telling the truth and I am sending you to Damascus tomorrow.'

Gunn gingerly tested the place where his molar had been with his tongue.

'What about my colleague?'

'Don't push it.'

In Tel Aviv, David had been reading Alaikum's report. Sol normally ploughed through it for him, sorting the wheat from the chaff. Alaikum's description of his material as de luxe was risible although he wondered where the material on Israel was coming from. It was rather accurate. The sooner someone sorted out those two clowns, the better. Perhaps the girl who worked with Gunn could do the world a favour and take over the role. It would take time and she would require training, but Sol spoke highly of her. He looked up at the clock and wondered how the pair were faring. He had seen them being picked up, in the distance. Hopefully, they were well on their way to Damascus now.

Their quarry, Matthaus, had been listening to one of his lieder cycles. They always made him nostalgic, for his parents, long-since dead, and for the Germany he had once known. Under normal circumstances, he would have drowned his sorrows. He no longer had the wherewithal for that. He felt like a ghost, between two worlds. After wallowing in sadness for a moment, he decided he was damned if he was going to sit around and await his fate. He knew the identity of the pair who were after him; Otto had sent a message. They would have a surprise.

The sun had not crept up over the brittle cold of the Golan when Gunn and Sol were loaded, with scant ceremony, onto the back of a Syrian army truck. Their escort consisted of a couple of disinterested reservists going home on leave, a little too casual for the situation, both thought. Still, they would seize their chance at the right moment.

Sol was nursing a bruised face and a couple of broken fingers, roughly bound with tape and splints. He seemed in reasonable fettle. Gunn kept exploring the hole at the back of his mouth with his tongue. He tried to keep his temper in check. He looked over at Sol.

'Ready for the off, old boy?'

Sol motioned him to keep quiet; they would talk once the journey was under way and the noise of the engine would disguise their voices. Gunn settled back and let his thoughts drift to Posillipo Beach, the bonnet of the Horch and the hayloft. He began to feel calmer.

At Hawara, Edward was enjoying a few hours' break before he had to collect his next 'cargo' and take it on to Tripoli. He was becoming accustomed to his silent German passengers. The last pair were profoundly grateful to alight from the aircraft alive. They had congratulated him and shaken his hand before they went their separate ways. He was, he reckoned, somewhere near what was known as Crocodilopolis. The locals had worshipped a crocodile and adorned it with gold, keeping it in a special temple pond. He had a copy of Herodotus's Histories to read later. He was a world away from Mummy, Caroline and irascible old ladies wanting him to draft another codicil. He felt a hundred times better for it.

The only fly in the ointment was Alaikum's weekly briefing, in which he had featured, to Bonnard's delight.

'Not by name, I hope,' Edward was aghast.

'Just that you are an ex Spitfire pilot; great publicity,' responded Bonnard. 'You're making a name for us. No harm in it, surely?'

'If it emerges that a former Spitfire pilot is ferrying well-dressed Germans around, many of whom have Prussian haircuts and carry themselves as if they were parading through Paris in 1940, that

395

could be harmful,' Edward pointed out. 'There are certain things one does not do. It appears I am doing them. Best keep me out of it.'

In Brighton, it had been another late night in the bar at the Gunn House Hotel. Inspector Gunn stood on the steps, taking in the sea air, before locking up. It was warm out there. All the residents were in for the night. Something was troubling him, a sixth sense. An air of menace but something good too, perhaps a homecoming some way off; it was strange. Following the routine he had adopted during the war, he climbed the stairs to Mark's room and stood there for a moment. He lit a candle and placed it in the window, and a few minutes later went back downstairs.

In Bavaria, Wirth was in thoughtful mood, following morning meditation with his acolytes. He would have to explain its mandatory nature more clearly to his young friend, Dieter, but there was no immediate hurry. As he did his rounds, from the weather station in the grounds and back to the main office, or 'engine room,' as they all thought of it, he reflected on the community now being built in Argentina. Mueller and Cumberland had put no thought into it, he thought angrily. Some of the people they had sent over should have been left to rot. Scientists were short on the ground. He knew of at least one 'facility,' deep underground in Austria that had never been found. Perhaps Adler could make some calls.

Adler was tapping his pencil abstractedly against an ashtray, reading through the latest Alaikum special.

'They're in thrall to someone,' he said to Wirth, who was standing beside his desk. 'It's obvious. That's why their intelligence is rubbish.'

'Maybe,' said Wirth. 'We'll just have to treat it all with a pinch of salt and draw our own conclusions. Anything of interest?'

'Former spitfire pilot recruited by Bonnard.'

'Fischer said he had taken on somebody good. Well, there's an irony.' Wirth gave a short laugh and continued with his perambulations. In a moment, he had made his decision. He crossed back over to Adler.

'Get Fischer on the telephone for me.'

In Hawara, while Edward settled down with Herodotus and a glass of mint tea, the two Germans he had dropped off earlier were waiting, sweating in their Northern European suits, in a fly-frequented hotel on the outskirts of town. They grumbled a little, missing decent beer and mountains, and waited for the contact to pick them up; they had been told he was German and would be coming from Cairo.

Dieter, almost having to pinch himself, was having lunch in the Grill Room at the Heliopolis Palace Hotel with Otto and Alaikum, having already been out with them first thing to see the sun coming up over the pyramids and the sphinx. He could put up with the creepiness of Wirth and his entourage, he decided, if it involved travel like this. The only other place he had travelled to so far, outside Germany, had been Russia, and not as a tourist.

The Heliopolis Palace was, they told him, known as the Taj Mahal of the desert, and was once frequented by the King of Belgium, Milton S Hershey and John Pierpoint Morgan. As the son of a hotelier, albeit on a far smaller scale, he was captivated, staring in wonder at the great dome as they walked through.

'Not quite as it was though,' Alaikum explained. 'The Australians used it as a hospital. Made a bloody awful mess of it.'

'We're trying to incorporate elements of the design into our new house out here,' Otto put in. 'It's taking a while, but we want to get it right.'

Money was clearly no object with these two, thought Dieter. Like Adler, he had concluded that they were in thrall to another wealthy pay master, and utterly corrupt. Unlike Adler, he sensed that they did not respond to bullying and rudeness. They could be bought, at a price, but it would be a steep one. Looking at his watch, he realised that his 'charges' would be nearing Hawara by now. He thanked his hosts and took his leave.

'Delightful young man,' Alaikum sighed, watching Dieter walking briskly down the steps to meet his driver.

'Don't you go getting any ideas,' Otto was amused. 'But yes, it makes a change not to be dealing with a rude, arrogant idiot.'

At Hawara, Dieter greeted his two charges, and asked them how their flight had been. They were very complimentary about the pilot.

'Ah yes, I think he may have been flown Spitfires in the war.'

'That explains a lot.'

Dieter knew that Egypt had been emerging as an alternative destination to Argentina: King Farouk was already finding a lot of work for his 'assets' to do. These two were to be no exception. They were to join the Egyptian secret police, after a debriefing which he was also to attend. He settled back to enjoy the ride.

In the back of the truck, Sol and Gunn were talking in hushed whispers. The two reservists were having an animated discussion, probably about their plans for the weekend.

'It's been fairly straightforward so far, hasn't it,' Gunn commented. 'I mean, they roughed us up a bit but now they've let us go, with just these two in charge.'

'We're probably not that important, in the wider scheme of things,' Sol replied. 'Just a couple of strays, only useful to a point.'

Gunn shifted a leg, to ease a spasm of cramp. He had been trying to recall the landscape from his previous time in Syria, to get his bearings.

'How far are we from Damascus?'

Sol peered through the slats of the truck at the road.

'Not much sign of habitation here. At a guess, a couple of hours.'

The truck was following an ancient trade route, along the Great Trunk Road towards Damascus, across hills and plains towards the city

399

whose name had an almost mythical ring to it. Neither man was handcuffed. That gave them options. Outside the city and they would make less noise; inside its walls, there would be a tumult and that would allow them to disappear like smoke. As Sol observed, it was simply a matter of timing and location.

Gunn shifted round. His fatigues were uncomfortable; he itched like mad. It had been a while since he was in uniform. He longed for a cigarette and a cup of tea.

'I meant to ask, what's the story between you and Riordan? You were at school together but you don't seem to like him?' asked Sol.

Gunn explained how Riordan had treated him and the other new boys, singling him out for special treatment, sensing the differences in his background; the usual thing, making toast, cleaning the study, keeping the fire going, and hell to pay if it wasn't done properly. One day, he had turned on Riordan and nearly smashed his head in. They had been alone in Riordan's study; nobody else had witnessed it. After that, the prefect had given him grudging respect and left him alone.

'You British and your public schools,' Sol began.

'I wouldn't send a dog to that establishment,' Gunn told him. 'Let alone a child. I always thought Riordan was a foul excuse for a human being. You obviously rate him. What's he doing here? Liaison of some sort?'

'You could call it that,' Sol replied, enigmatically.

400

They fell silent and Gunn drifted into a deep sleep. He was in the middle of a vivid dream about Sylvia. She seemed to want to tell him something and was being very persistent, in her own inimitable fashion. Just as she was about to reveal what it was, he came to with a start, as the truck veered off the road. He shook himself awake, slightly irritated, wondering momentarily where he was.

'Pit stop,' I reckon,' murmured Sol.

Gunn seized the chance, counting on Sol following. He swung off the metal frame struts at the rear of the truck and his boots caught a Syrian, who was minding his own business and smoking a cigarette, full on the temple. The Syrian crumpled and hit the rocky strand of the road like a dropped strand of coal.

Not stopping, Gunn lifted the Syrian's handgun and put one in the head of the other Syrian, as he turned, his mouth a dark O of surprise.

Sol was following, via a different route. He hoisted himself up onto a metal framework and swung back and forth, gaining the purchase of momentum. He went boot first through the back light of the truck's cabin, the driver's face bouncing off the steering wheel with the impact. The driver slumped sideways onto the passenger seat. Sol opened the cabin door and dragged him out. He dropped his cargo against a rock and turned. Gunn was walking towards him, a tight smile on his face. He was armed.

'What have you got?'

'One dead,' Gunn noted, 'and another who probably won't make it.'

'Doubt if this one will either; I hit him hard.'

'Well, they can rest in paradise.' Gunn looked around. The landscape was unfolding below them, green fields and signs of life. He looked behind them. There was sufficient cover in any one of the dried up rills and folds a little way back up the road.

'We can leave them there. Nobody will see them for a while.'

A few minutes later, having relieved their escorts of their arms and their papers, they began their descent onto the plains.

'Should give us a decent start, remarked Gunn, looking behind him. 'Next stop Damascus.'

'Hope we have a smooth run through,' muttered Sol. 'Checkpoint ahead.'

Their papers passed muster with the sentry, another reservist, who looked bored and sleepy.

'So this geezer,' Gunn said, putting the truck back into gear, 'lives by the old citadel?'

'So it seems,' replied Sol. 'Ever been to Damascus?'

'Oh yes. How long have you got?'

Wirth's castle in Bavaria was a hive of activity. They had got four assets out this week; two more to Egypt and two to Buenos Aires. Under the regime of Mueller and Cumberland, things had stalled. Dieter was sitting with Wirth in his inner sanctum, sipping vintage brandy out of an antique glass.

'You're doing well, my young friend,' Wirth smiled encouragingly. 'How did you get on with Alaikum and Otto?'

Dieter told him about the high life they were living, the house they were building in Heliopolis and his suspicions about their paymaster.

'They're coining it. Alaikum did have one too many over lunch though. Mentioned, and these were his words, an 'interesting duo' heading for Syria. Mark Gunn, who is British, and Sol Kalinsky, an Israeli. Both ex British forces. Reckons they're going to liquidate Matthaus. He's been causing mayhem in Israel, operating as a hitman.'

'Matthaus,' said Wirth slowly, 'can go to hell. As a traitor to the Reich, he deserves everything coming to him. I've no doubt this 'duo' will do a good job. Maybe run those names past Adler after lunch. Now, how is everything in Munich? How is your delightful young lady?'

Telling his driver to go and have fun on the pier for the rest of the evening, Howard Riordan ascended the steps of the Gunn House Hotel, taking in the chipped paintwork and the air of a building that needed money spending on it. This was more what he would have expected of Gunn. Some might describe him as nosey; he would call it 'doing his job.' There was little on the official files on Gunn, apart from a note of his war service with Stirling and the LRDG and a mention in the dispatches; interesting. The usual old school network had let him down; Gunn hadn't kept in touch with anyone. He went over to greet Inspector Gunn, who was opening up the bar while the young barman was changing a barrel in the cellar. The likeness was unmistakeable.

Several hours later, and distinctly the worse for wear, Riordan staggered back down the steps where his driver was still waiting patiently. He had the distinct impression that he had talked more about himself than they had spoken about Gunn, which was unusual for him. Still, it had been fun and he was always partial to a drop of decent bitter. He nodded off and slept all the way back to London.

Wondering not for the first time what Mark was up to, Inspector Gunn helped the young lad wash the glasses, leaving him to mop the floor. He had been curious to meet a school friend, which was how the man had introduced himself, although Mark had not, to his knowledge, made any particular friends at school. He still remembered dropping him off with the Brothers, in a bleak building with black walls on the outside and a hall panelled with honours boards, where several other young lads were saying goodbye to their parents. The sky had been black too.

'Don't leave me here, Dad,' Mark had said.

'You'll love it, son' he had responded. 'Lots of sport, new friends.' With that, he had gone, leaving Mark standing on the steps. He hadn't looked back, he couldn't bear to. He had headed off to drown his sorrows in a nearby pub.

He hadn't had a choice really. In the aftermath of Annette's death due to a late miscarriage, which Mark had witnessed, something to which no child should ever be subjected, he had been staring into a bottle most of the time, barely holding his job down. Mark had made friends with the local 'petits voyous.' A visit from his formidable sister Vi (to this day the family matriarch) had shaken him to the core, after an incident where the gendarmerie had become involved.

'That boy' she told him disapprovingly,' is running wild. You need to send him to school in England. Pull yourself together, Dom.'

He had let Vi make the arrangements. Mark, being a clever lad, had got a scholarship. His father had hoped school would be the making of him. However, Mark had said nothing in the holidays, other than 'I hate it,' and 'When can I leave?' Mark had passed some exams, but then taken matters into his own hands. His son had always been strong-willed. He had never said what the final catalyst was. Still, he had certainly done all right for himself now.

This evening, Inspector Gunn had got Riordan's measure straightaway. Army intelligence; he could tell them a mile off. In his usual fashion, Inspector Gunn had listened carefully and dispensed pints, while Riordan became more loquacious than was probably judicious, and spoke a little of the work Mark would be doing in Israel and the organisation he was working with. Having said goodnight to the barman and bolted the doors, Inspector Gunn went upstairs to light the candle in Mark's room, wondering who would arrive on the doorstep next. First Collins, now Riordan. None of them would get anything out of him. On an impulse, he lit another candle, for little Josephine Amelie, out there somewhere in France. He had never given up hope. He never would.

Chapter 27

The drive into the city walls of Damascus was remarkably straightforward. Near the old citadel, the sun was setting in a rose and gold sky, and the muezzin man was calling the faithful to prayer, his voice soaring to a crescendo. Sol and Gunn were walking towards it, having left the truck a few streets away.

'Being used as a prison and a barracks now the French have pulled out,' Sol explained, seeing Gunn looking curiously around him. 'Taken something of a pounding in recent years.'

'Where are we heading,' asked Gunn, noticing Sol's purposeful stride.

'Dr Weitz. Old friend of mine. Jewish physician. Family's been here thousands of years apparently. Quite some feat when you think about it.'

'I think I've heard of him,' Gunn remarked. 'Last time I was here.'

As the sun finally went down over the city, and the starlings fled the kites, a climb up over the walls and into the courtyard was the work of an instant. They found themselves in a neat and tidy courtyard, with well-tended lemon trees and rose bushes. There was no water in the fountain. The house itself had a wary, battened-down look, almost as if it was defending itself.

Sol frowned.

'Hope he's all right,' he murmured. 'I've heard some bad things.'

'If there is trouble here,' Gunn observed, leaning against a big terracotta pot containing a rosemary bush, 'We are not going to be helping the situation'

'True,' Sol nipped at his lip. 'We may need to get the family out'

Gunn was thinking of the phrase Sylv had used, probably something she'd read – 'a country without maps'; exactly where they were now. Matthaus was one thing; this was something different altogether. This was like his war service, thinking on his feet.

Karl Adler had also been thinking on his feet, inside Wirth's castle. His family came from the Black Forest, not far from the border with France. He prided himself on his fluent French, as well as his capacious memory. His older brother (Karl had idolised him) had spent the war in France, only to end up being killed in Paris in August 44. He himself, as one of Wirth's most talented doctoral students, had spent his war service with the Ahnenerbe. Some whispered that this had been a cushy number. He was always happy to take them to task.

On the way to meditation, he told Wirth he had just remembered where he had previously seen the name Mark Gunn; it was in some reports about an Englishman murdered in France in July. He had put the cuttings on one side already.

'He was on holiday with his fiancée, apparently,' Adler said sceptically. 'And now he has found himself a job with the Israelis.'

'I'm not too concerned about him being employed to take out scum like Matthaus,' Wirth replied, thoughtfully. 'I will, however, be most annoyed when they start targeting the pipeline. And it will be 'when,' not 'if.' You might mention the name to that idiot tailor in London; we ought to keep him on his toes. Well done, anyway. Keep up the good work, my young friend.'

The idiot tailor was giving Galland some tuna fish at that precise moment, with a saucer of whisky to follow, wondering what he was going to say to Adler at their weekly scheduled telephone call. He always used the same telephone box at the top of St Anne's Court. He had been perhaps been a tad remiss of late. He had done nothing about the files; Adler had not been pressing him and he was mindful of Louis's warning about the Cable Street boys. Putting himself in the direct line of fire was not his style now.

In the event, Adler had been in an uncharacteristically jovial mood. He had simply asked Juncker to keep an eye open for any mention of Mark Gunn, ex British army, now working for the Israelis. The name seemed familiar. It would come to him; he had perhaps been over-indulging in Galland's whisky of late. Exchanging the usual pleasantries with Adler, and promising he would indeed keep an eye open, Juncker returned to the shop with a spring in his step. He tickled Galland under the chin and began to leaf through his notebook.

In the doctor's courtyard in Damascus, Sol beckoned the object of Adler's attention over.

'Someone's moving about inside,' he whispered. Gunn allowed his right hand to move to his waistband and ease free the Browning 9mm he had taken from one of the Syrians. He stepped back a little, allowing himself a decent line of fire into the house. A key grated in the lock of the courtyard doors and a bolt was drawn back, slowly. A woman, her face tired beyond her years, peered out.

'Can I help you?' she asked.

Her face lit up when she recognised Sol. 'Thank goodness,' she whispered. 'Come in.'

Sara Weitz was twenty-four and the doctor's daughter and general 'aide de camp.' A gentle girl, she recalled Sol from years previously and was pleased to see him. He brought good memories in his wake. Sol introduced Gunn to her and he followed them inside, adjusting to the cool, dark interior, taking in every detail.

'What happened to your eye?' she asked Sol.

'That's a long story,' he replied. 'What's been going on here? We've heard a few things. Where's your father?'

'In the library; I'll take you through. But I must warn you, he won't be the way you remember him. And yes, it's been terrible.' She turned to Sol. 'I'm not sure we can stay here; I'm so worried. Let's not go into that in front of him for now, though.'

Dr Weitz was in the small library, his chair facing the courtyard, to catch the cooling evening breezes and to hear the sounds of the night and the city. His hair was thinning now, and he was as spare as a pared down lathe. A copy of the Iliad rested on his knee. He had always used the classics as an escape. He did not get up but his eyes caught the light and held it at the sight of Sol. He extended a thin hand.

'It's been a long time.'

'Perhaps a little too long,' Sol smiled. He could see that Dr Weitz had been made to suffer. Perhaps only the memories of what his family had done for so long and for so many had prevented his death. Then again, from the pain etched into the old man's face, death might have been the more generous option.

'Please sit.' Weitz offered Sol a place. Gunn lingered in the doorway, not wanting to intrude. Sol looked up and shook his head. Gunn understood, stepped back into the corridor and went to find Sara.

Gunn sat on the worn stone of the back step, his legs stretched out onto the stone slabs below. He looked at them for a moment, as he sipped the cinnamon tea Sara had shyly offered him, turning his head to examine their marks and notches. The stones were old, bible-old and with stories untold. He laughed out loud at his moment of fancy. His laugh echoed around the courtyard.

'It's been a while since any laughter was heard here. It is good to hear'

Gunn looked up to see Sara, a blanket in her hands, smiling.

'Sol and I will find a way to help you.' He made the promise before sense caught him. He groaned inwardly, knowing he would have to follow through now.

'You and Sol,' she turned to him. 'I take it this is more than just a social call?'

'You could say that,' Gunn replied, carefully. He did not wish to burden her with their mission; she had enough to deal with already. 'Are you and your father alone here now?'

'We are. My brother and my mother were arrested last year. They never made it back. It was a pure fluke that my father and I were left alone. I'm under no illusions.' She bit her lip. 'Many of our community left in 1946, when the French mandate ended. But Father refused   to go. I don't think he'll ever leave.'

Sol came out to join them. He took Sara into his arms.

'I'm so sorry,' he said.

Gunn walked over to the fountain, to give them some privacy and to try to think things through. Sara's plight – and her father's - was grave. He was well aware that he and Sol had a limited window of opportunity before the reservists who had formed their escort were missed, at home or back at the barracks. They were probably safe enough inside Dr Weitz's house for now; he noted how the windows all faced onto the courtyard, not the street. The authorities wouldn't necessarily connect two English soldiers with Dr Weitz. But they were going to have to break cover before long.

'Sol, I've been thinking,' he called, dragging on a cigarette, watching its smoke rise like a ghost into the city night. Sol came over and cadged one of Gunn's supply (Egyptian tobacco, pretty good).

'Come to any conclusions?'

'Well, we've hardly got time to acquire suitable attire for cover, have we?'

411

Sol nodded and motioned for him to continue. Gunn lit another cigarette and smoked rapidly while thinking.

'I'm sure the good Doctor has a jacket or two and a hat that I can borrow; disguise me enough in the dark to get by. I was thinking, I'll do Matthaus tonight and in the meantime you acquire a car and we get out of the city tonight with these good people. I think their line in this city is fading.'

Gunn dropped his cigarette and ground it into the stone with his heel. He looked at Sol.

'Not a great plan but probably the best we can do in the circumstances.'

'Then a race for the border?' Sol grinned. 'You're driving. Let's speak with Sara and her father.'

They all went through to the library. Sol and Gunn outlined their plans, while Sara tucked a blanket around her father as he listened attentively.

'I know Matthaus,' Doctor Weitz said thoughtfully. 'A little too fond of spirits for his own good. Oddly enough, I helped him once or twice when he first arrived here. Before he got 'established,' so to speak. Do you remember, Sara? But don't under-estimate Matthaus. He has quite a following. Did you know he was born in Alexandria? Speaks Arabic like a native.'

'No,' said Sol. 'We were told not to under-estimate him though. So you think he might have reinforcements?'

'Yes. You will need to be very careful. Now, for the next stage of your plan, if you need a car, take ours. I won't need it. I won't be coming with you.'

412

'Well, I'm not leaving you,' began Sara resolutely.

Weitz's voice took on a strength he had not felt for years.

'You are going with Sol. You are going to Israel. I am going to stay here, with my books and my good brandy, and take my leave on my terms at my choosing. He paused and coughed, a grim sound, the bare rattle of bones on wood.

'I cannot run – I'm too old, too tired. And despite everything, Damascus is my city, my place. I have made my decision. It will be as I say.'

Sara simply nodded, lost for words, and went to pack a bag for herself. Most of her luggage would be memories, nothing heavy. Sol pecked her on the forehead, holding her to him briefly. 'Go.'

'We will get her out, Dr Weitz,' Sol observed, and Gunn nodded in agreement.

'Good.' Weitz smiled faintly. 'Now pass me my copy of The Odyssey, my brandy and that old Webley you left me last time you were here. It's in my desk, bottom left drawer. I am left handed, after all.'

While Gunn went off in search of a shower and some spare clothes, Sol set about making Doctor Weitz as comfortable as he could. He poured him a brandy and found The Odyssey on the shelves.

'Thank you,' said Weitz, putting the book aside for a moment. 'You and Sara have my blessing. You know what I mean by that. She ought to finish her medical training. She only has two years or so left.'

'I'll make sure she does,' Sol replied. 'And thank you.'

Sol was touched by the doctor's faith in him, but he was under no illusions as to what lay ahead. They would be lucky if they made it back alive. That was all he was going to focus on for now. Leaving the doctor for a moment, he went to find Sara and Gunn, to make arrangements and to have a look at the car, a sleek black 1937 Delahaye Cabriolet. It had a tank of petrol but had not been driven for some time.

Gunn was wearing a jacket of the doctor's over his fatigues. He checked the Browning 9mm. Ideally, he would have had something else up his sleeve. This would have to do.

'I'll see you on the highway, where we came into the city, at 1 am,' he told them. 'If I'm not there by half past one, just go. Don't wait.'

Sol shook his head in disagreement. Gunn slapped him across the face.

'Listen, don't wait. This is a rough game. We both know it. So get on with it. You've seen me drive enough to know how to really put your foot down.

'All right.' Sol was a little chastened. 'Not sure that car is up to your Horch.'

'Very little is.' Gunn grinned. 'Now I am off to pay a call.'

Matthaus lived on Terek ben Ziad, as he had himself observed with a sour irony, not far from Dr Weitz's house in the old Jewish quarter and a stone's throw from the Umayyad Mosque. He did not share Hitler's admiration for Islam, despite his early childhood spent in Alexandria. In his cups, he often

414

recalled the observations of an old Berber he had met a year or so ago on one of his trips south, who had noted that the Arabs deserved Islam as they were such a rabble.

Gunn kept his head down, his brim snapped low and his eyes up. He did not stop as he ducked up an alley, headed towards Al Azm Palace and then turned left on Mou'aeiyah, where he hit a right into Terek ben Ziad. He walked past Matthaus's house, noting the two minders outside, and paused for a cigarette out of their eyeline to consider. He smoked quickly and walked on, finally finding a cut through. He ducked in and then, losing the jacket and hat in a drain, hauled himself up onto a crumbling wall. He looked back. He could see Matthaus's house, two buildings back. He climbed and soft shoed across the roof tops, avoiding loose tiles. He could see the minaret of the Umayyad and the Barada River to the north, and he tossed a sardonic salute in the direction of Saladin's Mausoleum. He had already decided he would take his leave via the rooftops.

Gunn knew that Matthaus was on the second floor, with at least one window overlooking the street. He peered over the edge of the rooftop, his fingers poised on the lip of the roof. There was a light below and a narrow balcony, with room for a chair and nothing else. The window was ajar and Gunn could make out German songs coming from the interior. He grinned at his quarry's resistance to the call to prayer.

Lifting himself up carefully, Gunn crept to the opposite edge, where there was a narrow ladder down; some kind of maintenance arrangement. It was near another window which again was ajar but which

415

appeared to be, judging by the scents smoking upwards, a kitchen. Gunn rolled back onto his haunches and then fished into his pocket for a silver coin Dr Weitz had given him as a remembrance. The coin had the stamp of Alexander the Great with the horns of Amun. Gun considered Alexander lucky. He flipped the coin. It settled in the palm of his hand, horns up. He smiled, and slipped it back in his pocket. Ladder it was.

In Brighton, having awoken from an uneasy sleep, Inspector Gunn padded back upstairs to Gunn's room, being careful not to disturb the slumbers of his 'residents,' the usual crowd of little old ladies and elderly ex-Army officers. They were no trouble at all; actually, they paid well. It was late though. Mark and Josephine's candles had burnt down. He replaced them.

He looked out over the Channel, where there was a full moon, darting in and out of clouds. Normally, the sight stirred him. Now, he was distracted. 'Come on, son, where are you?' he muttered.

He tried to picture where Mark was. The Holy Land; only familiar to him through newsreels and stories from long ago. Mark had been in some scrapes before. He remembered sitting up waiting for him in Paris when he was a teenager and roaming the streets. He remembered Mark's war service. This scrape seemed different somehow. Shaking his head, he made his way back downstairs. That carpet was almost threadbare. He was going to have to bite the bullet and replace it.

Sylvia woke with a start in her hotel room in Cognac, from a vivid dream which had started with her and Gunn at the demeure, but which now featured him alone, in some sort of biblical scenery with rooftops. She had arrived in Cognac only that morning, after a drive through fields of sunflowers. They always made her smile. She was wearing a shirt of Gunn's which he had discarded, nothing else. She went over to the window and looked out over the square. It was deserted, apart from a black cat weaving in and out of the shadows. A squally wind, a harbinger of cooler weather ahead, was stirring up the detritus from the market. She missed Gunn's arms around her and the warmth of him next to her.

'Go back to sleep, sweetheart,' he would have told her. She felt uneasy. With a shiver, she climbed back into bed and reaching for the notepad so she could continue the letter she had started to write.

At the doctor's house, Sara had said a final goodbye to her father and a prayer, before Sol drove her away, through the narrow streets. He was, in spite of the situation they were in, excited about driving the car. It started like a dream.

'We'll make our way towards the Highway now, and we'll be in plenty of time to meet up with Gunn,' he told her. Sara was in a world of her own. She sat back and let the memories tumble in her mind, like pebbles in a running stream. She knew she would not see Damascus again and that her father would soon be one of the memories. Damascus was all she knew. She knew she had to go; she was grateful to Sol, but she could not yet bring herself to say so.

Sol slipped the car into gear, and the long snout guided them out of the Jewish Quarter, through quiet streets towards the gates. Sara did not look back, although once or twice she glanced up towards the rear view mirror.

Matthaus emptied into a glass the last of a bottle of brandy sent to him with the compliments of Otto and Alaikum in Cairo, and delivered by one of his minders. Decent of them, he thought. He had enjoyed his chats with Otto. His gramophone records had put him in a sentimental mood; they invariably did. His thoughts drifted back not to his childhood in Alexandria but to the summer home his family had owned, high in the Bavarian Alps, with a little hotel at the bottom of the track. As a small boy, he would always wake up when they reached it, and his mother always told him and his brother they were nearly home. Sometimes, they used to stop at the hotel for a drink. Maybe it was time to leave this shithole and go back there. Doubtless, he would find a very different country from the one he had walked out of. Nonetheless, he had no desire to end his days here.

'Come on, whoever you are,' he muttered. 'I'm ready for you.'

The answer came from the shadows, with a glancing blow to the back of his head. Matthaus barked in surprise and stumbled forward, his shins cracking against a wooden table, his hands fumbling for his revolver. Booted feet swept his ankles away, and he lay, looking up at the fan turning heavily on the ceiling and into the face of the Englishman.

'Evening, old chap.'

Matthaus did not answer. He looked about him. His temple was bleeding and his nose was flattened. His revolver was resting up against his armchair; it was out of reach. He dismissed it from his mind and looked up at Gunn.

'What do you want?'

'Payment,' came the reply.

'Payment?'

'Retribution then.' Gunn placed a pillow over the nose of his Browning. 'But consider it a mercy, I am sending you home.'

Home. That was the only place Matthaus wanted to be. If this was what it took to get him there, then so be it.

'Get on with it and make it quick.'

Gunn did. He set the pillow under Matthaus's head and restored the revolver to his possession. Rather a clumsy-looking suicide, he reflected, but it might buy him a few minutes start or even an hour.

In his library, Dr Weitz was sitting quietly where Sara and Sol had left him. His leather-bound edition of The Odyssey in ancient Greek (which he had been given as a present as a young man upon starting medical school), lay open on his lap, his finger upon the opening lines. The description of Odysseus the Wanderer had seemed appropriate in the closing moments of his life.

He let his finger drift across Homer's words and smiled to himself as he raised the revolver to his temple. He would soon feel the sea's good wind on his face and would be standing on the deck of a ship straining hard to fair Ithaca. That was his wish; his final wish. He pulled the trigger and departed this world.

After a wonderful evening in Heliopolis, inspecting their new property and choosing light fittings and paint schemes, Alaikum and Otto were surveying a report which had come in on the ticker tape machine from Scheherezade.

'That woman must survive on scarcely any sleep,' marvelled Alaikum. 'However does she manage it? Anyway, sounds as if it's all kicking off on the Golan; flurry of activity on the Syrian side. Word is that two reservists and their driver have been reported missing. And two British prisoners. Bet that's Kalinsky and Gunn.'

'Should we pass that on?' asked Otto.

'I'll sleep on it for now,' Alaikum replied. 'Looking at our two main paymasters, the Israelis will be perfectly able to see from their positions that something is kicking off. I don't have the impression that Wirth is that interested in Matthaus. I'm fairly sure that's who the two 'Brits' have gone to get.'

'Poor old Matthaus,' said Otto. 'Hope he enjoyed his brandy. You're right though; Wirth's main preoccupation is that pipeline of his. It's obvious from the money he is throwing at it. Bet that nice-looking young lawyer we met doesn't come cheap. Best wait and see what happens when the dynamic duo come charging back over the border.'

'If indeed they do,' replied Alaikum.

Parked neatly in the shadows near the city gate, Sol checked his watch again; it had just gone one. There was nobody about.

'Gunn should be here any time,' he reassured Sara. Sara did not usually smoke but she took a drag on his cigarette. She could see the white ribbon of the Kings' Highway heading south. She was anxious to go; it would only be a matter of time before her father's car was recognised, especially in Damascus.

'What if he doesn't make it?'

'He will.'

'If not?'

'If is a big word,' Sol smiled and lit another cigarette. 'If not, we go on and Gunn will try to make it back.'

'What happens if he doesn't?'

'Oh, I suspect a lot of Syrians will die hard.'

In Tel Aviv, David was still at the office, pacing up and down. He had, as Alaikum had predicted, been briefed about the activity on the Syrian side, with trucks now racing down the highway towards Damascus. He had every confidence in Sol; he had worked with him long enough for that. Gunn had already impressed him. Even so, this was worrying. He hoped they had been able to make use of whatever windows of opportunity were available.

Matthaus's gramophone was still playing as Gunn scaled the ladder back onto the roof. He looked down. One of the minders had moved round to his side of the building and was peering up.

421

'Bugger!' muttered Gunn. He felt for his Browning and flattened himself against the wall while he took stock quickly. He felt the outline of the Alexander coin in his pocket and that decided him. Luck would favour one who did not cower. He looked down, straight into the face of the minder, and dropped, boots first. The soles of his boots hit the Syrian full in the face. His neck snapped at the impact. Gunn stepped across the alley, leaving the man dead, his head lolling at a twisted angle. He hoisted himself up. He was going across the rooftops.

Gunn was away, kicking loose tiles as he went. Every so often, he had to hurdle somebody prone and asleep on their own patch of rooftop. He needed to shift. Shouts and one or two gunshots behind him indicated that the minder had been found and, pound to an Alexandrian coin, Matthaus would be found any time now. He paused for a second to look at his watch. He knew he shouldn't have done that; he slipped and fell first into a stack of tiles, scattering them like shells across the sea floor. He blew out his cheeks, spat out a gobbet of blood and hauled himself up, Glancing over his shoulder, he spotted two men, armed and pointing his way, three roofs back. He knelt, picked up a broken tile and another, and sent them spinning and scudding across the gap. The tiles splintered as they skidded and broke, and Gunn's pursuers ducked. That would buy a few more seconds.

The shouts and gunfire were becoming louder and more intense. He was going to be surrounded at this rate. Meeting up with Sol and Sara would be impossible now; he would make them targets too. He stopped by a huge pigeon loft to consider.

Half past one, murmured Sol. There was no sign of Gunn but he could hear gunshots and shouting. He could guess what had happened. Uttering a prayer for his friend, and seizing a slim chance for himself and Sara, he put the car in gear and made his way onto the highway. Ignoring her look of enquiry, he guided the car down the highway at the kind of speed which would not attract a second glance. He would push hard when out of sight. He shrugged.

'Got no choice.'

By the pigeon loft, which was affording a little shelter, Gunn picked up a bucket and filled it with tiles and pots. He moved forward, hefted it by its rope and swung it over his head four times gathering pace, his shoulders cracking. He let go of the rope at the fourth pass and at the peak of the arc. The bucket flew across two alleys, pottery and tiles spinning out like seeds, and crashed down into a wall two streets over. He heard voices converging on the unfortunate bucket and he was gone. He was late; Sol should be on the road south now. Time to improvise.

Gunn landed as lightly as a cat on the solid roof. It was just inside the city gates. He spared a moment to glance over the edge of the eaves. It was an army post. A truck was parked outside, nose pointing south. He heard the murmur of tired voices. A patrol just in, end of shift and ready to sleep. That would do. He leaned forward and let himself fall, twisting as he did so, and flew, boot first, through a still open door. One man raised a rifle. It was instinct but, in a confined space, foolish. Gunn ducked and rolled up and grabbed the barrel, gave it a twist and cracked the soldier across the jaw.

As the Syrian went down, eyes rolling back in his head, Gunn dropped the rifle and ploughed head first into another soldier's midriff, knocking him down. Gunn knocked the man out with a flick of his Browning. One left. He stood, turned and smiled and extended his hand.

'Keys.'

'Keys?'

'To the truck.' Gunn stepped forward a pace. 'Give them to me nicely and I will hit you hard enough so you won't get into any trouble. Get me out of the city and I will dump you a few miles out with a canteen, and you'll have a walk back. Your choice. '

To his surprise, the Syrian chose the latter option and handed him the keys.

'It can't be this easy, surely,' thought Gunn, as they set off through the city gates.

Away from the city, Sol was putting the Delahaye through its paces. It was a joy to drive. He was anticipating road blocks; so far so good. He knew this would not last. He felt discreetly in his pocket for the Browning he had taken from the reservists.

Sara looked over at him.

'There's somebody following us,' she said. She had been expecting this, watching for them in the mirror.

'I know,' Sol replied. 'I've been watching for a few minutes. It could be an army patrol truck. They're some way back. I'm not hanging around for them. Hold on tight.'

Gunn glanced at his passenger. Around eighteen years old, he estimated, and probably a conscript. He looked terrified. He'd picked a right one there. Ahead of them, he could make out another army truck and, beyond that, the Delahaye. It certainly looked as if Sol was getting his foot down, and indeed the car could outrun most things in a straight line. On the twisting ribbon of an ancient highway, however, things were a little equalised. He noticed the sparks of barrel flash as somebody took a shot or two at Sol and Sara. That didn't trouble him overly, as a swaying truck did not make the most stable of gun platforms. But he did need them to get away. He glanced over at his passenger and warned:

'Hold on. This may get a little rough,' as he pressed the accelerator to the floor.

In the Delahaye, Sara was starting to panic. 'Sol, they just fired at us.'

'Yes, something of a forlorn hope.' Sol gave her what he hoped was a reassuring smile. 'They won't get us now.'

Gunn was gaining on the truck. He noticed that his passenger was as pale as a shade from campfire tales and, feeling a spasm of sympathy for him, slowed at an approaching bend. He leaned across and opened the door.

'Off you go, chum.'

The Syrian rolled out and down a scree of loose rocks and sand before coming to a bruised and battered halt in a dirty stream. He lay there for a moment and then lifted himself slowly up, to begin a somewhat limping progress back to the city.

Gunn pressed his boot down and gave the heavy steering wheel a sideways flick. The long bonnet of the truck shied like a kicking mule, and the left wing smacked the right flank of the truck ahead. It fishtailed as the driver wrestled, and coughed, kicked and then settled, the troops in the rear concentrating on hanging on for the ride rather than their pursuer.

There was a left bend ahead, a slight twist in the highway. That would do. Gunn weaved his trunk left and right, his shoulders protesting at the effort. He flicked the wheel again. The smack was more inclined this time around, and there was a ripping of metal as his truck shook itself free, leaving its bumper behind and, he was relieved to observe, a darkening around the petrol tank. Some damage.

'One more time,' thought Gunn, 'and I should have them out of action altogether.'

A final twist of the wheel from Gunn, his shoulder muscles singing like a bow string, and his truck crashed into Sol's pursuer like a trireme into a slow-moving galley. Metal twisted and tore, and the two beasts rolled away together, wheels spinning, seeking purchase on desert air, off the King's Highway and spiralled away, across rock and sand. Gunn was thrown around the cabin and then tossed clear like a rag doll discarded by a brat.

426

He lay bruised, winded, with at least one rib cracked and his left ankle sprained. He shook his head and looked up. A Syrian was staggering towards him. Gunn felt for his pistol. It had gone. As the Syrian bent down, blade in hand, Gunn stove his temple in with a piece of rock the size of his fist. He hauled himself to his heels, dragged the dead Syrian back to the wreckage and dropped him beside a boulder. After a quick examination of the trucks, he took a flask of water, a blanket, a pistol and a few clips and loped off up into the rocks.

Sara noticed the army truck behind them had disappeared. She did not mention it. There was nothing ahead of them, simply darkness. She shivered a little.

'How long now?' she asked, anxiously.

'We'll be at the border in about forty minutes if we carry on at this rate,' Sol replied. He was spot on with his timing. As he approached the border, he could see a small checkpoint; it looked unmanned.

'Keep on holding tight,' he told her. As the Delahaye flew past, two bewildered Syrians emerged from the sentry box, rubbing the sleep from their eyes. They shook their heads in bewilderment and went back inside, resolving to say nothing if asked.

The Delahaye passed them like the shade of a hound rippling through the grass on a summer's night and kept going. Sol finally slew to a halt well into Israel. He got out for a stretch. Sara followed. They sat on the ground by the car, sharing a cigarette.

'Welcome home,' he said, putting his arm round her.

'And it will be home, I promise,' he said, gently. 'I still miss things about Warsaw, but I really couldn't call it home now'

'Where are we going?' she asked.

'My place, if that's all right. For tonight, or what's left of it. I share it with Gunn.'

'Fine by me.'

Chapter 28

Sara stood downstairs, in the house in Tiberias which Sol and Gunn had rented only the previous week, her bag clasped tightly in her arms, looking round her. It was almost empty.

'We've only just moved in,' Sol explained. 'We've hardly been here. You have my room; I'll sleep on the roof.'

Someone had dropped their post round. David, he suspected. There was a letter from his aunt in Paris, which he tucked into his pocket to read later, a note from their landlord and another postcard for Gunn from Sylvia. The line of kisses caught his eye; he didn't read it. He put it carefully on one side. He really hoped Gunn was safely on his way back.

Having made sure Sara was comfortable, Sol settled down on a mat on the roof with a cigarette and tried to relax. He loved the view over Galilee from up here; it was one of the reasons they had chosen the house. He drifted into an uneasy sleep for a while.

On the other side of the Sea of Galilee, it had been a long, cold night for Gunn, who had stuffed himself and a blanket found in the wreckage of the trucks into a fissure in some rocks and scree. He woke with the first vague glimmerings of dawn after a fitful sleep. Instinctively, he reached for Sylvia. Then he remembered where he was. He lifted his head slightly, and through slitted eyes, watched as the Syrian camp below unfurled into life. From a professional perspective, he was less than impressed by what he saw, but that was moot.

So near and yet so far; he could almost see Tiberias. He grunted in sour amusement and wondered what the chances were of a sinner such as he walking on water. He had to find a way back.

Sol could hear Sara moving around. He found her in the kitchen, in tears.

'I couldn't sleep.'

'Come up on the roof,' he suggested gently, taking her by the hand. 'It's cooler up there. We'll watch the sun come up later.'

'How could I have left my father?'

'Your father was a brave and honourable man,' he said, kissing her tears away. 'You know he wanted this for you. And I'm going to take care of you. If you want me to, that is. But we should try and get some rest for now,' he told her, settling her down on the mat. 'Busy day ahead.'

Not that he had a clue what the day would hold, he thought to himself.

'Hold me,' she whispered. 'Please.'

He lay next to her, breathing in the faint scent of lemons from her long dark hair. He felt her relax against him, and she went to sleep. He could feel her heart beating. He thought back to when he had first met her, in Damascus; it seemed a lifetime ago. She would have been eighteen then, just a girl. He had made promises to her father before they left yesterday. He would keep them, although he was not sure how at the moment. For now, he drew Sara closer to him. It had been a long time since he had held a pretty girl in his arms. He kissed her gently and joined her in a deep sleep.

Edward Cumberland was looking out over a different sea. He was in Bandol, one of his favourite spots. He had the day off from flying today, after a particularly action-packed schedule in recent days. He was learning to switch off completely from thinking about his 'cargo.' Life was good. Louis had sent him a little money, and he had signed the lease on an apartment near the harbour. He was meeting Bonnard for dinner here this evening. He beckoned the waitress over and ordered a coffee and a croissant. He had been watching the fishing boats manoeuvring in and out of the harbour and had another chapter of Herodotus to read with his breakfast. He stretched luxuriously.

'Wind, sand and stars,' he thought happily.

He didn't notice the ghastly apparition approaching from his left until it was too late, and a bony hand had grabbed him by the ear, with a triumphant hiss of 'Got you.'

Edward got up, in horror, ready to run, but thought better of it. He would face the old cow down. How dare she appear in his new life? He motioned the waitress over again and ordered his mother the same as him.

'What are you doing here, Mother?' he asked, when their breakfast arrived. He noted her grimace at the bitterness of the coffee with childish satisfaction; he had acquired a taste for it. She had always hated black coffee. Winifred noted for her part that she was now 'Mother,' not Mummy. She didn't like that.

'I want you to face up to your responsibilities,' Winifred told him. 'Did you know

Mr. and Mrs. Andrews are going to put the baby in a children's home, when it's born? Is that what you want for your son?'

Edward had to admit, he did not want that. He had always thought of his sons following in his footsteps to Wellington. But he was never going home and that was that. He told his mother so in no uncertain terms.

'Have you been seeing that little bitch while you've been over here?' she asked, shocked at his uncouthness. 'I heard she was in France. Is that where your attitudes are coming from?'

'Of course not,' he told her. He had heard Sylvia was in France too but he did not know where. If only, he thought. Perhaps she would find him attractive now that he was a pilot again and had a little flat by the sea. Although from what he had been able to make out, she and Gunn were definitely together. Whatever did she see in him?

'Anyway, what if it's a girl?' he objected, changing the subject.

'Don't be ridiculous,' Winifred countered. 'There is another way, of course.'

Picking at her croissant, Winifred outlined her plan. Caroline and Edward would marry quietly abroad, to give the baby a name. Caroline would return to England and move in with Winifred until the birth. She would then give the baby to Winifred to bring up and afterwards she would be free.

'I don't see how that assists,' Edward commented, draining his coffee cup. 'We wouldn't be able to get divorced for years. She'd follow me out here, and I am absolutely not having that. And how do you think you are going to persuade her to give the baby to you anyway?'

'Oh, she won't have much choice, don't worry,' Winifred told him, her eyes glittering. 'But this way, you're officially the baby's father, whatever happens. And she doesn't have any money of her own, so she can't follow you out here.'

'Well, I'm not coming back to England or having anything else to do with her,' Edward said wearily, wondering how he had become embroiled in these distasteful matters. All he wanted to do was fly. 'So long as that's abundantly clear, you do what you want.'

'That's settled then,' Winifred said happily. 'I'll make the arrangements. Better get her out here as soon as we can; poor girl looks like the back of a bus already.'

'She always did,' Edward thought, motioning the waitress to bring the bill.

Far away, in their Bavarian hideaway, Adler finally caught up with Wirth, who was having what he described as an 'early morning stroll' around the castle grounds. Not much of a stroll, reflected Adler, more of a route march. He wondered, not for the first time, how old Wirth actually was; he seemed ageless, somehow. It had just started to rain; a soft but persistent drizzle. He unfurled a large black umbrella and held it over his professor, as he still liked to think of him.

'Matthaus is dead,' he announced. 'Otto just called.'

Wirth paused for a moment. Years ago, in more innocent times, he had played with Matthaus and his brother at the little hotel in the mountains owned by an aunt of his, when they used to visit from Egypt, a place which had seemed so exotic and faraway to him then. He shrugged. Matthaus had turned into something else altogether, a traitor. That disgusted him. He had got his come-uppance.

'There will be plenty more where he came from,' he observed. 'And if it keeps the attention of the Israelis away from our little operation, all well and good. There is still much to be done.'

He looked across at Adler. Yes, a true believer. Fischer was efficient, hard-working and good at his job, but that was as far as it went. Nobody would suspect what he was involved in. Yet there were certain things he could not and would not share with him. Perhaps he should consider involving young Adler at a deeper level.

In Tiberias, Sol came to with a start. Somebody was at the door downstairs. He peered down. It was David.

'Be with you in a minute,' he called.

'No need,' David noted. 'I will come up. Nice car, by the way.'

He climbed the stairs and then the short wooden ladder onto the flat roof. He shook Sara's hand and then hugged her, whispering a welcome into her ear. He accepted a cigarette from Sol and sat on the low lip of the roof.

'So, my boy, you get the job done but you leave the Englishman in the dirty stuff.'

'Gunn got the job done and he got us out.' Sol's reply was brittle. 'We owe him.'

434

'No, we don't. We are grateful.' David blew a smoke ring across the roof. 'But he'd better come back. I have a lot more work for the pair of you. Where did you last see him?'

'At the house in Damascus; we agreed we wouldn't wait if he was later than half past one. I had to get my foot down, there was an army truck in hot pursuit of us most of the way. It disappeared about forty minutes from the border. I wonder if he had anything to do with it.'

Sol chewed at his finger.

'I'll go and make some enquiries,' David said. 'Back here in an hour or two. Let you get sorted.'

In Cairo, Alaikum had got up early. He had been to the souk. Having grown up in and around it, he loved shopping there, especially now he had money, always on the lookout for items for the new house. He kicked the door open to the office; his hands were full of his purchases.

Otto had been up for hours. Matthaus's death was confirmed. He felt genuinely sad about that and had been quite taken aback by Adler's offhand reaction to the news.

'Traitor to the Reich. He had it coming to him. Let us know about his killers when you hear anything. They'll have their hands full now, that's for sure.'

Scheherezade had been up early too, sending reports of trucks lying beside the King's Highway and fatalities.

'Word is that Kalinsky got out, with a girl, and Gunn was in one of the trucks - ran the other one off the road and killed everyone in it. The Syrians are hopping mad. It would be better if he was dead, actually. Because if he isn't, and they catch him...'

'Keep me posted,' Otto told her. 'Wonder who the girl was. What a morning,' he said, turning to Alaikum, smiling indulgently at all the shopping. 'And I haven't even had breakfast yet.'

As David walked back, he could see Sol and Sara having breakfast on the roof. Sol had been to the little shop around the corner and Sara, anxious to keep busy, had been investigating the contents of the cupboards for crockery and cutlery and chatting to Sol about her studies.

'I got my medical degree in Damascus. I need to do the practical stage now, in a hospital.'

'Well, that should be easy to arrange, 'Sol told her. 'We need doctors here.'

'Oh to be young again,' David thought to himself, amused, hauling himself carefully up the rickety ladder.

'Not good news, I'm afraid. There are reports of the mangled wreckage of two Syrian army trucks on the Kings Highway. Gunn pushed your pursuer off the road all right but he may have killed himself in the process.'

'We'll find out more soon,' he added, helping himself to a glass of orange juice. Sol and Sara were visibly shaken and upset. 'There's not a lot we can do for now. I would suggest you get some rest and come in for a briefing this evening.'

Gunn felt in the pocket of his fatigues. He was down to his last cigarette; it was battered. Still, he would save it. There was no point in giving himself away. He lifted the blanket and let the breeze filter into his hideaway. The trucks would be discovered before too long. Even the most casual of patrols would not miss the wreckage. The sun was coming up. It was time to make a move; keep the red stuff flowing through his veins.

He lifted himself carefully from his billet and crawled slowly back to the far side of the slope, away from the Sea of Galilee. Spurs of rock and clusters of thorns snagged and caught at his fatigues as he went. He reflected, as he inched his way painfully along, that he was not in a good place, and from what he could deduce, a long way from anywhere he could safely lay his head. It was pretty exposed up here. Still, he was alive. That would do for now. He would make the most of the time before him. He had once read a Norse legend to the effect that the skein of a man's life was woven long before he was born, and the knot would be snapped at the appointed time, no sooner and no later. There was nothing to fear in that, he reflected; the Norsemen had probably been onto something.

His ankle was throbbing and he was dehydrated. He drained the last drops of water from the water flask and threw it away, into a large thorn bush. Making his way slowly along the ridge, he thought about the vivid dream he had just had about France and another night on scrubby high ground, watching the dawn coming up over an army camp. This time, the uniforms were grey, and there was a fearless girl beside him, with tawny hair and high cheekbones, a rifle in her hand.

'Mark, you need to go now, quickly,' she had said. 'Please. I've got you covered. Just go.'

He shook his head. Why the hell had he been dreaming about that bitch? Why was there such a sense of urgency in her voice? She had hardly shown him any concern, had she, or the baby for that matter? Well, he agreed with her about one thing anyway. It was time to get out of here.

Epilogue

From the vantage point of his apartment window, Pierre Billet could see the girl – so like her mother - cross the square, clutching the photographs and the piece of squared paper he had given her, her pale blue dress a contrast to the black mushrooms that grew on the surrounding walls, a by-product, as he loved to tell any tourists who would listen, of cognac production.

She was right. There was no time to lose. They'd promised to keep in touch but he had a feeling he would soon be joining Amelie in the vault in the little stone church on the corner. He waved cheerily to the old bat who had stopped outside, to let her minuscule, yappy dog do its business on his front step. She had spat at him in the street last week. Since his return, he had been shunned, appraised with narrowed eyes. Sometimes he found it hard to believe how rapid his fall from grace had been. Perhaps, by his actions just now, he could make amends and at least assuage his guilt.

He watched the girl stop and reach into her handbag, a gesture so reminiscent of her mother that he could have wept, for her car keys, and then observed her driving off, slowly and with care. As she disappeared round the corner, he reached for Amelie's old address book and took a deep breath; he had a few calls to make.

Printed in Poland
by Amazon Fulfillment
Poland Sp. z o.o., Wrocław

62273404R00258